Chi's Sweet Home

チーズ スイートホーム

7

Konami Kanata

contents
homemade 111~128 +

homemade 111: a cat tags along

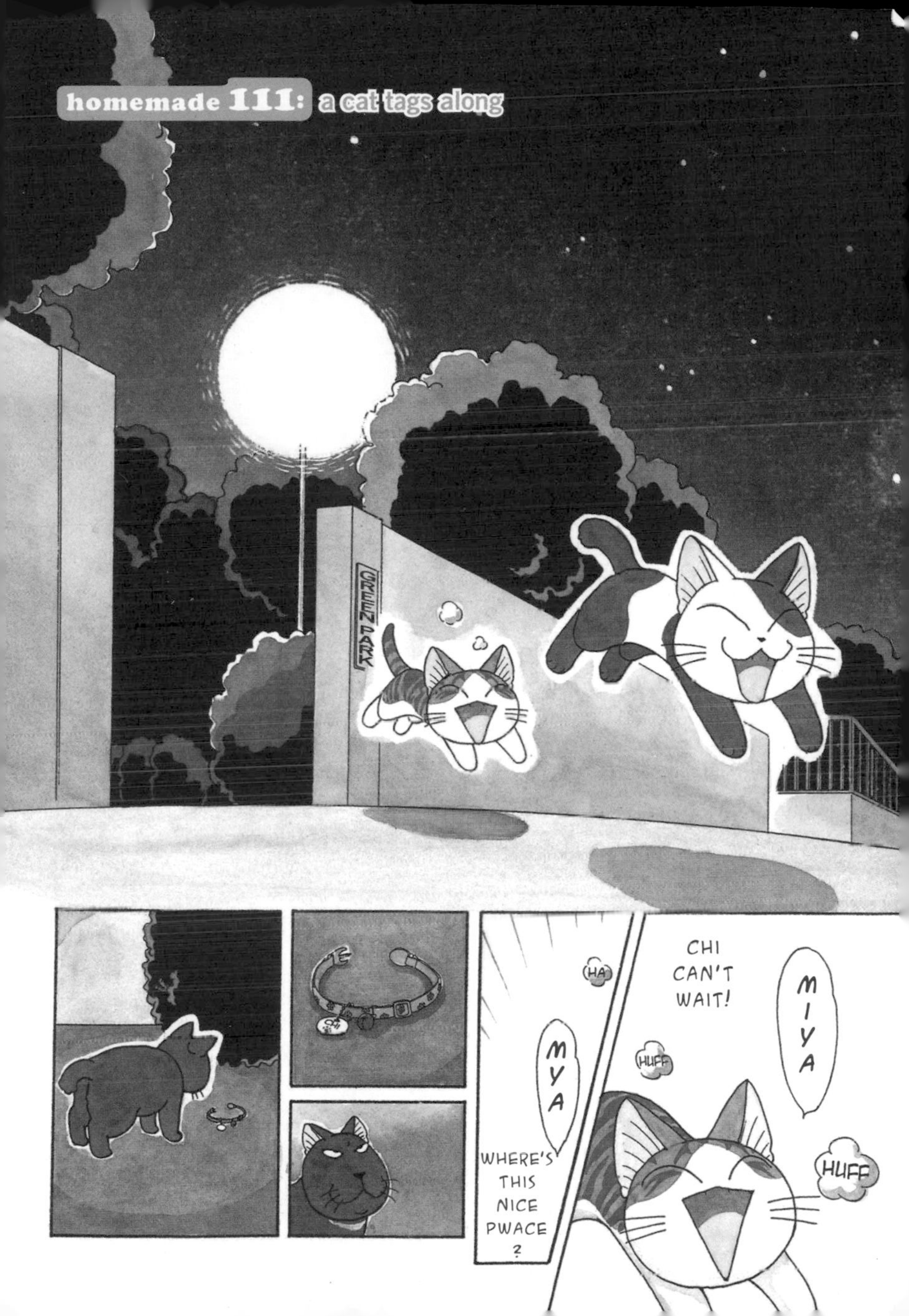

GREEN PARK
HA
CHI CAN'T WAIT!
MIYA
MYA
HUFF
WHERE'S THIS NICE PWACE?
HUFF

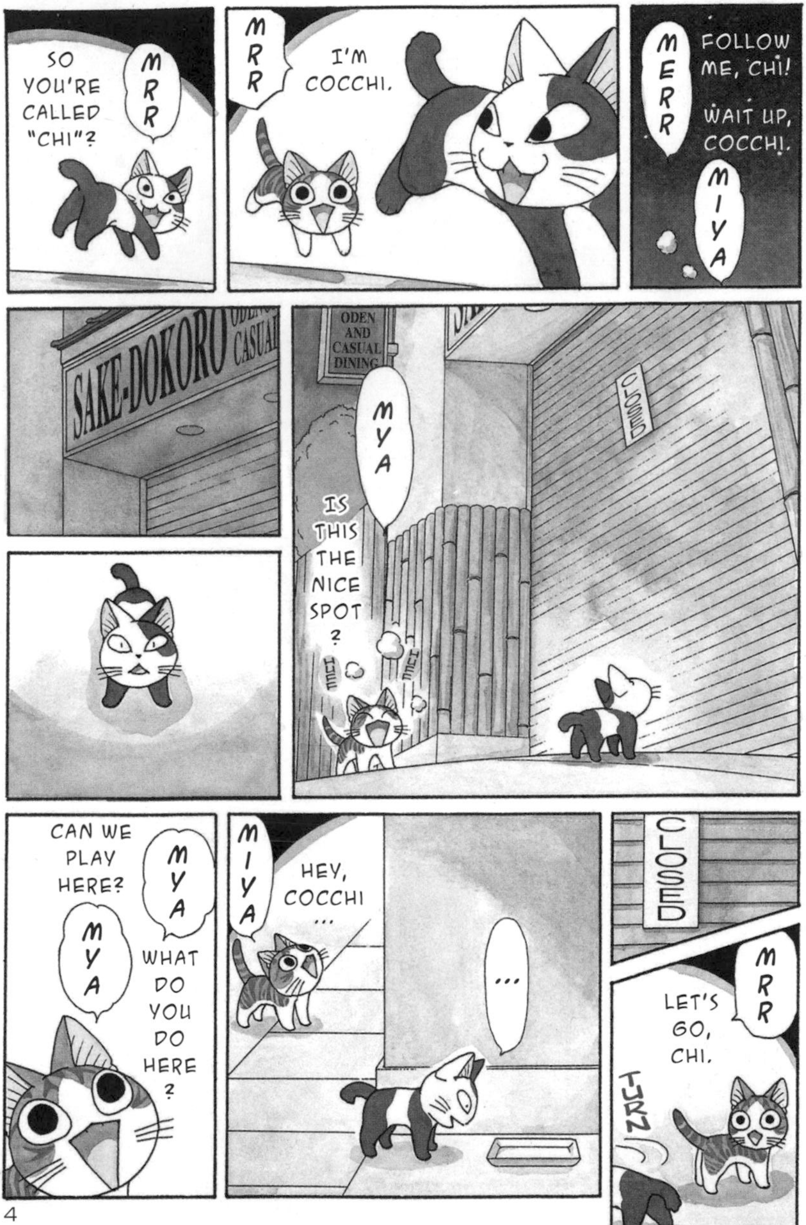
SO YOU'RE CALLED "CHI"?
MRR
MRR
I'M COCCHI.
MERR
FOLLOW ME, CHI!
WAIT UP, COCCHI.
MIYA
SAKE-DOKORO
ODEN AND CASUAL DINING
MYA
IS THIS THE NICE SPOT?
HUE
HUE
CLOSED
CAN WE PLAY HERE?
MYA
MYA
WHAT DO YOU DO HERE?
MIYA
HEY, COCCHI ...
...
CLOSED
MRR
LET'S GO, CHI.
TURN

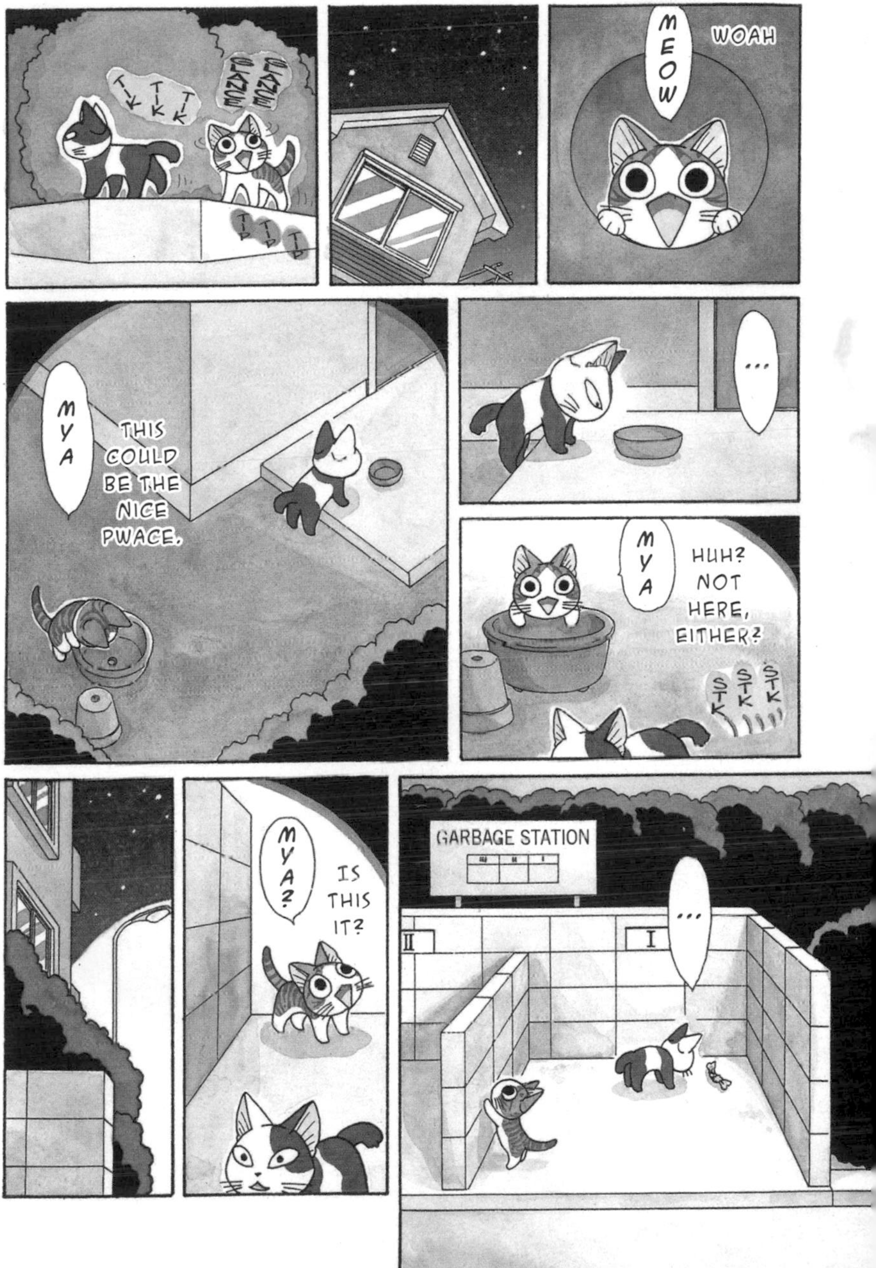
TIK TIK TIK
GLANCE GLANCE
TIP TIP TIP
MEOW
WOAH
MYA
THIS COULD BE THE NICE PWACE.
...
MYA
HUH? NOT HERE, EITHER?
STK STK STK
MYA?
IS THIS IT?
GARBAGE STATION
II
I
...

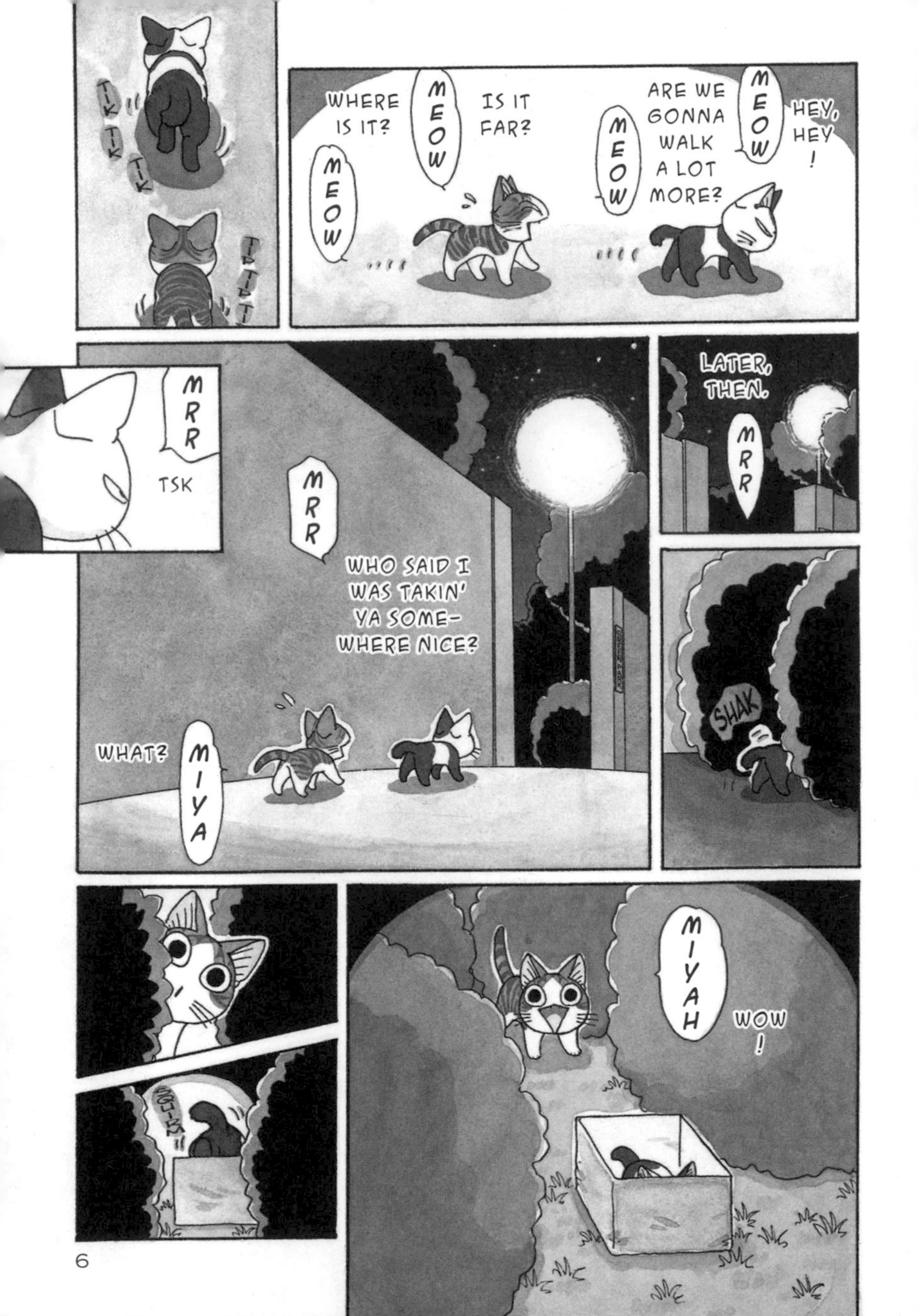
TIK TIK TIK
TIP TIP TIP
WHERE IS IT?
MEOW
MEOW
IS IT FAR?
MEOW
ARE WE GONNA WALK A LOT MORE?
MEOW
HEY, HEY!
MRR
TSK
MRR
WHO SAID I WAS TAKIN' YA SOME-WHERE NICE?
WHAT?
MIYA
LATER, THEN.
MRR
SHAK
SQUIRM
MIYAH
WOW!

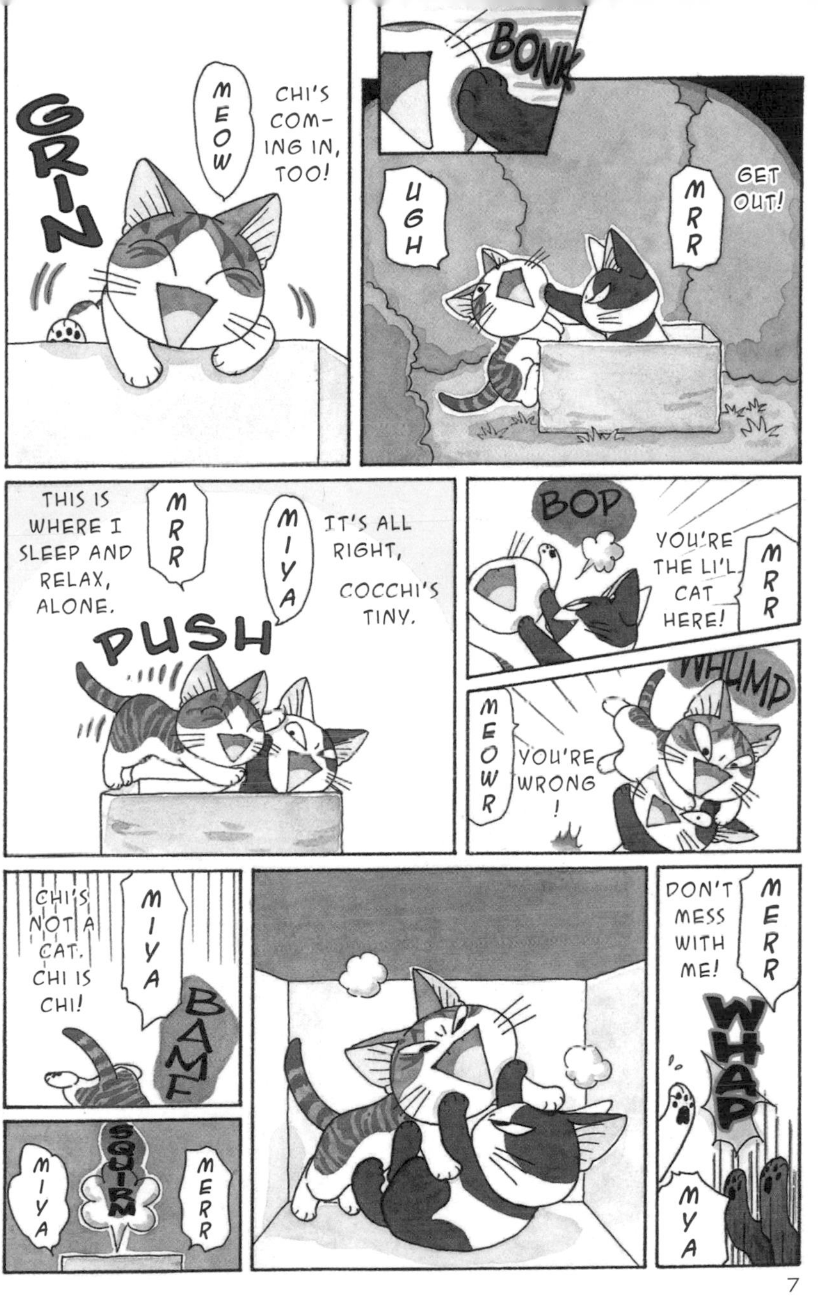
GRIN
MEOW
CHI'S COM-ING IN, TOO!
BONK
UGH
MRR
GET OUT!
THIS IS WHERE I SLEEP AND RELAX, ALONE.
MRR
MIYA
IT'S ALL RIGHT, COCCHI'S TINY.
PUSH
BOP
YOU'RE THE LI'L CAT HERE!
MRR
WHUMP
MEOWR
YOU'RE WRONG!
CHI'S NOT A CAT. CHI IS CHI!
MIYA
BAMF
MIYA
SQUIRM
MERR
DON'T MESS WITH ME!
MERR
WHAP
MYA

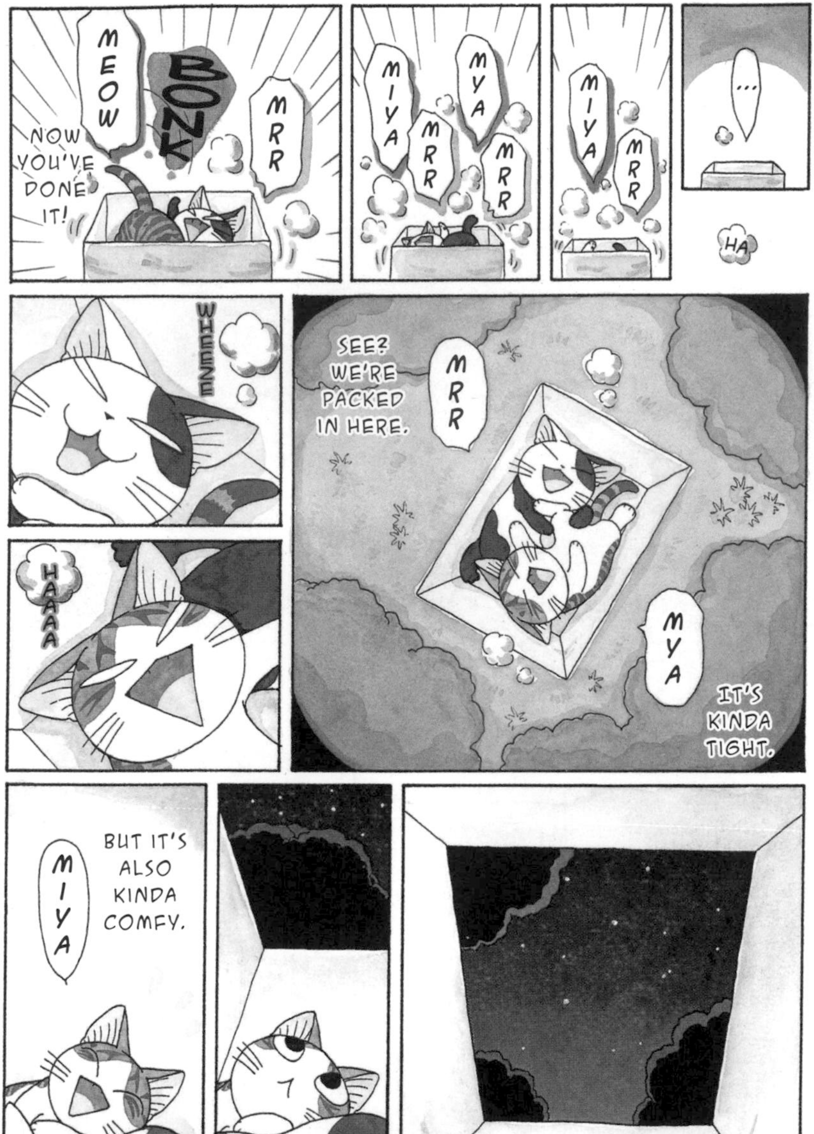
MEOW
BONK
NOW YOU'VE DONE IT!
MRR
MIYA
MYA
MRR
MRR
MIYA
MRR
...
HA
WHEEZE
HAAAAA
SEE? WE'RE PACKED IN HERE.
MRR
MYA
IT'S KINDA TIGHT.
MIYA
BUT IT'S ALSO KINDA COMFY.

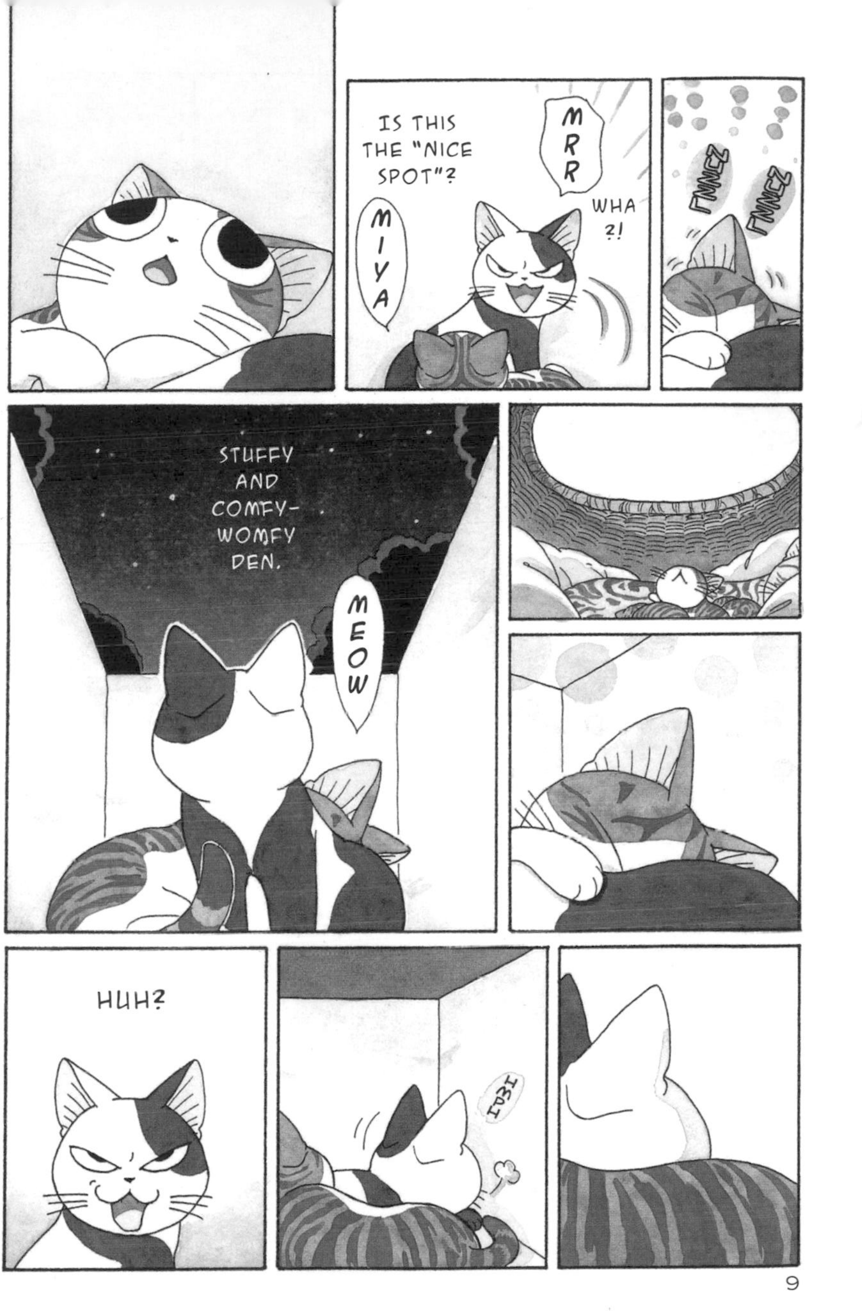
IS THIS THE "NICE SPOT"?
MRR
MIYA
WHA ?!
STUFFY AND COMFY-WOMFY DEN.
MEOW
HUH?

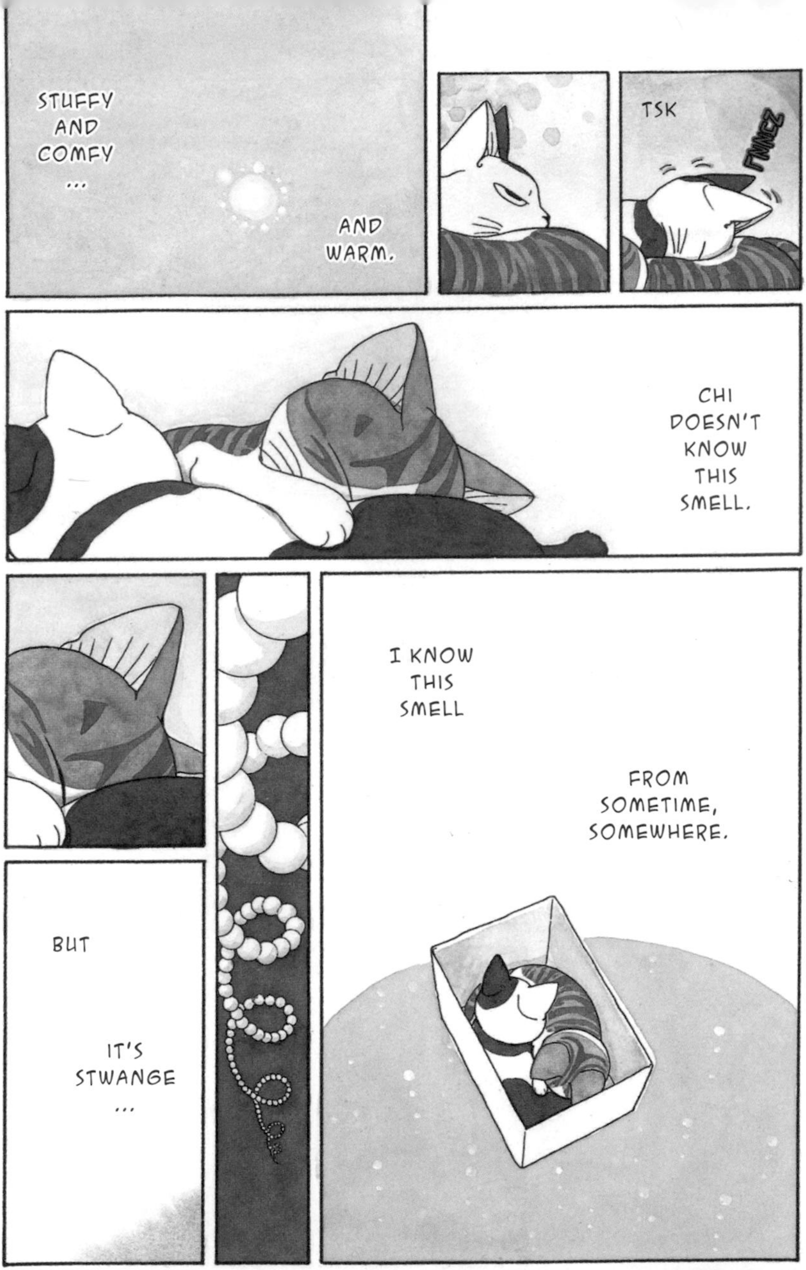

STUFFY AND COMFY ...
AND WARM.
TSK
CHI DOESN'T KNOW THIS SMELL.
BUT
IT'S STWANGE ...
I KNOW THIS SMELL
FROM SOMETIME, SOMEWHERE.

the end

homemade 112: a cat over-reaches

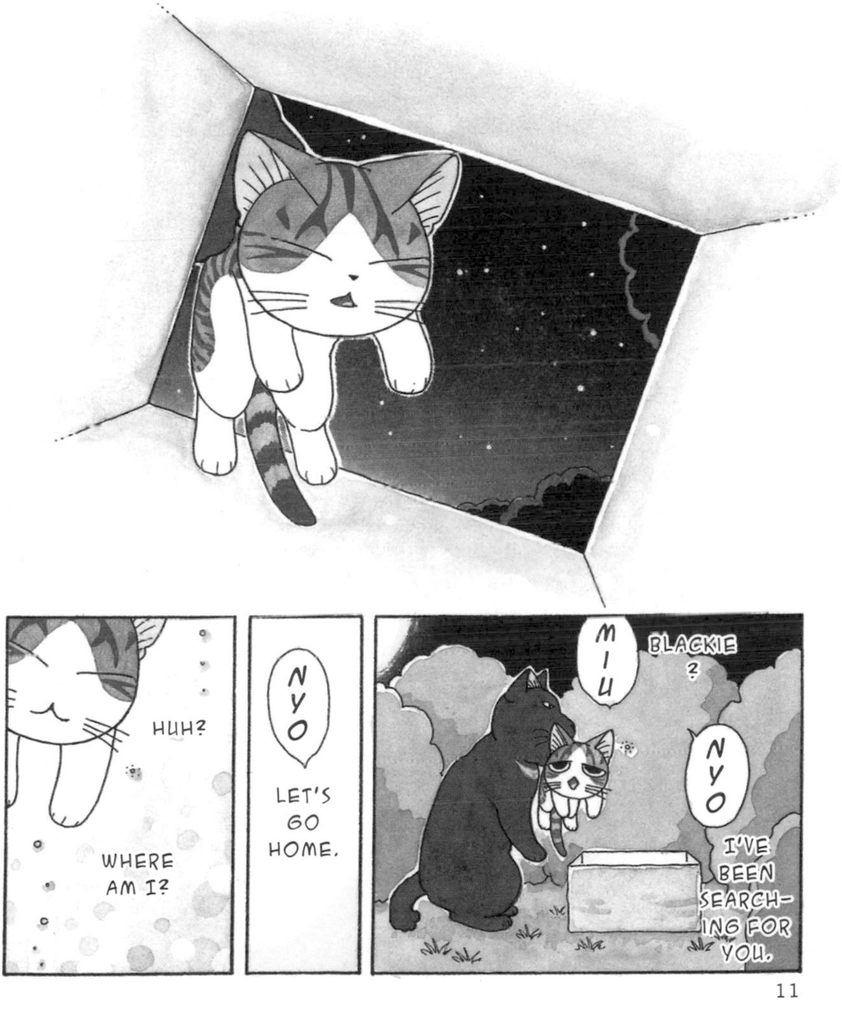
HUH?
WHERE AM I?
NYO
LET'S GO HOME.
MIU
BLACKIE?
NYO
I'VE BEEN SEARCHING FOR YOU.

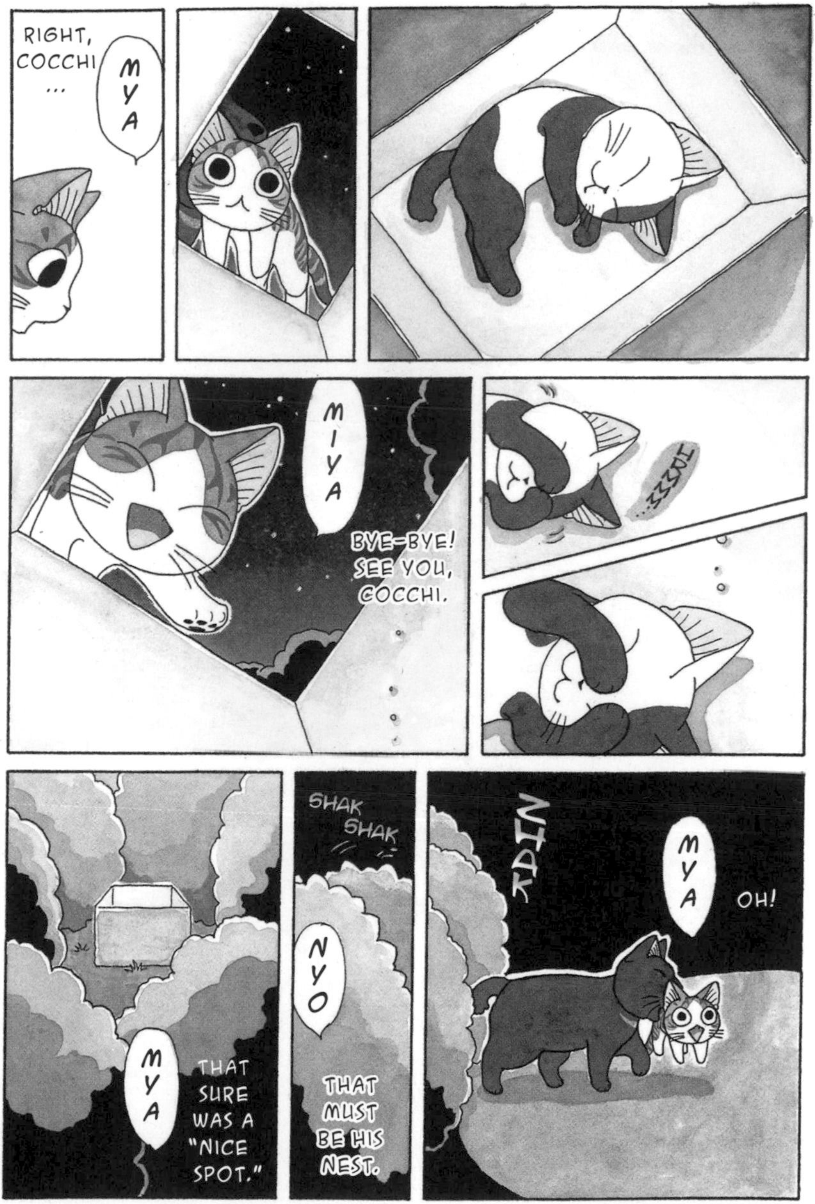
RIGHT, COCCHI ...
MYA
MIYA
BYE-BYE! SEE YOU, COCCHI.
SHAK SHAK
NYO
MYA
THAT SURE WAS A "NICE SPOT."
THAT MUST BE HIS NEST.
SHAK
MYA
OH!

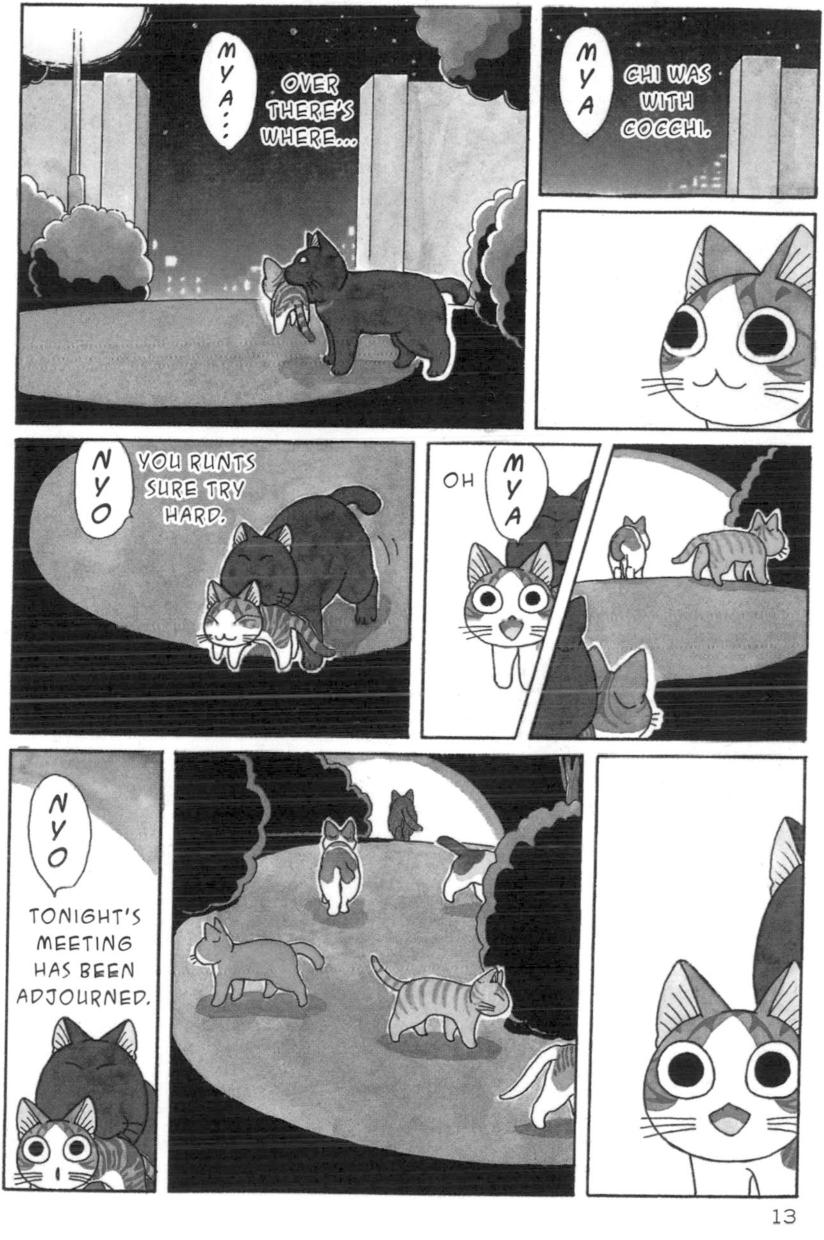
MYA...
OVER THERE'S WHERE...
MYA
CHI WAS WITH COCCHI.
NYO
YOU RUNTS SURE TRY HARD.
OH
MYA
NYO
TONIGHT'S MEETING HAS BEEN ADJOURNED.

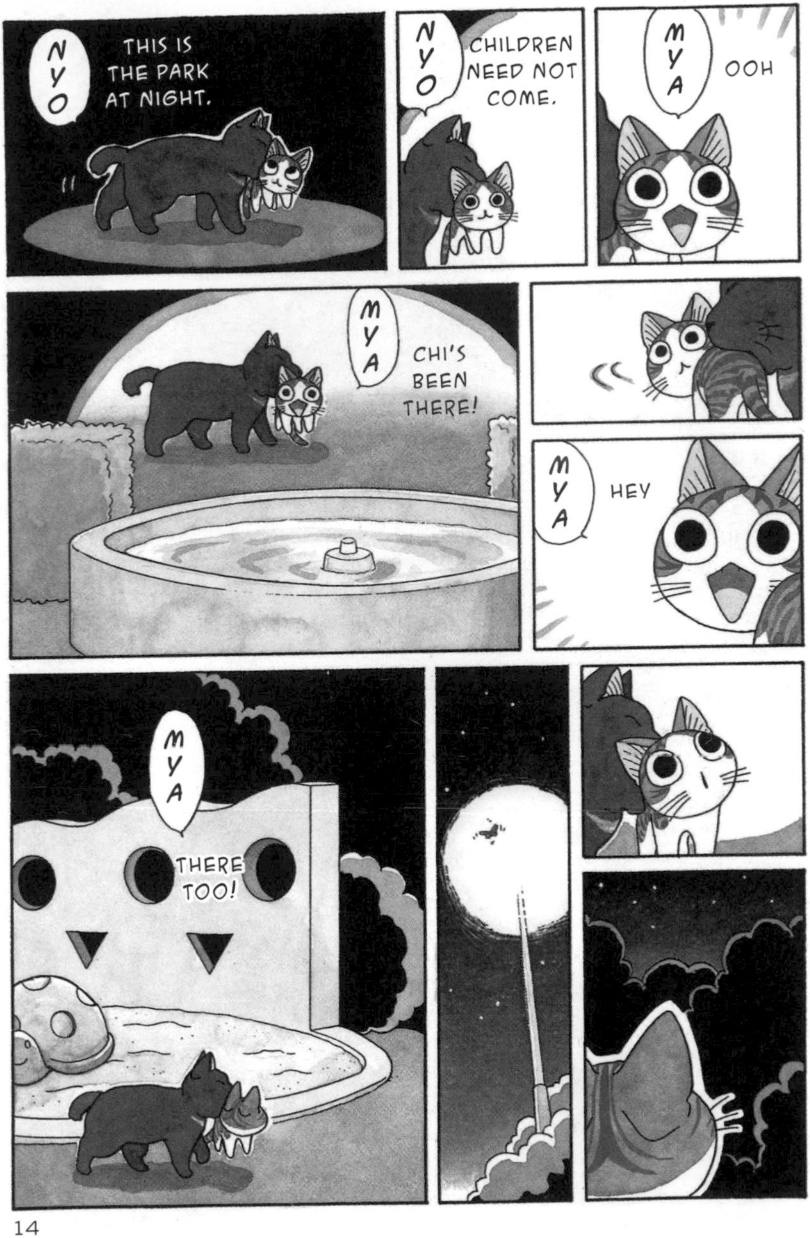
NYO
THIS IS THE PARK AT NIGHT.
NYO
CHILDREN NEED NOT COME.
MYA
OOH
MYA
CHI'S BEEN THERE!
MYA
HEY
MYA
THERE TOO!

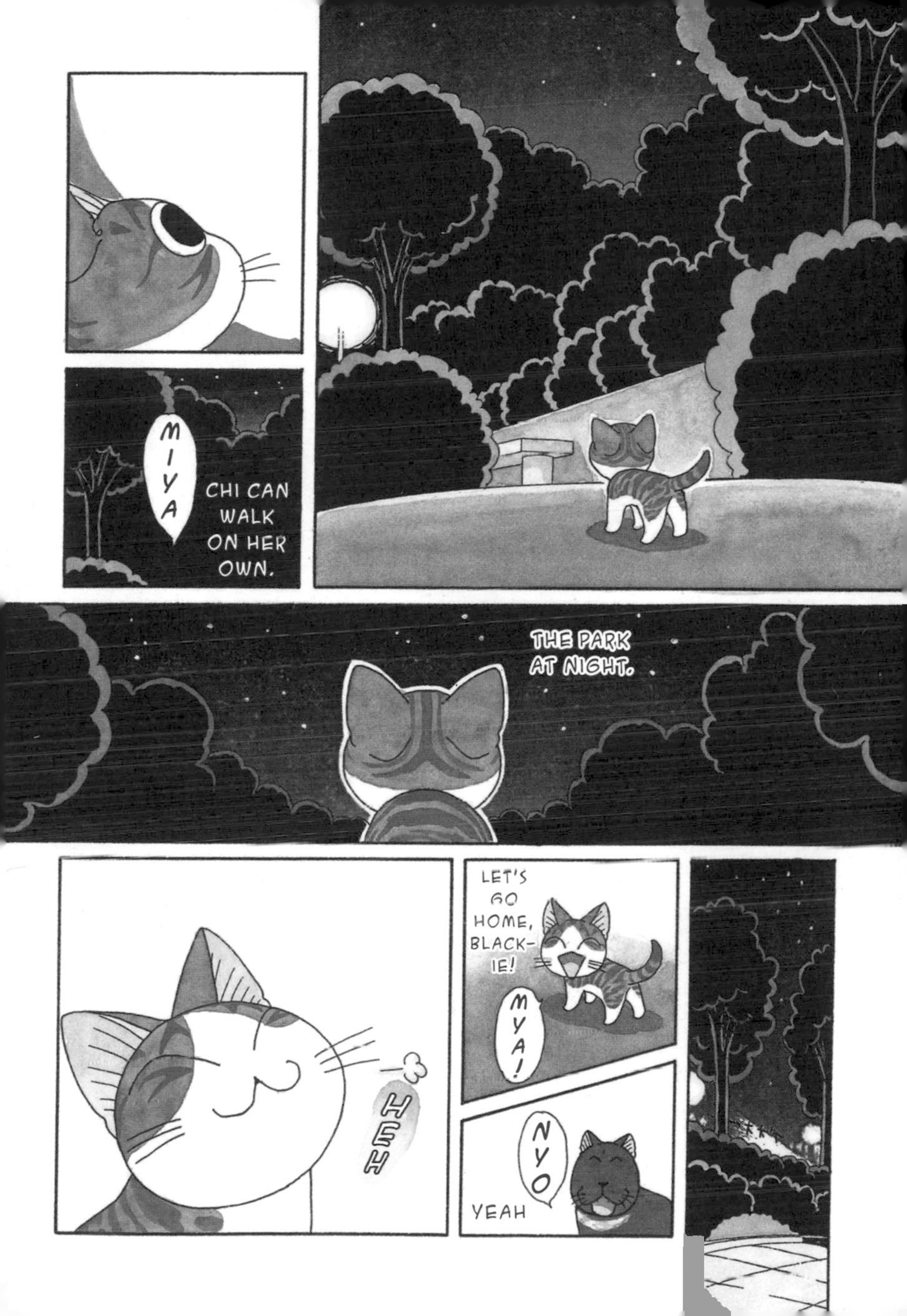
MIYA
CHI CAN WALK ON HER OWN.
THE PARK AT NIGHT.
HEH
LET'S GO HOME, BLACKIE!
MYA!
NYO
YEAH

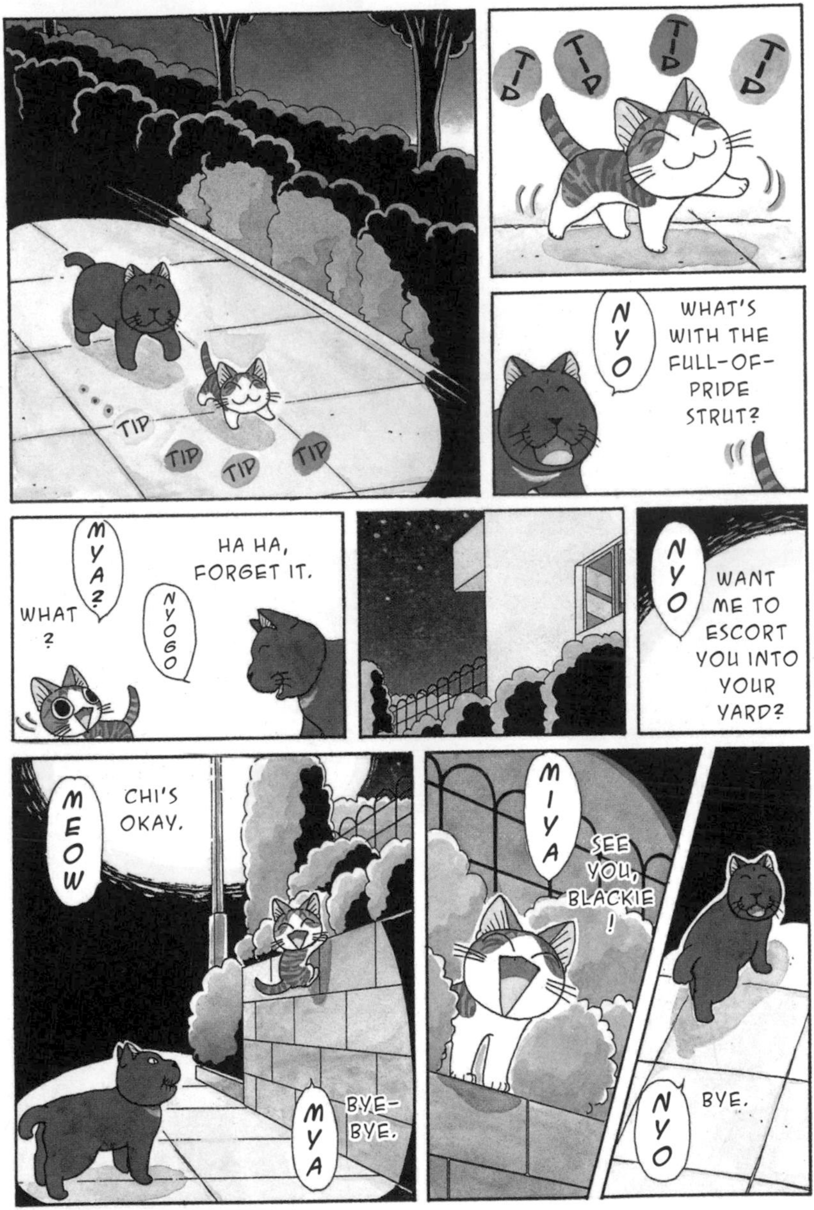
TIP
TIP
TIP
TIP
TID
TID
TID
TID
NYO
WHAT'S WITH THE FULL-OF-PRIDE STRUT?
MYA?
WHAT?
NYOGO
HA HA, FORGET IT.
NYO
WANT ME TO ESCORT YOU INTO YOUR YARD?
MEOW
CHI'S OKAY.
MYA
BYE-BYE.
MIYA
SEE YOU, BLACKIE!
NYO
BYE.

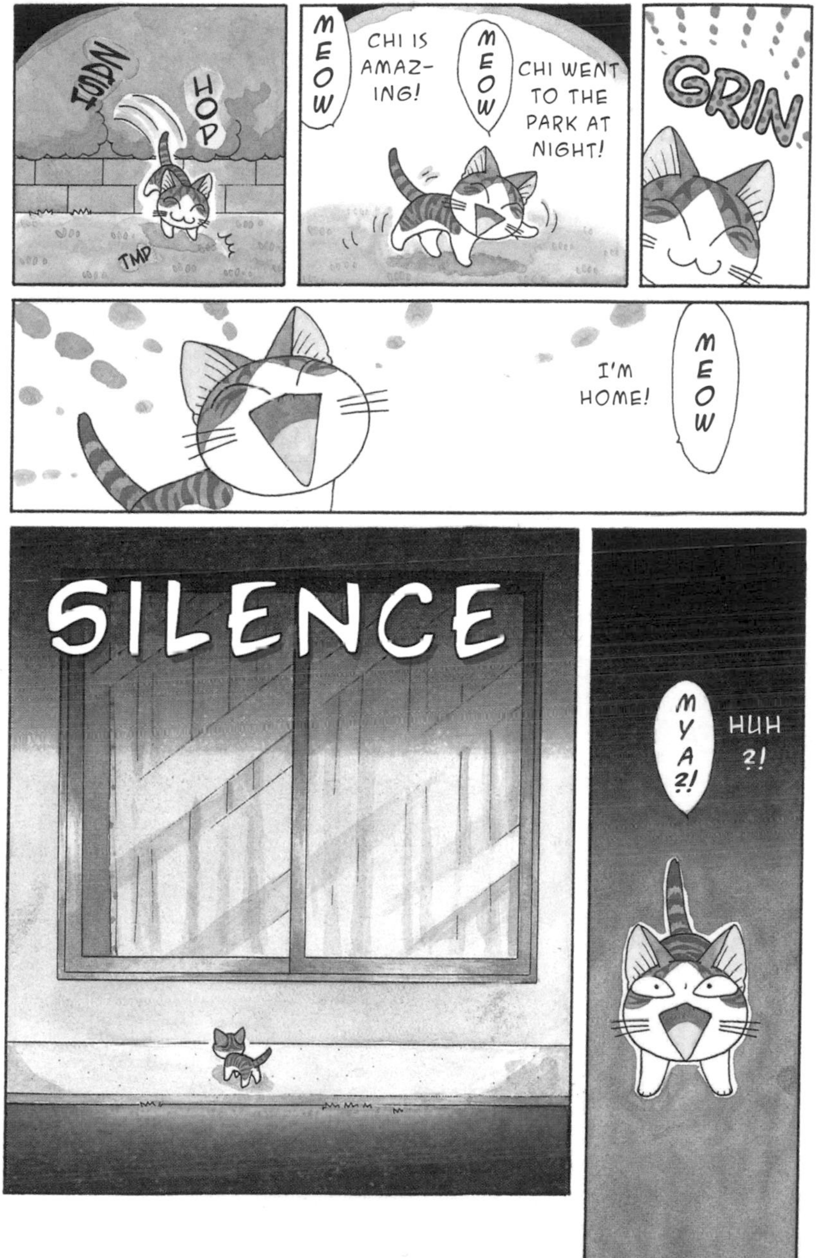
TODDLE
HOP
TMP
MEOW
CHI IS AMAZ-ING!
MEOW
CHI WENT TO THE PARK AT NIGHT!
GRIN
MEOW
I'M HOME!
SILENCE
MYA?!
HUH ?!

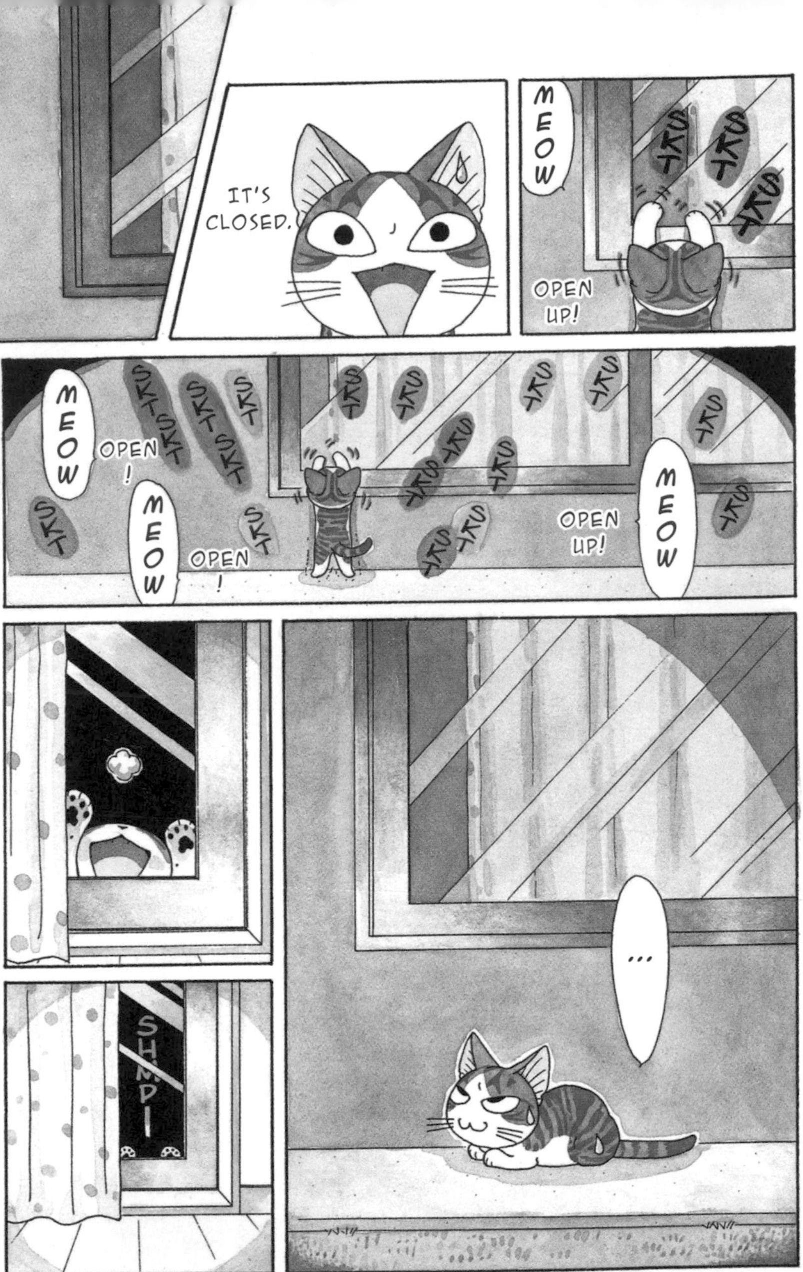
IT'S CLOSED.
MEOW
SKT SKT SKT
OPEN UP!
MEOW
OPEN !
SKT SKT SKT SKT SKT SKT SKT SKT
MEOW
OPEN !
SKT SKT SKT SKT SKT SKT SKT SKT SKT SKT SKT SKT
OPEN UP!
MEOW
SHMP!
...

the end

homemade 113: a cat is shut out

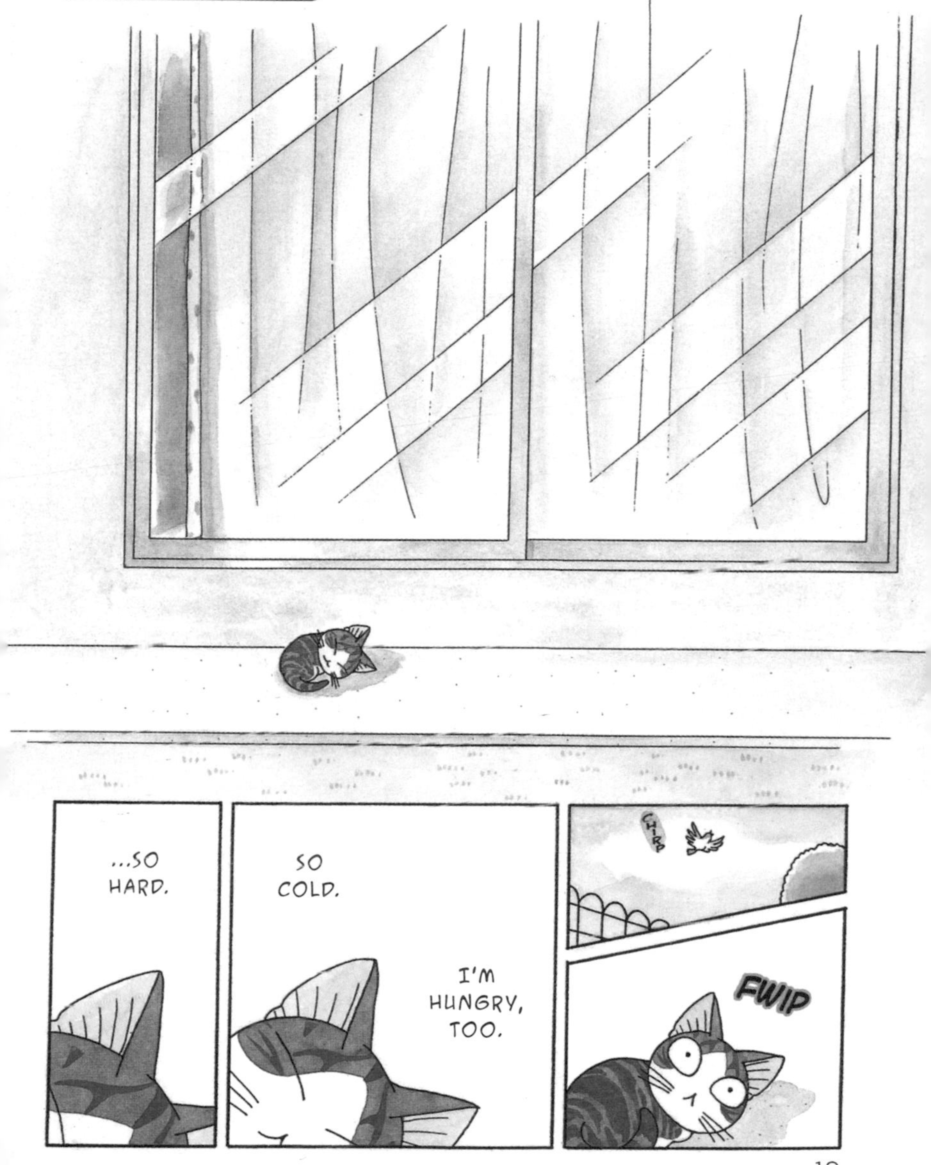
...SO HARD.
SO COLD.
I'M HUNGRY, TOO.
CHIRP
FWIP

IT'S MORN-ING.

AND CHI SLEPT OUT HERE...

'CAUSE "DOOR" IS CLOSED.

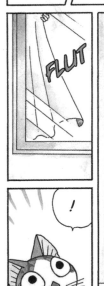

FLUT

WOOSH

!

IT'S MOMMY!

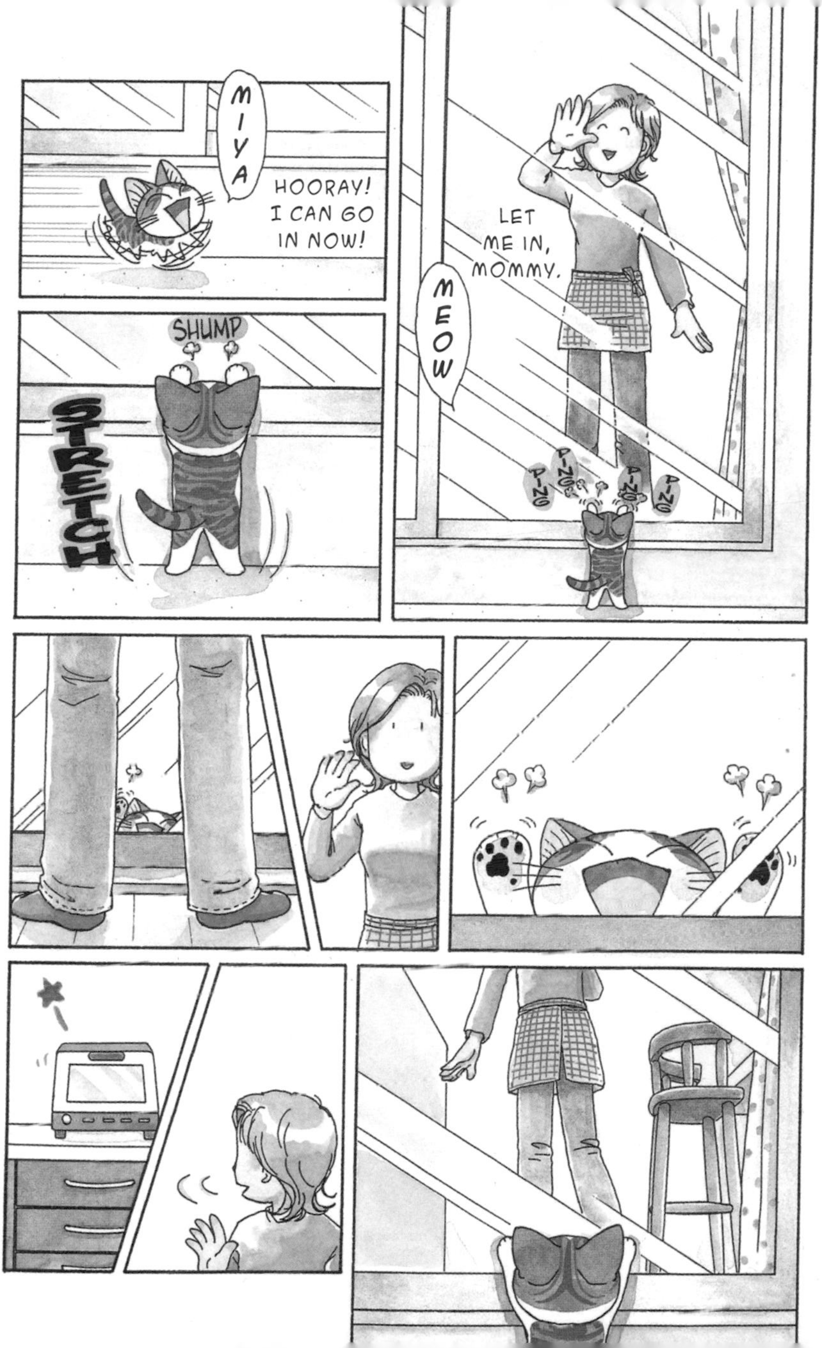
MIYA
HOORAY! I CAN GO IN NOW!
SHUMP
STRETCH
LET ME IN, MOMMY.
MEOW
PING
PING
PING
PING

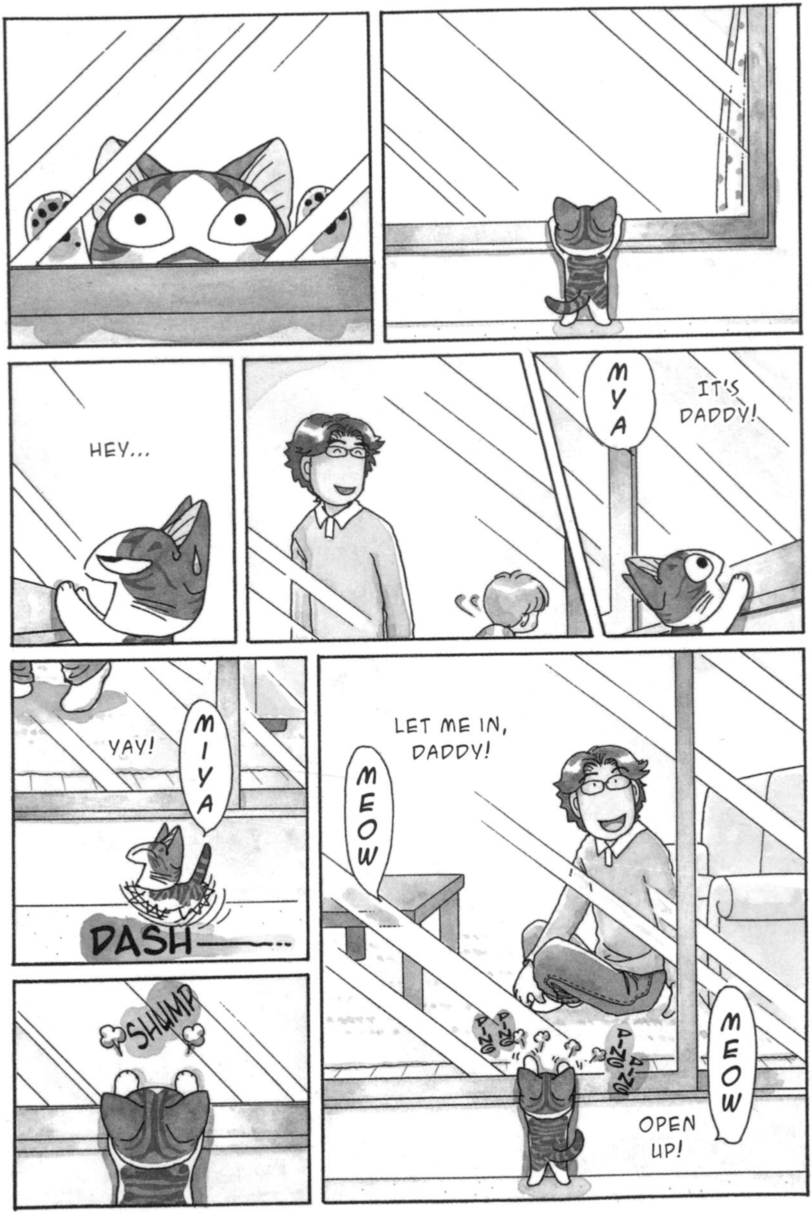
HEY...
MYA
IT'S DADDY!
YAY!
MIYA
DASH
SHUMP
LET ME IN, DADDY!
MEOW
PING PING
PING PING
MEOW
OPEN UP!

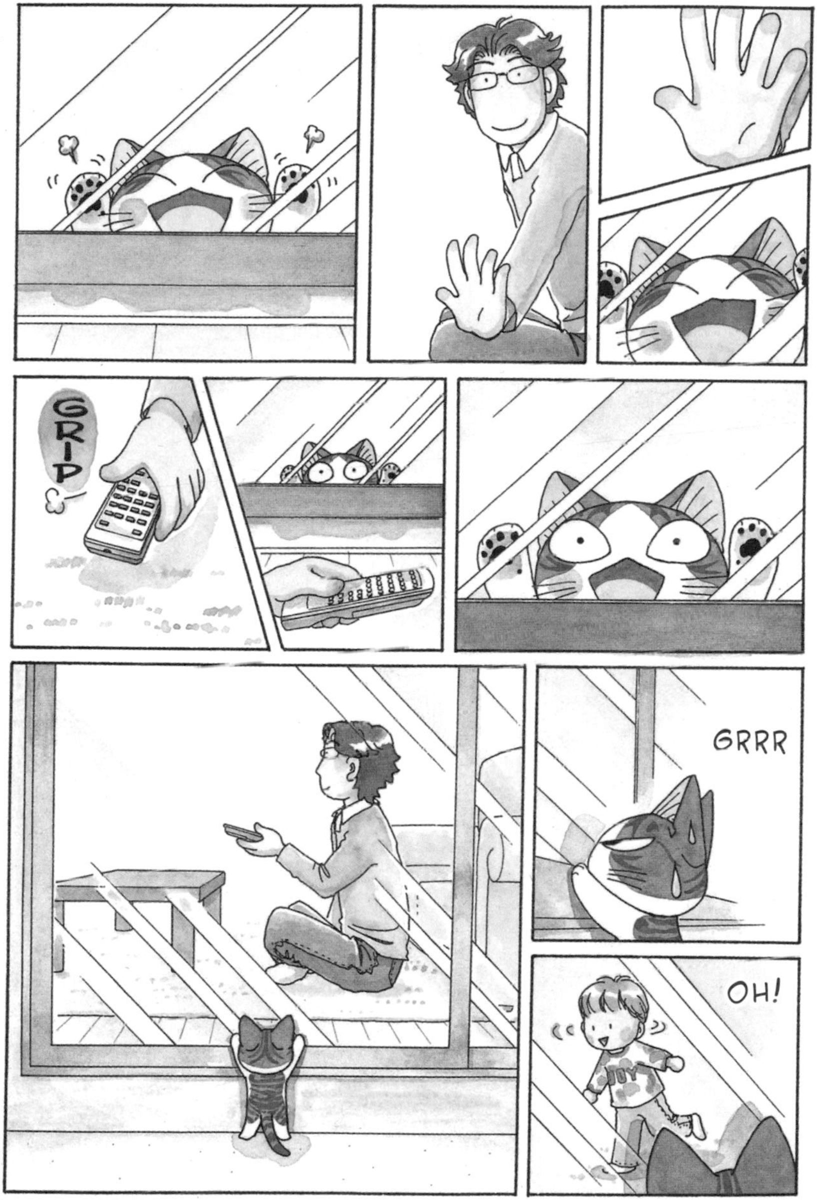
GRIP
GRRR
OH!
BOY

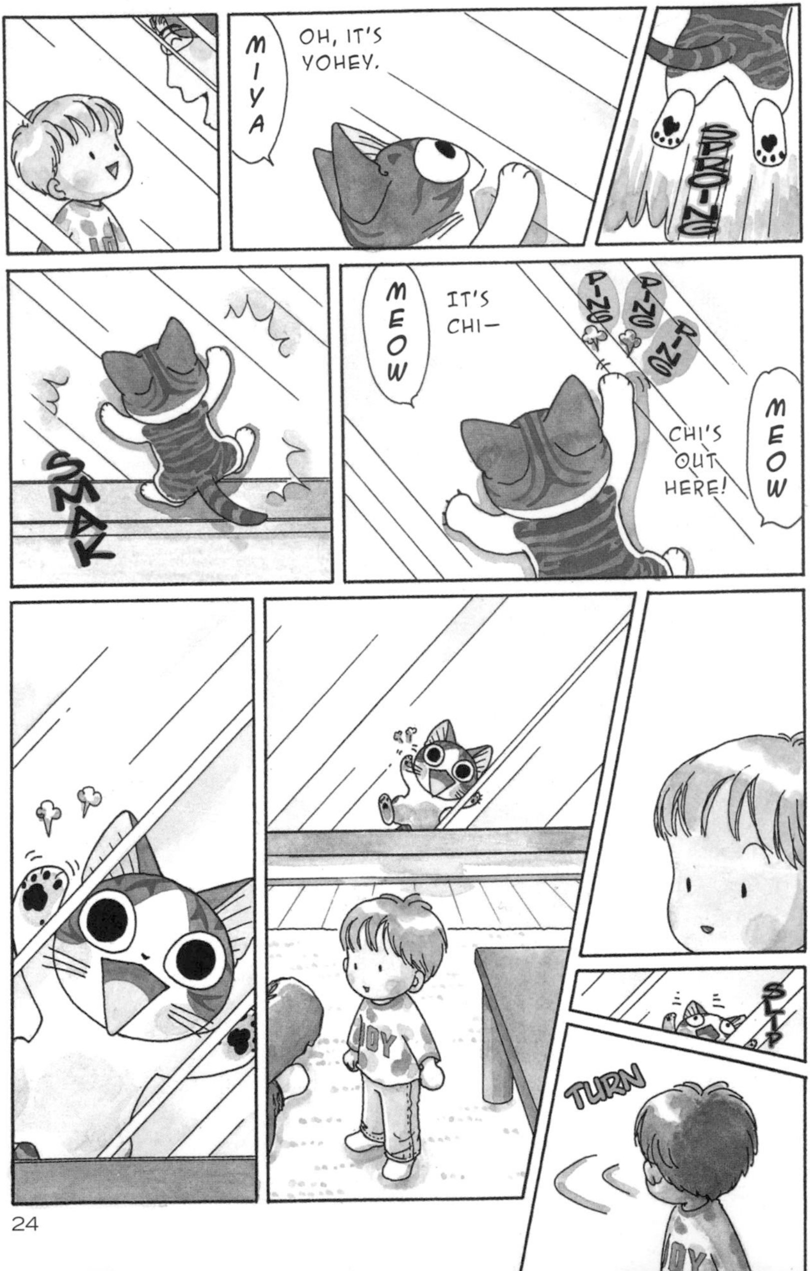
MIYA
OH, IT'S YOHEY.
SPROING
SMAK
MEOW
IT'S CHI—
PING PING PING
CHI'S OUT HERE!
MEOW
SLIP
TURN

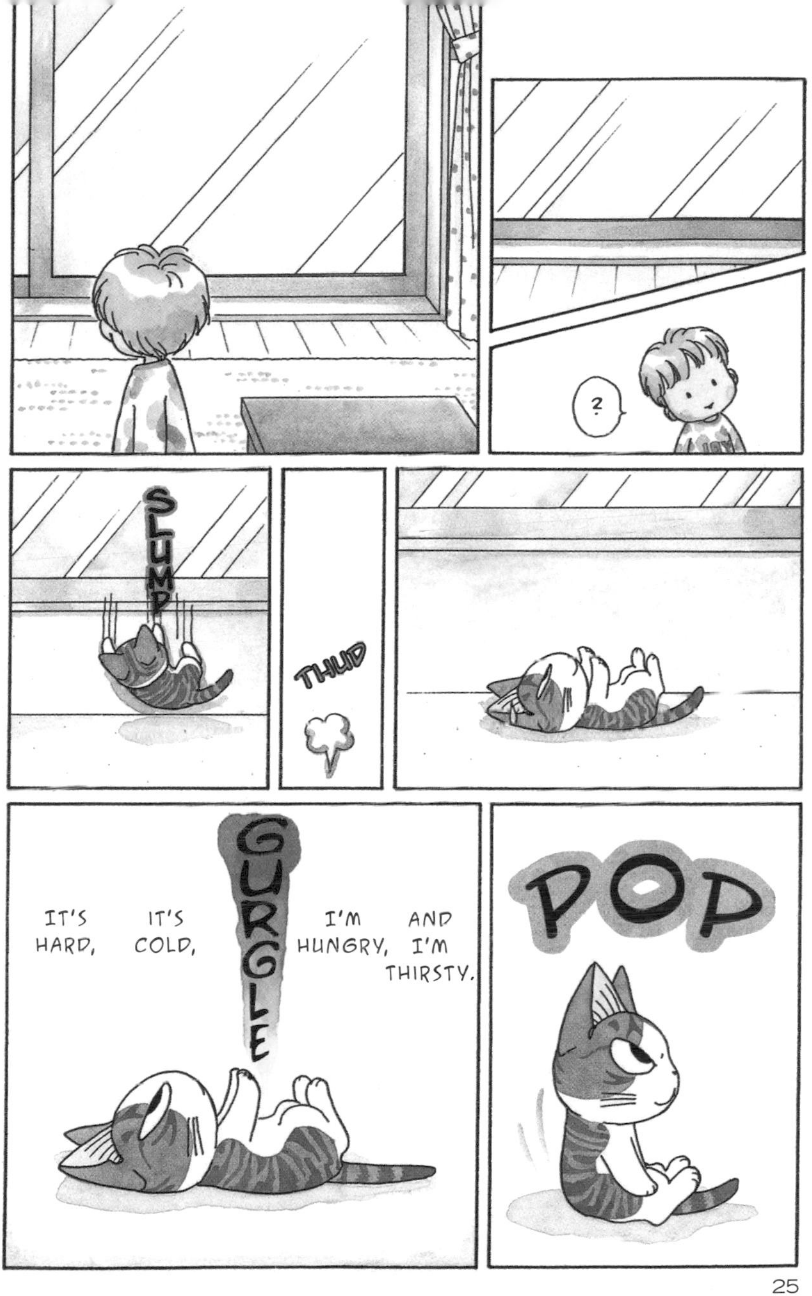
?
SLUMP
THUD
IT'S HARD,
IT'S COLD,
GURGLE
I'M HUNGRY,
AND I'M THIRSTY.
POP

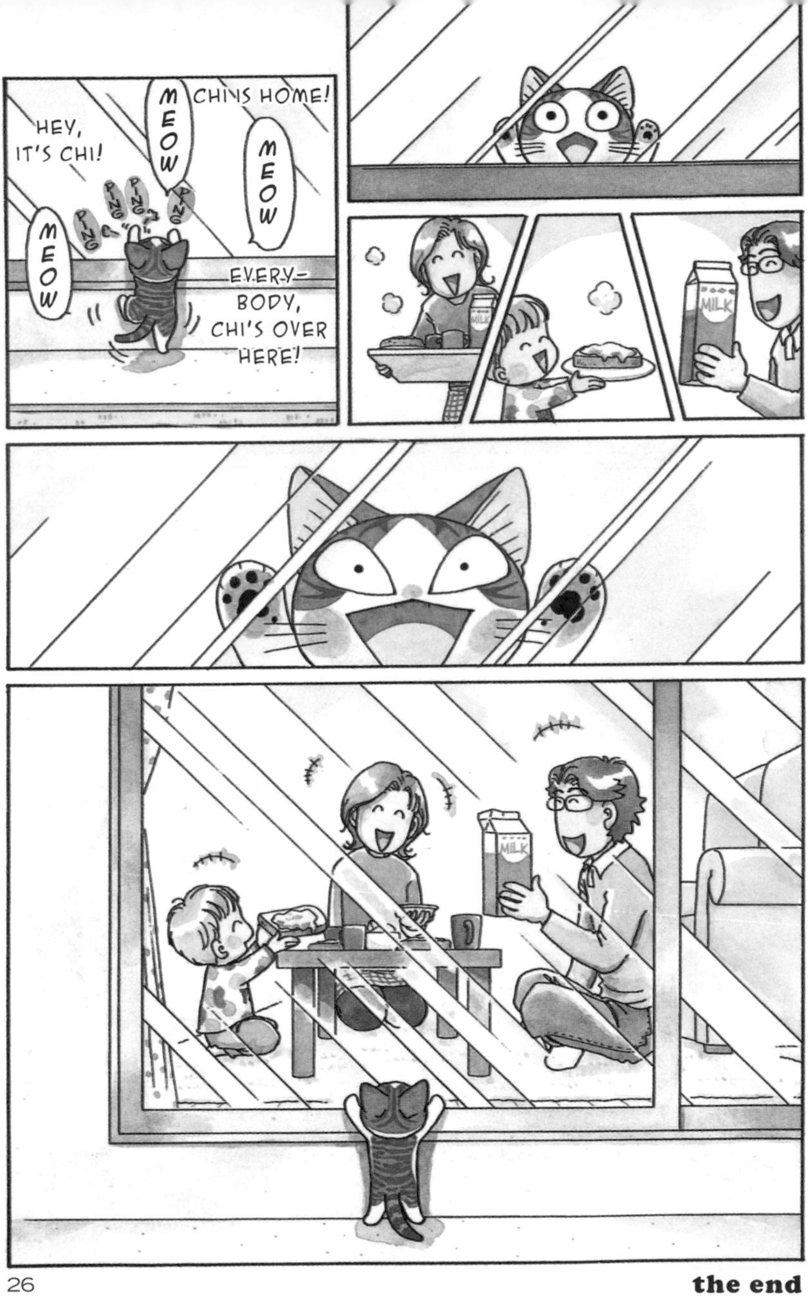
MEOW
CHI'S HOME!
HEY, IT'S CHI!
MEOW
PING PING PING PING
MEOW
EVERY-BODY, CHI'S OVER HERE!
MILK
MILK

the end

homemade 114: a cat comes back

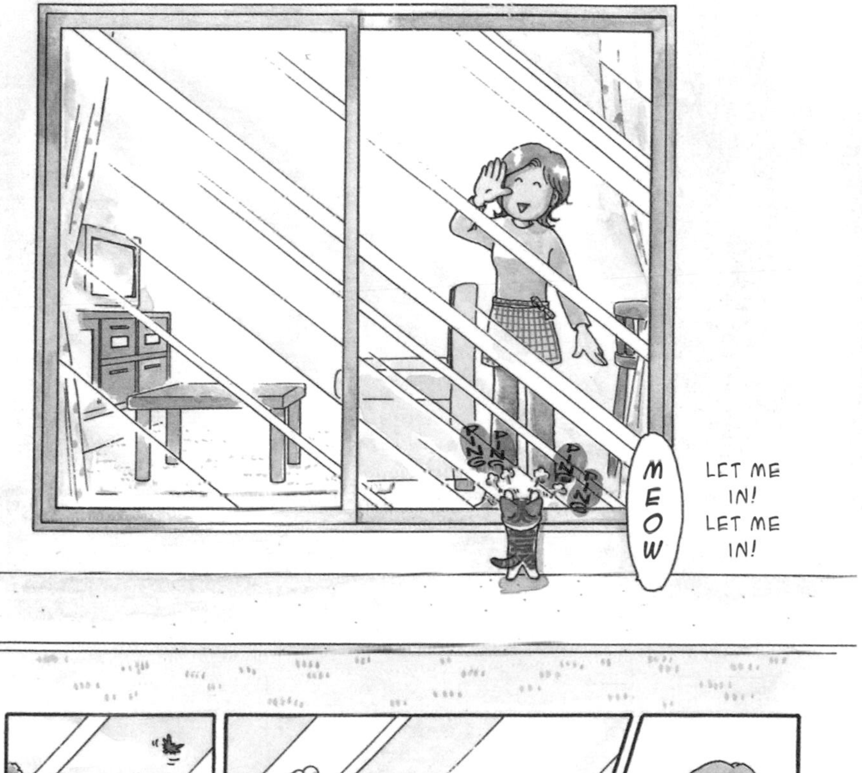
PING
PING
PING
PING
MEOW
LET ME IN! LET ME IN!
BRIGHT
IT'S NICE OUT.
HM?

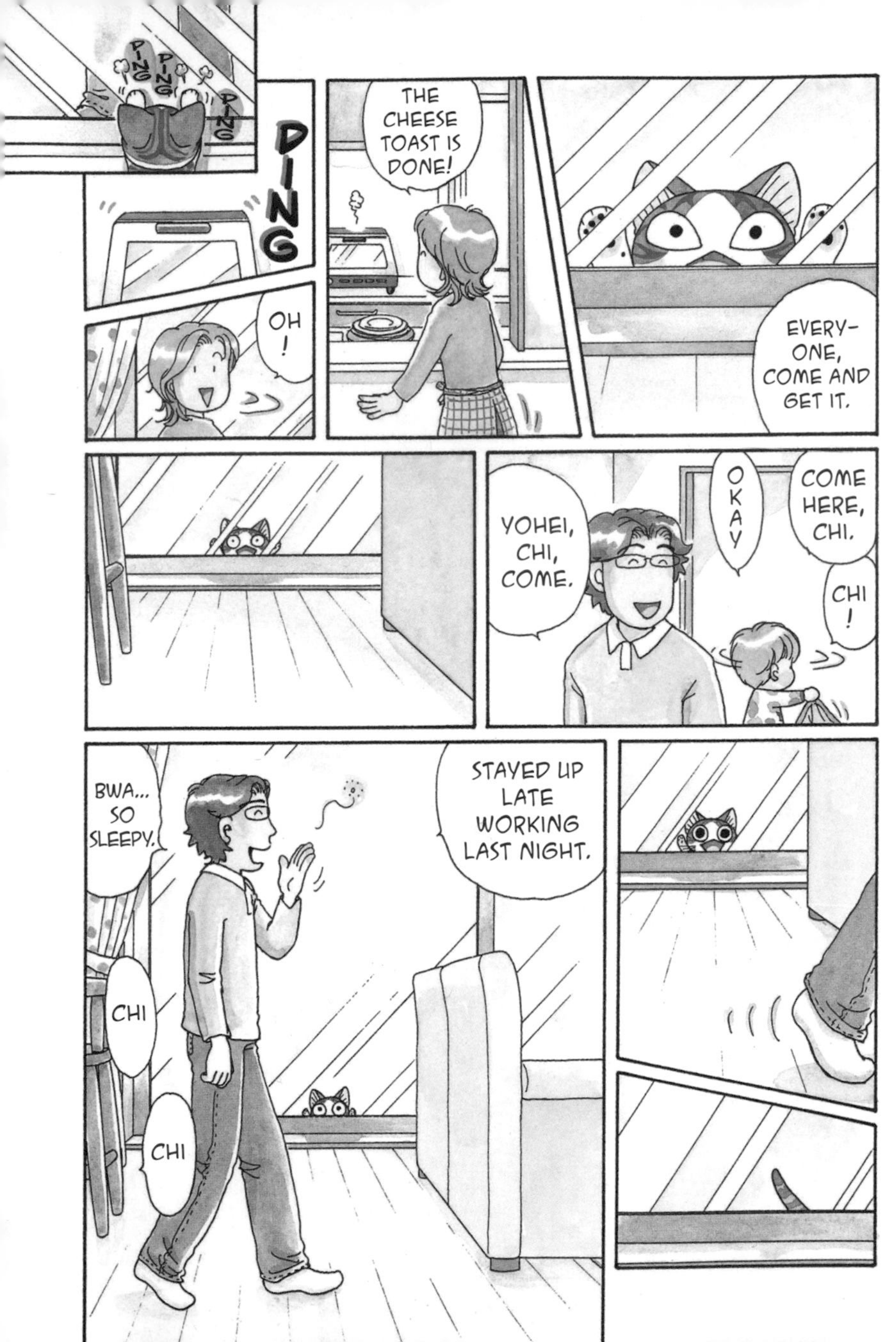

PING
PING
PING
DING
OH!
THE CHEESE TOAST IS DONE!
EVERYONE, COME AND GET IT.
YOHEI, CHI, COME.
OKAY
COME HERE, CHI.
CHI!
BWA... SO SLEEPY.
STAYED UP LATE WORKING LAST NIGHT.
CHI
CHI

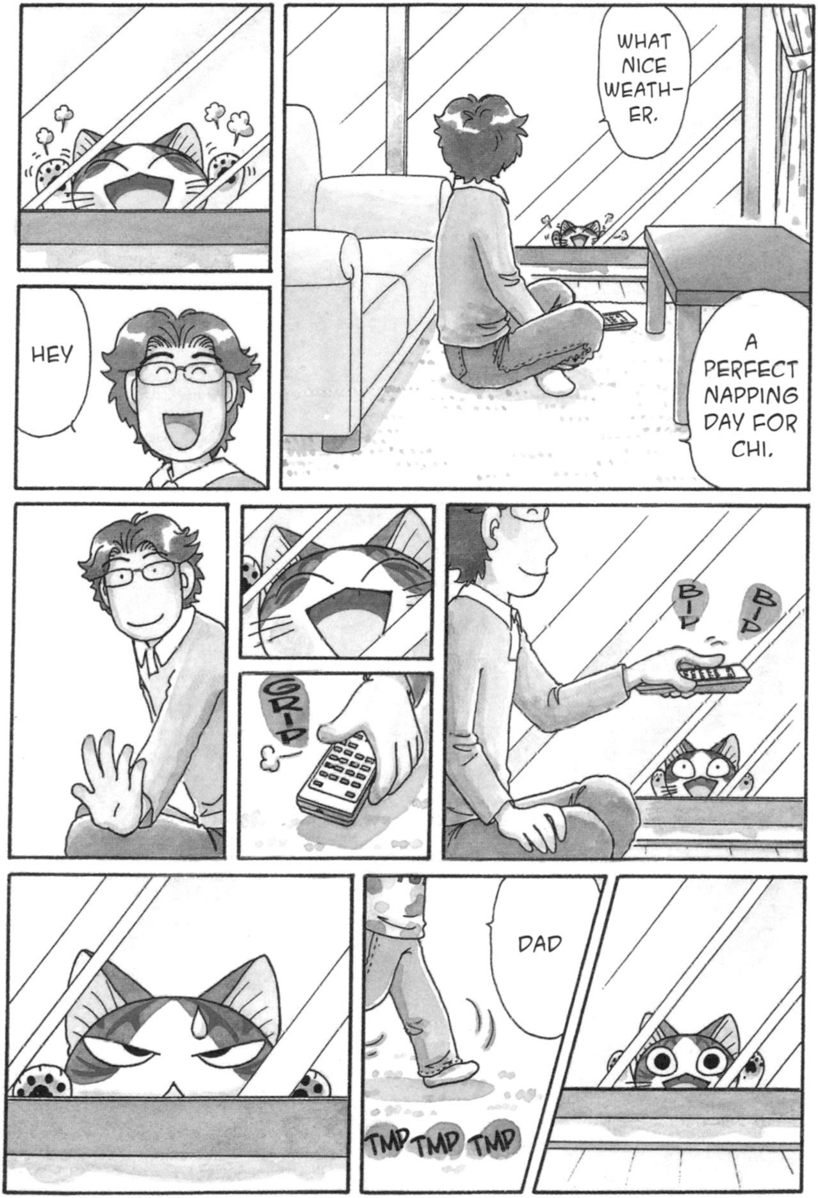
WHAT NICE WEATH- ER.
A PERFECT NAPPING DAY FOR CHI.
HEY
GRIP
BIP
BIP
DAD
TMP TMP TMP

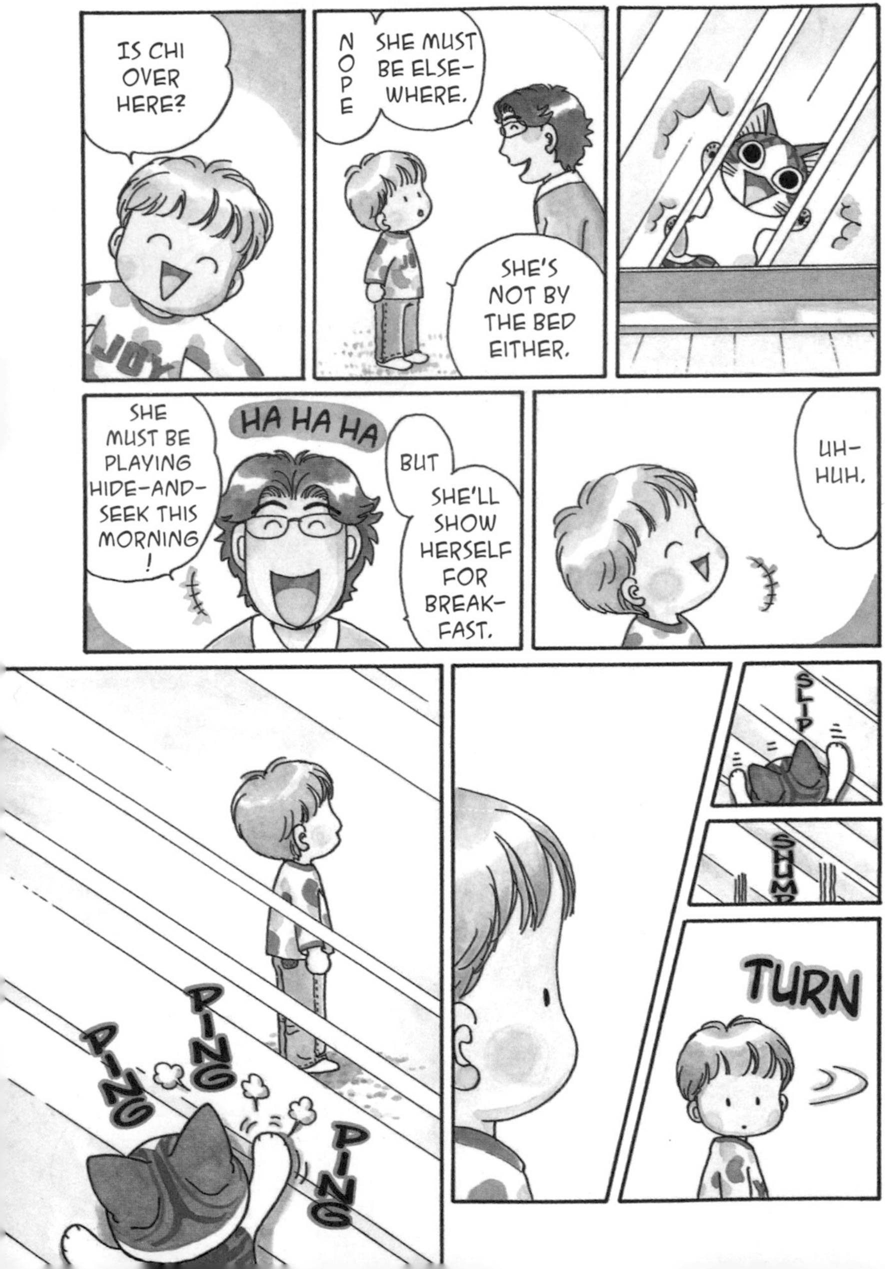
IS CHI OVER HERE?
NOPE
SHE MUST BE ELSE-WHERE.
SHE'S NOT BY THE BED EITHER.
SHE MUST BE PLAYING HIDE-AND-SEEK THIS MORNING!
HA HA HA
BUT SHE'LL SHOW HERSELF FOR BREAK-FAST.
UH-HUH.
PING
PING
PING
SLIP
SHUMP
TURN

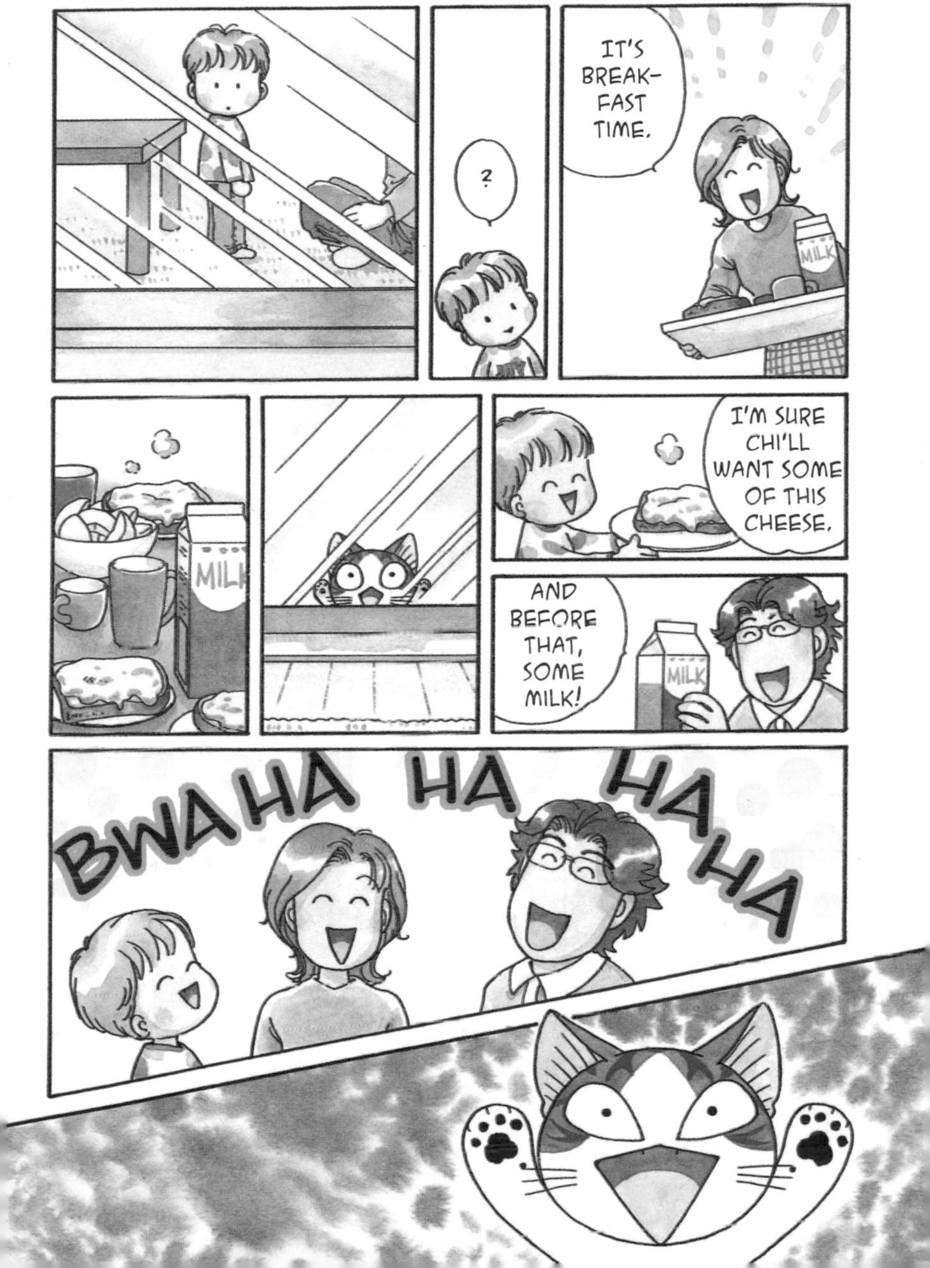
?
IT'S SURE BREAK-FAST TIME.
I'M SURE CHI'LL WANT SOME OF THIS CHEESE.
AND BEFORE THAT, SOME MILK!
BWAHA HA HA HA HA

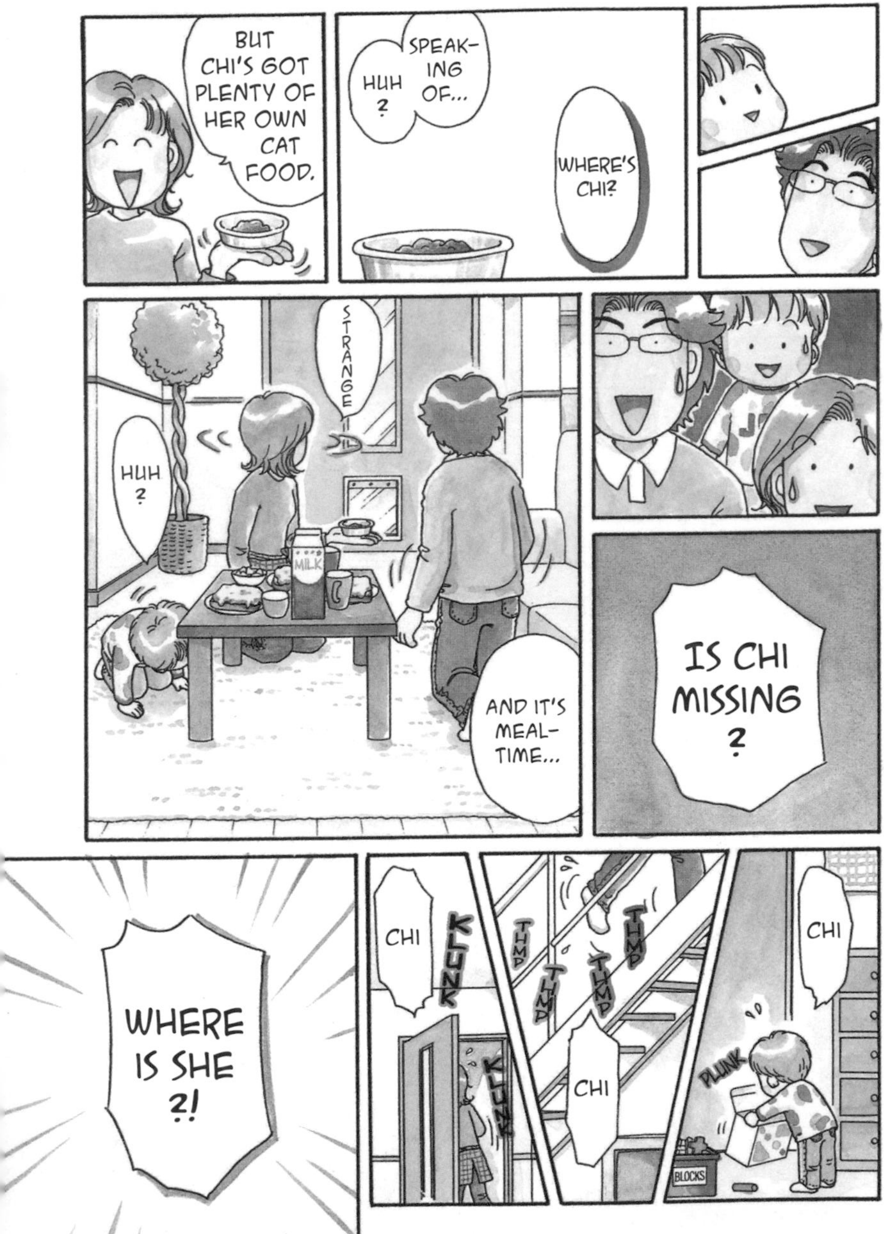
BUT CHI'S GOT PLENTY OF HER OWN CAT FOOD.
HUH?
SPEAKING OF...
WHERE'S CHI?
STRANGE
HUH?
AND IT'S MEALTIME...
IS CHI MISSING?
WHERE IS SHE?!
CHI
KLUNK
KLUNK
THMP THMP THMP THMP
CHI
CHI
PLINK
BLOCKS
MILK

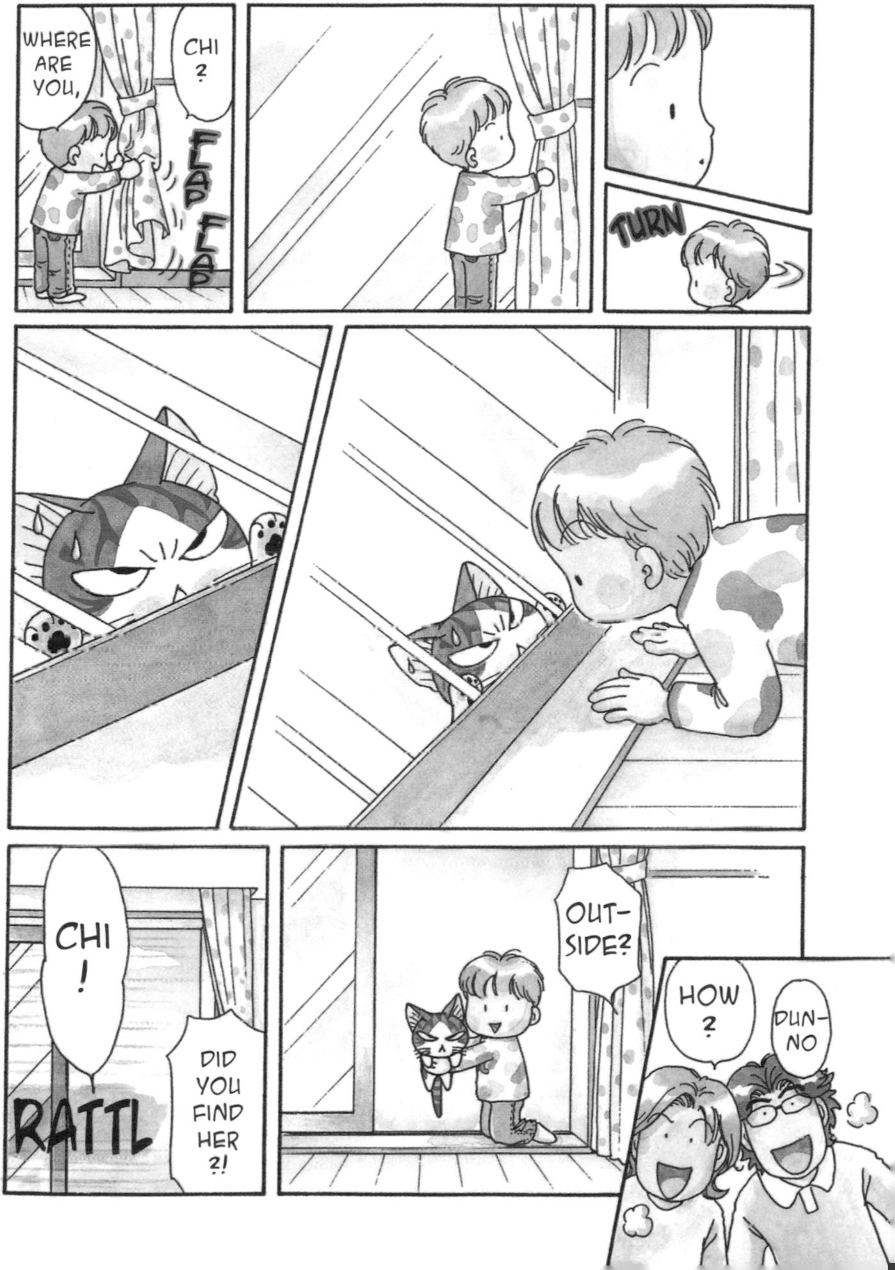
WHERE ARE YOU,
CHI?
FLAP FLAP
TURN
CHI!
RATTL
DID YOU FIND HER?!
OUT-SIDE?
HOW?
DUN-NO

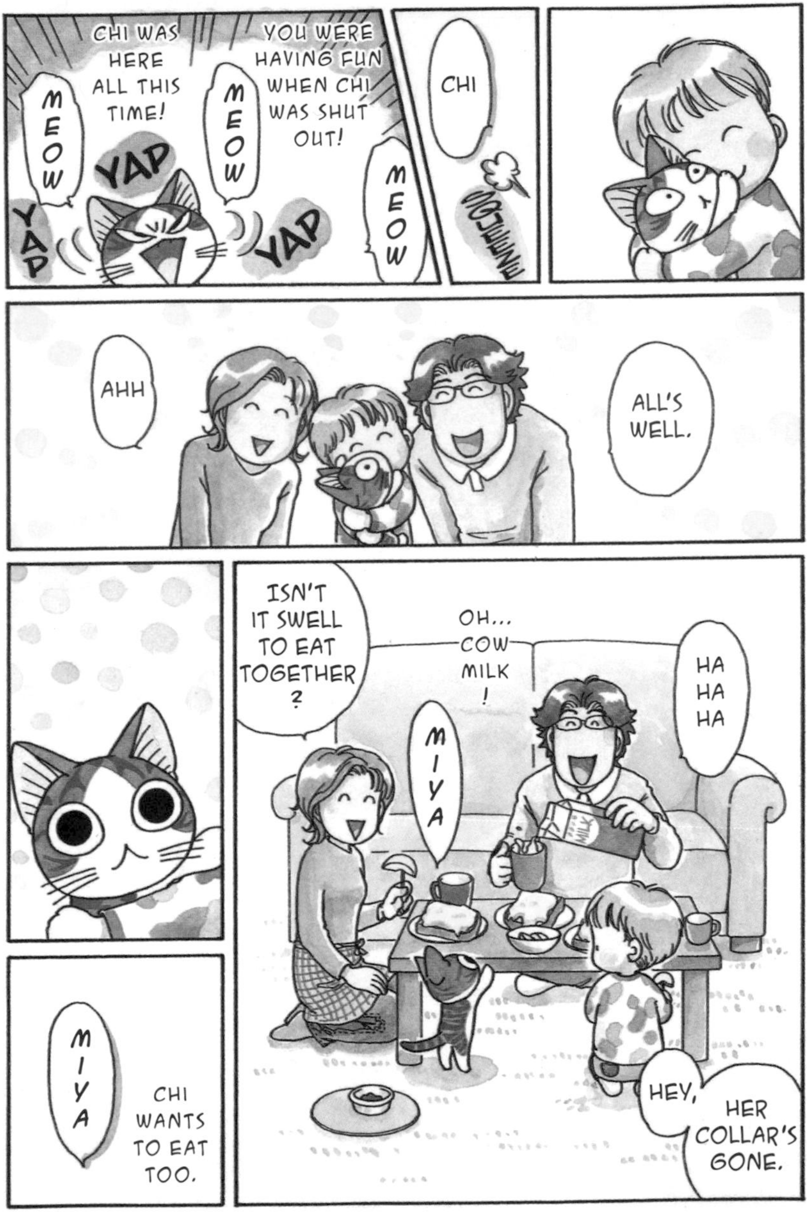
MEOW
YAP
CHI WAS HERE ALL THIS TIME!
MEOW
YAP
YOU WERE HAVING FUN WHEN CHI WAS SHUT OUT!
YAP
MEOW
CHI
AHH
ALL'S WELL.
MIYA
CHI WANTS TO EAT TOO.
ISN'T IT SWELL TO EAT TOGETHER?
OH... COW MILK!
HA HA HA
MIYA
HEY, HER COLLAR'S GONE.

the end

homemade 115: a cat gives up

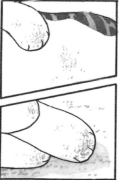

CHI'S A MESS.

HUH ?

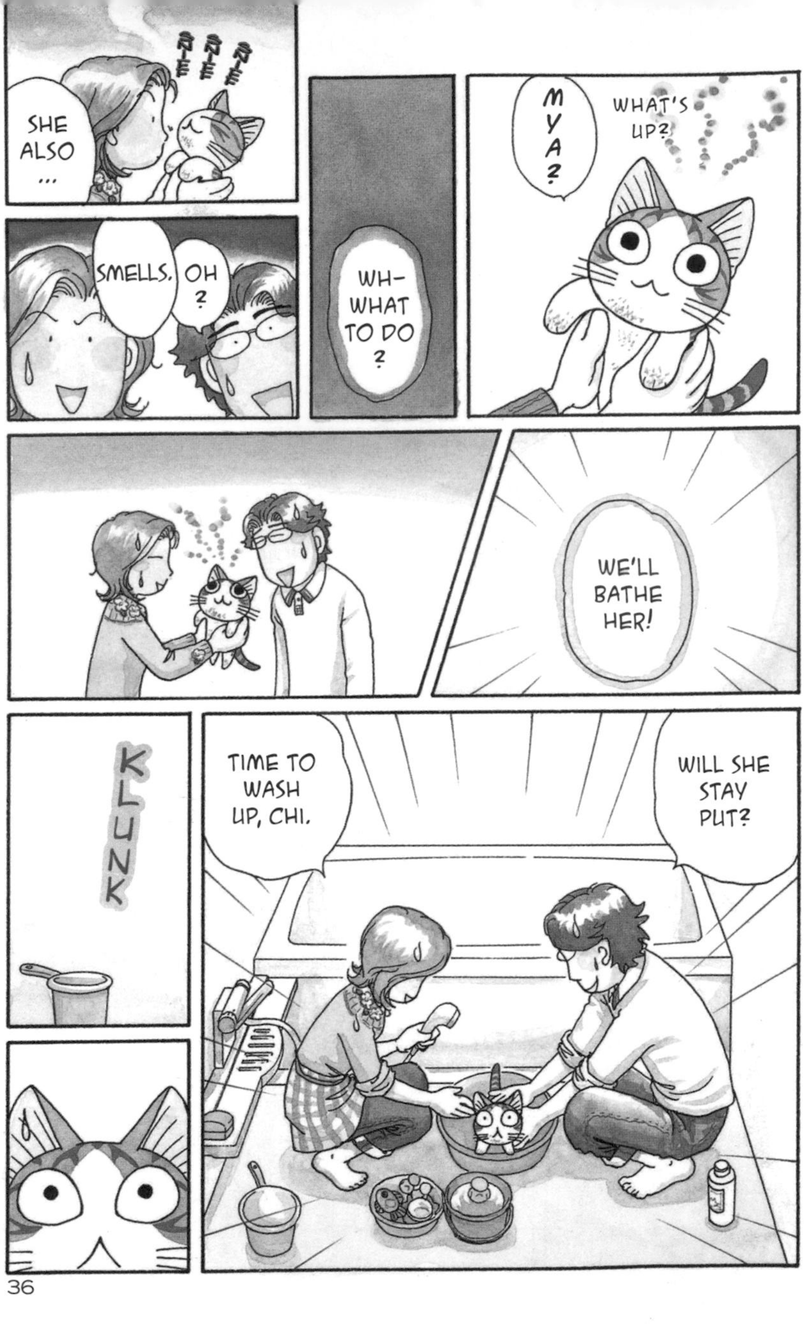
SNIF SNIF SNIF
SHE ALSO ...
SMELLS.
OH?
WH-WHAT TO DO?
MYA?
WHAT'S UP?
WE'LL BATHE HER!
KLUNK
TIME TO WASH UP, CHI.
WILL SHE STAY PUT?

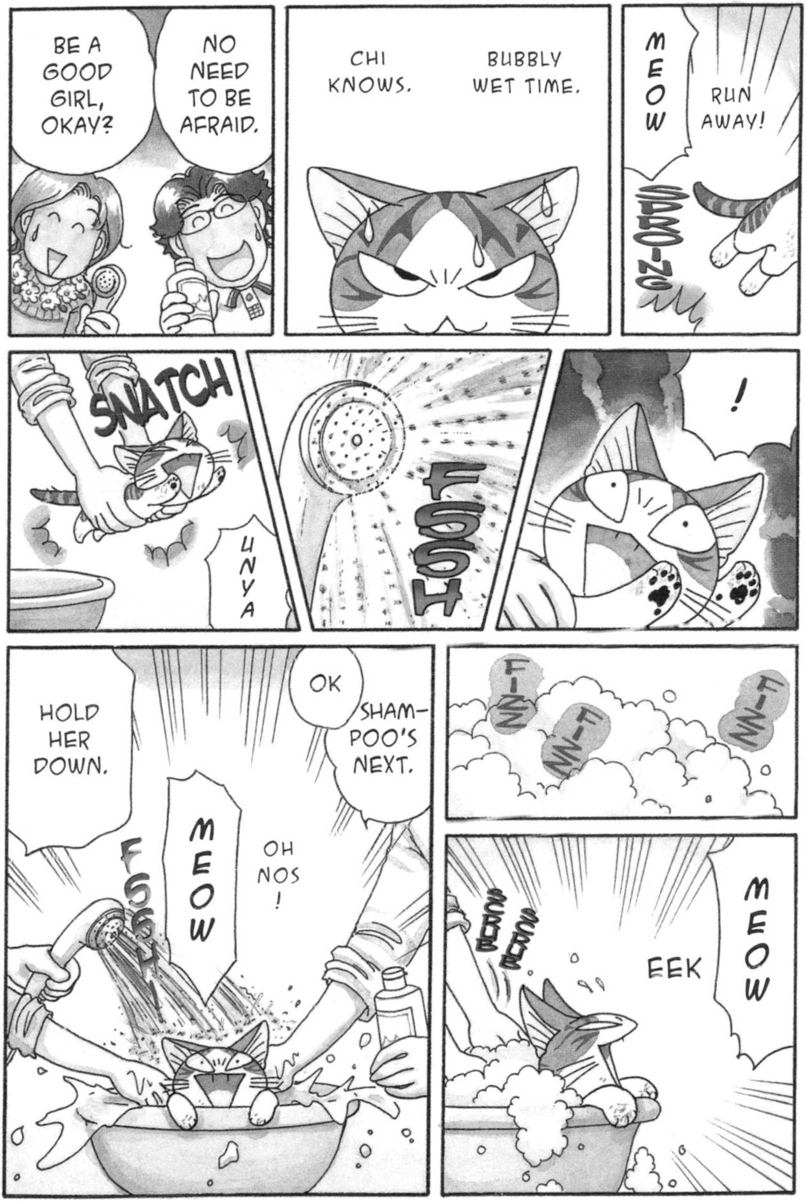
BE A GOOD GIRL, OKAY?
NO NEED TO BE AFRAID.
CHI KNOWS.
BUBBLY WET TIME.
MEOW
RUN AWAY!
SPROING
SNATCH
UNYA
FSSH
!
HOLD HER DOWN.
OK
SHAMPOO'S NEXT.
FSSH
MEOW
OH NOS!
FIZZ
FIZZ
FIZZ
SCRUB
SCRUB
EEK
MEOW

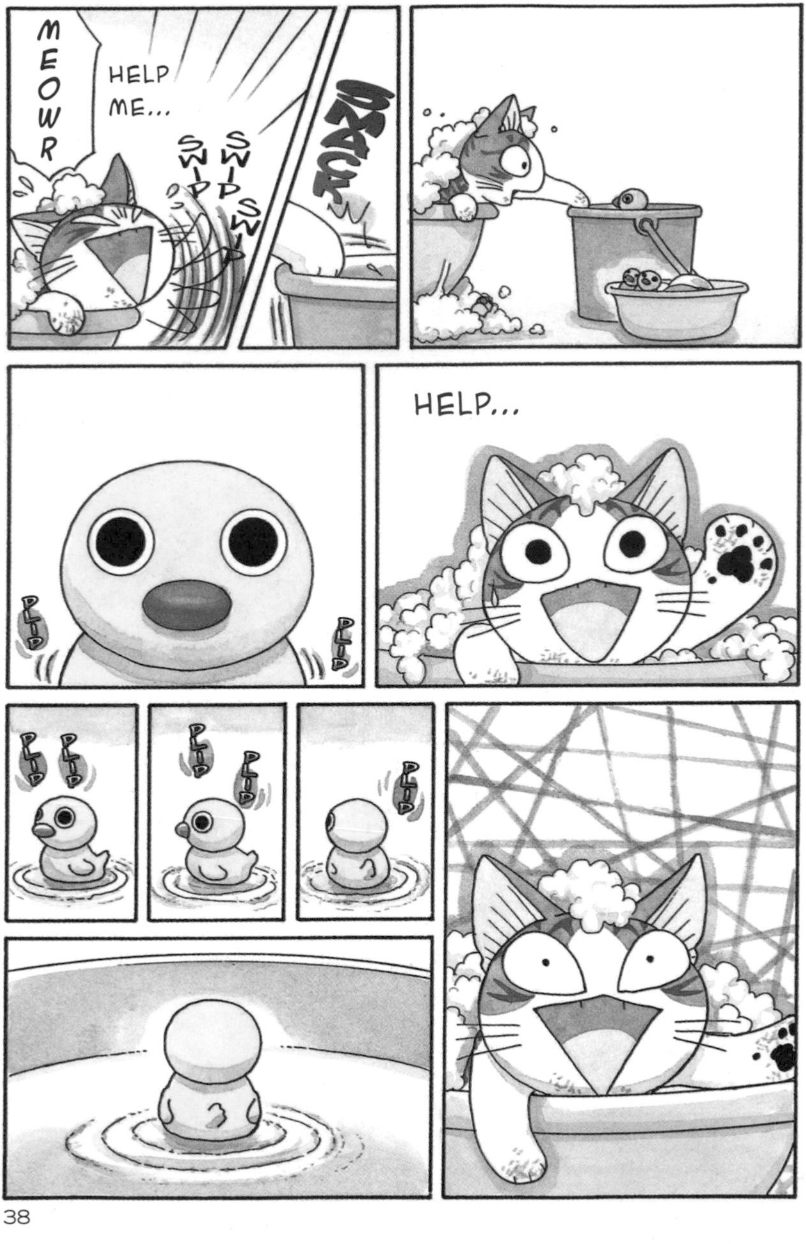
MEOWR
HELP ME...
SWIP SWIP SWI
SMACK
HELP...
PLIP
PLIP
PLIP PLIP
PLIP
PLIP
PLIP

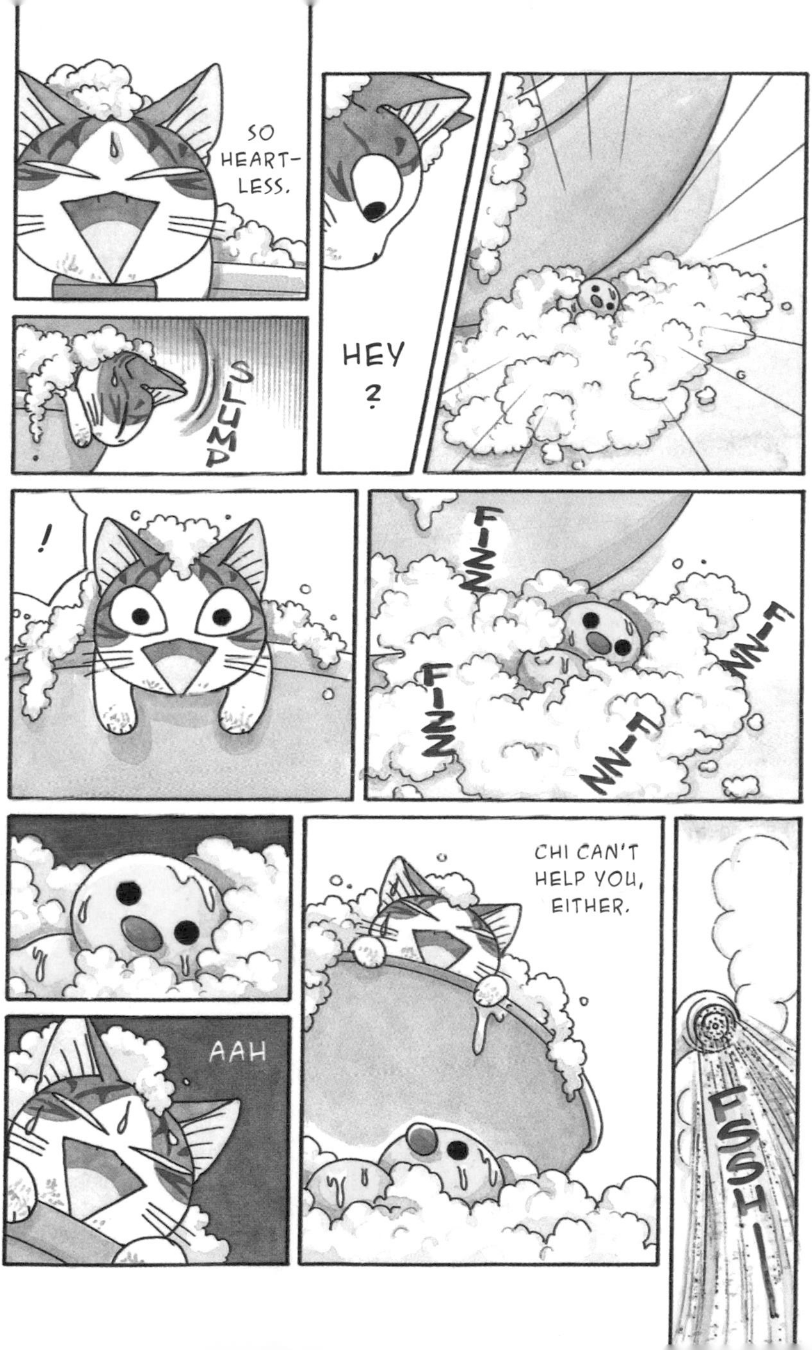
SO HEART-LESS.
HEY ?
SLUMP
!
FIZZ
FIZZ
NN-FI
NN-FI
CHI CAN'T HELP YOU, EITHER.
AAH
FSSH

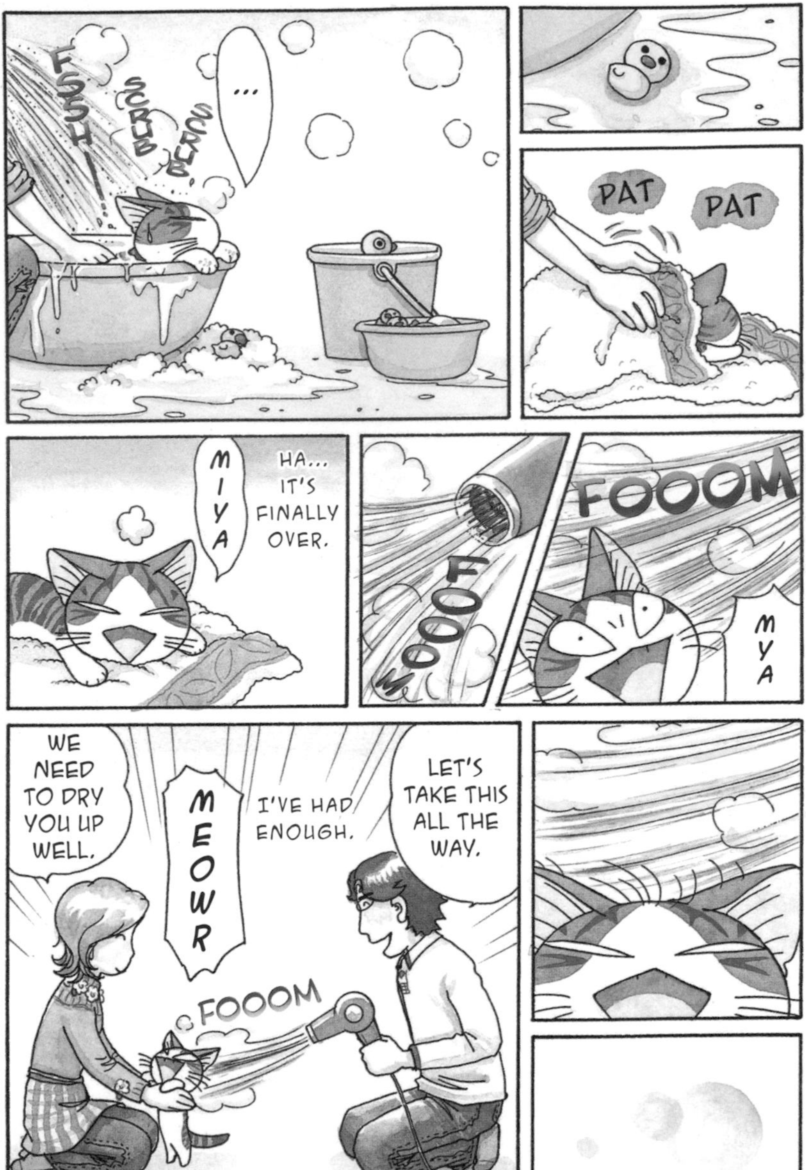
FSSH!
SCRUB
SCRUB
...
PAT
PAT
MIYA
HA... IT'S FINALLY OVER.
FOOOM
FOOOM
MYA
WE NEED TO DRY YOU UP WELL.
MEOWR
I'VE HAD ENOUGH.
LET'S TAKE THIS ALL THE WAY.
FOOOM

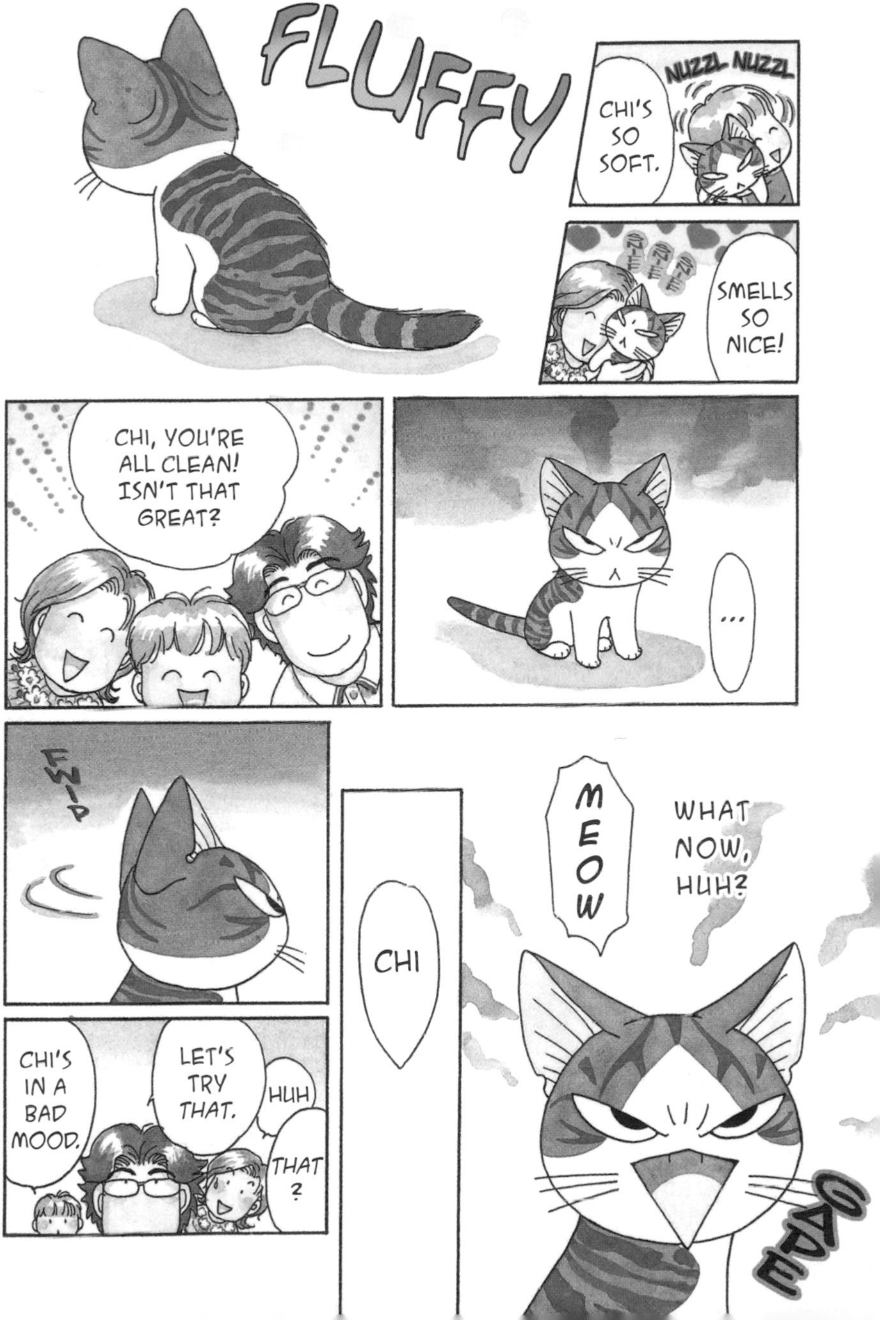
FLUFFY
NUZZL NUZZL
CHI'S SO SOFT.
SNIFF SNIFF SNIFF
SMELLS SO NICE!
CHI, YOU'RE ALL CLEAN! ISN'T THAT GREAT?
...
FWIP
CHI'S IN A BAD MOOD.
LET'S TRY THAT.
HUH
THAT?
CHI
MEOW
WHAT NOW, HUH?

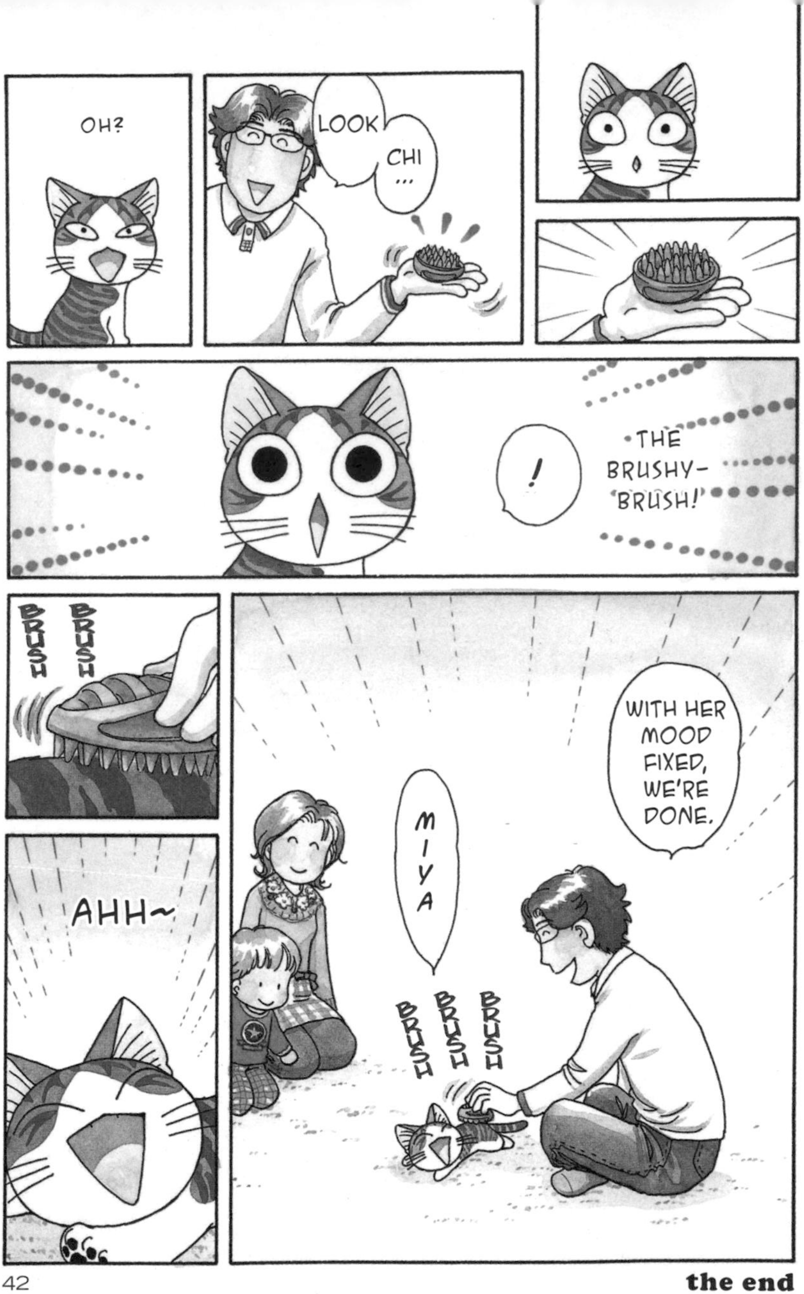
OH?
LOOK
CHI ...
THE BRUSHY-BRUSH!
!
BRUSH BRUSH
WITH HER MOOD FIXED, WE'RE DONE.
MIYA
BRUSH BRUSH BRUSH
AHH~

the end

homemade 116: a cat observes

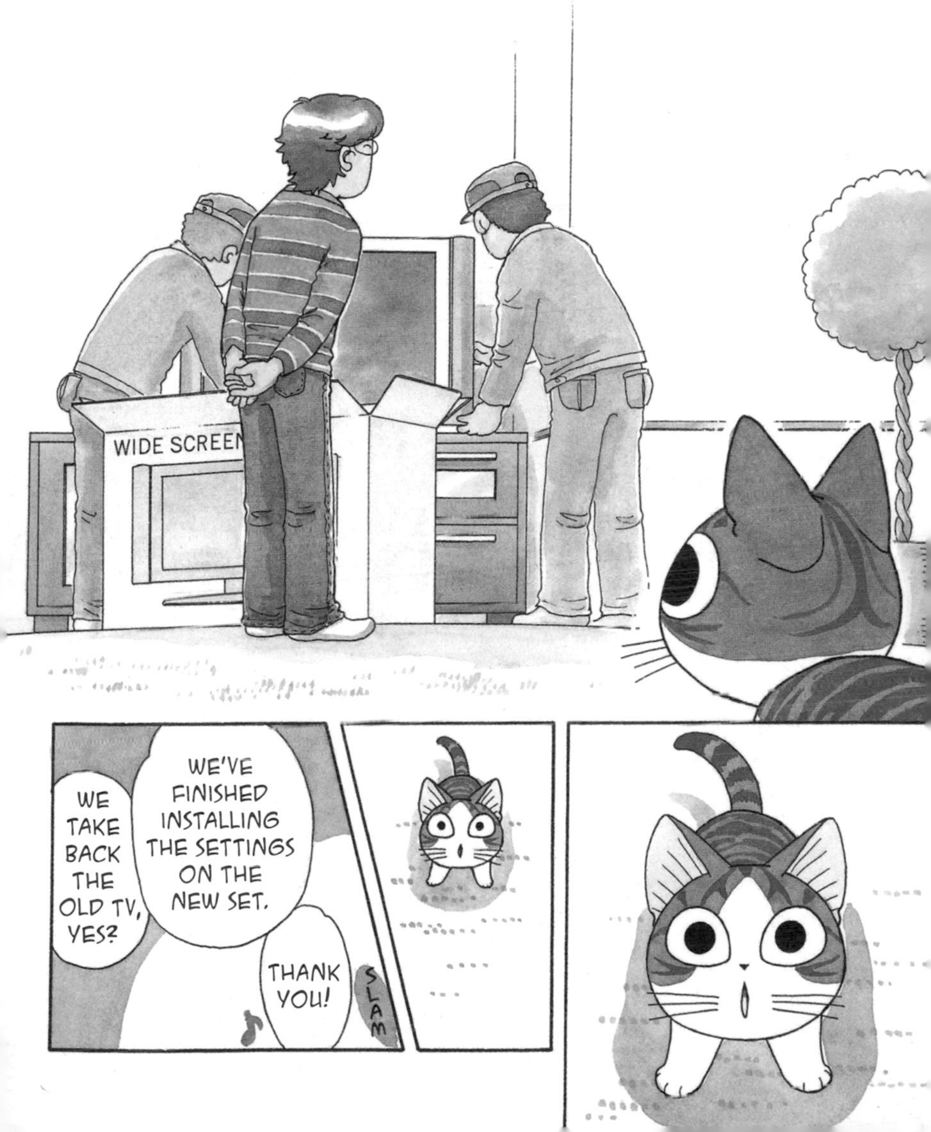
WIDE SCREEN
WE'VE FINISHED INSTALLING THE SETTINGS ON THE NEW SET.
WE TAKE BACK THE OLD TV, YES?
THANK YOU!
SLAM

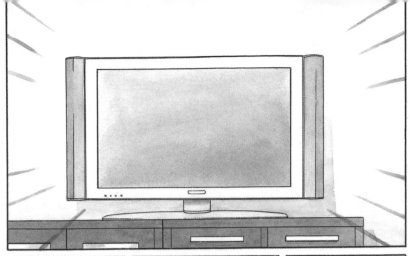

IT'S SO THIN! AND WHAT A BIG SCREEN.

IT'S SO COOL!

YUP

YUP

THERE ARE SO MANY BUTTONS. HDTV, SATELLITE...

IT'S DIGITAL SO THERE'S EVEN A PROGRAMMING GUIDE MENU.

STARE

WHAT'S THAT?

MIYA

POWER ON!

BIP

44

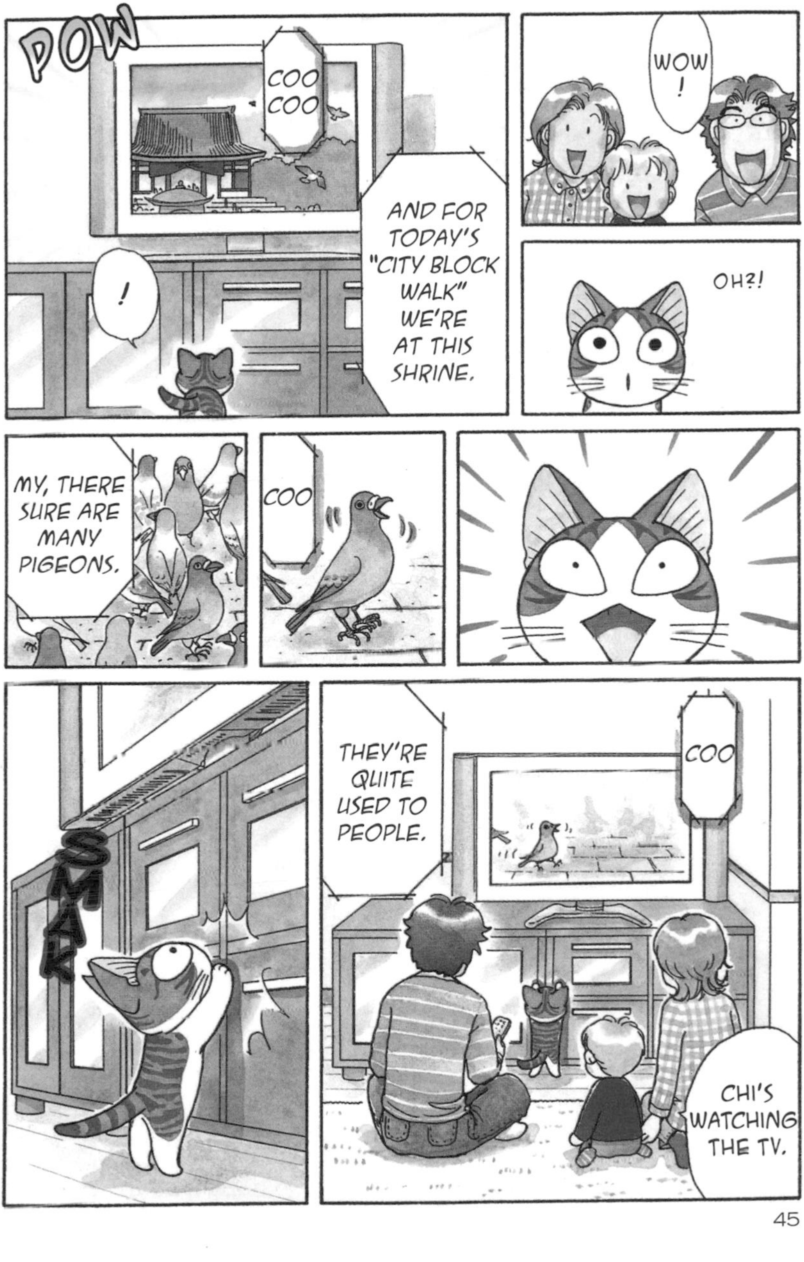
POW
COO COO
!
AND FOR TODAY'S "CITY BLOCK WALK" WE'RE AT THIS SHRINE.
WOW!
OH?!
MY, THERE SURE ARE MANY PIGEONS.
COO
SMAK
THEY'RE QUITE USED TO PEOPLE.
COO
CHI'S WATCHING THE TV.

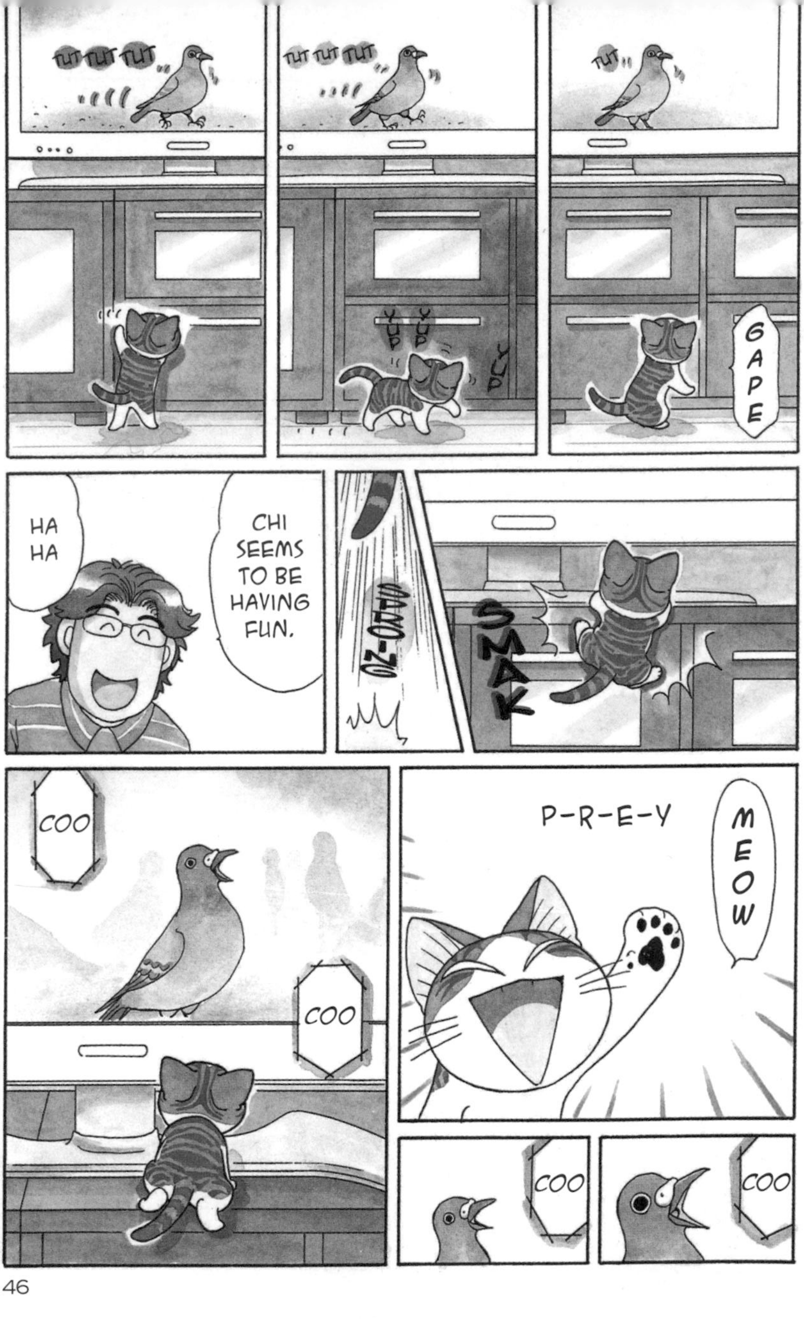
TUT TUT TUT
TUT TUT TUT
YUP YUP
YUP
TUT
GAPE
HA HA
CHI SEEMS TO BE HAVING FUN.
SMAK
COO
COO
P-R-E-Y
MEOW
COO
COO

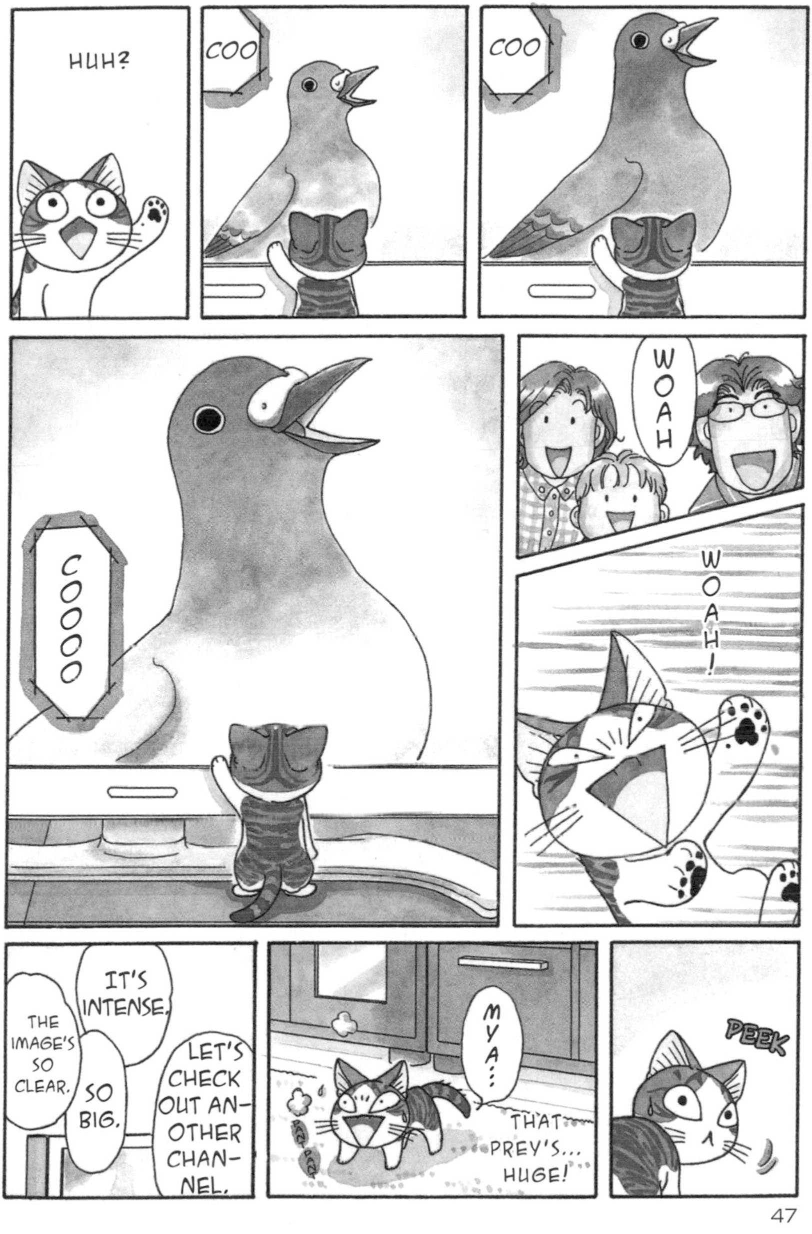
HUH?
COO
COO
COOOOO
WOAH
WOAH!
IT'S INTENSE.
THE IMAGE'S SO CLEAR.
SO BIG.
LET'S CHECK OUT AN-OTHER CHAN-NEL.
MYA...
THAT PREY'S... HUGE!
PEEK

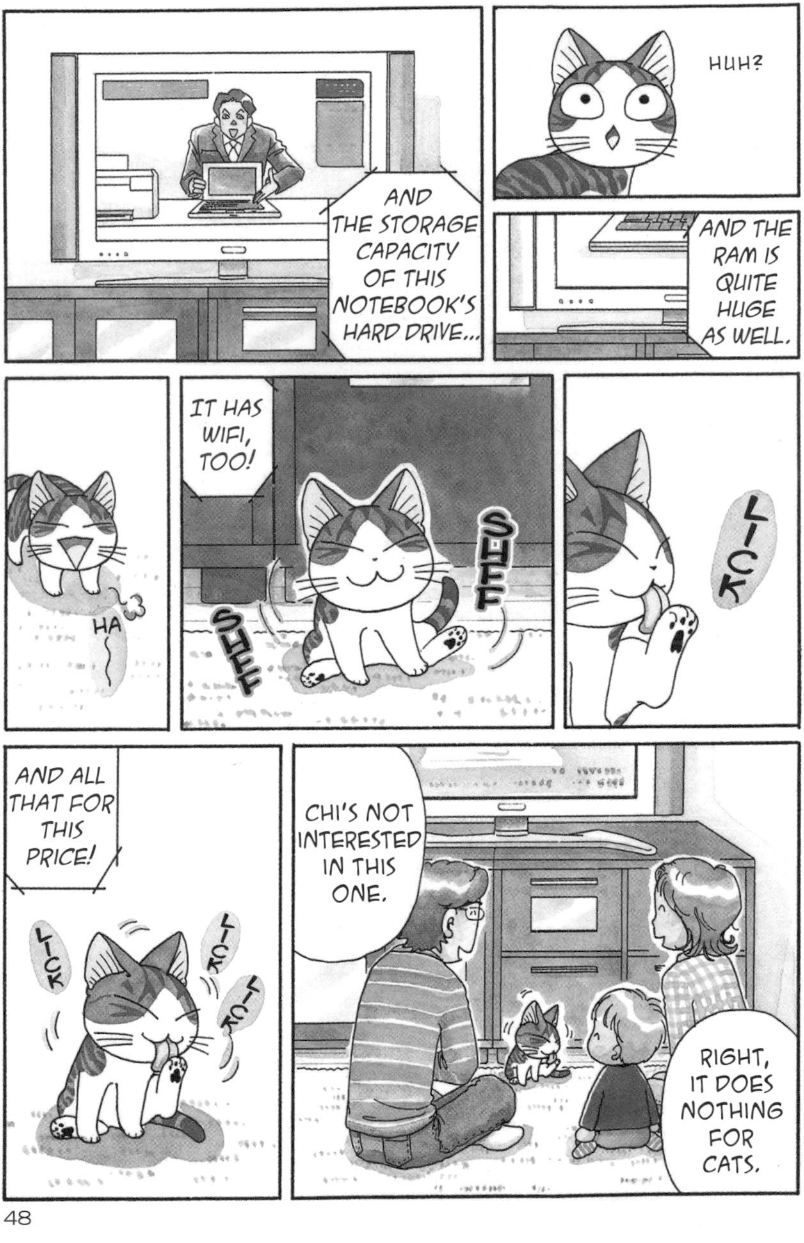
AND THE STORAGE CAPACITY OF THIS NOTEBOOK'S HARD DRIVE...
HUH?
AND THE RAM IS QUITE HUGE AS WELL.
HA
IT HAS WIFI, TOO!
SHUFF
SHUFF
LICK
AND ALL THAT FOR THIS PRICE!
LICK
LICK
LICK
CHI'S NOT INTERESTED IN THIS ONE.
RIGHT, IT DOES NOTHING FOR CATS.

HOW ABOUT AN-OTHER CHAN-NEL?

HEH

THERE! A SCHOOL OF MACK-EREL!

OH

CHI'S GONNA LIKE THIS!

HERE, CHI...

HUP

FLICK

CHECK IT OUT.

LOOK, CHI... FISH!

HMM?

WHAT DO YOU THINK? FUN, HUH?

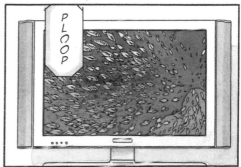

PLOOP

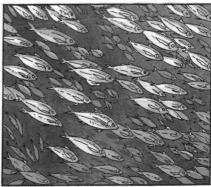

49

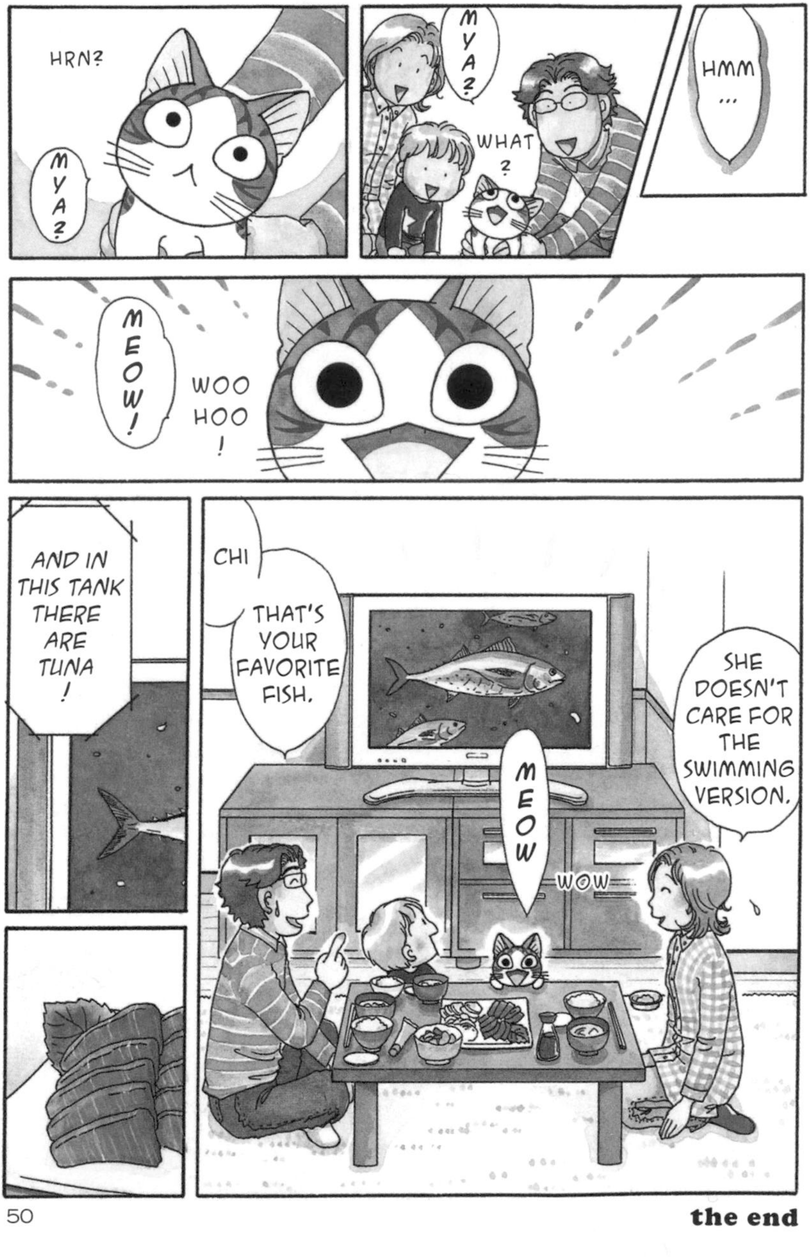
HRN?
MYA?
MYA?
WHAT?
HMM...
MEOW!
WOO HOO!
AND IN THIS TANK THERE ARE TUNA!
CHI
THAT'S YOUR FAVORITE FISH.
MEOW
WOW
SHE DOESN'T CARE FOR THE SWIMMING VERSION.

the end

homemade 117: a cat is astounded

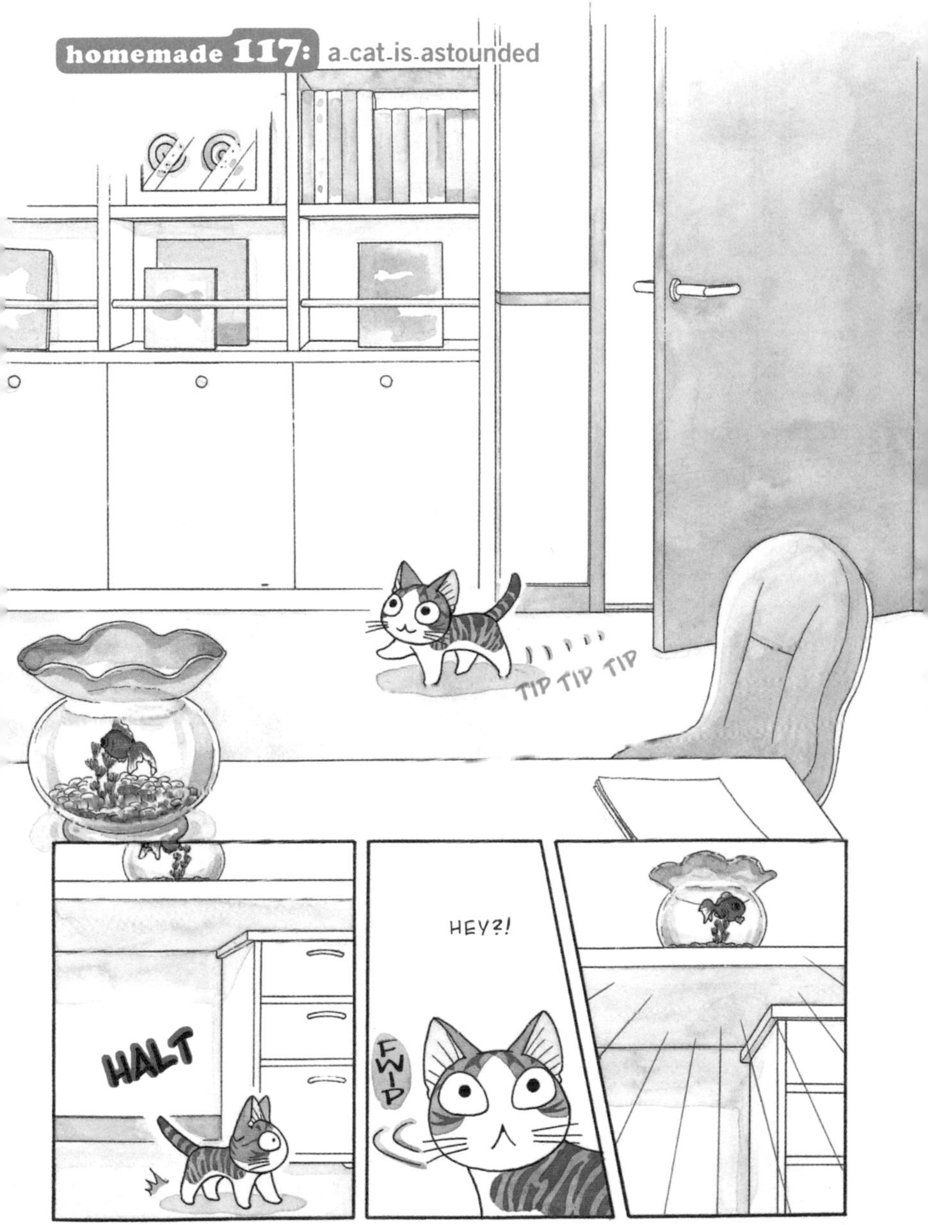
TIP TIP TIP
HALT
HEY?!
FWIP

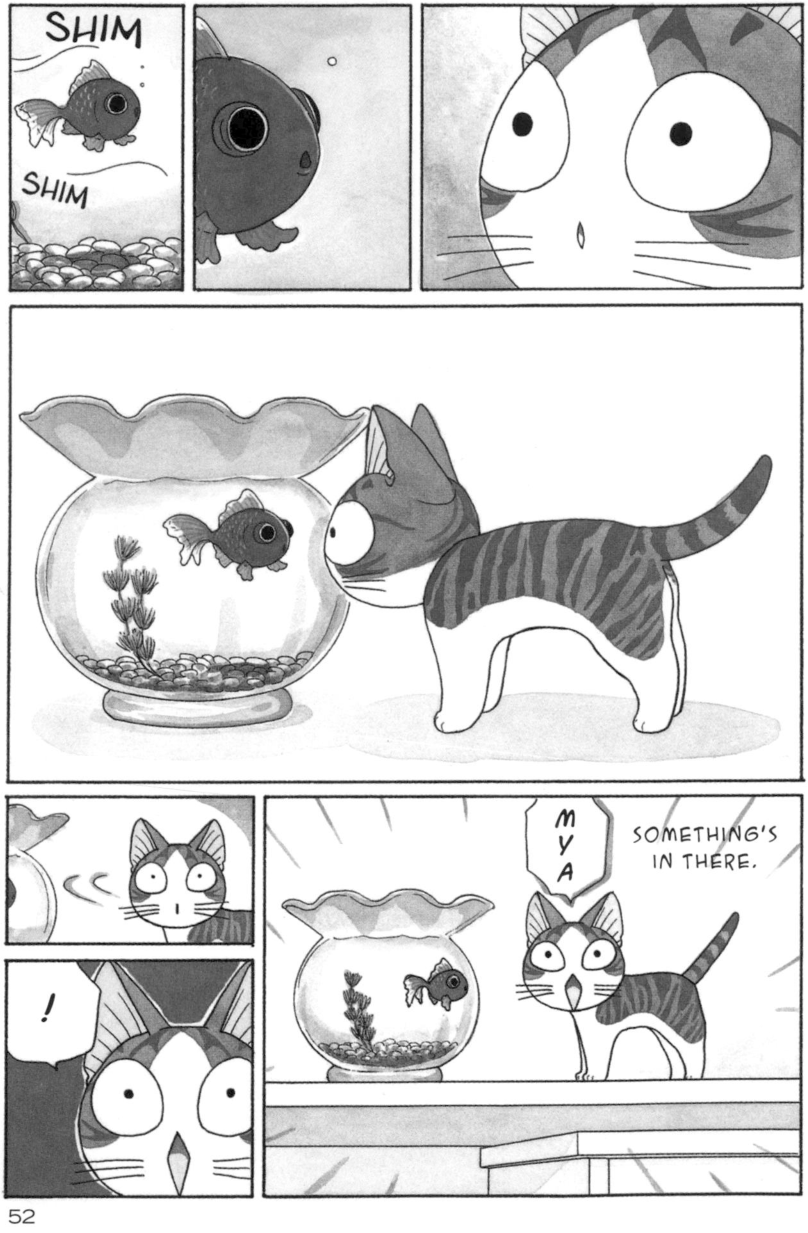
SHIM
SHIM
MYA
SOMETHING'S IN THERE.
!

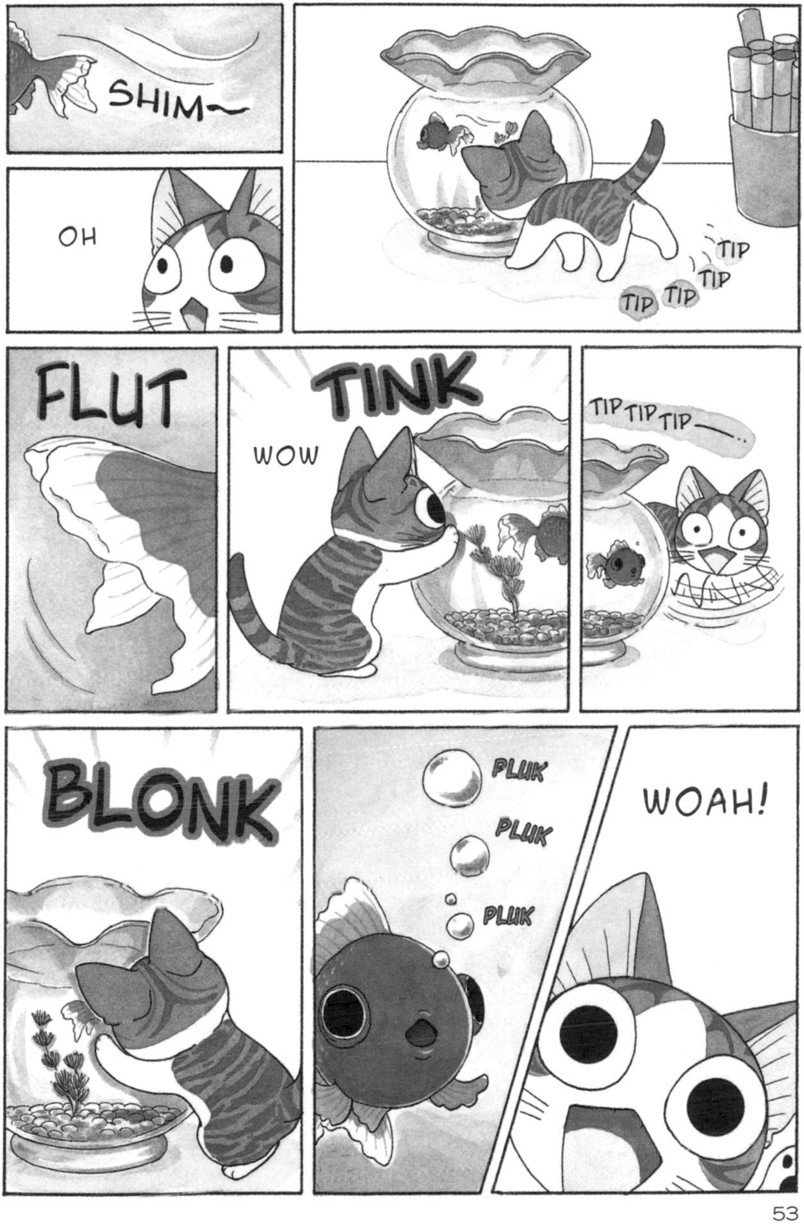
SHIM~
OH
TIP
TIP
TIP
TIP
FLUT
TINK
WOW
TIP TIP TIP——..
BLONK
PLUK
PLUK
PLUK
WOAH!

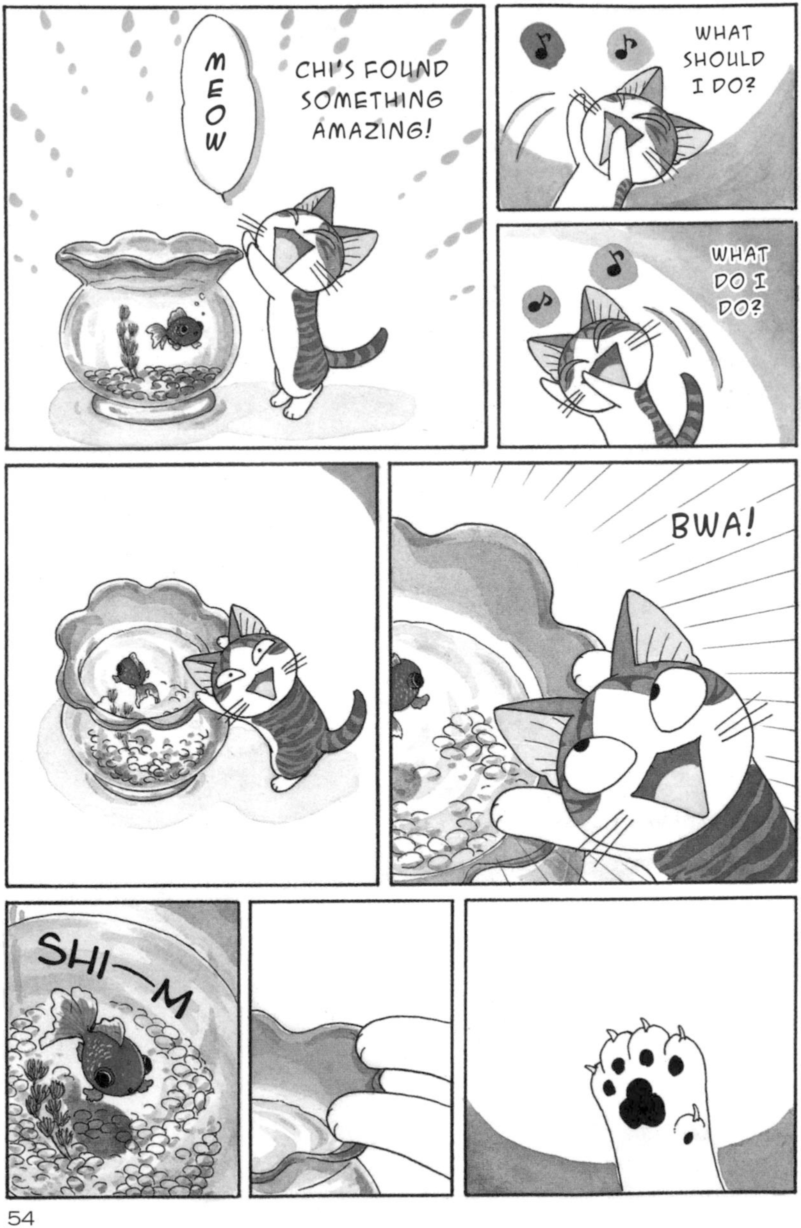
MEOW
CHI'S FOUND SOMETHING AMAZING!
WHAT SHOULD I DO?
WHAT DO I DO?
BWA!
SHI—M

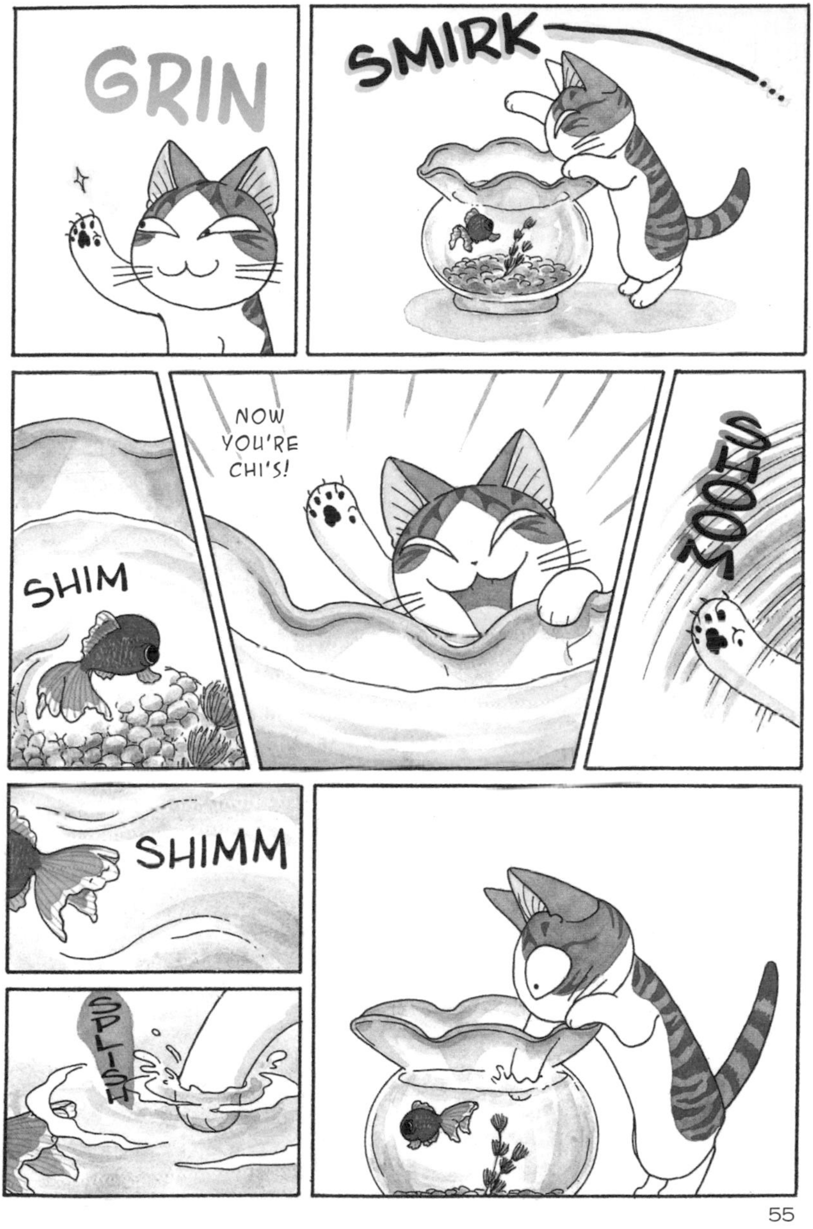
GRIN
SMIRK...
SHIM
NOW YOU'RE CHI'S!
SHOOM
SHIMM
SPLISH

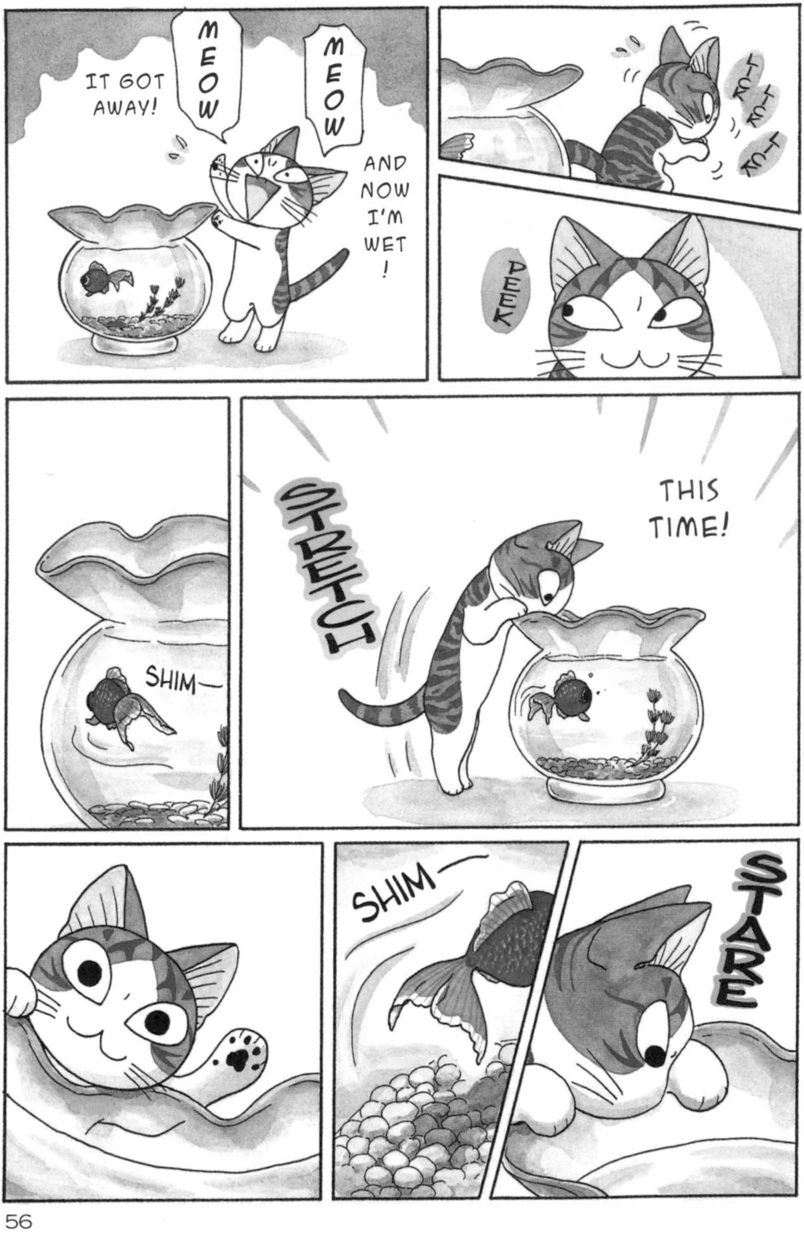

IT GOT AWAY!
MEOW
MEOW
AND NOW I'M WET!
LICK LICK LICK
PEEK
SHIM—
STRETCH
THIS TIME!
SHIM—
STARE

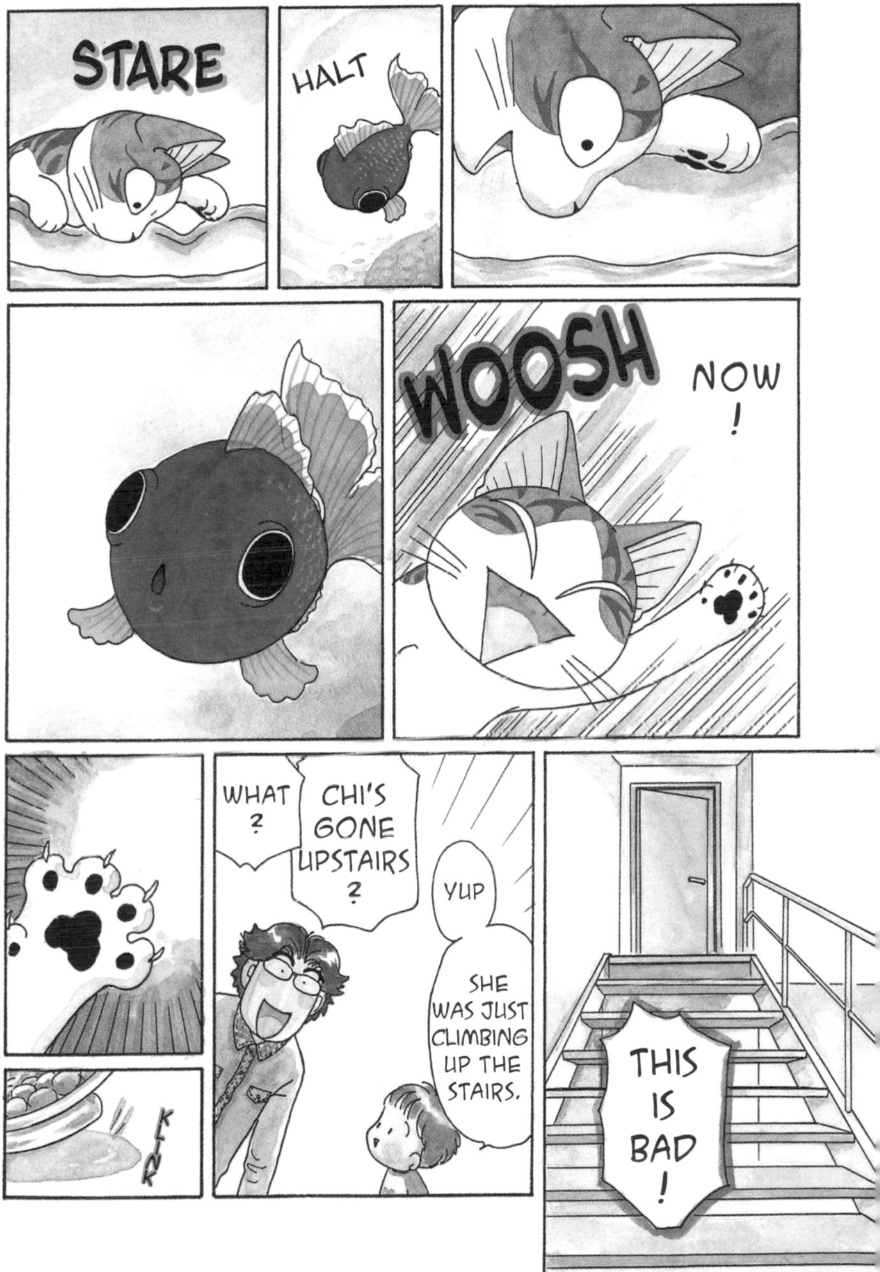
STARE
HALT
WOOSH
NOW!
KLINK
WHAT?
CHI'S GONE UPSTAIRS?
YUP
SHE WAS JUST CLIMBING UP THE STAIRS.
THIS IS BAD!

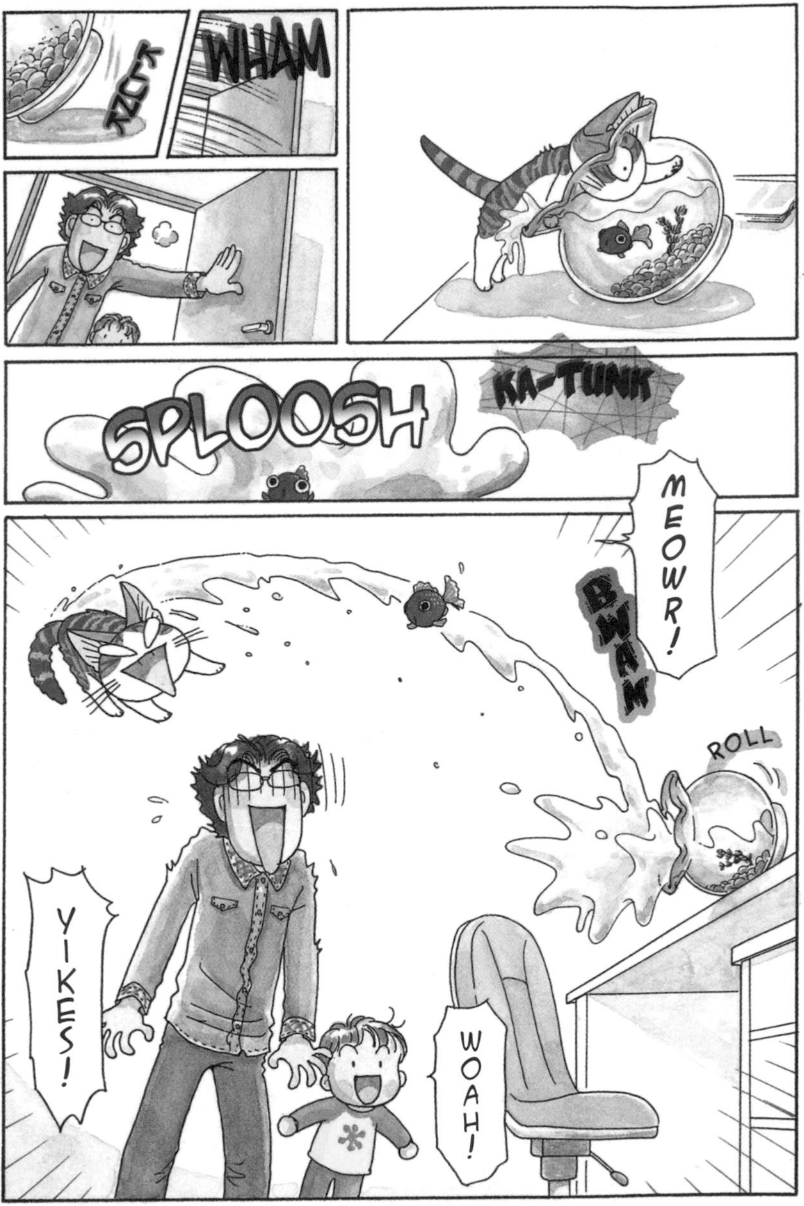
KLUNK
WHAM
SPLOOSH
KA-TUNK
MEOWR!
BWAM
ROLL
YIKES!
WOAH!

the end

homemade 118: a cat's heart is stolen

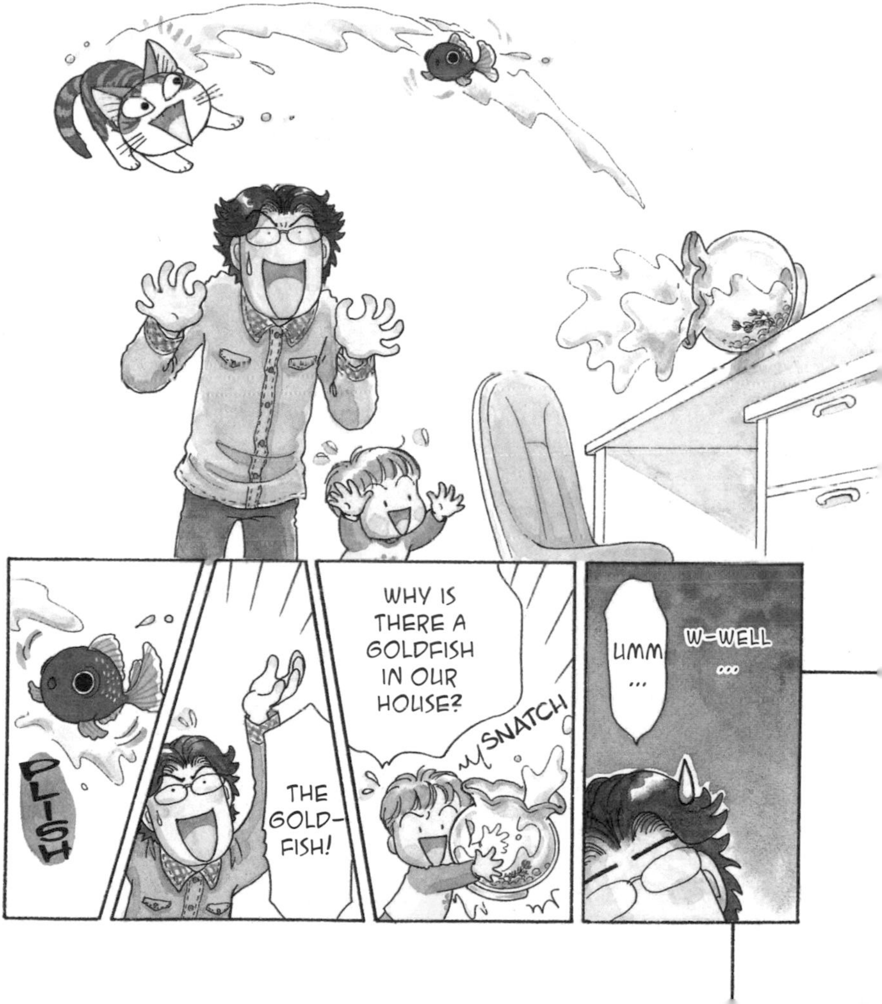
PLISH
THE GOLD-FISH!
WHY IS THERE A GOLDFISH IN OUR HOUSE?
SNATCH
UMM ...
W-WELL ...

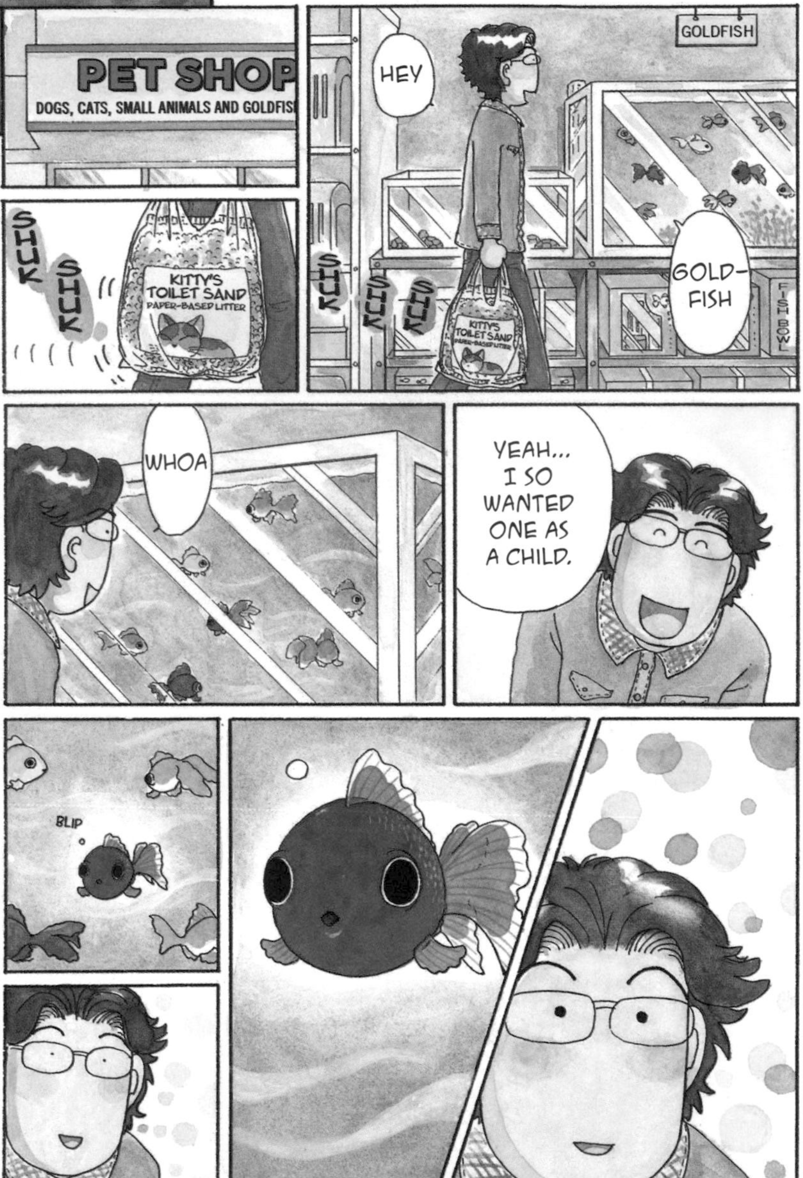
PET SHOP
DOGS, CATS, SMALL ANIMALS AND GOLDFISH
SHUK SHUK
KITTY'S TOILET SAND PAPER-BASED LITTER
HEY
GOLDFISH
SHUK SHUK SHUK
KITTY'S TOILET SAND PAPER-BASED LITTER
GOLD-FISH
FISH BOWL
WHOA
YEAH... I SO WANTED ONE AS A CHILD.
BLIP

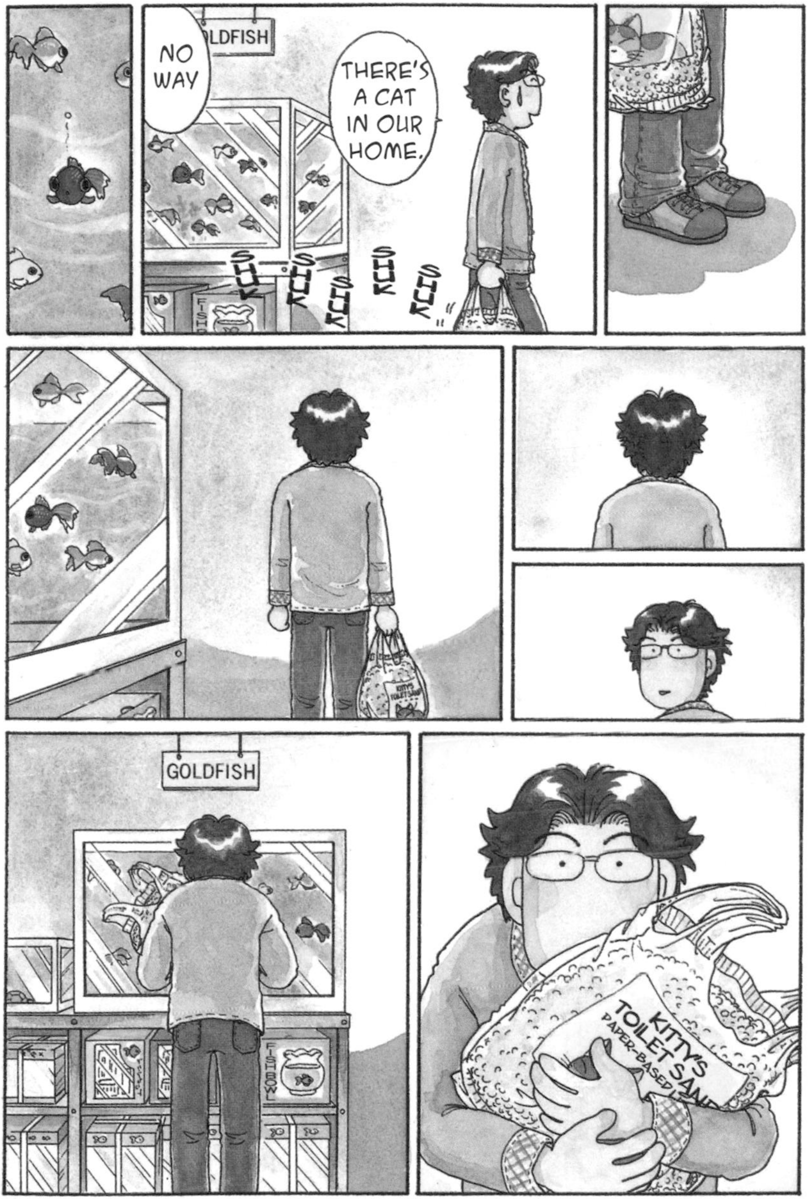
THERE'S A CAT IN OUR HOME.
NO WAY
SHUK
SHUK
SHUK
SHUK
SHUK
KITTY'S TOILET SAND
GOLDFISH
FISHBOWL

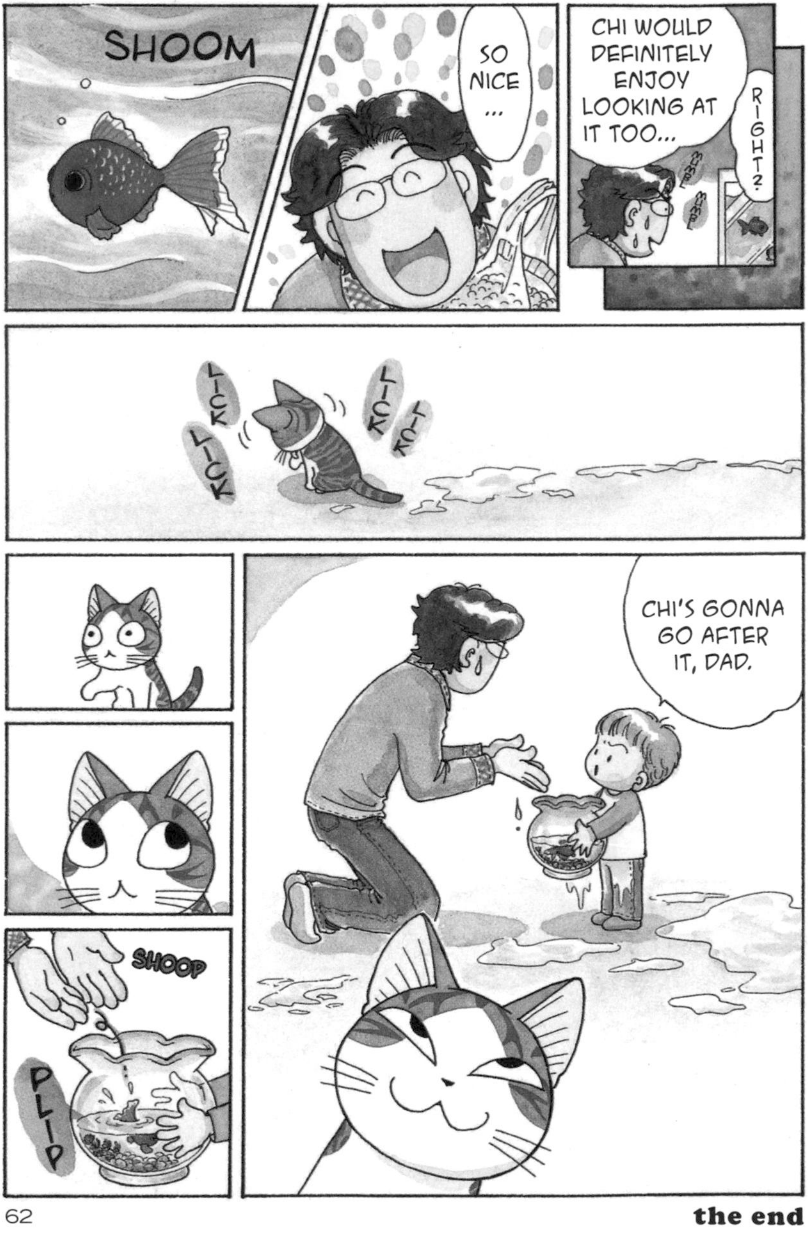
SHOOM
SO NICE ...
CHI WOULD DEFINITELY ENJOY LOOKING AT IT TOO...
MUMBL
MUMBL
RIGHT?
LICK
LICK
LICK
LICK
SHOOP
PLIP
CHI'S GONNA GO AFTER IT, DAD.

the end

homemade 119: a cat reaches

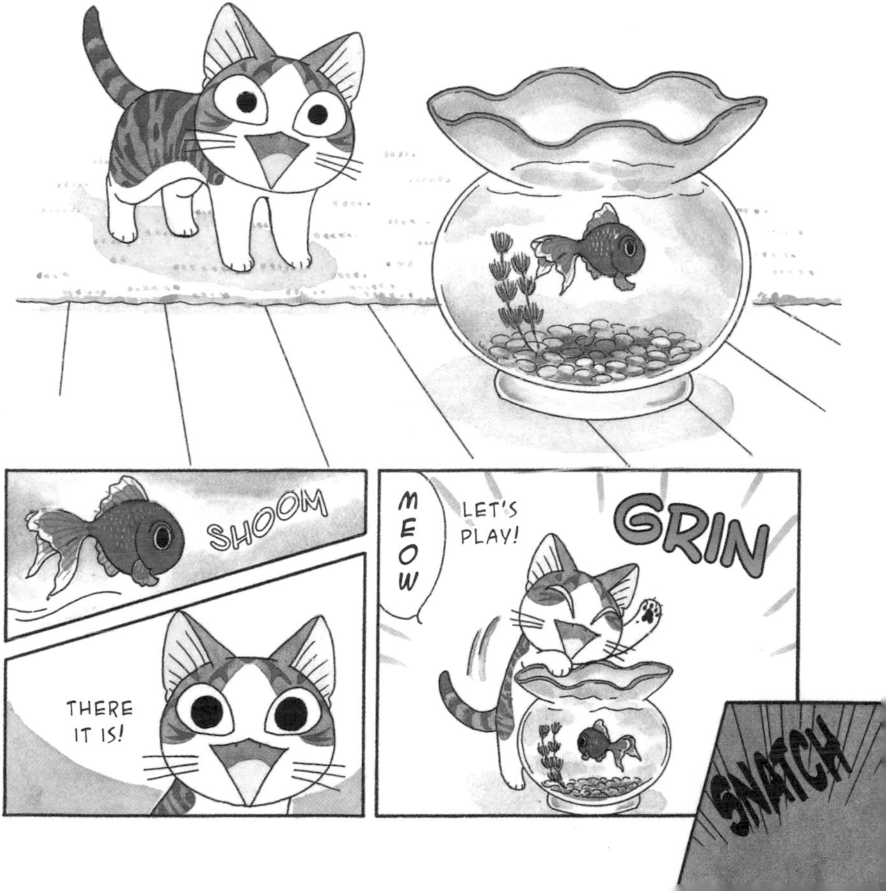
SHOOM
THERE IT IS!
MEOW
LET'S PLAY!
GRIN
SNATCH

MEOWR?!

DON'T GO CATCHING THAT GOLDFISH, OKAY?

STOP THAT, CHI.

TURN

BUT CHI JUST WANTED TO PLAY.

DASH—

MIYA

DADDY, CHI WANTS TO PLAY TOO...

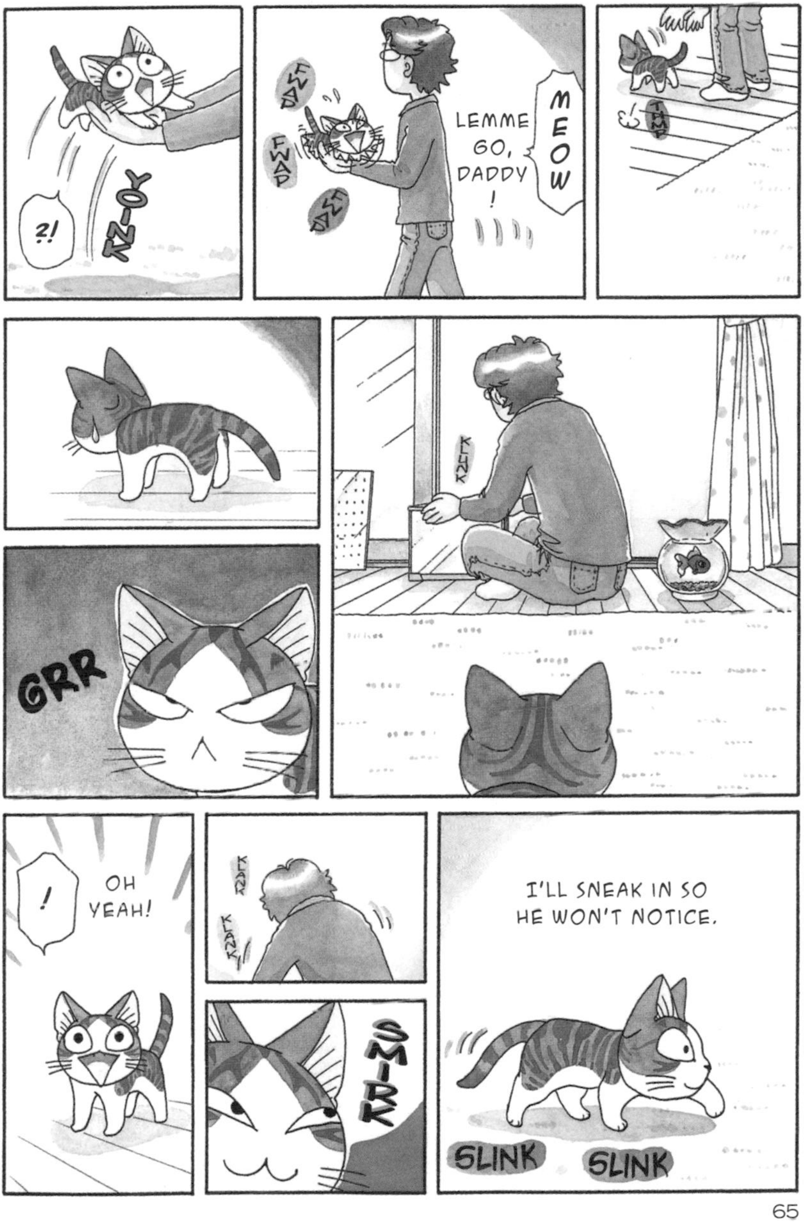
YOINK
?!
FWAP
FWAP
FWAP
LEMME GO, DADDY!
MEOW
THMP
KLUNK
GRR
!
OH YEAH!
KLANK
KLANK
SMIRK
I'LL SNEAK IN SO HE WON'T NOTICE.
SLINK
SLINK

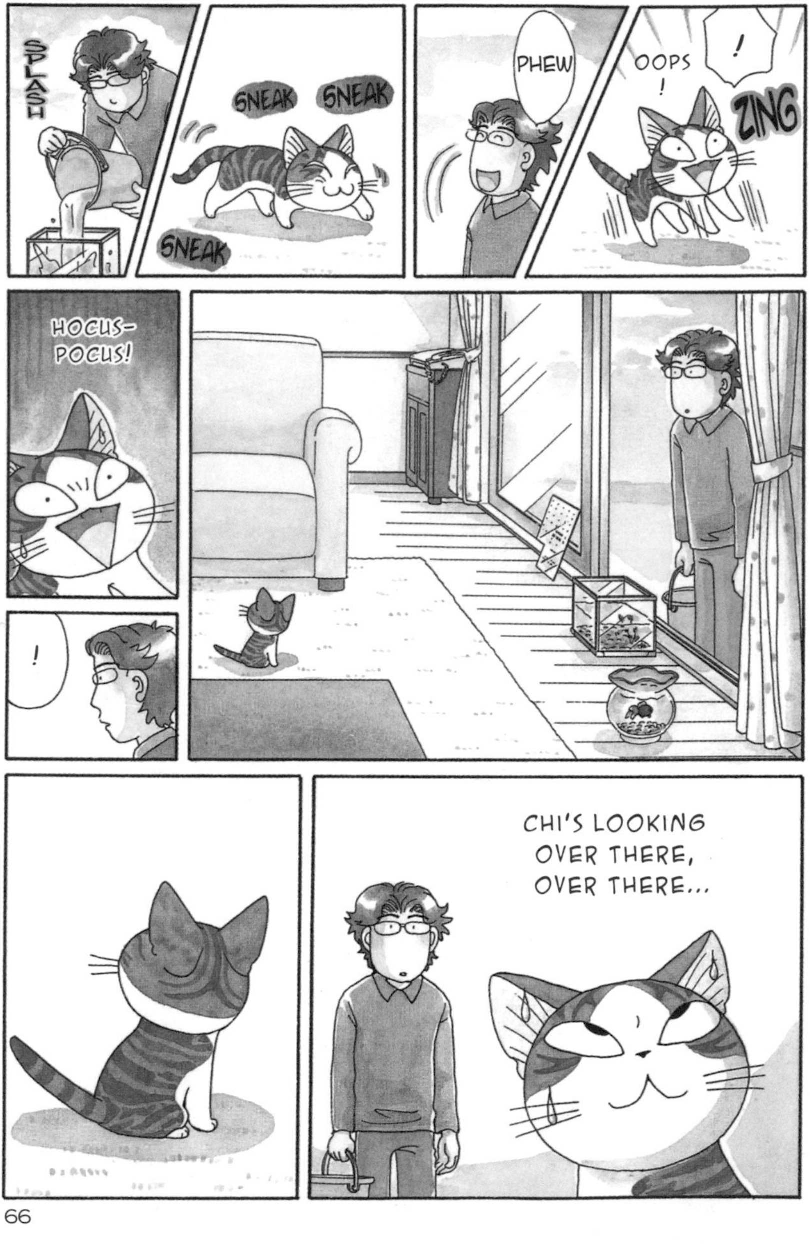
SPLASH
SNEAK SNEAK
SNEAK
PHEW
OOPS
!
!
ZING
HOCUS-POCUS!
!
CHI'S LOOKING OVER THERE, OVER THERE...

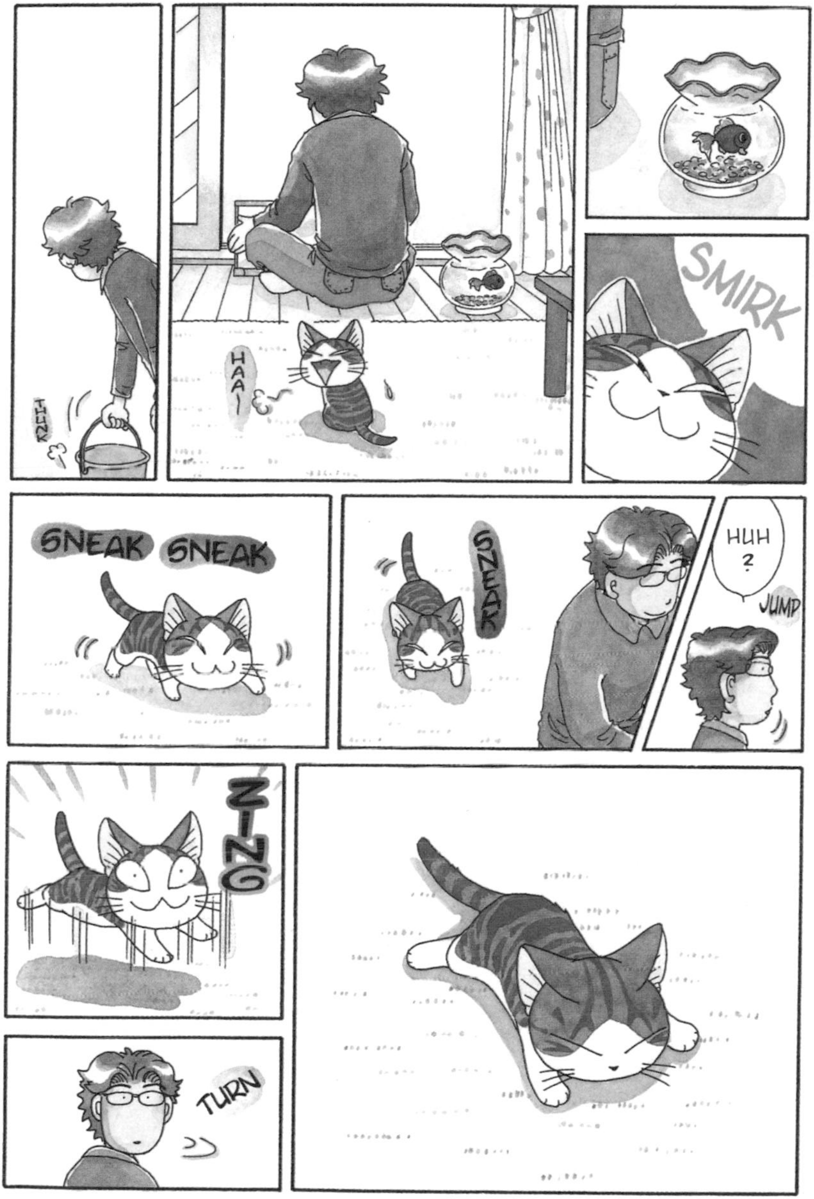
THUNK
HAA!
SMIRK
SNEAK SNEAK
SNEAK
HUH?
JUMP
ZING
TURN

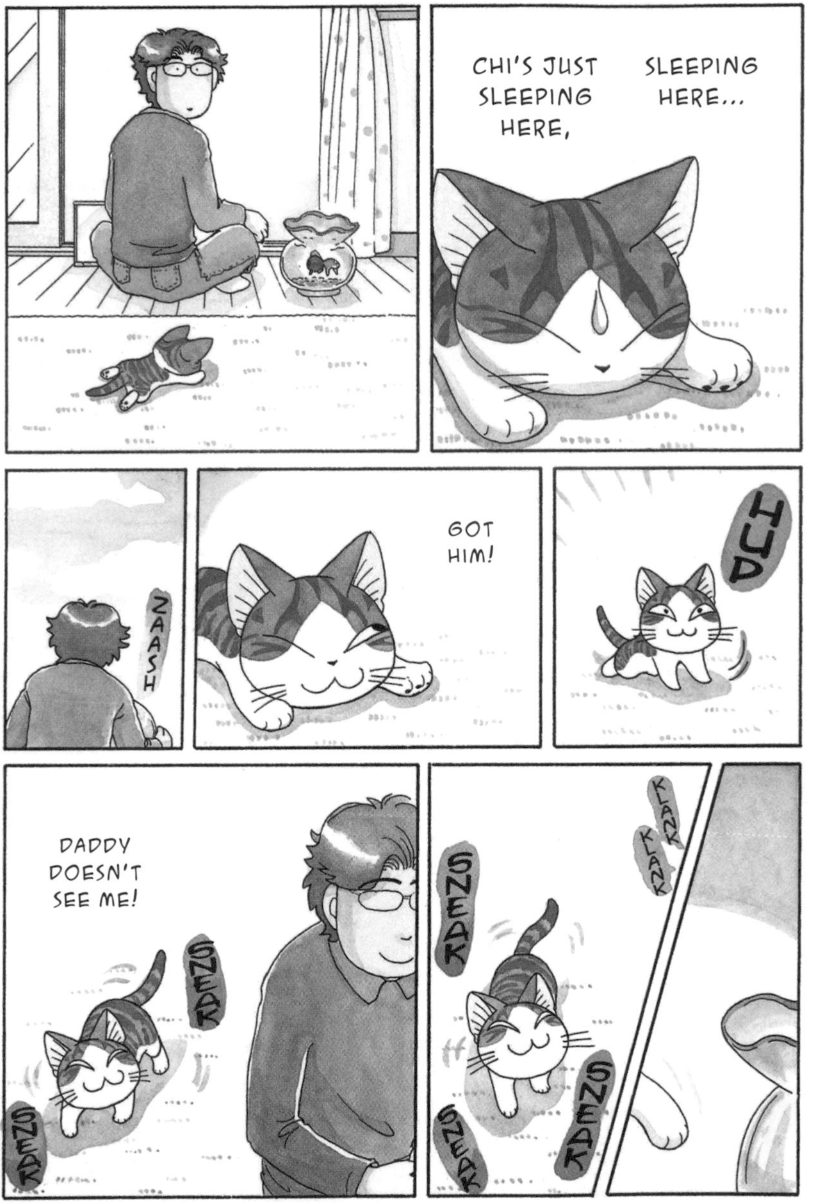
CHI'S JUST SLEEPING HERE,
SLEEPING HERE...
ZAASH
GOT HIM!
HUD
DADDY DOESN'T SEE ME!
SNEAK
SNEAK
SNEAK
KLANK KLANK
SNEAK
SNEAK

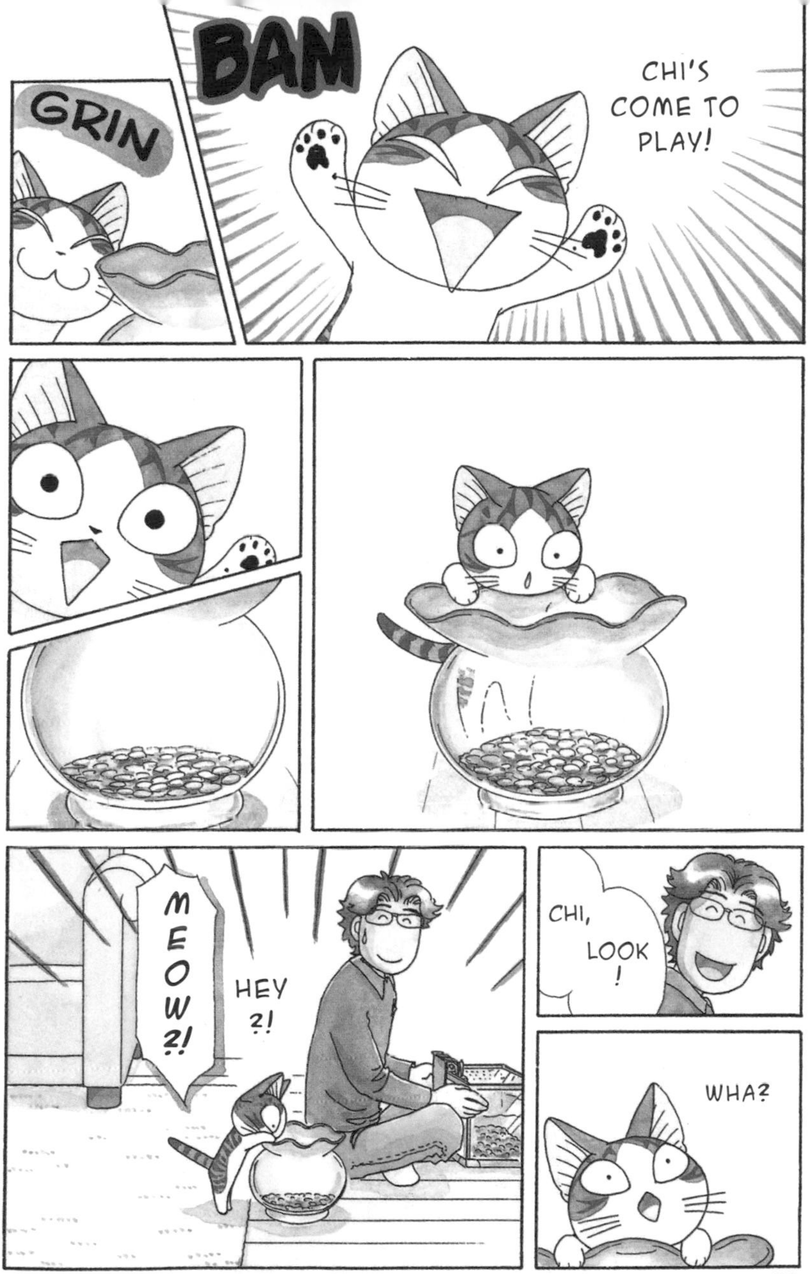
GRIN
BAM
CHI'S COME TO PLAY!
MEOW?!
HEY?!
CHI, LOOK!
WHA?

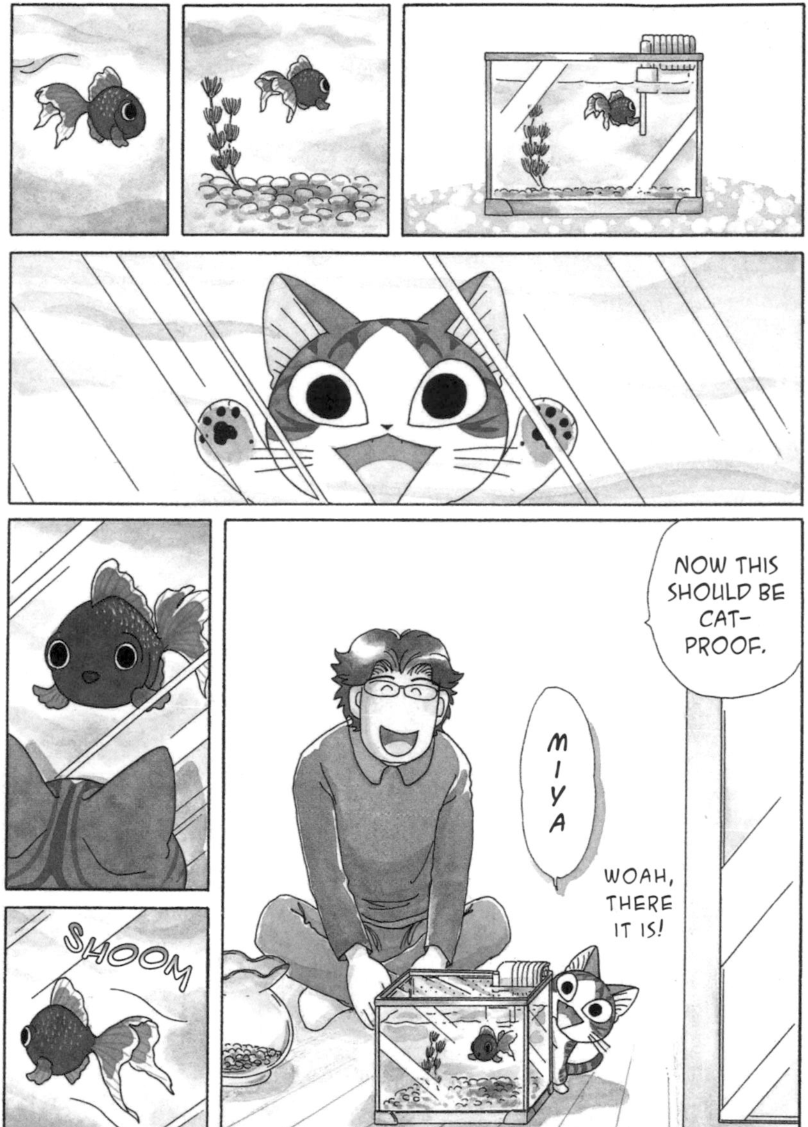
SHOOM
NOW THIS SHOULD BE CAT-PROOF.
MIYA
WOAH, THERE IT IS!

the end

homemade 120: a cat misunderstands

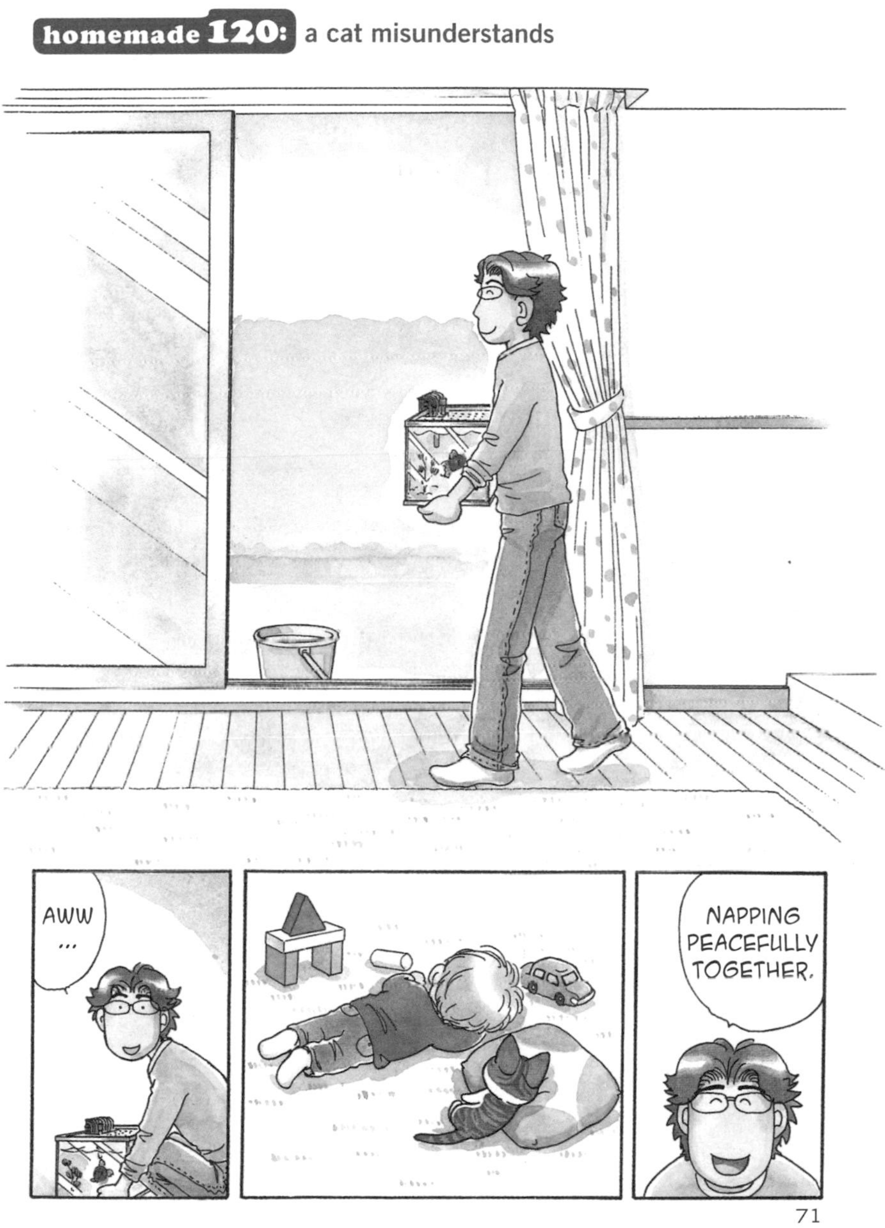
AWW ...
NAPPING PEACEFULLY TOGETHER.

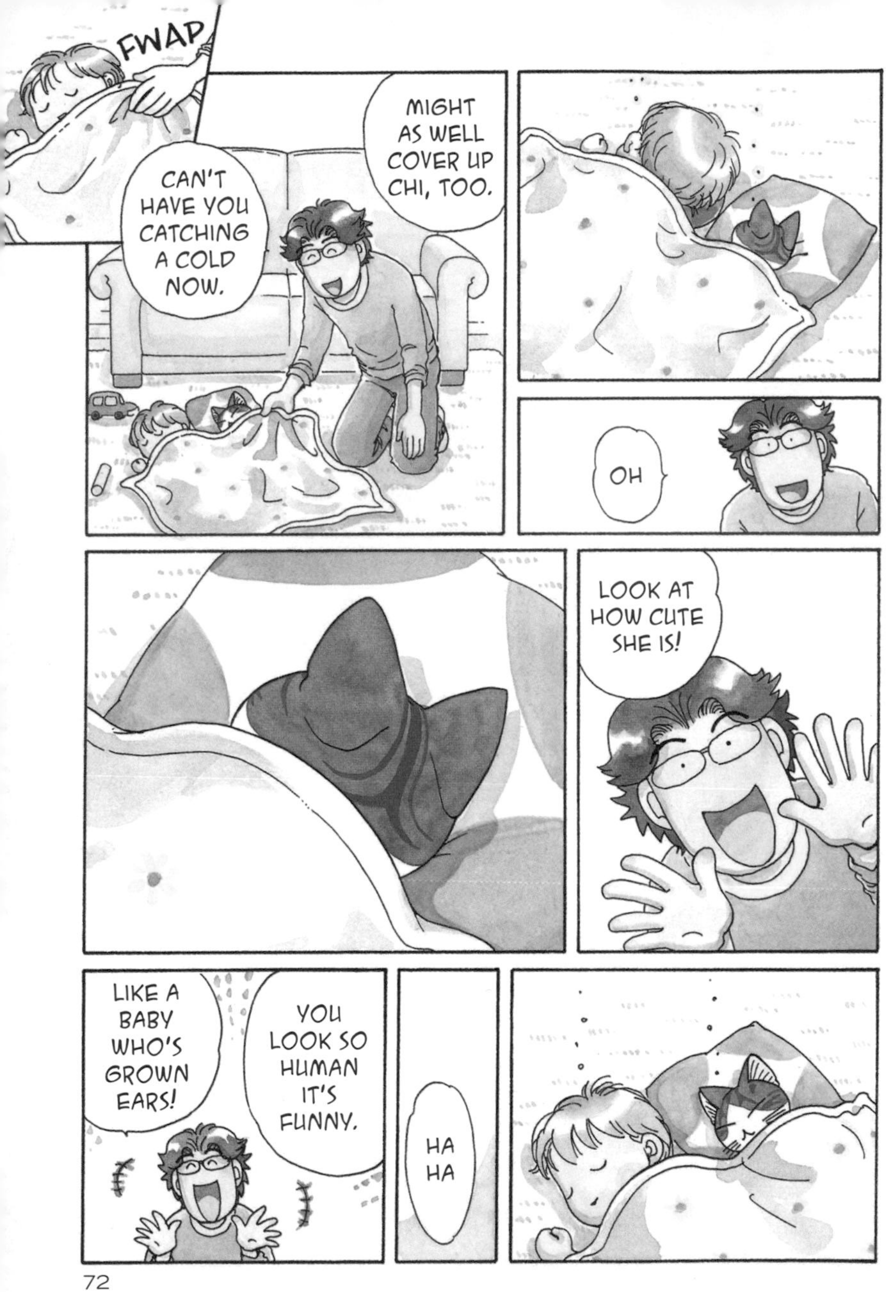
FWAP
CAN'T HAVE YOU CATCHING A COLD NOW.
MIGHT AS WELL COVER UP CHI, TOO.
OH
LOOK AT HOW CUTE SHE IS!
LIKE A BABY WHO'S GROWN EARS!
YOU LOOK SO HUMAN IT'S FUNNY.
HA HA

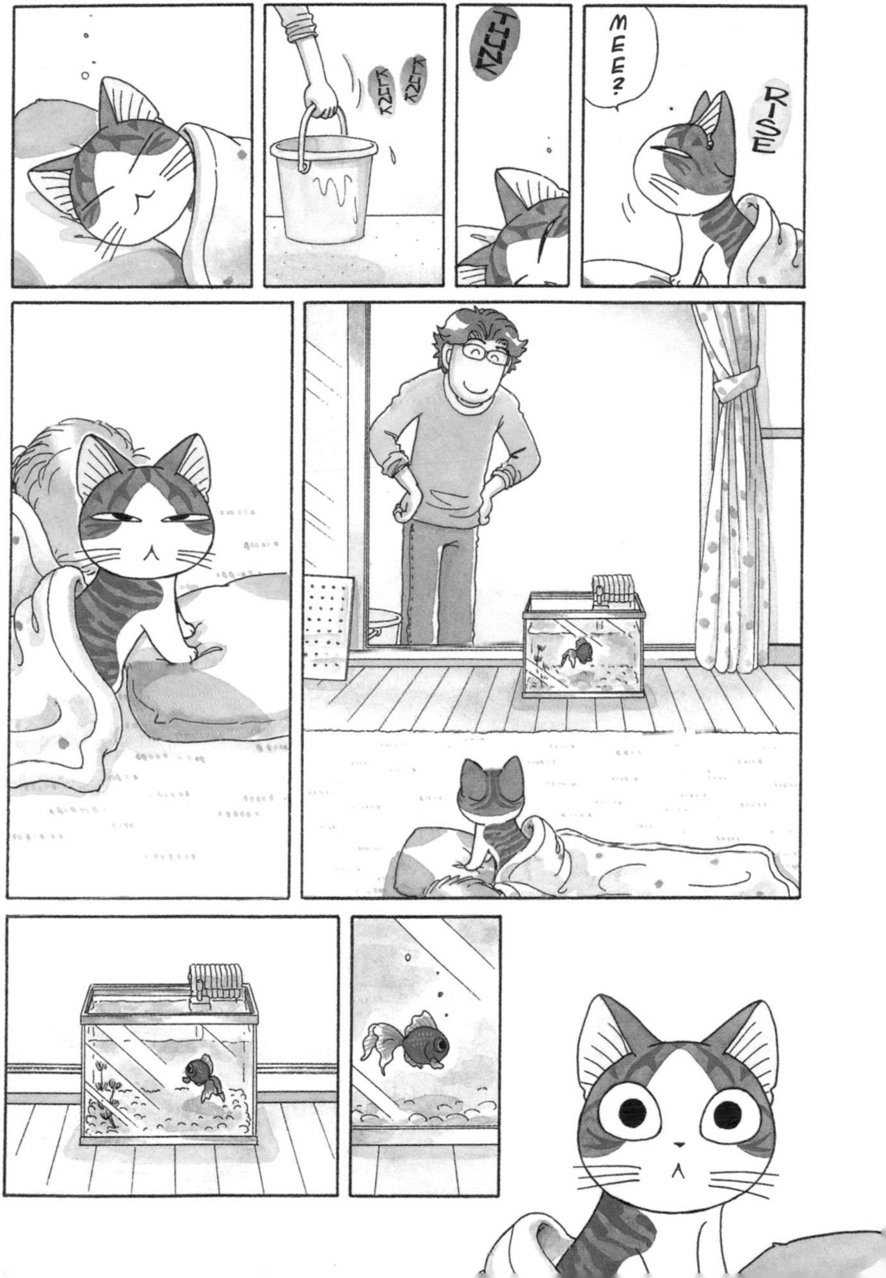
KLUNK
KLUNK
THUNK
MEEE?
RISE

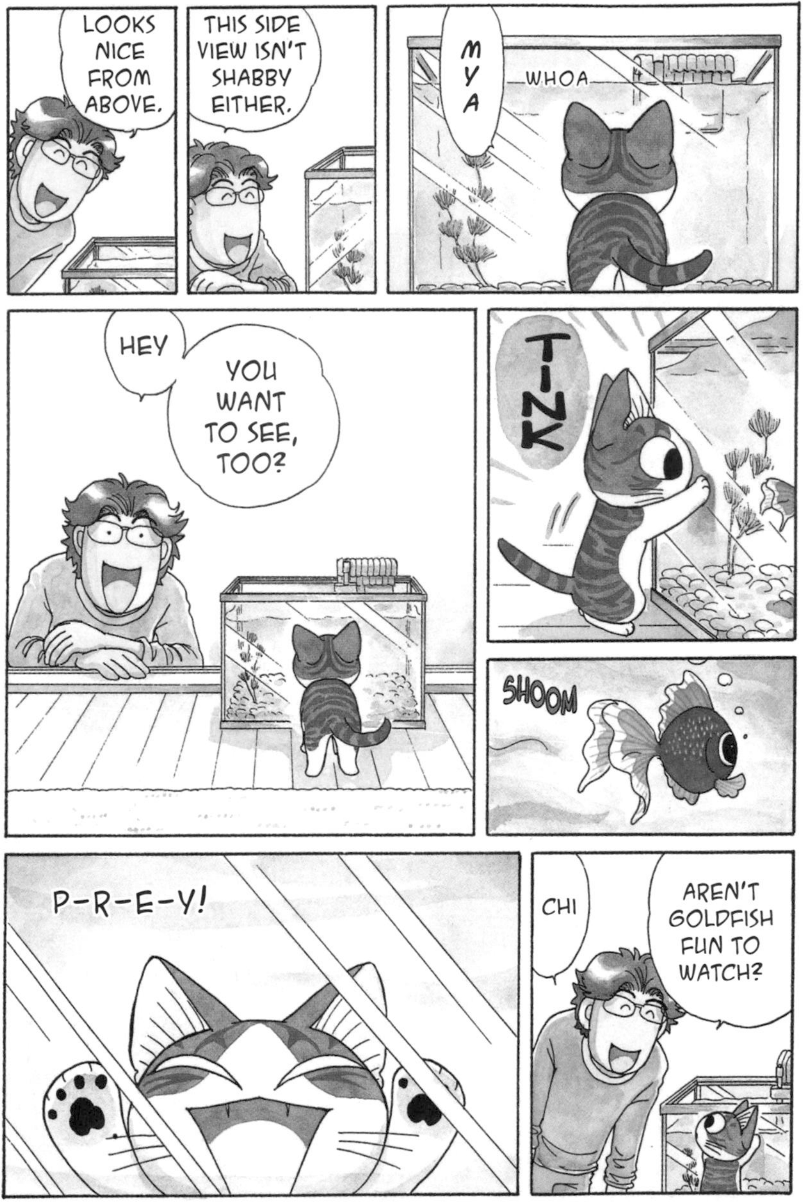
LOOKS NICE FROM ABOVE.
THIS SIDE VIEW ISN'T SHABBY EITHER.
MYA
WHOA
HEY
YOU WANT TO SEE, TOO?
TINK
SHOOM
P-R-E-Y!
CHI
AREN'T GOLDFISH FUN TO WATCH?

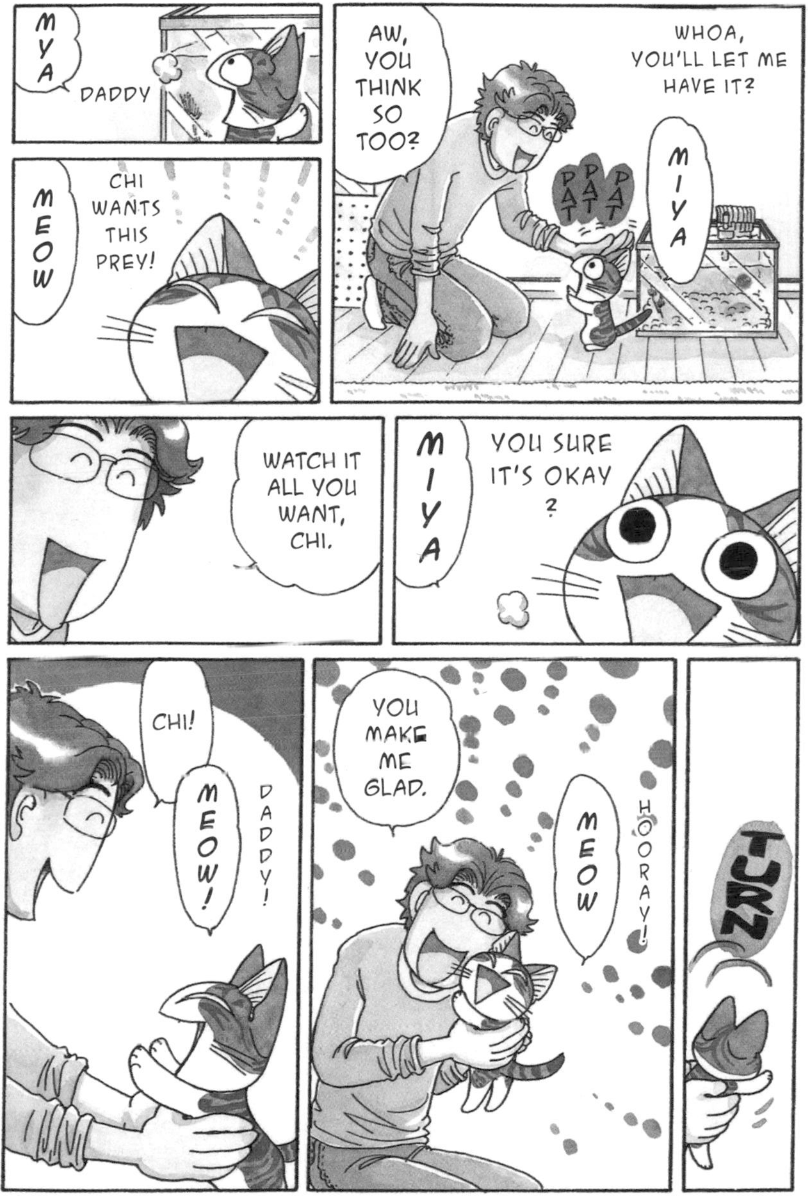

MYA
DADDY
MEOW
CHI WANTS THIS PREY!
AW, YOU THINK SO TOO?
WHOA, YOU'LL LET ME HAVE IT?
PAT PAT PAT
MIYA
WATCH IT ALL YOU WANT, CHI.
MIYA
YOU SURE IT'S OKAY?
CHI!
MEOW!
DADDY!
YOU MAKE ME GLAD.
MEOW
HOORAY!
TURN

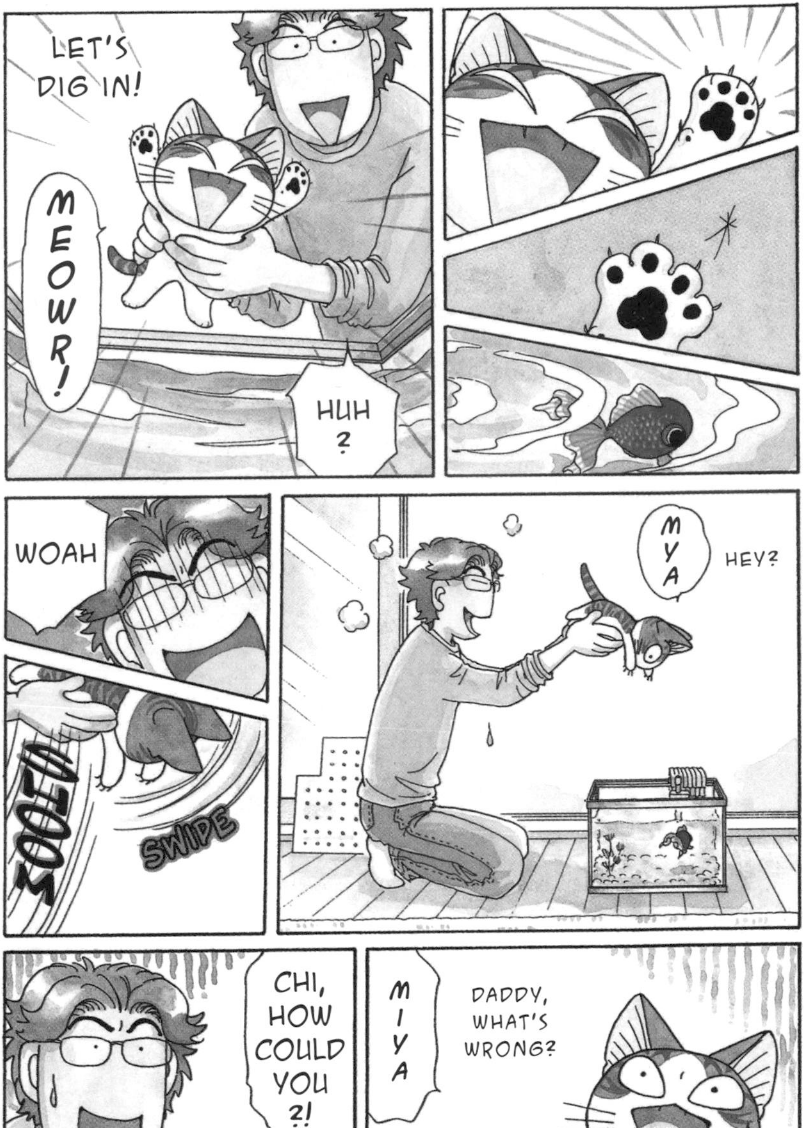
LET'S DIG IN!
MEOWR!
HUH?
WOAH
ZOOOM
SWIPE
MYA
HEY?
CHI, HOW COULD YOU?!
MIYA
DADDY, WHAT'S WRONG?

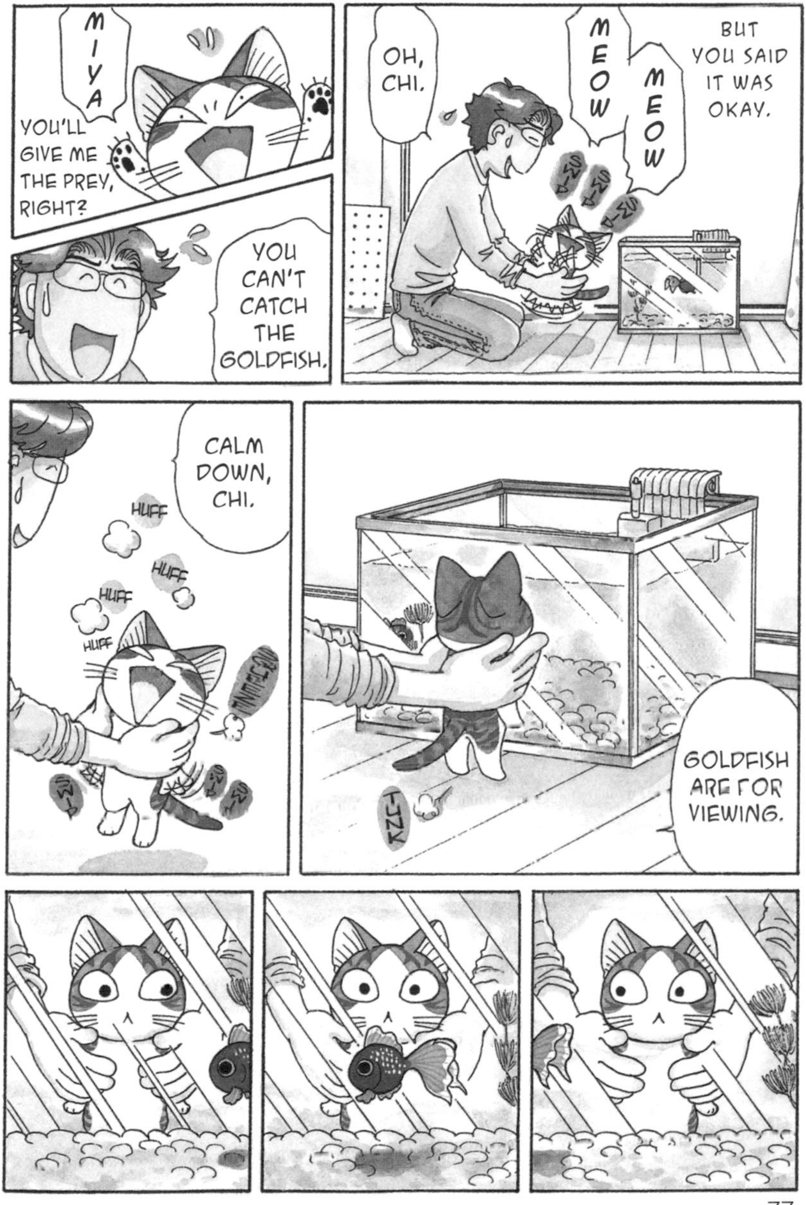
MIYA
YOU'LL GIVE ME THE PREY, RIGHT?
YOU CAN'T CATCH THE GOLDFISH.
OH, CHI.
MEOW
MEOW
BUT YOU SAID IT WAS OKAY.
SWIP
SWIP
SWIP
CALM DOWN, CHI.
HUFF
HUFF
HUFF
HUFF
SWIP
SWIP
SWIP
TUNK
GOLDFISH ARE FOR VIEWING.

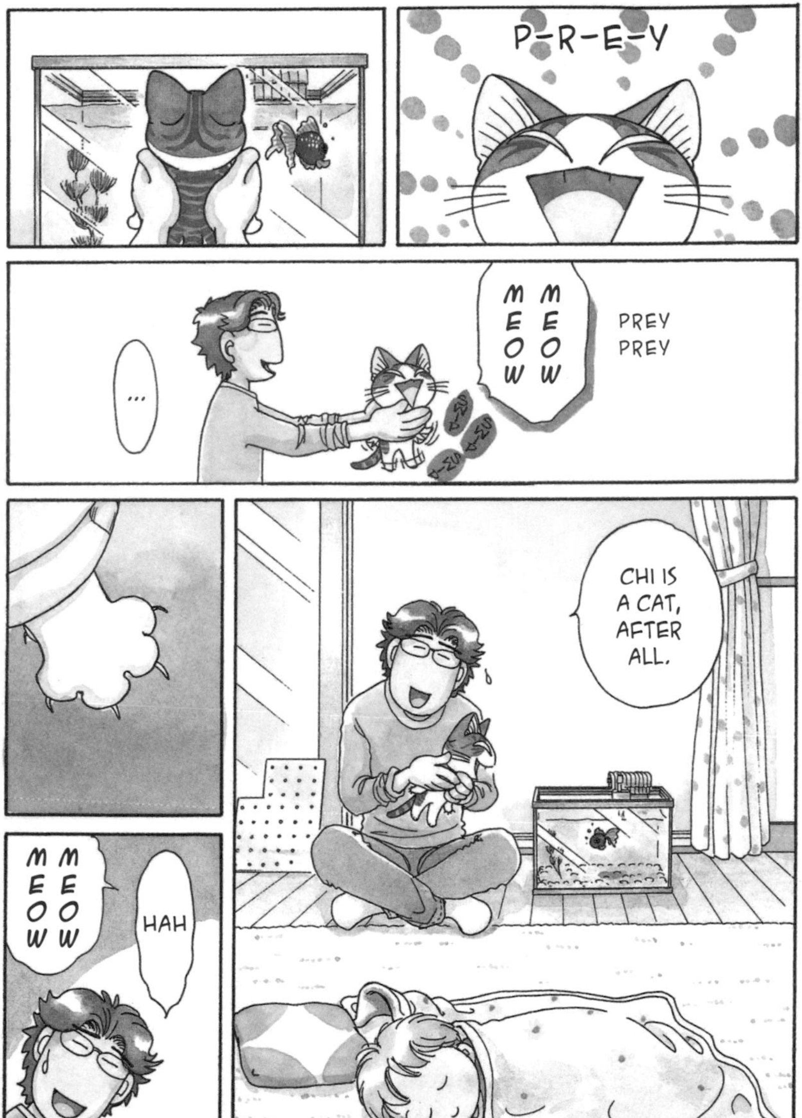
P-R-E-Y
...
MEOW MEOW
PREY PREY
MEOW MEOW
HAH
CHI IS A CAT, AFTER ALL.

the end

homemade 121: a cat is cheesed

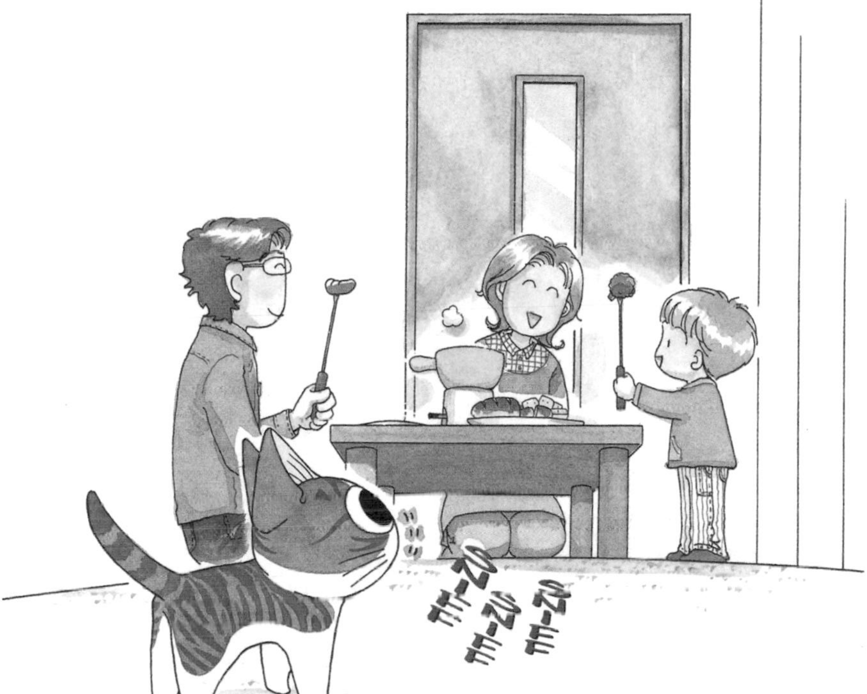
ZU-TETE
ZU-TETE
ZU-TETE

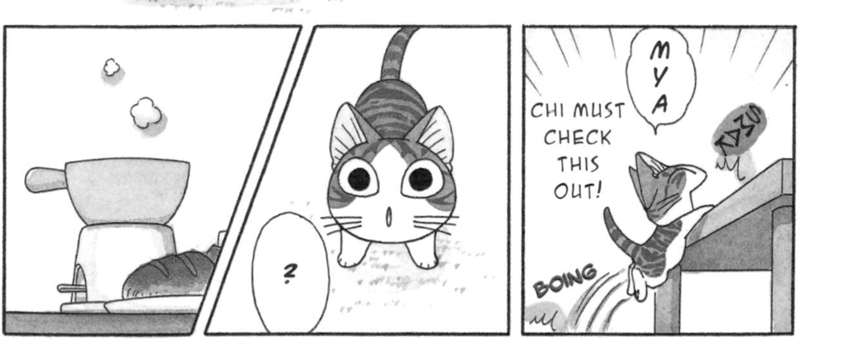
?
MYA
CHI MUST CHECK THIS OUT!
BOING

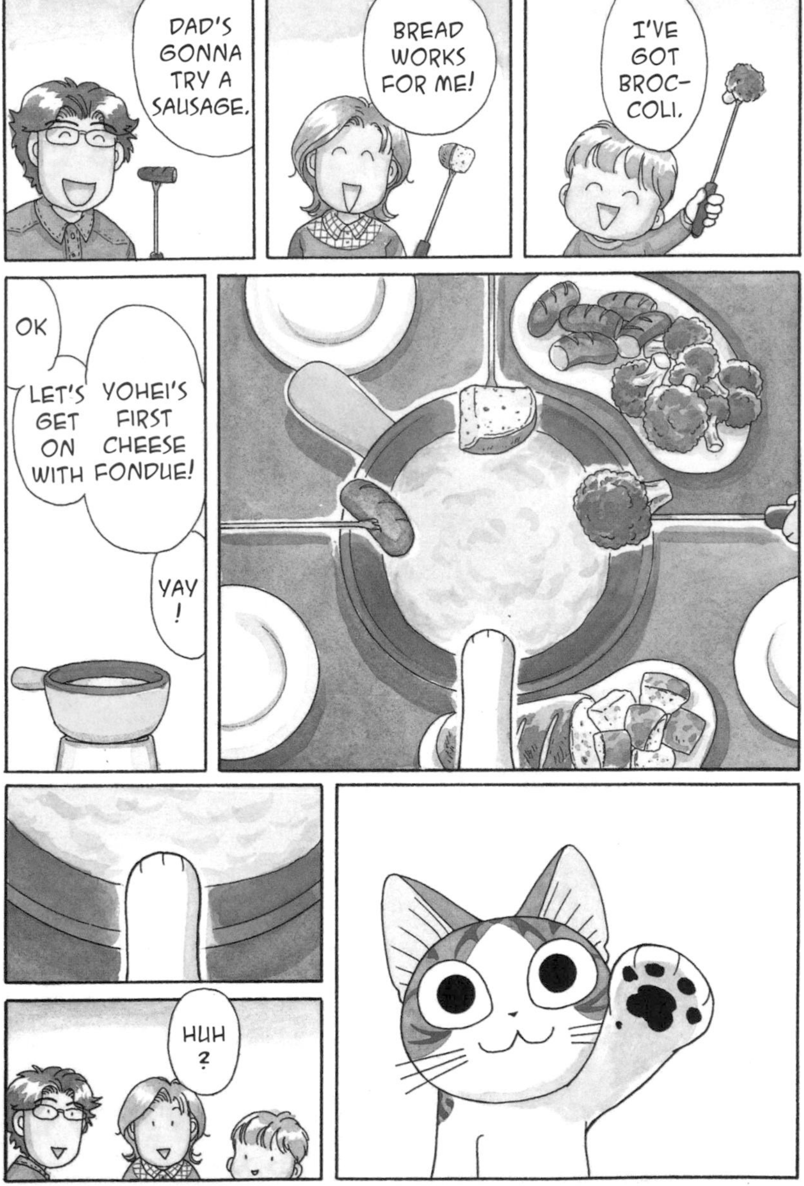
DAD'S GONNA TRY A SAUSAGE.
BREAD WORKS FOR ME!
I'VE GOT BROC-COLI.
OK
LET'S GET ON WITH
YOHEI'S FIRST CHEESE FONDUE!
YAY!
HUH?

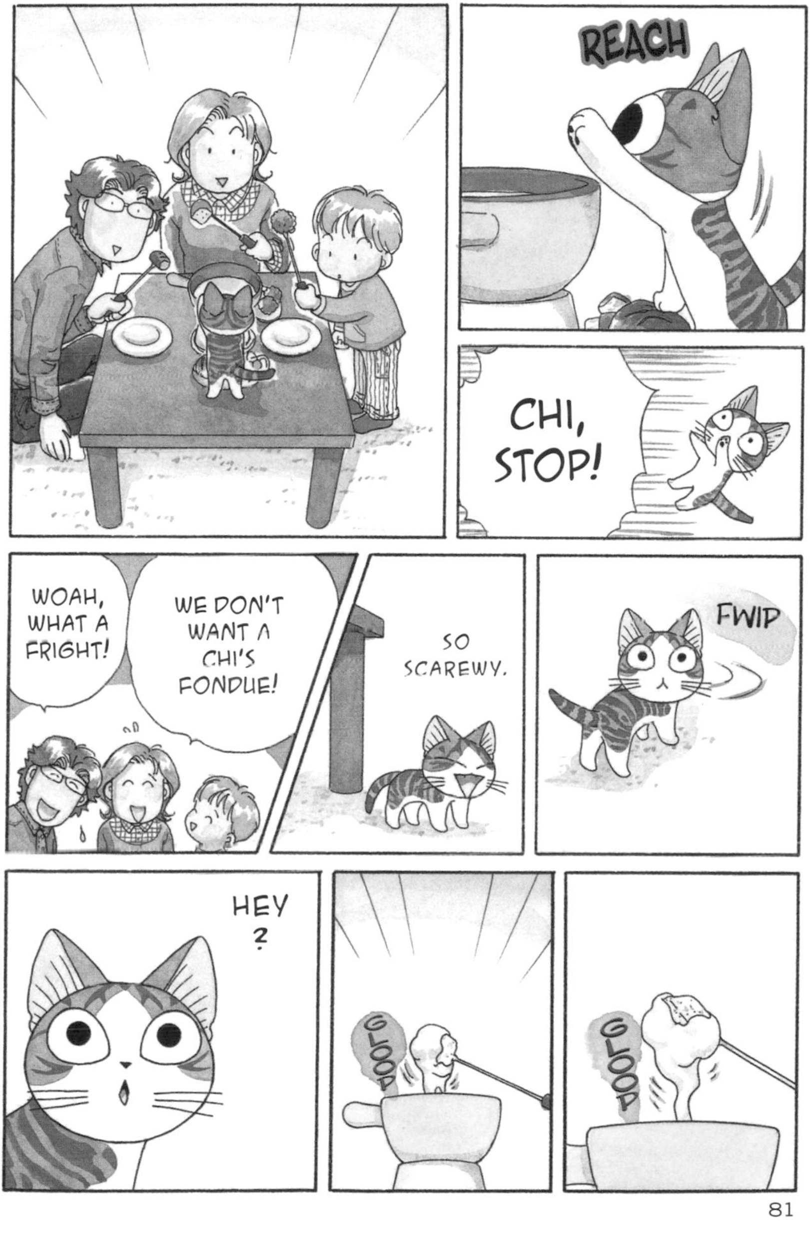
REACH
CHI, STOP!
WOAH, WHAT A FRIGHT!
WE DON'T WANT A CHI'S FONDUE!
SO SCAREWY.
FWIP
HEY ?
GLOOP
GLOOP

WHAT'S THAT?

TWIRL

TWIRL

WHAT IS THAT?

SPIN

I'M GONNA REALLY DIG IN.

SMACK

YUM!

BLOOP

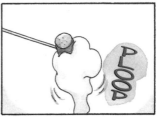

PLOOP

OH!

PLOOP

WHOA!

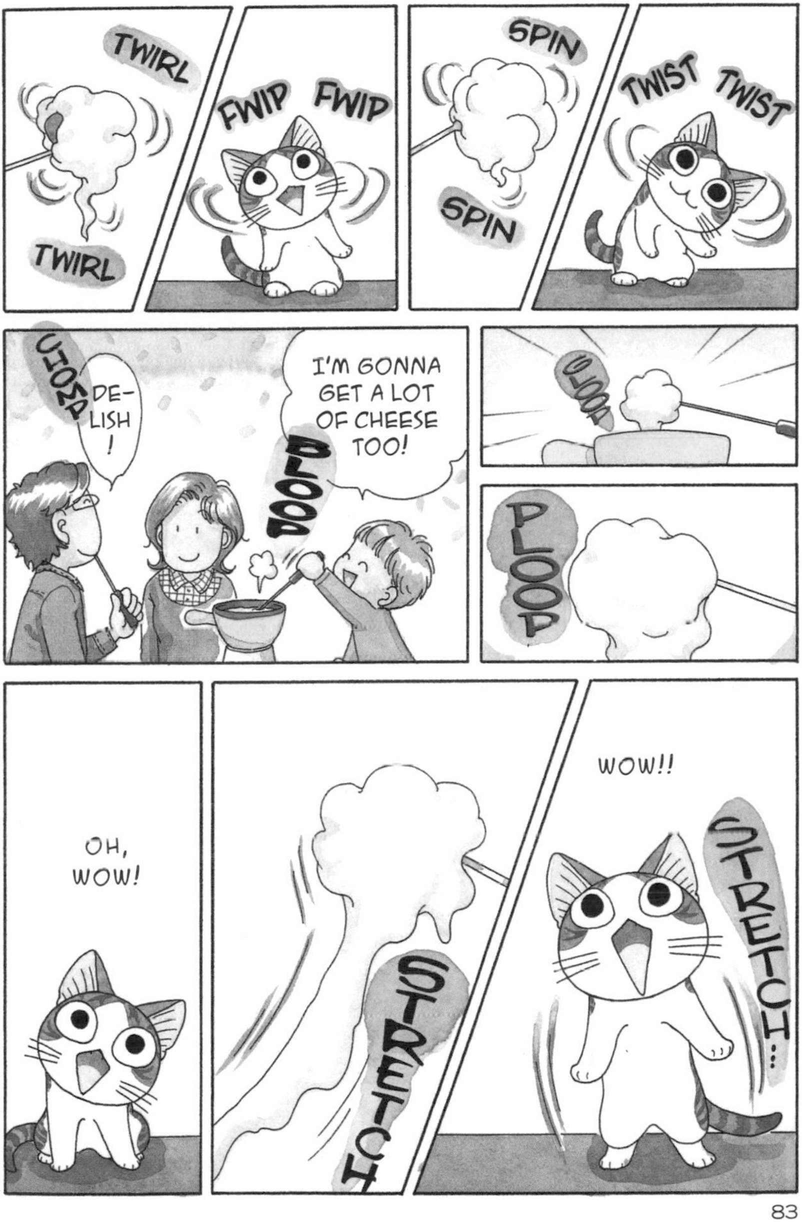

TWIRL
TWIRL
FWIP FWIP
SPIN
SPIN
TWIST TWIST
CHOMP
DE-LISH!
I'M GONNA GET A LOT OF CHEESE TOO!
PLOOP
GLOOP
PLOOP
OH, WOW!
STRETCH
WOW!!
STRETCH...

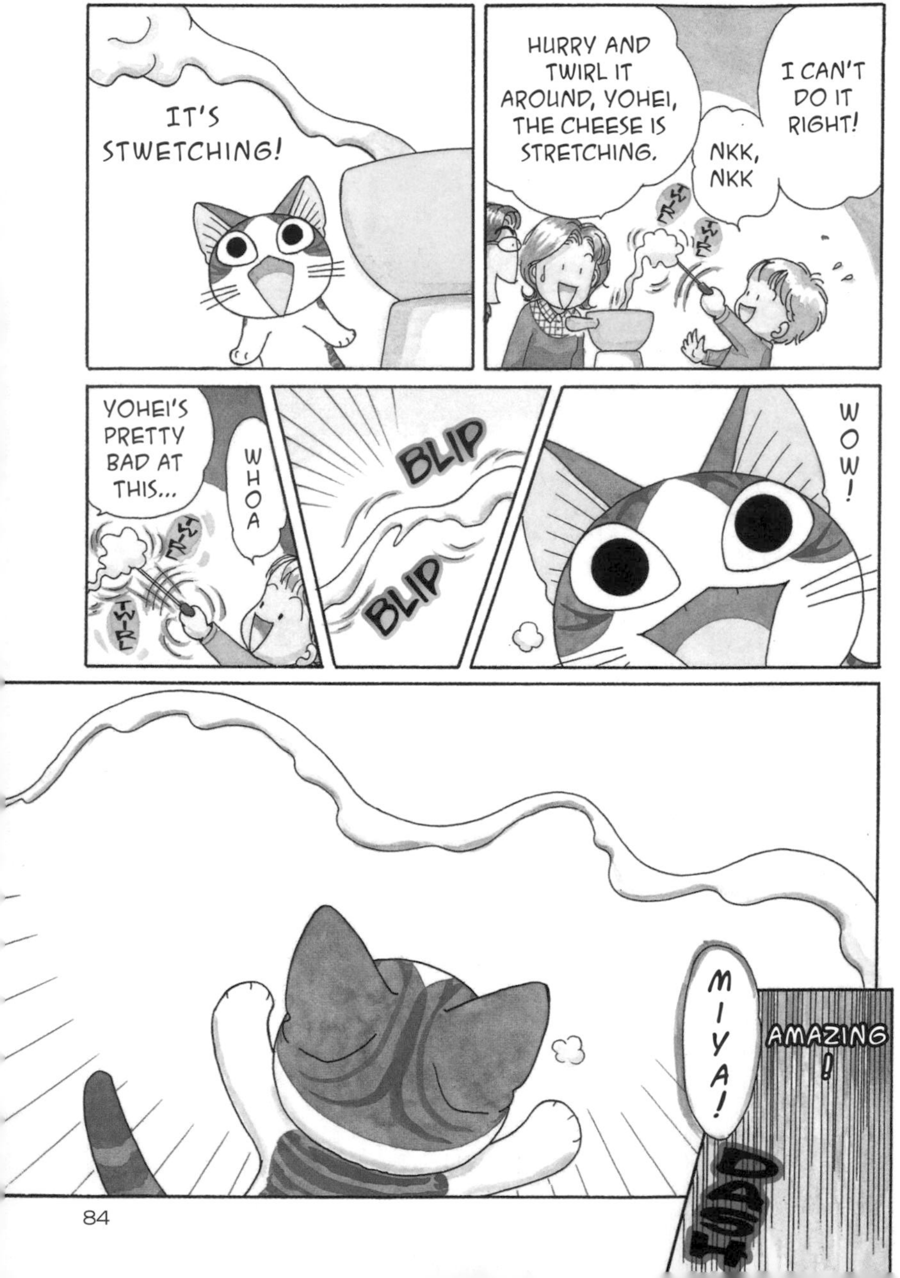
IT'S STWETCHING!
HURRY AND TWIRL IT AROUND, YOHEI, THE CHEESE IS STRETCHING.
I CAN'T DO IT RIGHT!
NKK, NKK
TWIRL
TWIRL
YOHEI'S PRETTY BAD AT THIS...
WHOA
TWIRL
TWIRL
BLIP
BLIP
WOW!
MIYA!
AMAZING!
DASH

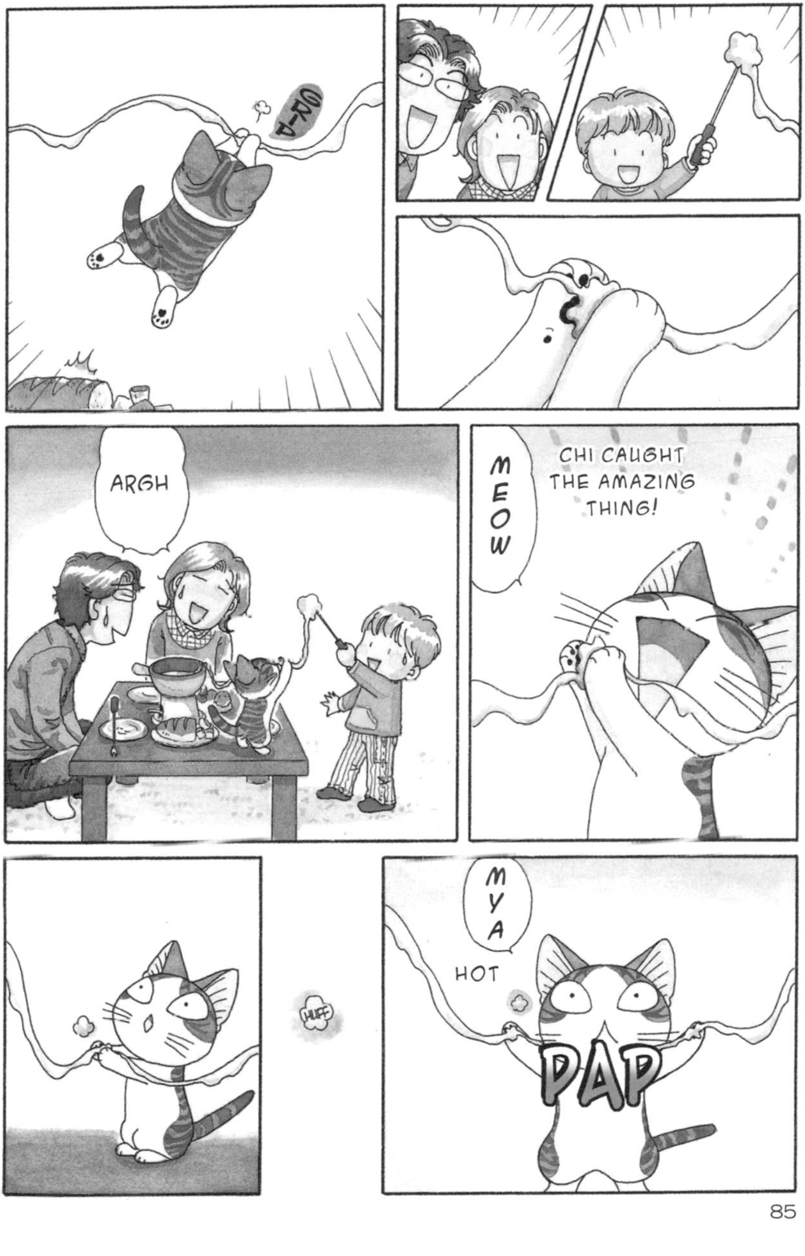
GRIP
ARGH
MEOW
CHI CAUGHT THE AMAZING THING!
HUFF
MYA
HOT
PAP

HUH ?!

STRETCH

SNIF

SNIF SNIF SNIF

AHHHHHHH

CLEAN UP CHI'S PAWS.

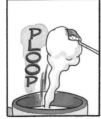

PLOOP

SEE HOW STWETCHY IT IS, YOHEY!

MEOW

MEOW

YUMMY, HUH.

the end

homemade 122: a cat feels a presence

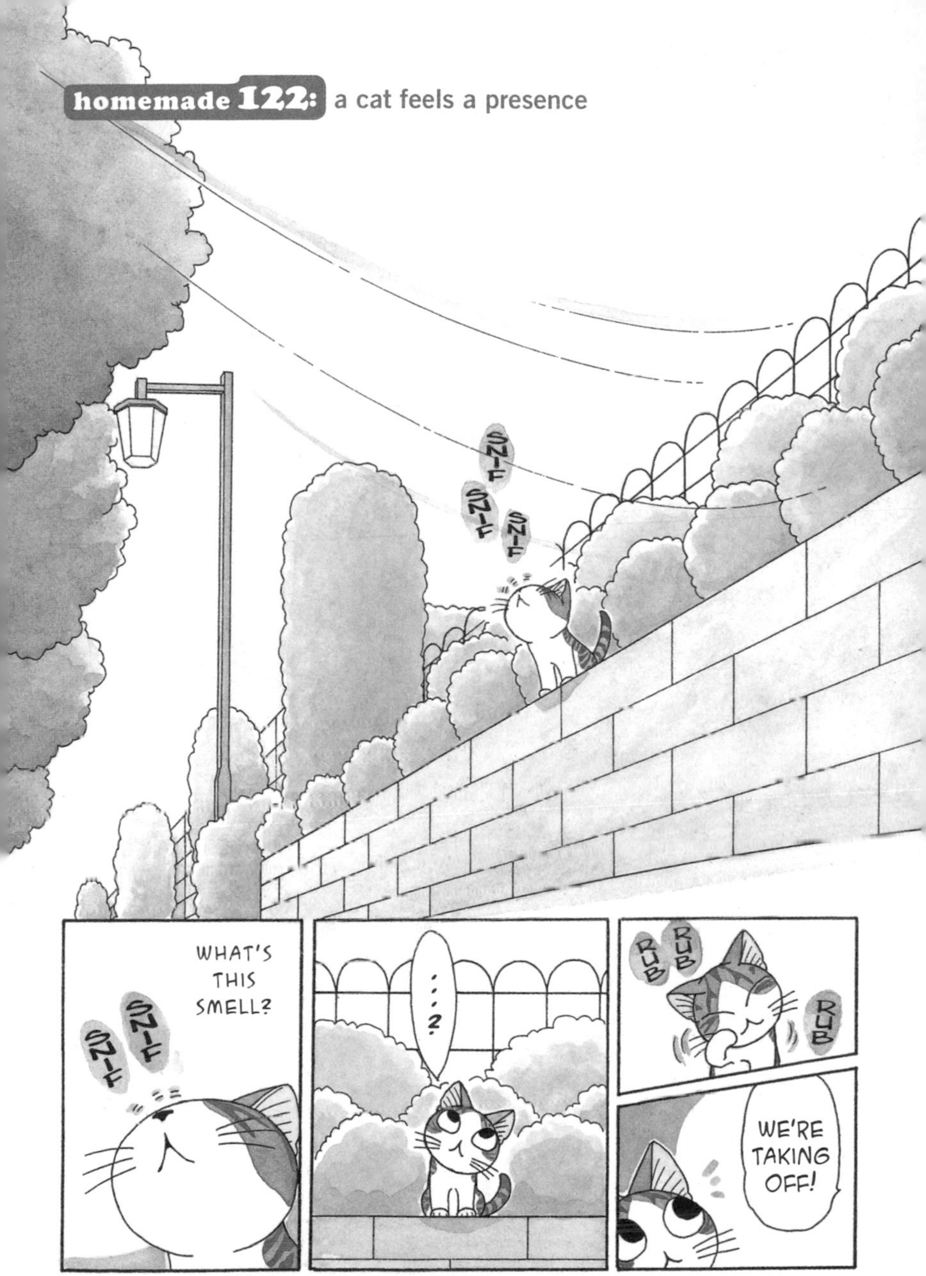
SNIF
SNIF
SNIF
WHAT'S THIS SMELL?
SNIF
SNIF
...?
RUB
RUB
RUB
WE'RE TAKING OFF!

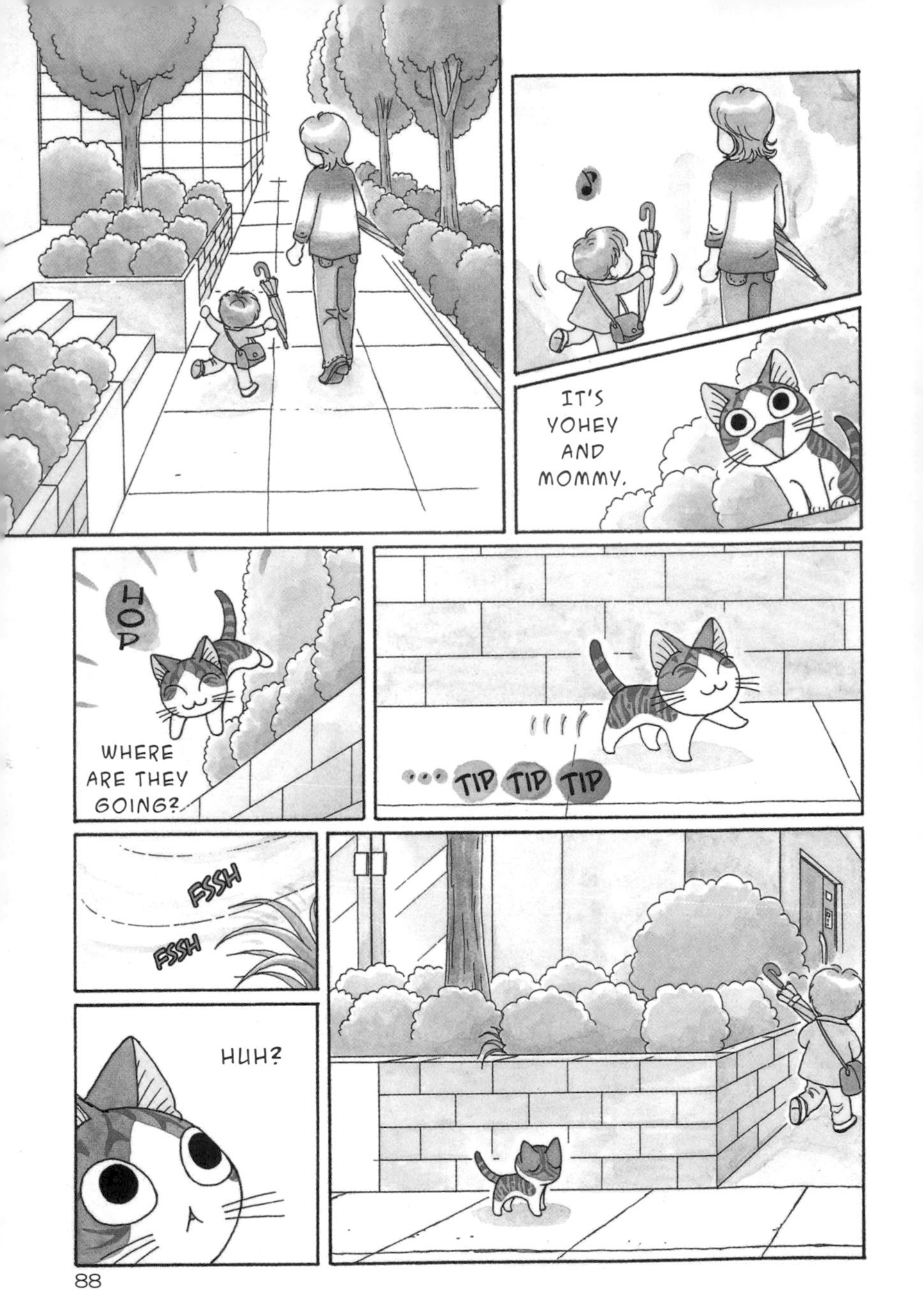
IT'S YOHEY AND MOMMY.
HOP
WHERE ARE THEY GOING?
...TIP TIP TIP
FSSH
FSSH
HUH?

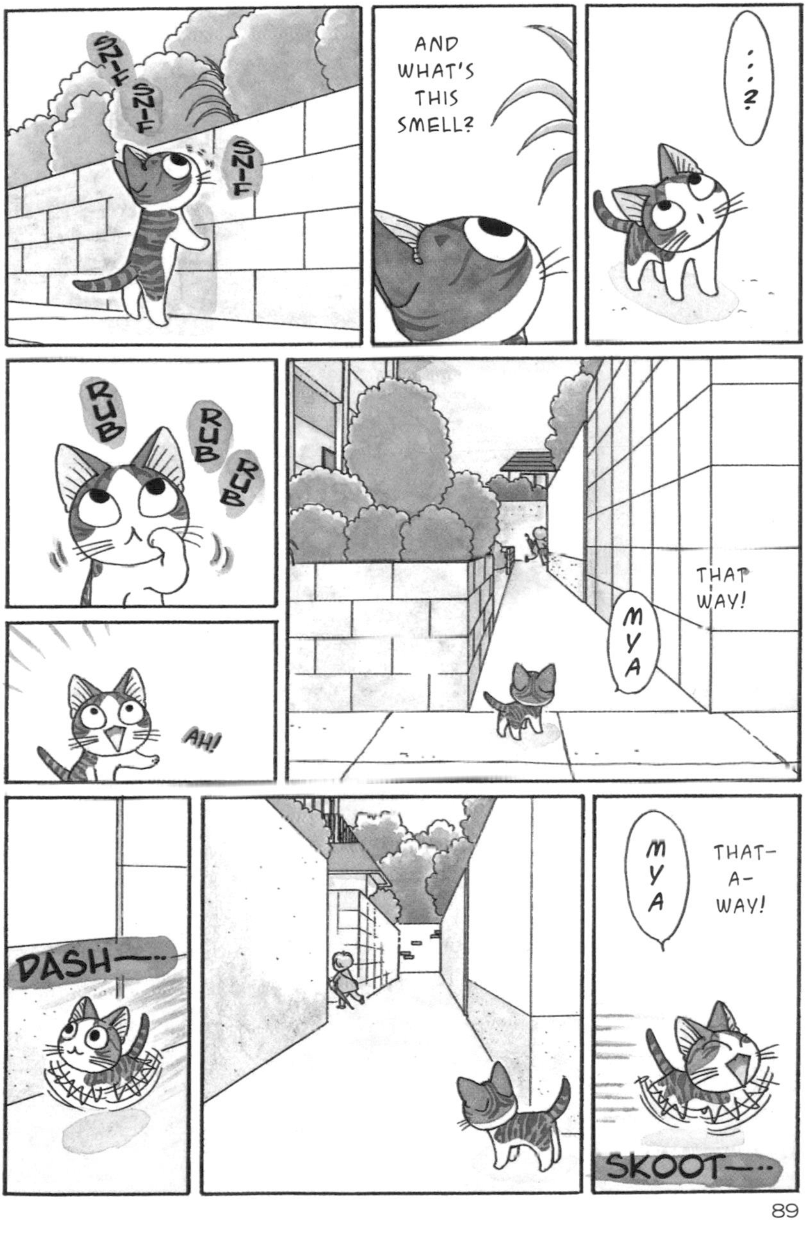
SNIF SNIF SNIF
AND WHAT'S THIS SMELL?
...?
RUB RUB RUB
AH!
THAT WAY!
MYA
DASH—...
MYA
THAT-A-WAY!
SKOOT—...

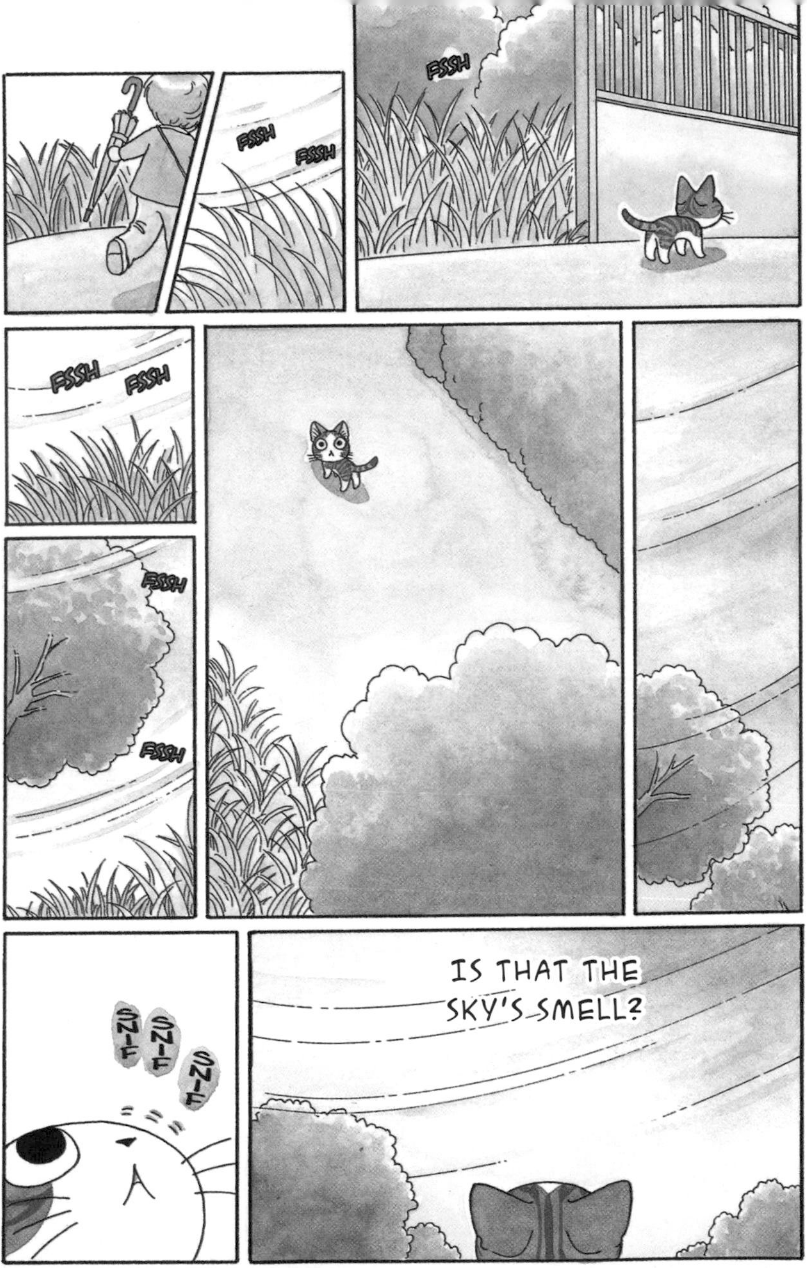
FSSH
FSSH
FSSH
FSSH
FSSH
FSSH
FSSH
SNIF
SNIF
SNIF
IS THAT THE SKY'S SMELL?

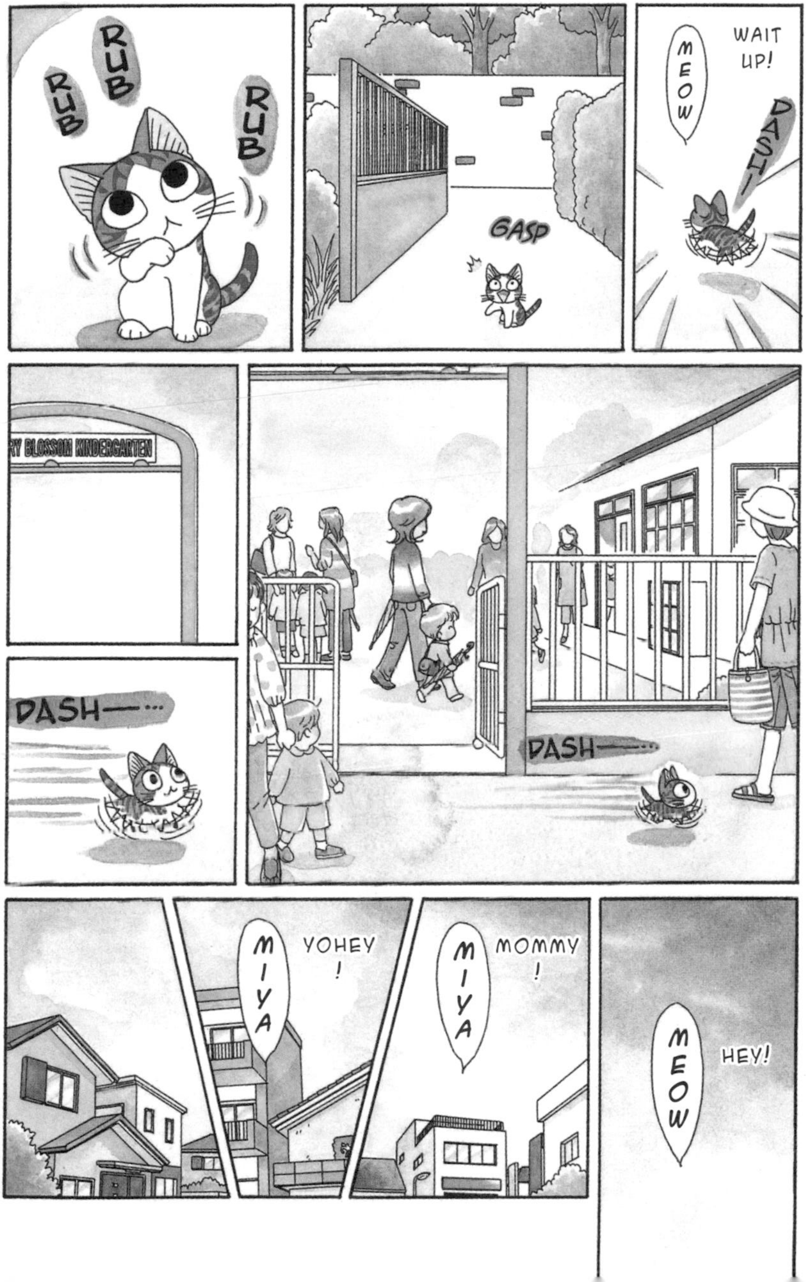
RUB
RUB
RUB
GASP
MEOW
WAIT UP!
DASH
RY BLOSSOM KINDERGARTEN
DASH—...
DASH——...
MIYA
YOHEY!
MIYA
MOMMY!
MEOW
HEY!

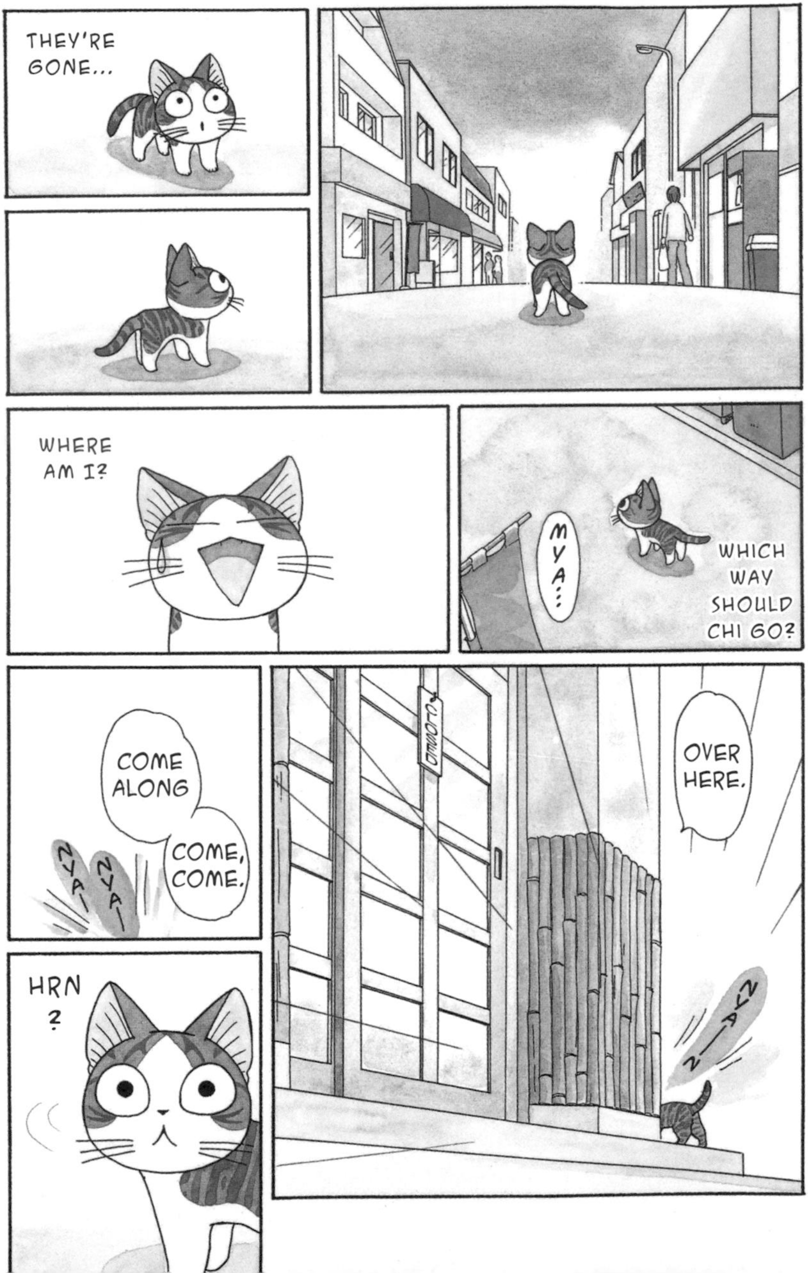
THEY'RE GONE...
WHERE AM I?
MYA...
WHICH WAY SHOULD CHI GO?
COME ALONG
COME, COME.
NYA!
NYA!
HRN?
CLOSED
OVER HERE.

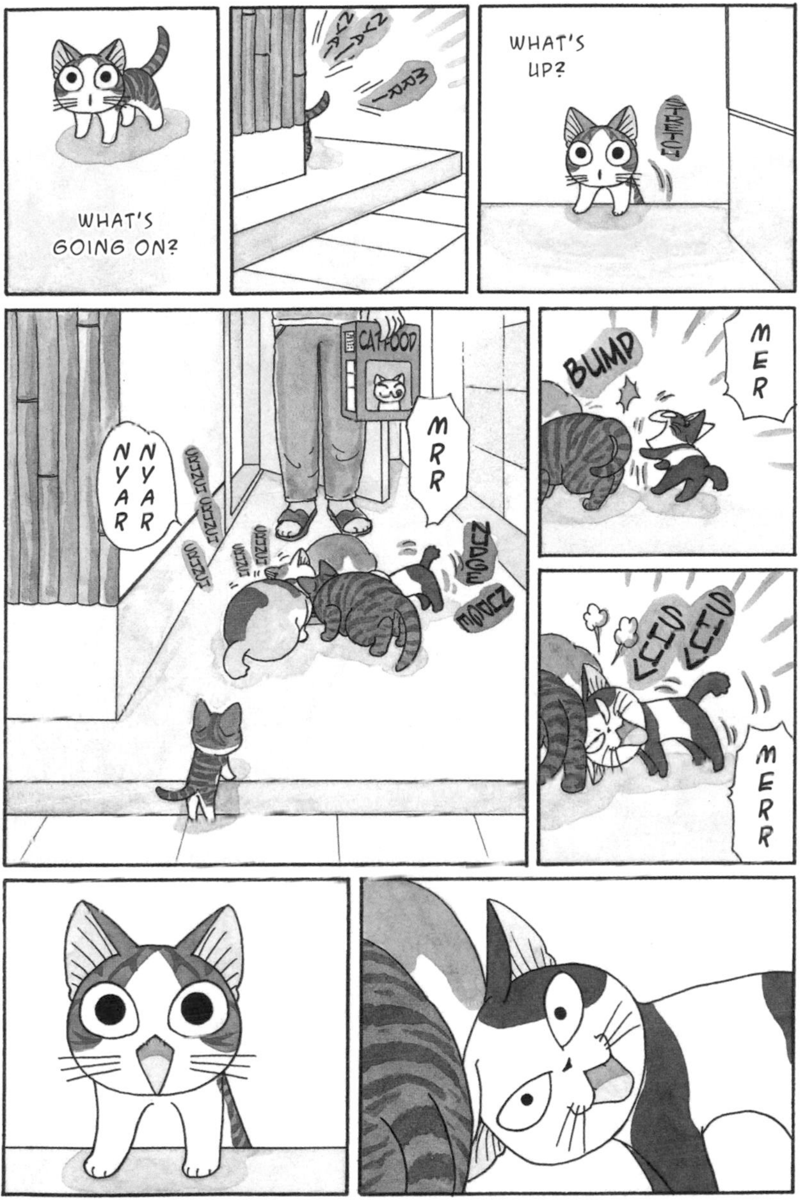
WHAT'S GOING ON?
NYA- NYA-
MRRR-
WHAT'S UP?
STRETCH
NYAR NYAR
NUZZLE NUZZLE
NUZZLE
NUZZLE NUZZLE
MRR
NUDGE
BUMP
MER
SHUV SHUV
MERR

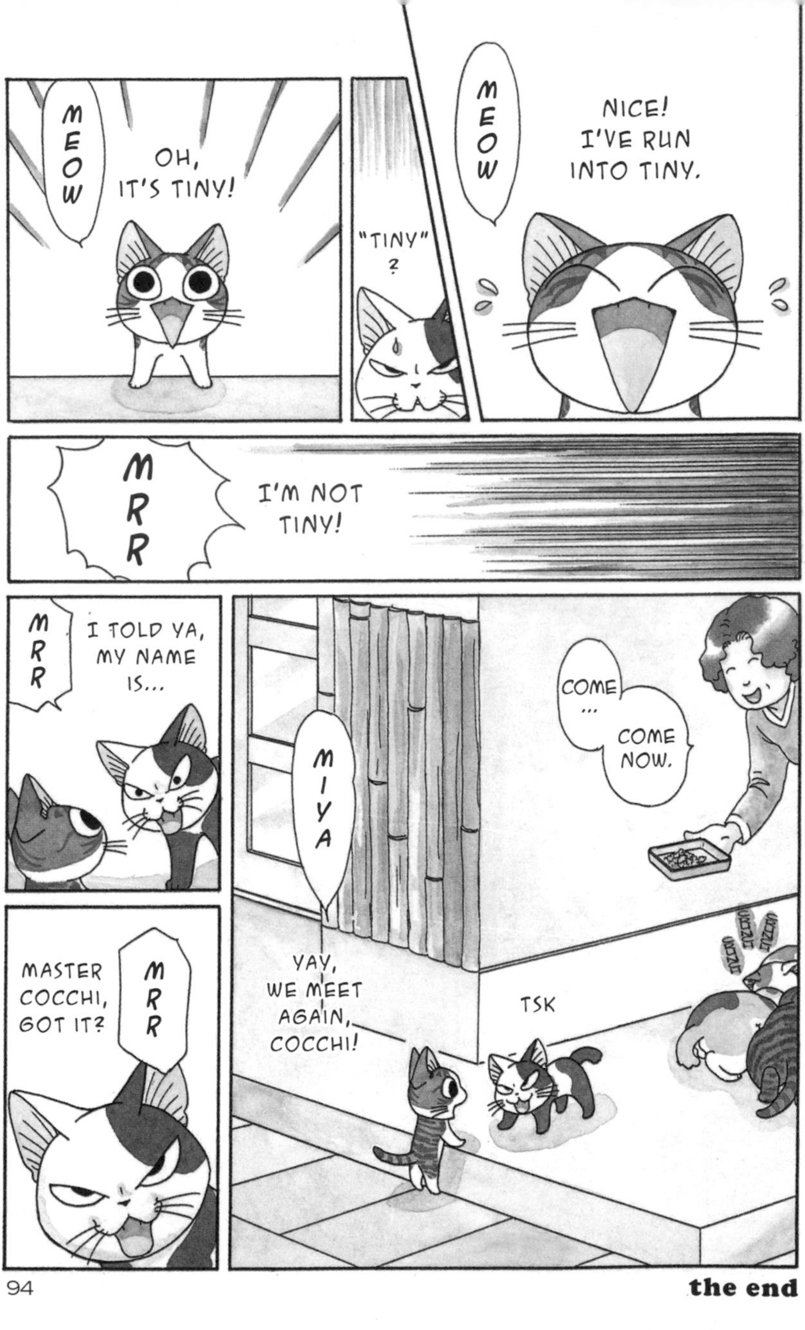
MEOW
OH, IT'S TINY!
"TINY" ?
MEOW
NICE! I'VE RUN INTO TINY.
MRR
I'M NOT TINY!
MRR
I TOLD YA, MY NAME IS...
MASTER COCCHI, GOT IT?
MRR
COME ... COME NOW.
MIYA
YAY, WE MEET AGAIN, COCCHI!
TSK

the end

homemade 123: a cat senses an anomaly

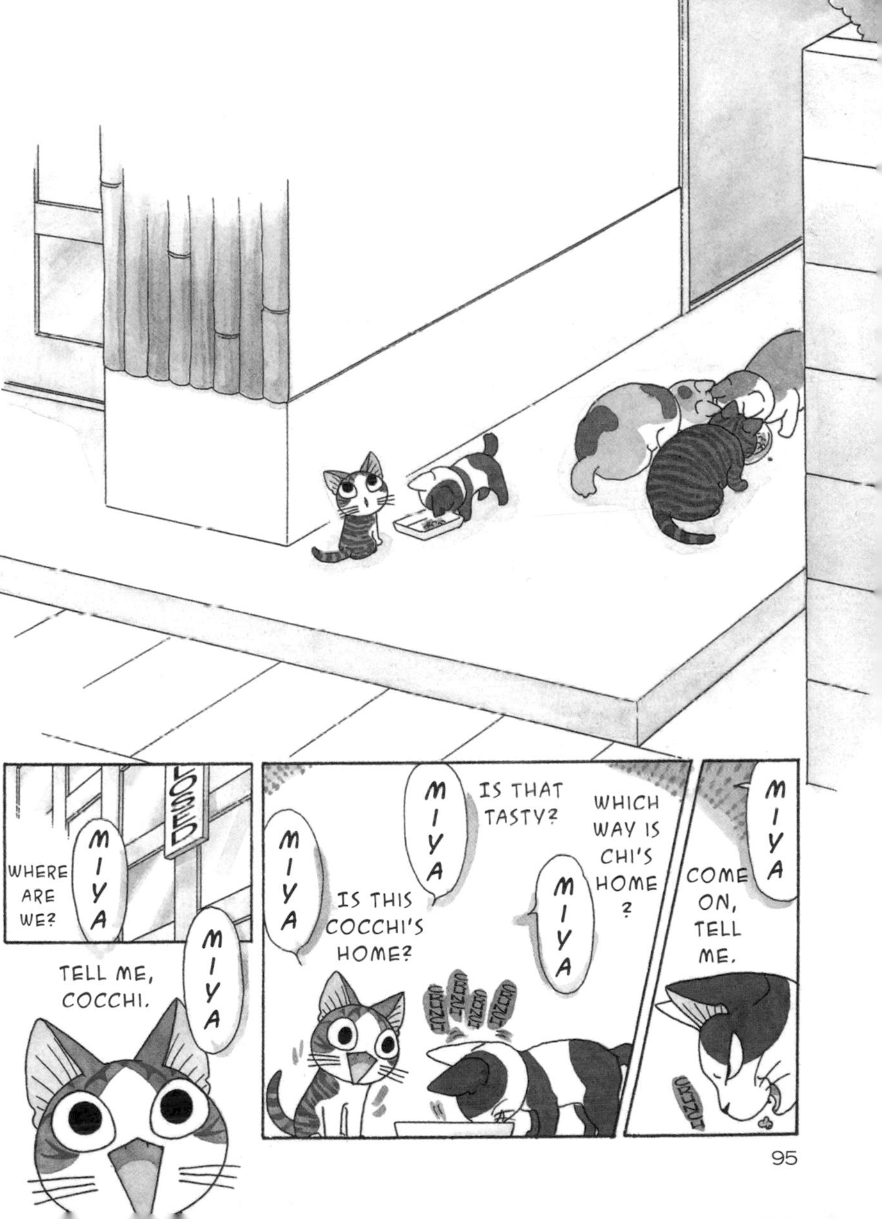
LOSED
WHERE ARE WE?
MIYA
TELL ME, COCCHI.
MIYA
MIYA
IS THIS COCCHI'S HOME?
MIYA
IS THAT TASTY?
WHICH WAY IS CHI'S HOME?
MIYA
COME ON, TELL ME.
MIYA

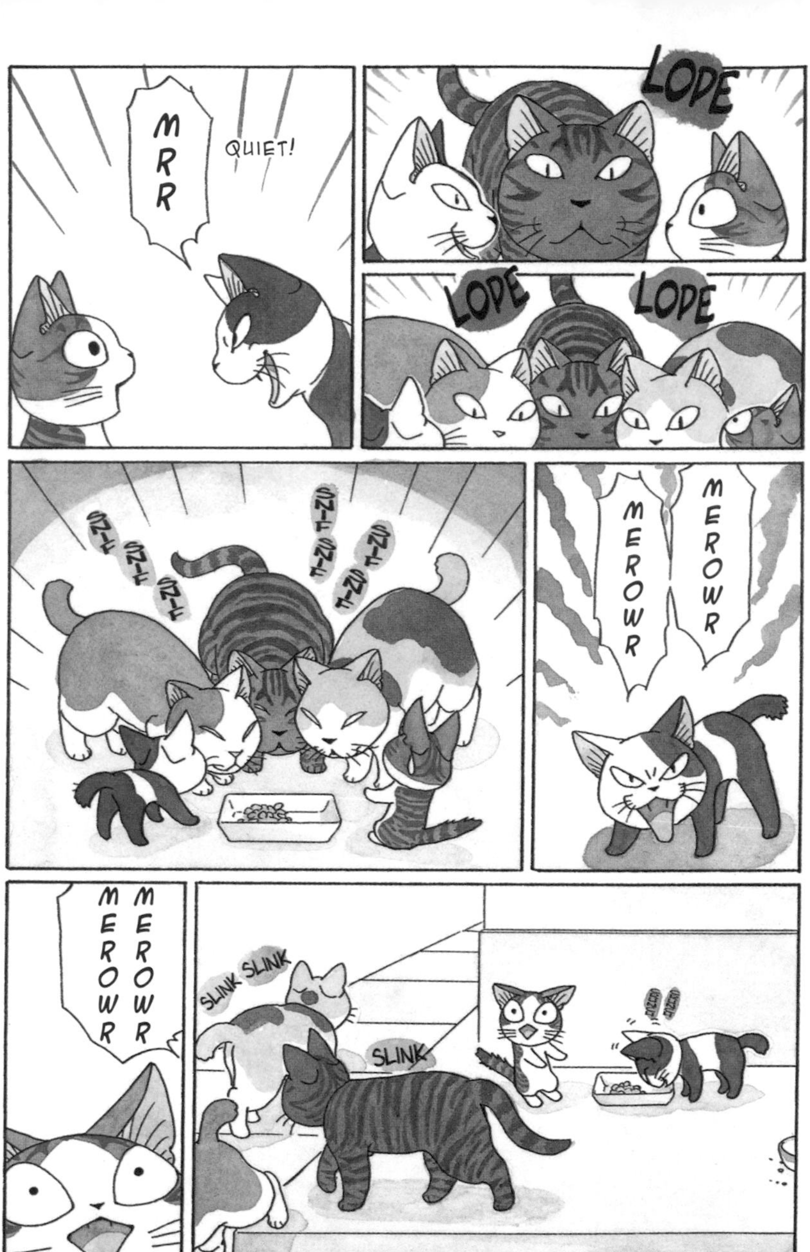
MRR
QUIET!
LODE
LODE
LODE
SNIF SNIF SNIF
SNIF SNIF
SNIF SNIF
MEROWR
MEROWR
MEROWR
MEROWR
SLINK SLINK
SLINK

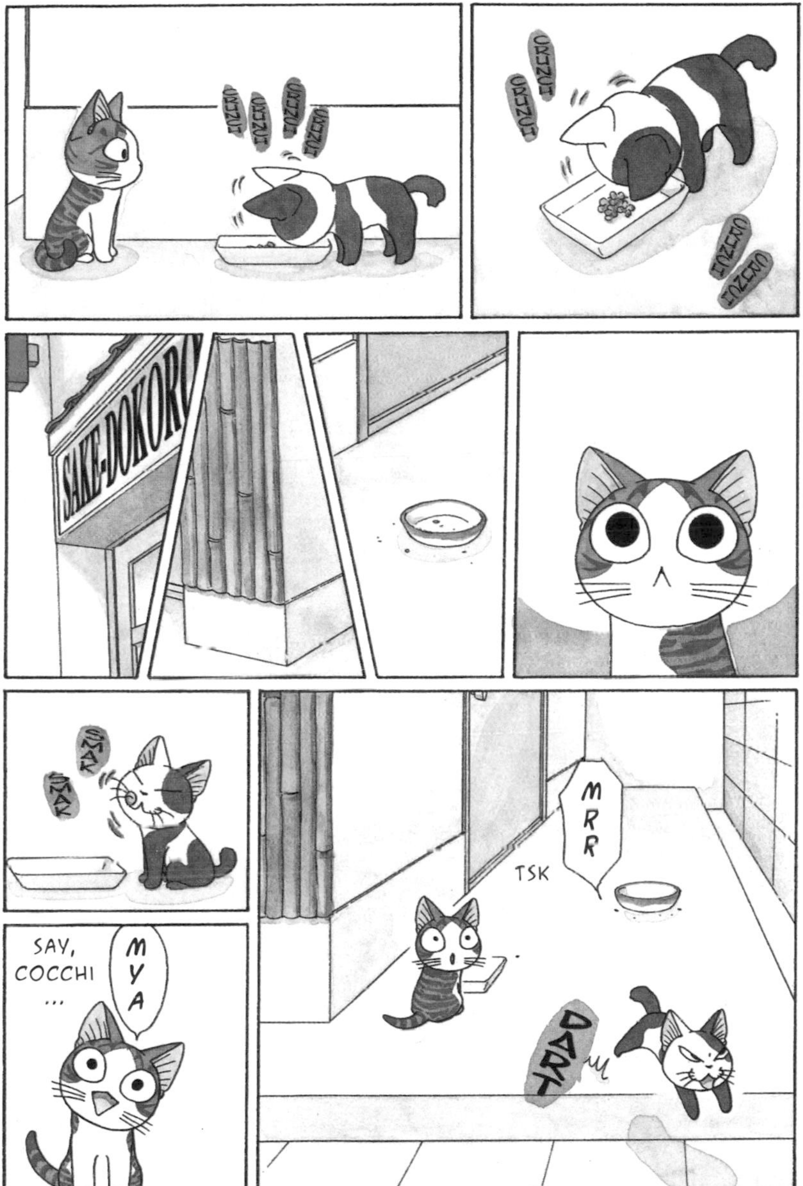
CRUNCH CRUNCH CRUNCH CRUNCH
CRUNCH CRUNCH
CRUNCH CRUNCH
SAKE-DOKORO
SMAK SMAK
SAY, COCCHI ...
MYA
MRR
TSK
DART

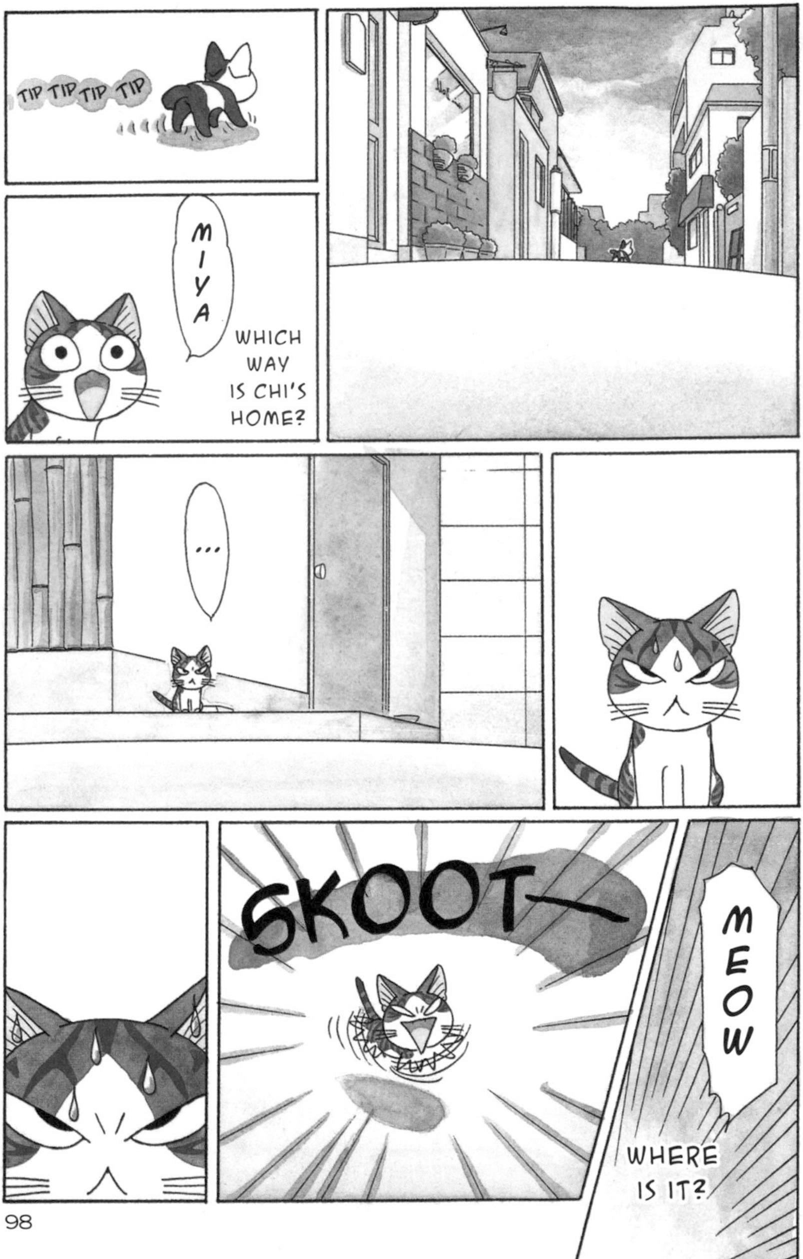
TIP TIP TIP TIP
MIYA
WHICH WAY IS CHI'S HOME?
...
SKOOT—
MEOW
WHERE IS IT?

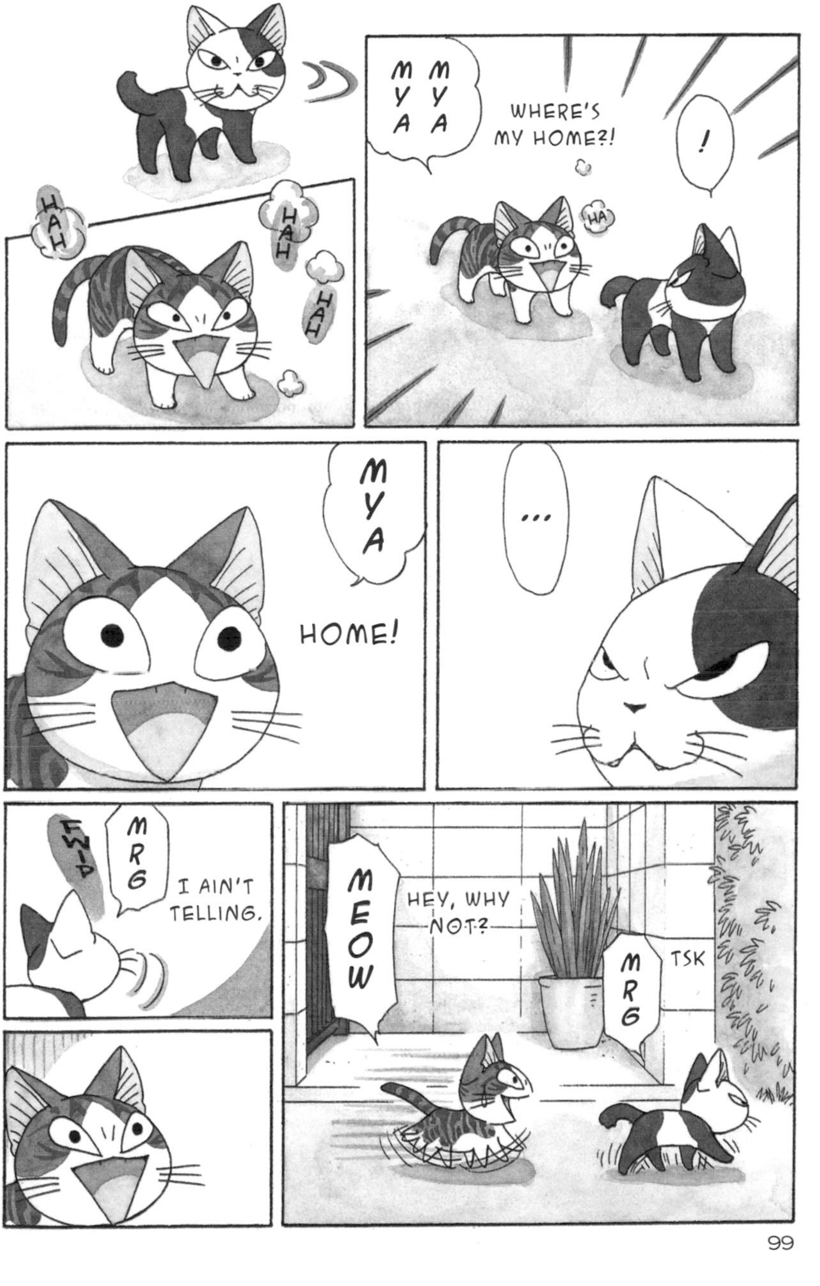
HAH
HAH
HAH
MYA
MYA
WHERE'S MY HOME?!
HA
!
MYA
HOME!
...
FWIP
MRG
I AIN'T TELLING.
MEOW
HEY, WHY NOT?
MRG
TSK

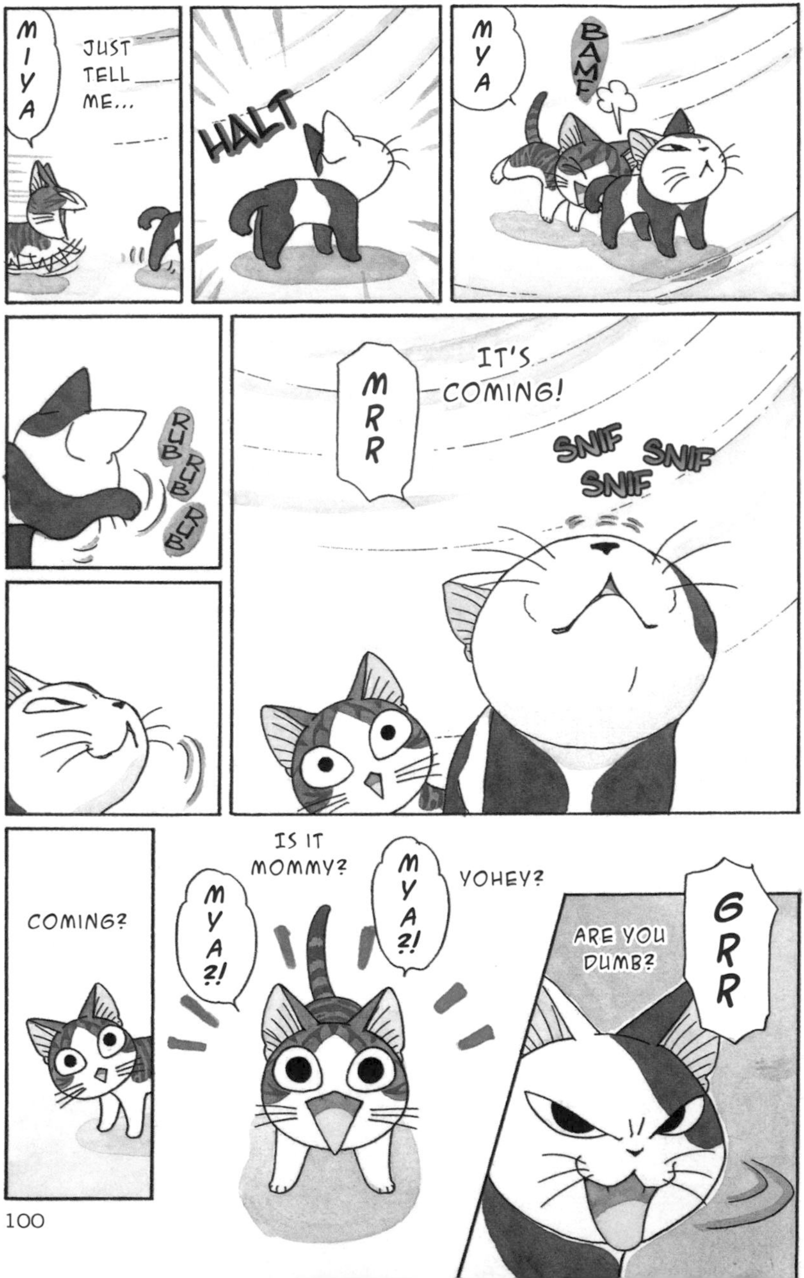
MIYA
JUST TELL ME...
HALT
MYA
BAMF
RUB RUB RUB
MRR
IT'S COMING!
SNIF SNIF SNIF
COMING?
MYA?!
IS IT MOMMY?
MYA?!
YOHEY?
GRR
ARE YOU DUMB?

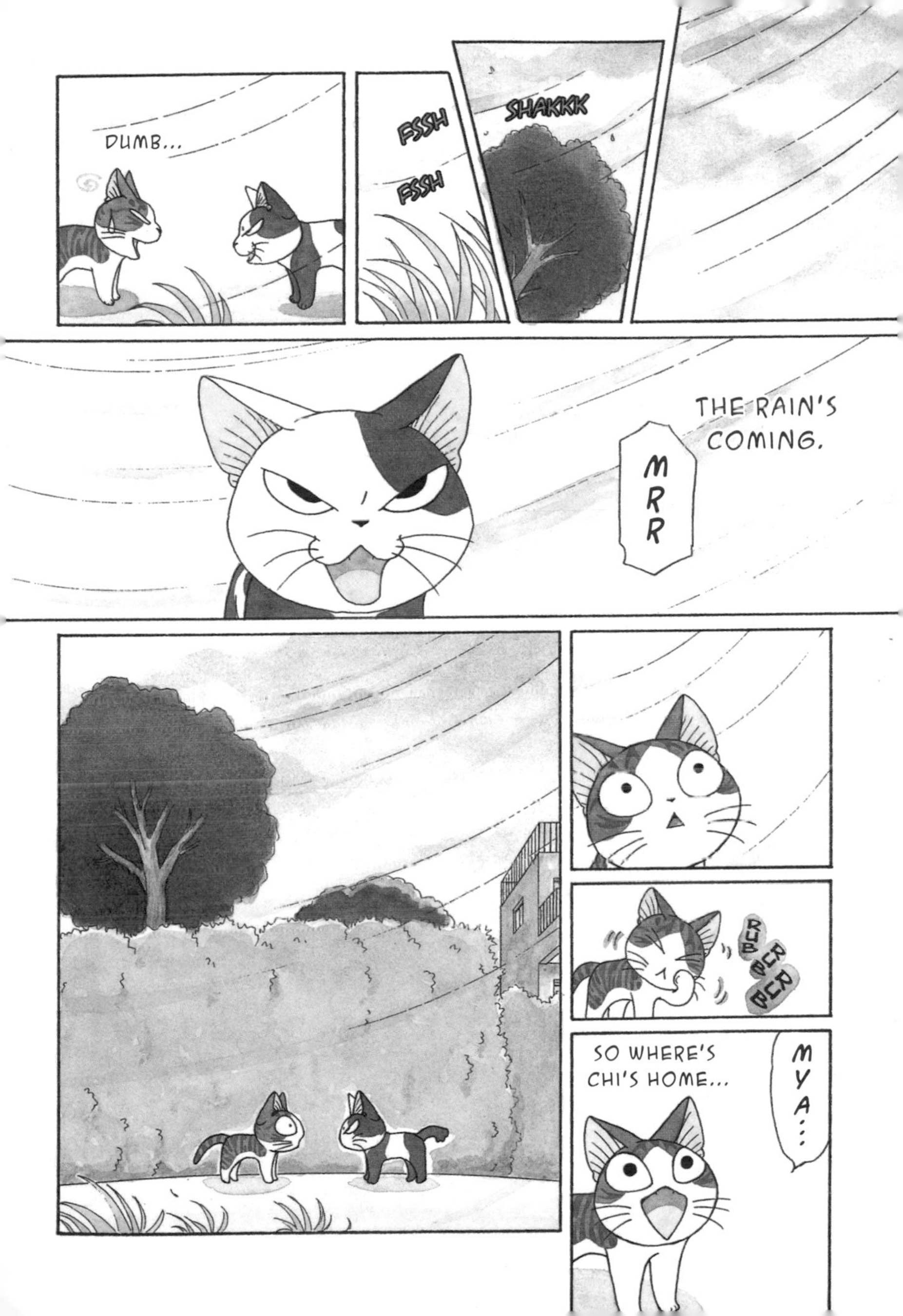
DUMB...
FSSH
FSSH
SHAKKK
THE RAIN'S COMING.
MRR
RUB
SO WHERE'S CHI'S HOME...
MYA...

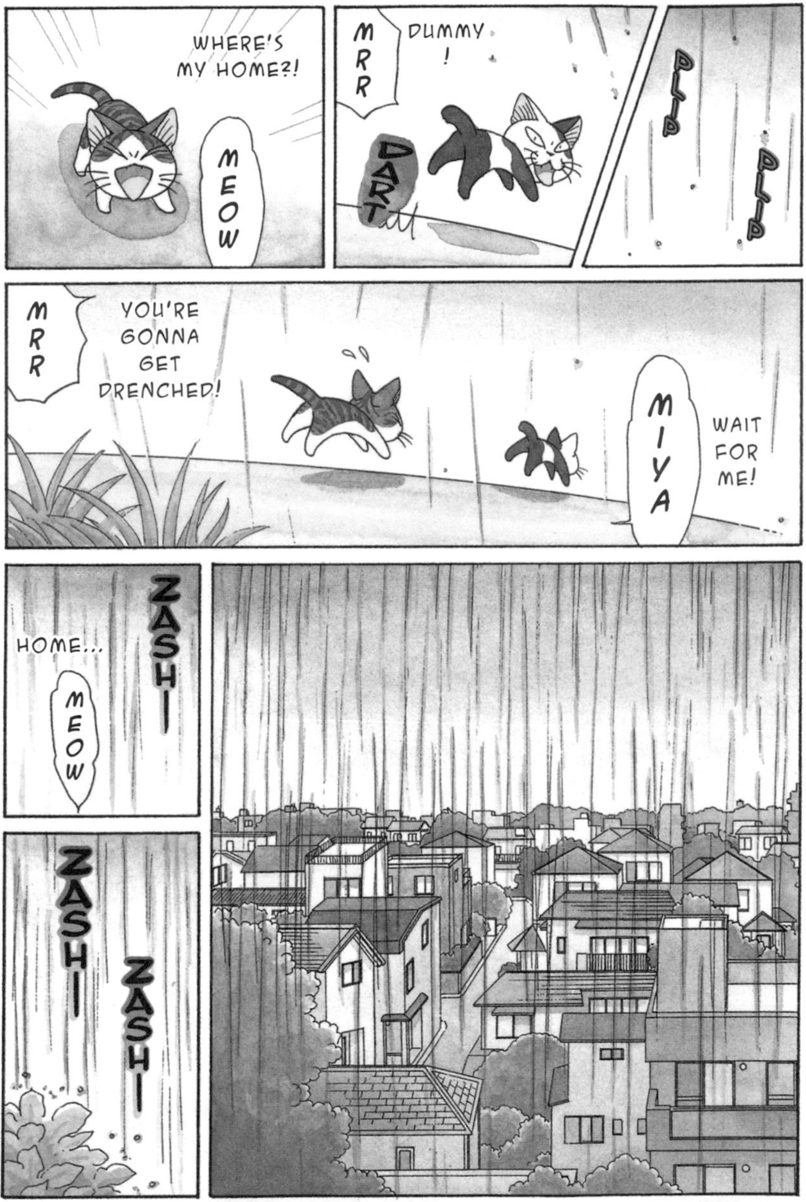
WHERE'S MY HOME?!
MEOW
MRR
DUMMY!
DART
PLIP
PLIP
MRR
YOU'RE GONNA GET DRENCHED!
MIYA
WAIT FOR ME!
HOME...
MEOW
ZASHI
ZASHI
ZASHI

the end

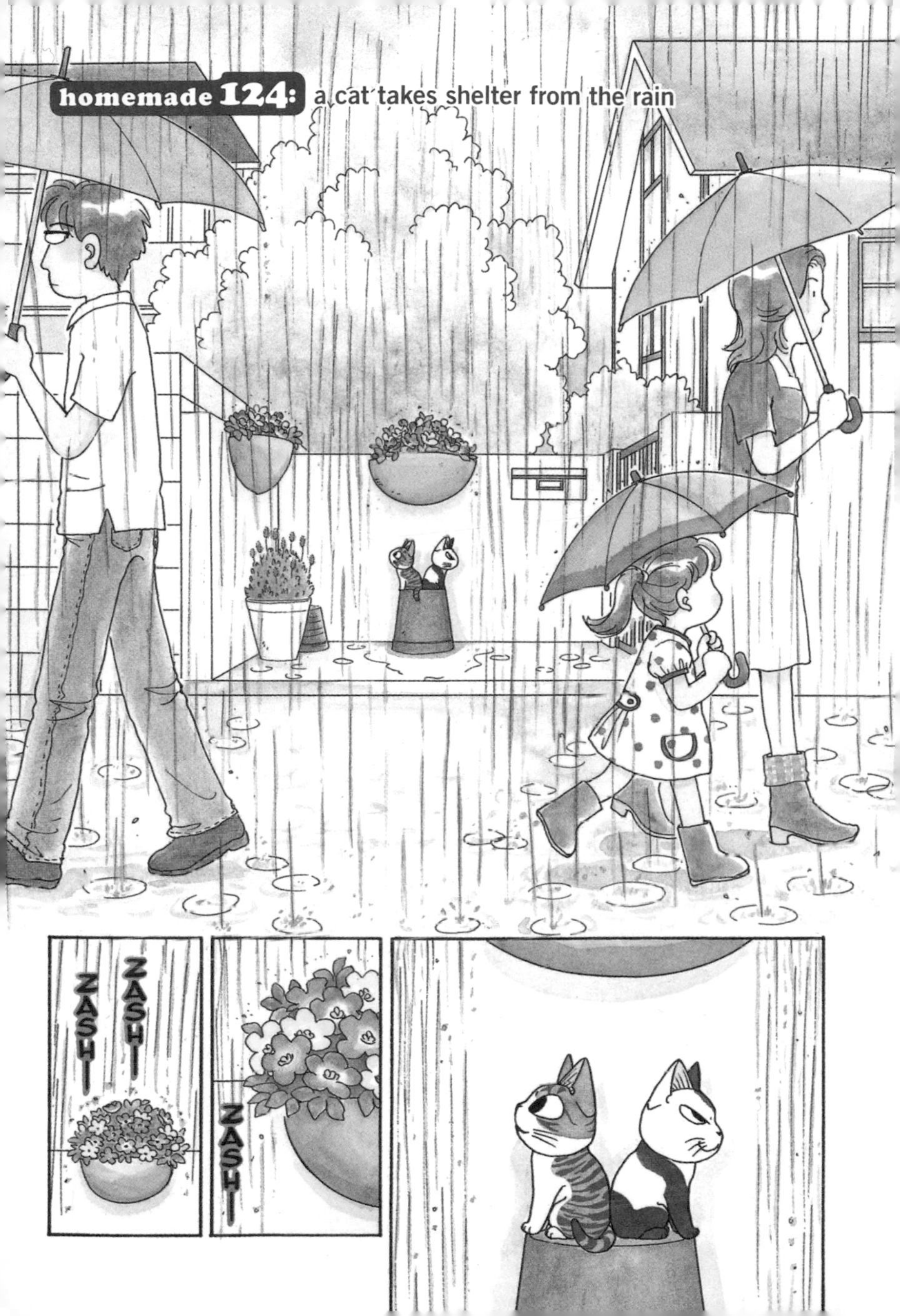
homemade 124: a cat takes shelter from the rain
ZASHI
ZASHI
ZASHI

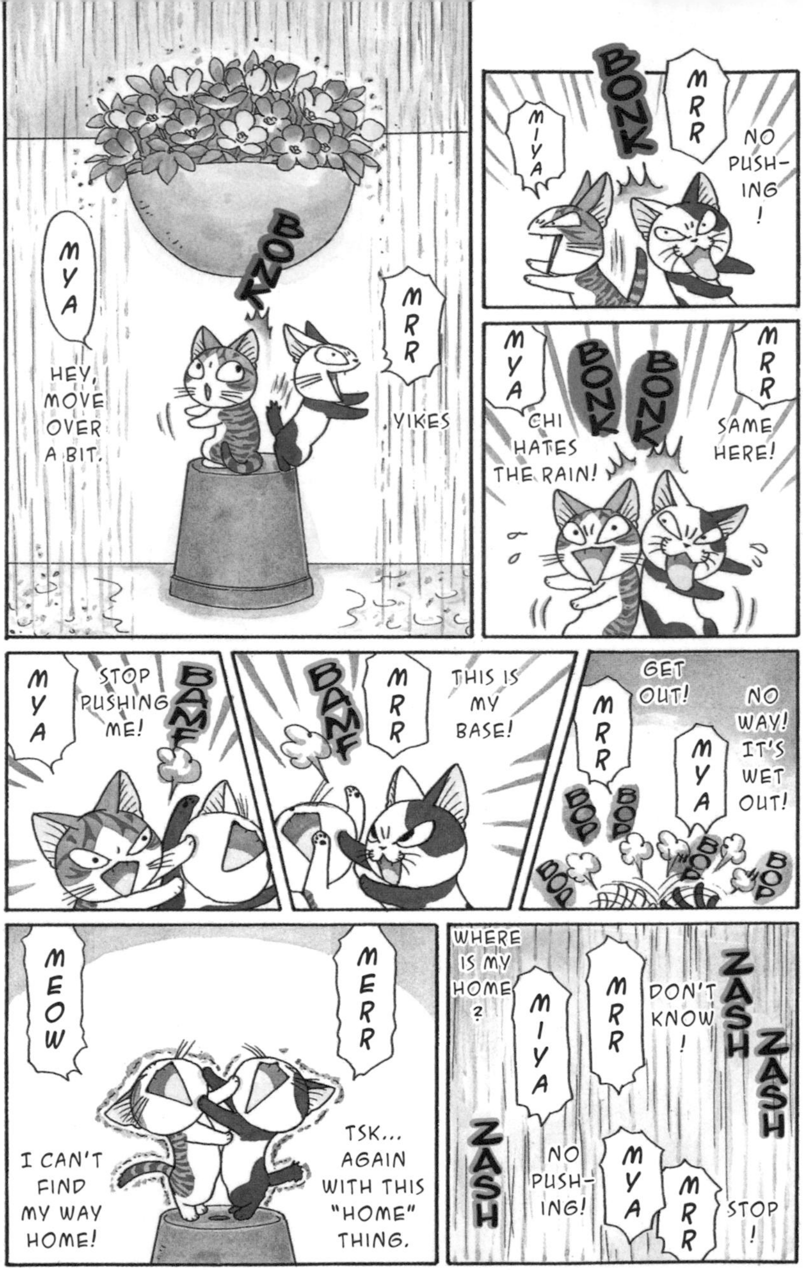
MYA
BONK
HEY, MOVE OVER A BIT.
MRR
YIKES
MIYA
BONK
MRR
NO PUSHING!
MYA
CHI HATES THE RAIN!
BONK
BONK
MRR
SAME HERE!
MYA
STOP PUSHING ME!
BAMF
BAMF
MRR
THIS IS MY BASE!
GET OUT!
MRR
NO WAY! IT'S WET OUT!
MYA
BOP
BOP
BOP
BOP
BOP
BOP
MEOW
I CAN'T FIND MY WAY HOME!
MERR
TSK... AGAIN WITH THIS "HOME" THING.
WHERE IS MY HOME?
MIYA
MRR
DON'T KNOW!
ZASH
ZASH
ZASH
NO PUSHING!
MYA
MRR
STOP!

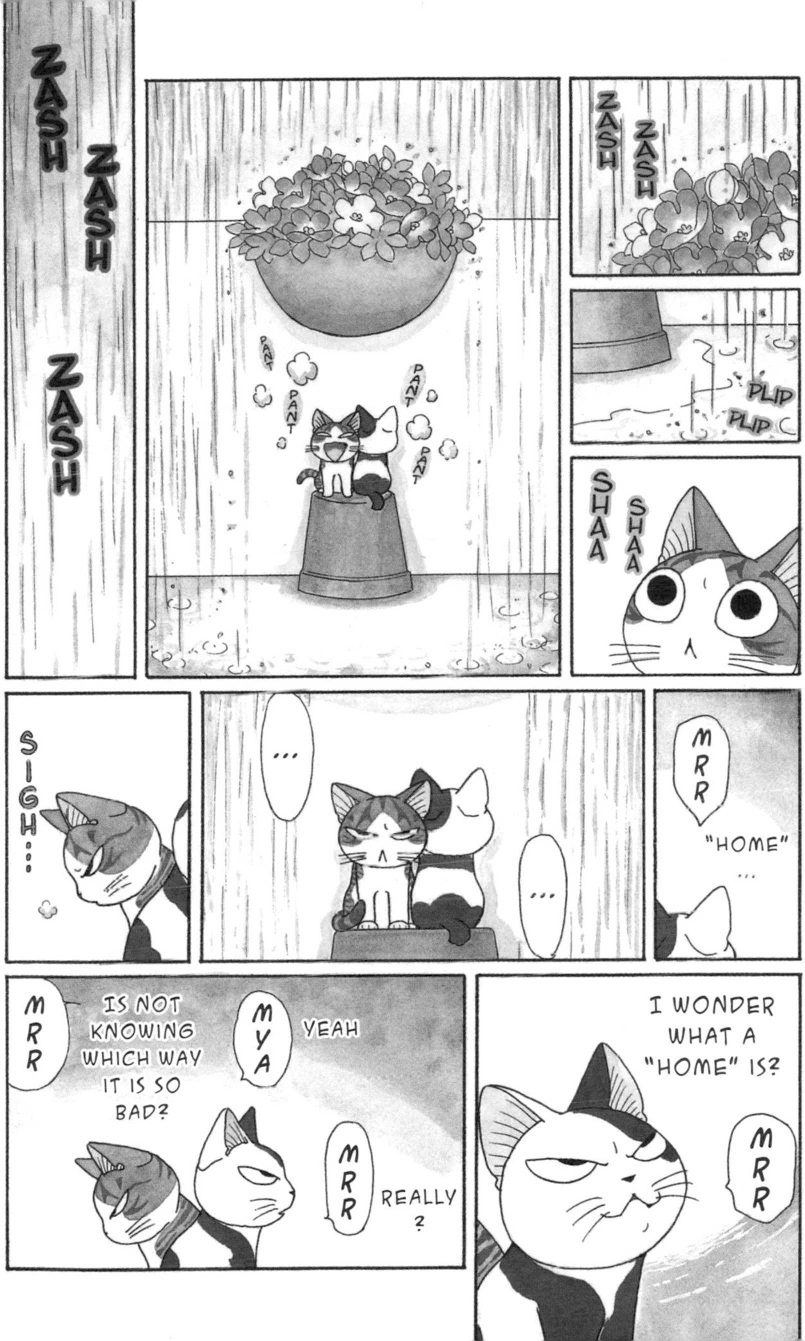

ZASH
ZASH
ZASH
PANT
PANT
PANT
PANT
ZASH
ZASH
PLIP
PLIP
SHAA
SHAA
SIGH...
...
...
MRR
"HOME"
...
MRR
IS NOT KNOWING WHICH WAY IT IS SO BAD?
MYA
YEAH
MRR
REALLY?
I WONDER WHAT A "HOME" IS?
MRR

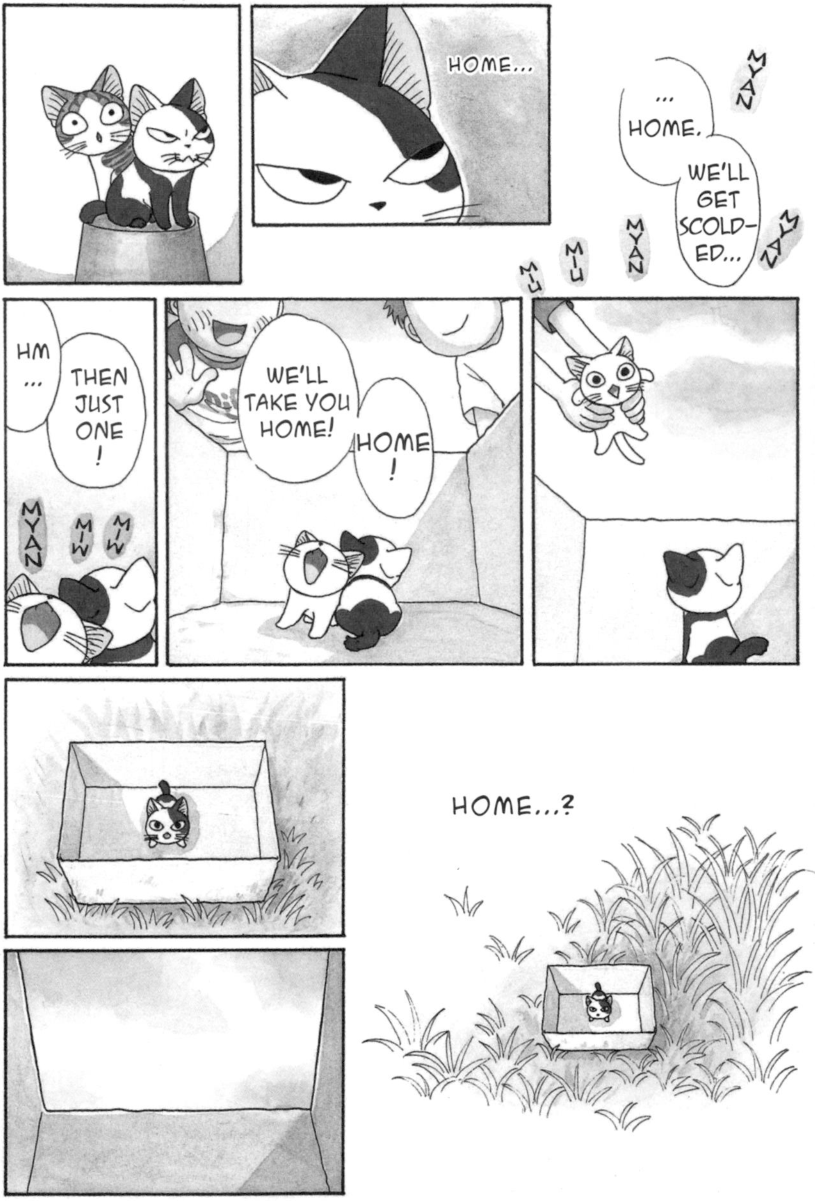
HOME...
... HOME.
MYAN
WE'LL GET SCOLD-ED...
MYAN
MYAN
MIU
MIU
HM ...
THEN JUST ONE!
MYAN
MIW
MIW
WE'LL TAKE YOU HOME!
HOME!
HOME...?

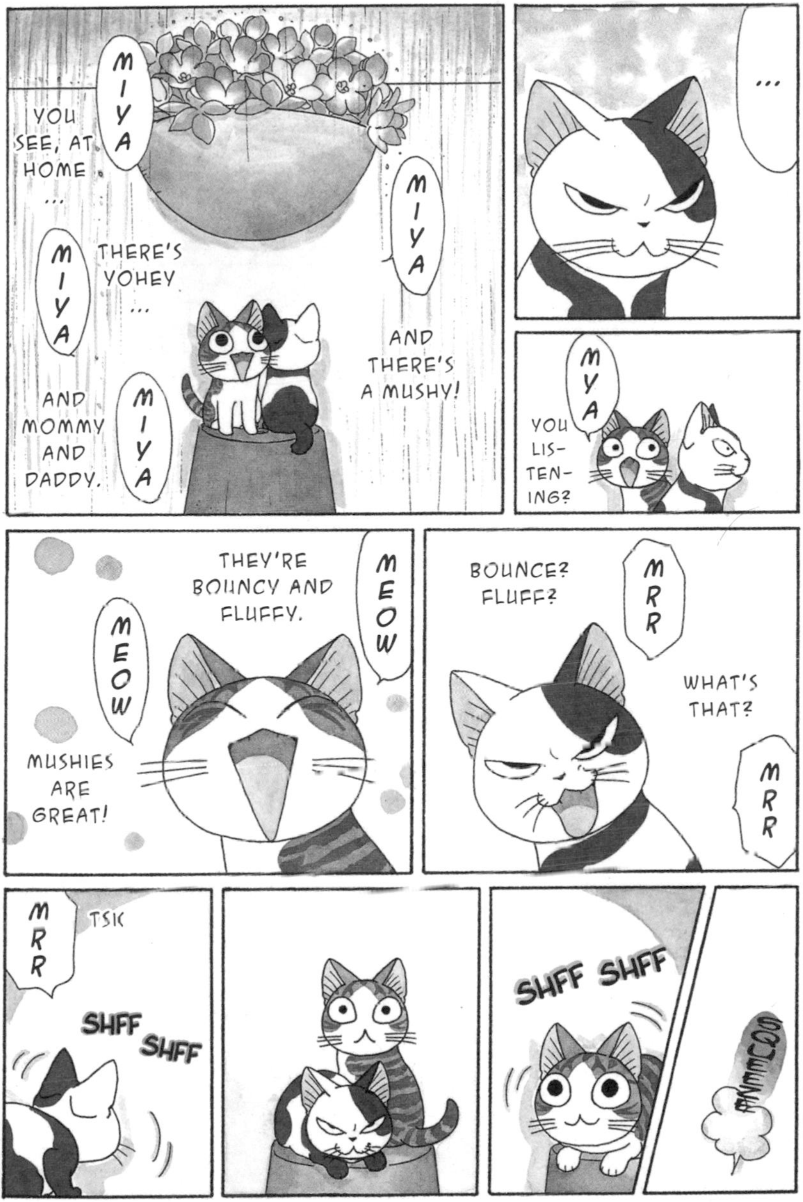
MIYA
YOU SEE, AT HOME ...
MIYA
MIYA
THERE'S YOHEY ...
AND THERE'S A MUSHY!
AND MOMMY AND DADDY.
MIYA
...
MYA
YOU LIS- TEN- ING?
THEY'RE BOUNCY AND FLUFFY.
MEOW
MEOW
MUSHIES ARE GREAT!
BOUNCE? FLUFF?
MRR
WHAT'S THAT?
MRR
MRR
TSK
SHFF SHFF
SHFF SHFF

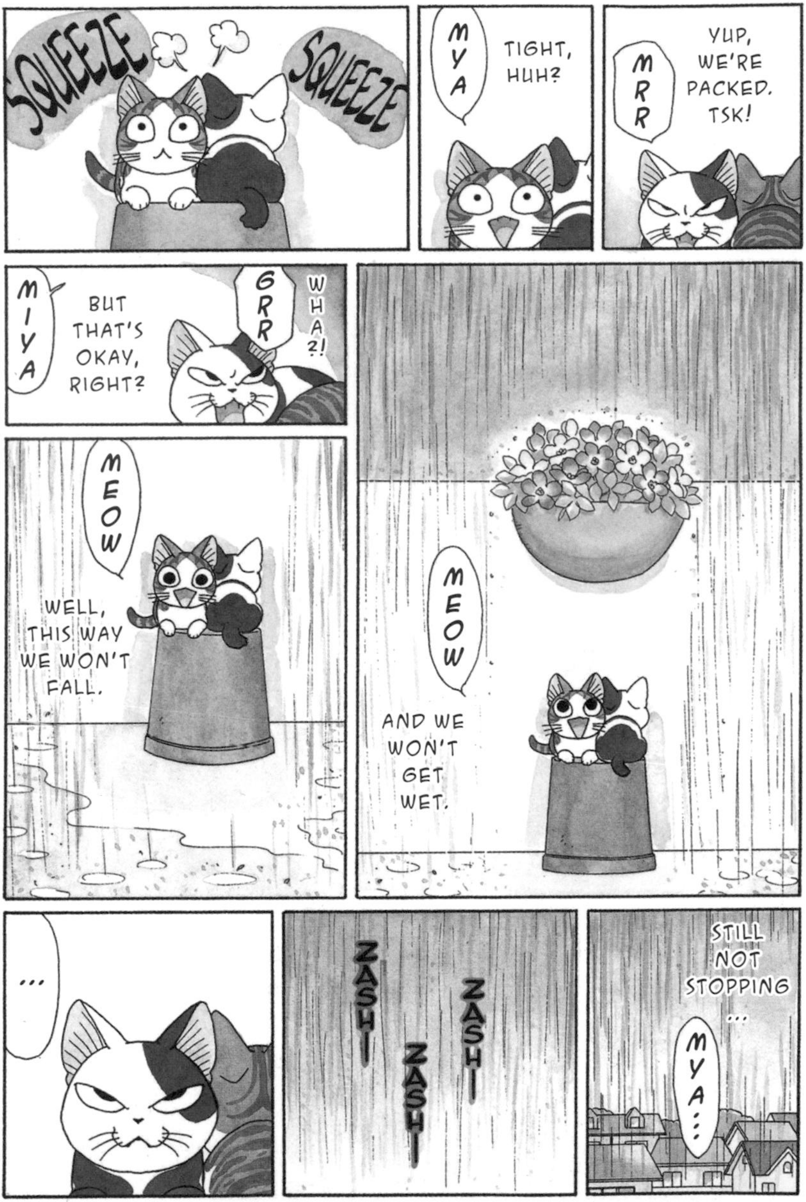
SQUEEZE
SQUEEZE
MYA
TIGHT, HUH?
MRR
YUP, WE'RE PACKED. TSK!
MIYA
BUT THAT'S OKAY, RIGHT?
GRR
WHA?!
MEOW
WELL, THIS WAY WE WON'T FALL.
MEOW
AND WE WON'T GET WET.
...
ZASHI
ZASHI
ZASHI
STILL NOT STOPPING...
MYA...

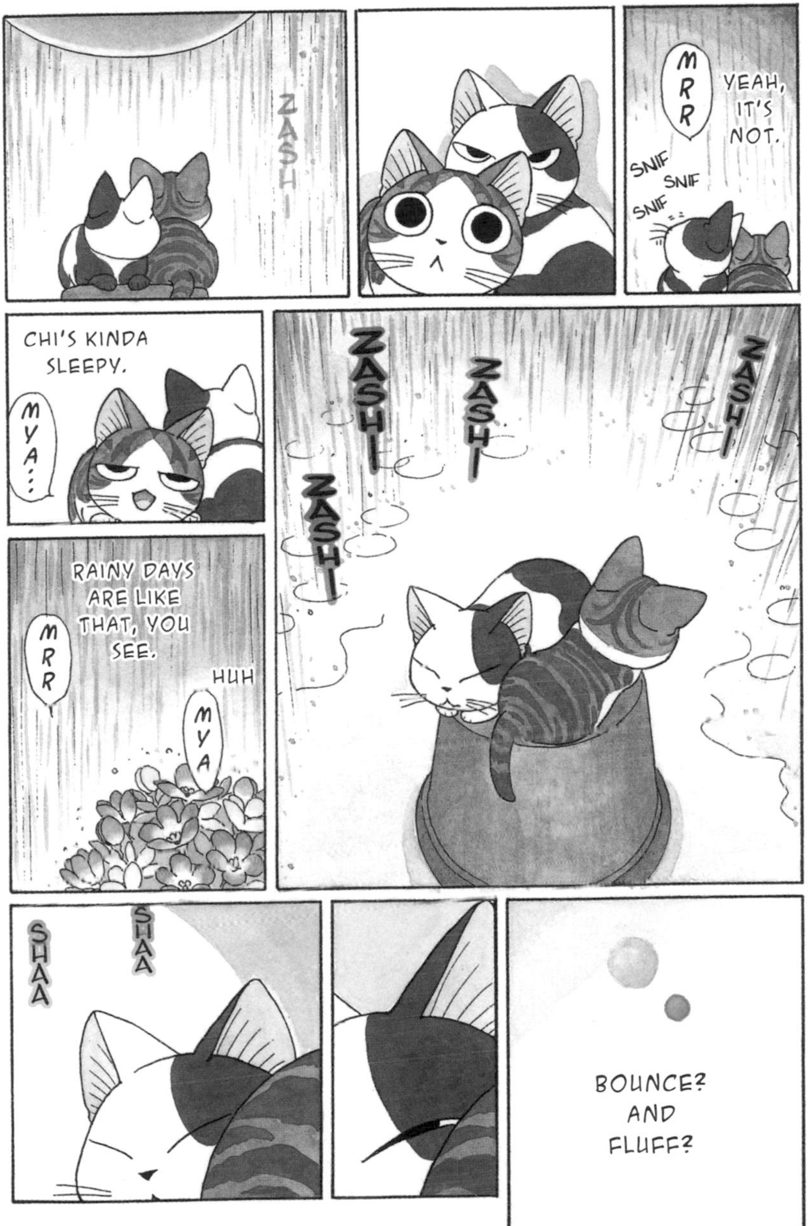
ZASHI
MRR
YEAH, IT'S NOT.
SNIF
SNIF
SNIF
CHI'S KINDA SLEEPY.
MYA...
RAINY DAYS ARE LIKE THAT, YOU SEE.
MRR
HUH
MYA
ZASHI
ZASHI
ZASHI
ZASHI
SHAA
SHAA
BOUNCE? AND FLUFF?

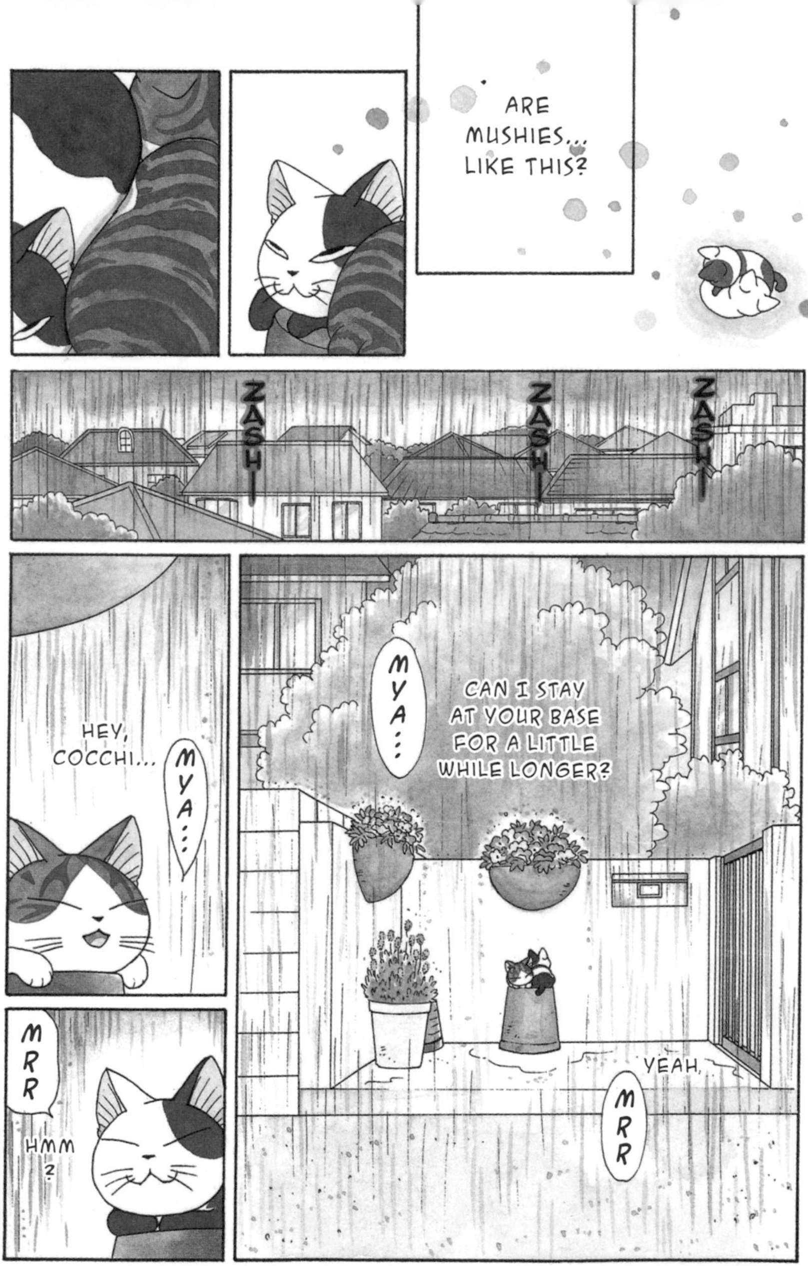
ARE MUSHIES... LIKE THIS?
ZASHI
ZASHI
ZASHI
HEY, COCCHI...
MYA...
MRR
HMM?
MYA...
CAN I STAY AT YOUR BASE FOR A LITTLE WHILE LONGER?
YEAH,
MRR

the end

homemade 125: a cat goes halves

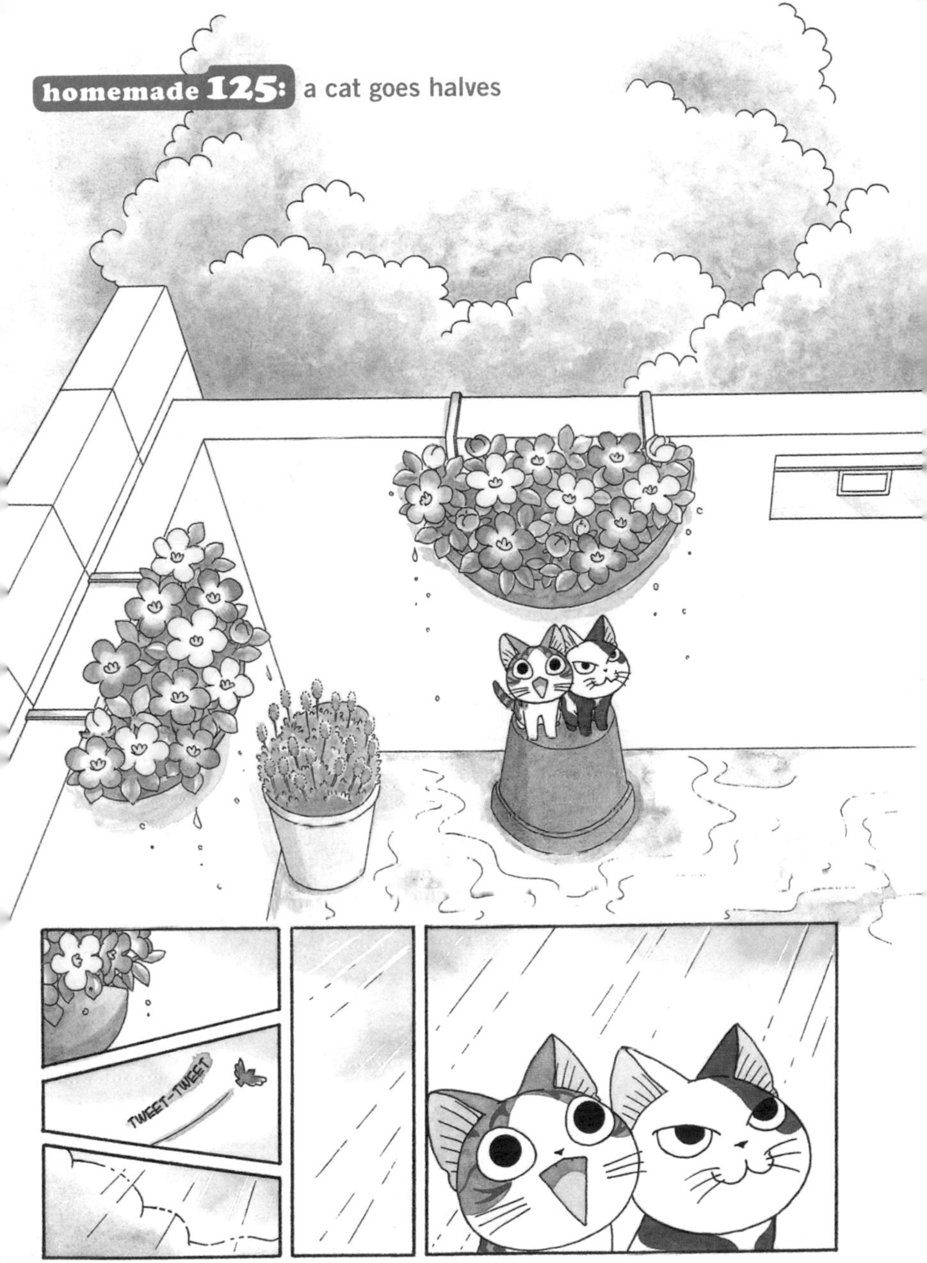
TWEET-TWEET

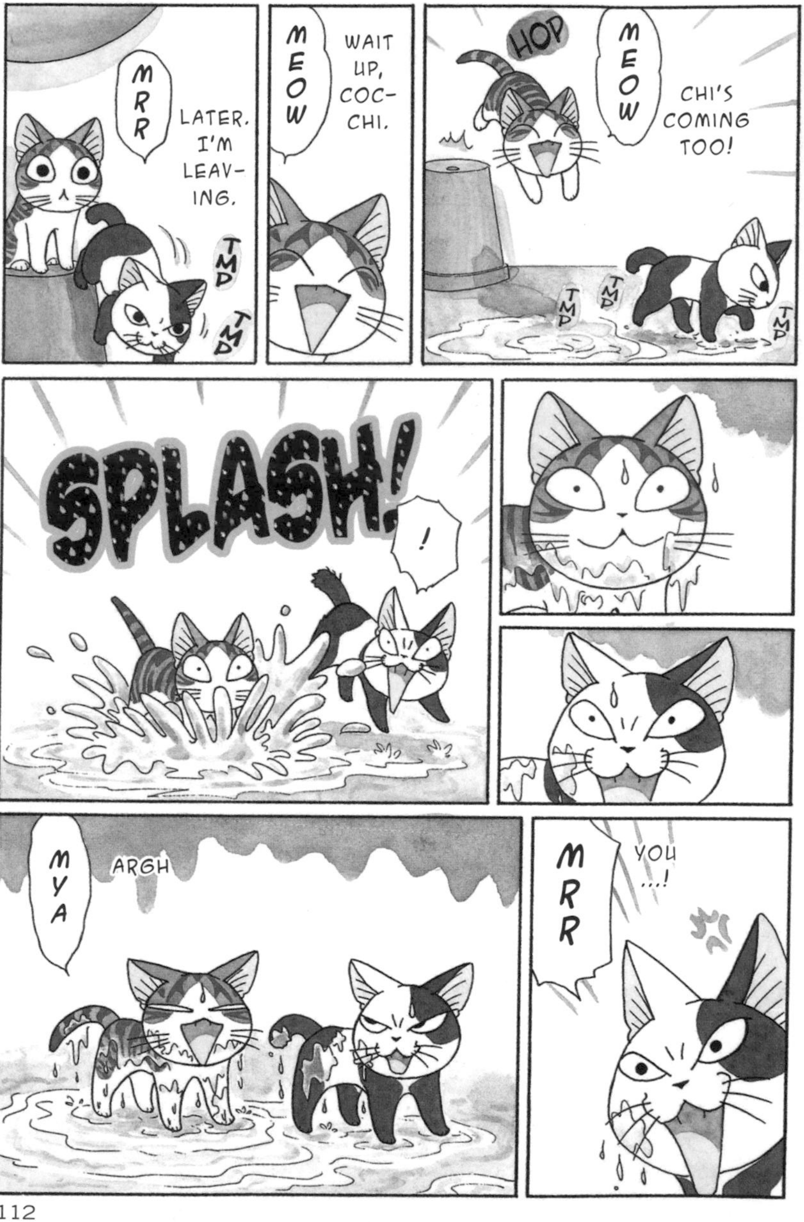
MRR
LATER. I'M LEAVING.
TMD
TMD
MEOW
WAIT UP, COCCHI.
HOP
MEOW
CHI'S COMING TOO!
TMP
TMP
TMP
SPLASH!
!
MYA
ARGH
MRR
YOU ...!

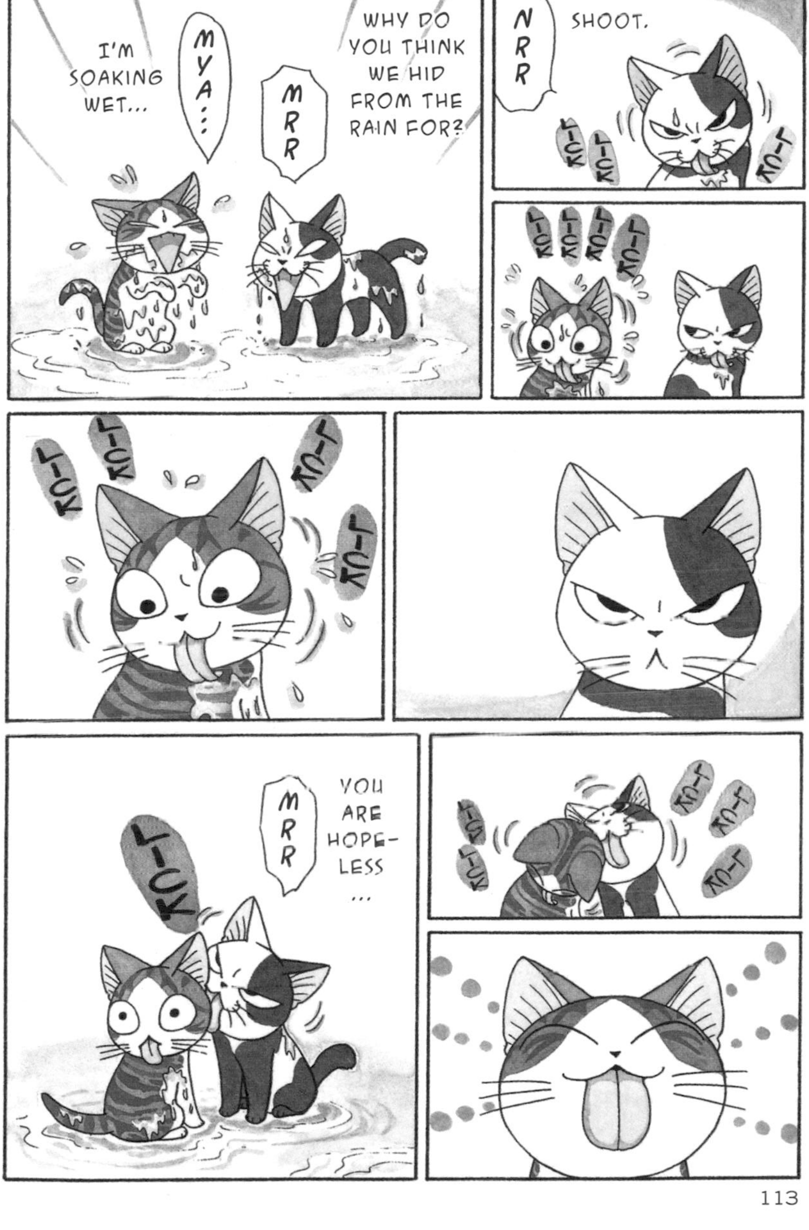
I'M SOAKING WET...
MYA...
MRR
WHY DO YOU THINK WE HID FROM THE RAIN FOR?
NRR
SHOOT.
LICK
LICK
LICK
LICK
LICK
LICK
LICK
LICK
LICK
LICK
LICK
MRR
YOU ARE HOPE-LESS ...
LICK
LICK
LICK
LICK
LICK
LICK

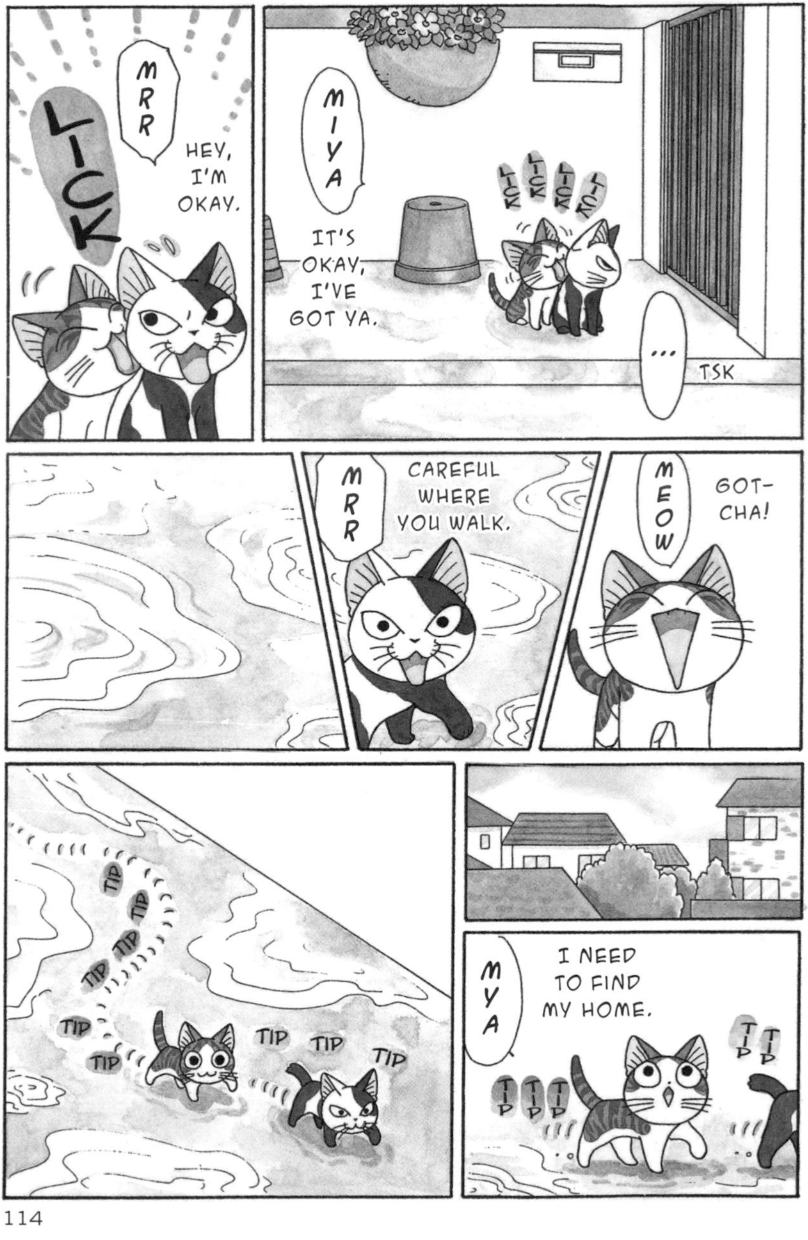
LICK
MRR
HEY, I'M OKAY.
MIYA
IT'S OKAY, I'VE GOT YA.
LICK LICK LICK LICK
...
TSK
MRR
CAREFUL WHERE YOU WALK.
MEOW
GOT-CHA!
TIP
TIP
TIP
TIP
TIP
TIP
TIP
TIP
TIP
MYA
I NEED TO FIND MY HOME.
TIP TIP TIP
TIP TIP

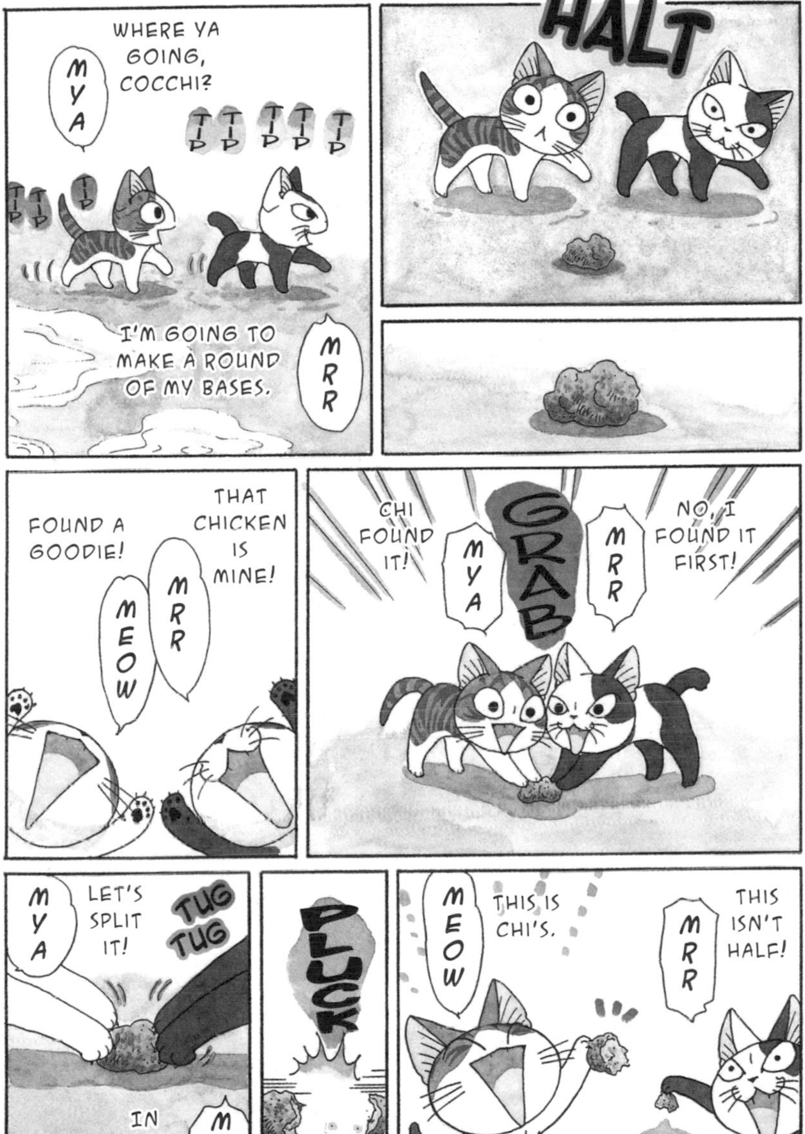
MYA
WHERE YA GOING, COCCHI?
TIP TIP TIP TIP TIP
TIP TIP TIP
I'M GOING TO MAKE A ROUND OF MY BASES.
MRR
HALT
FOUND A GOODIE!
MEOW
THAT CHICKEN IS MINE!
MRR
CHI FOUND IT!
MYA
GRAB
MRR
NO, I FOUND IT FIRST!
MYA
LET'S SPLIT IT!
TUG TUG
IN HALF, THEN.
MRR
PLUCK
MEOW
THIS IS CHI'S.
MRR
THIS ISN'T HALF!
PLINK

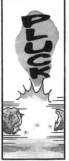

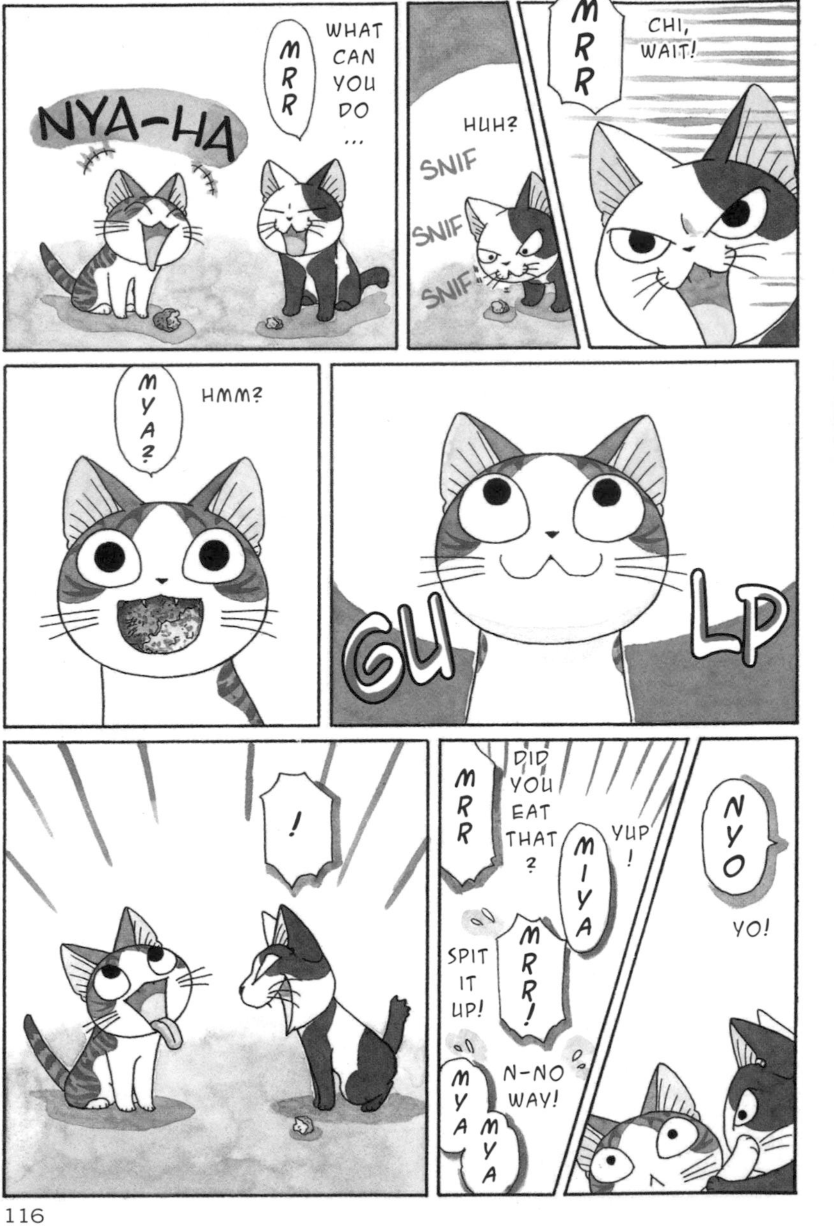
NYA-HA
MRR
WHAT CAN YOU DO ...
HUH?
SNIF
SNIF
SNIF
MRR
CHI, WAIT!
MYA?
HMM?
GU LP
!
MRR
DID YOU EAT THAT?
MIYA
YUP!
MRR!
SPIT IT UP!
MYA MYA
N-NO WAY!
NYO
YO!

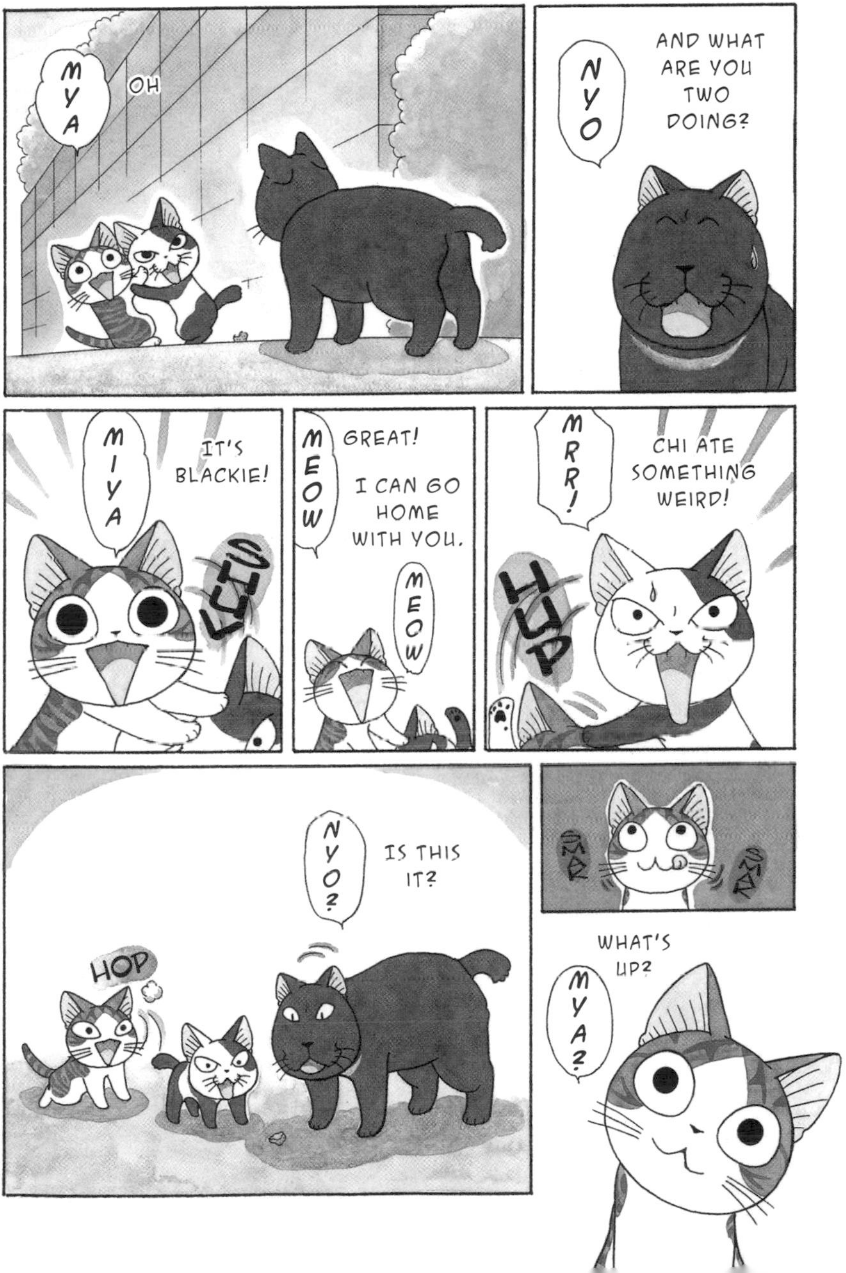
MYA
OH
NYO
AND WHAT ARE YOU TWO DOING?
MIYA
IT'S BLACKIE!
SHU
MEOW
GREAT!
I CAN GO HOME WITH YOU.
MEOW
MRR!
CHI ATE SOMETHING WEIRD!
HUP
NYO?
IS THIS IT?
HOP
WHAT'S UP?
MYA?

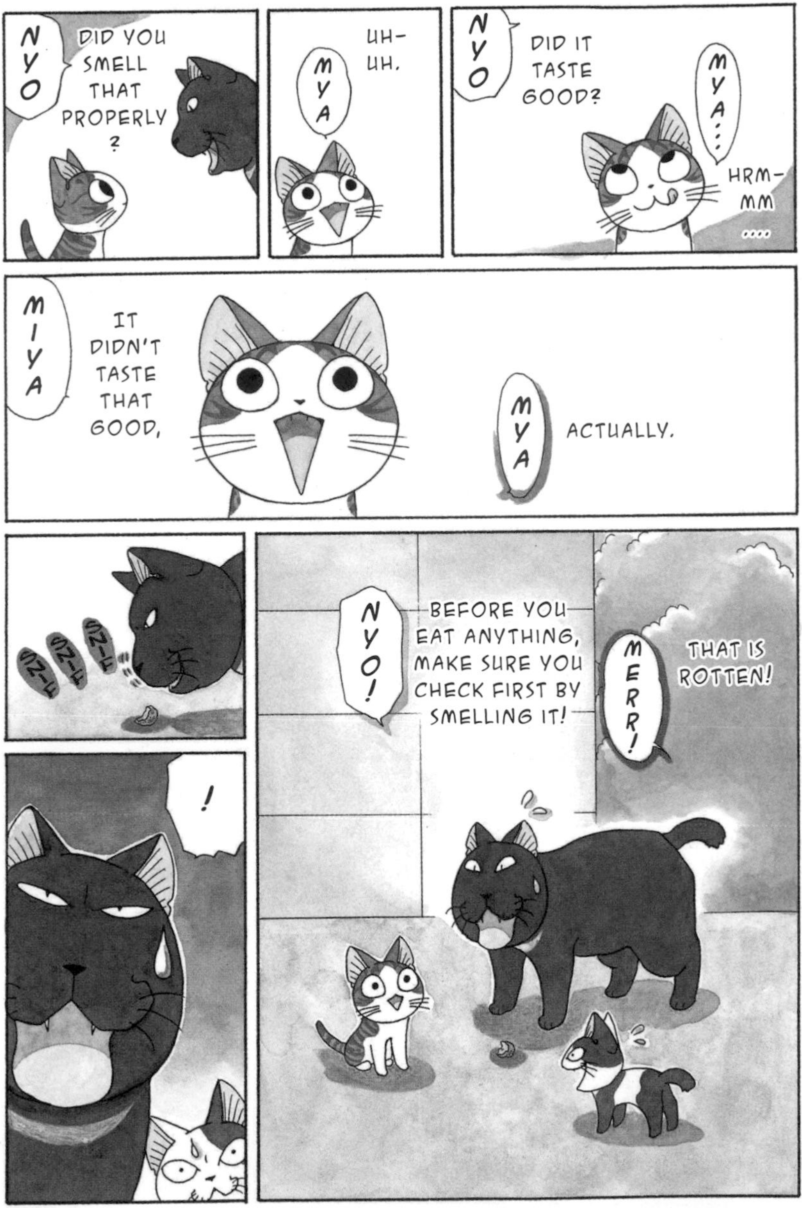
NYO
DID YOU SMELL THAT PROPERLY?
MYA
UH-UH.
NYO
DID IT TASTE GOOD?
MYA...
HRM-MM.....
MIYA
IT DIDN'T TASTE THAT GOOD,
MYA
ACTUALLY.
SNIF SNIF SNIF
!
NYO!
BEFORE YOU EAT ANYTHING, MAKE SURE YOU CHECK FIRST BY SMELLING IT!
MERR!
THAT IS ROTTEN!

the end

homemade 126: a cat has an emergency

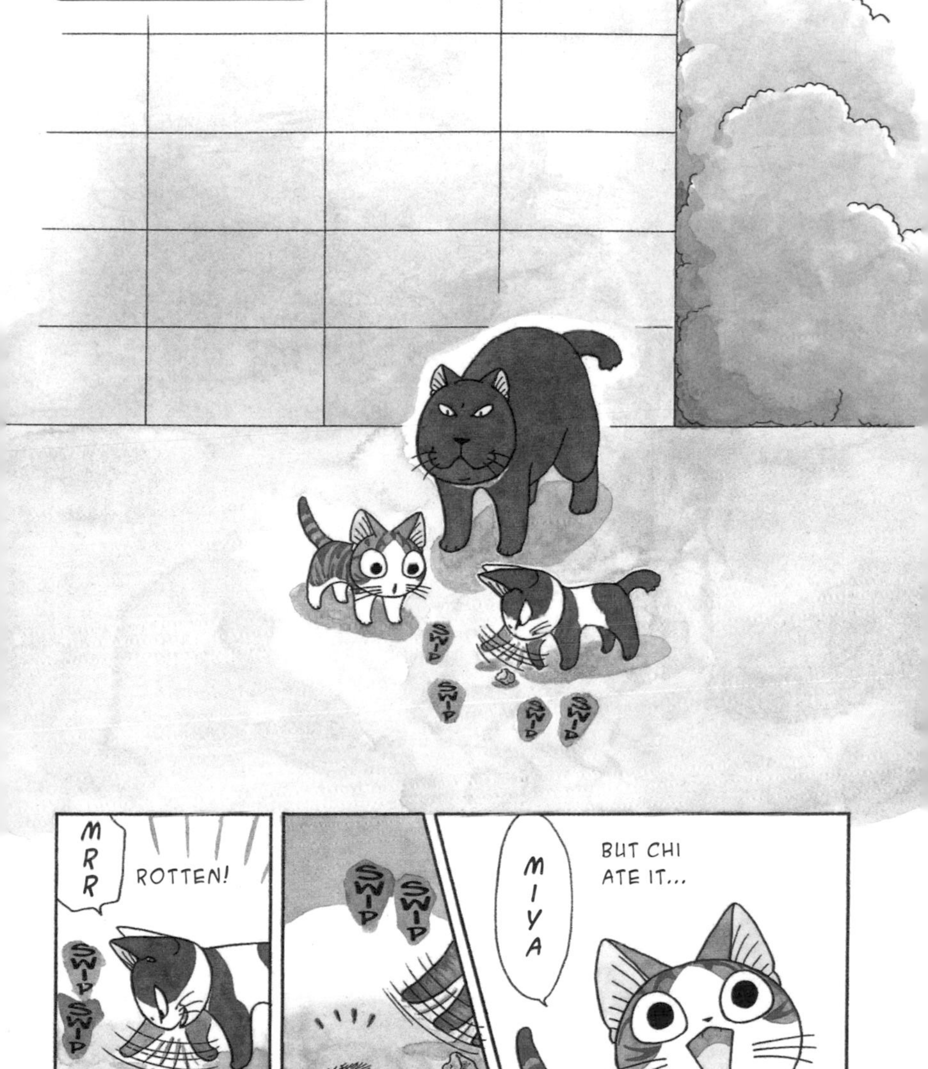
SWID
SWID
SWID
SWID
MRR
ROTTEN!
SWID
SWID
SWID
SWID
SWID
MIYA
BUT CHI ATE IT...

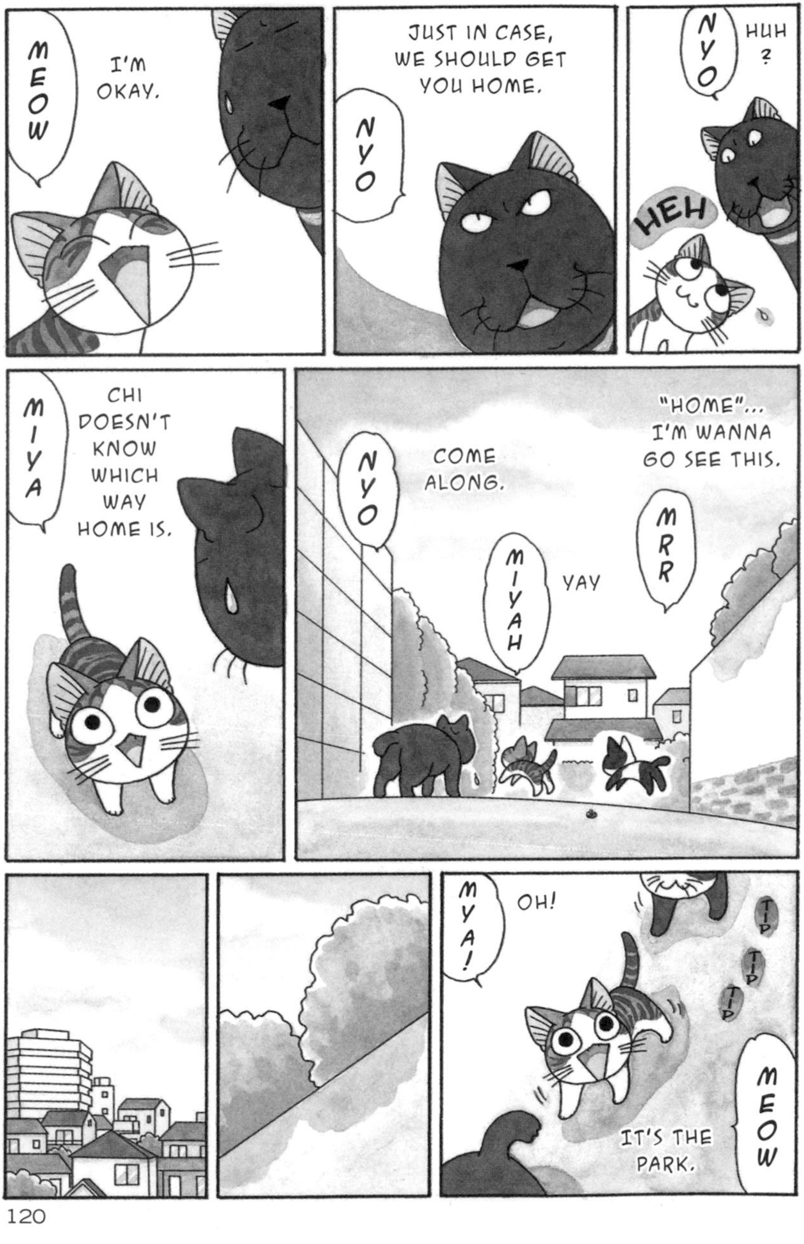
MEOW
I'M OKAY.
JUST IN CASE, WE SHOULD GET YOU HOME.
NYO
NYO
HUH?
HEH
MIYA
CHI DOESN'T KNOW WHICH WAY HOME IS.
NYO
COME ALONG.
MIYAH
YAY
MRR
"HOME"... I'M WANNA GO SEE THIS.
MYA!
OH!
TIP
TIP
TIP
IT'S THE PARK.
MEOW

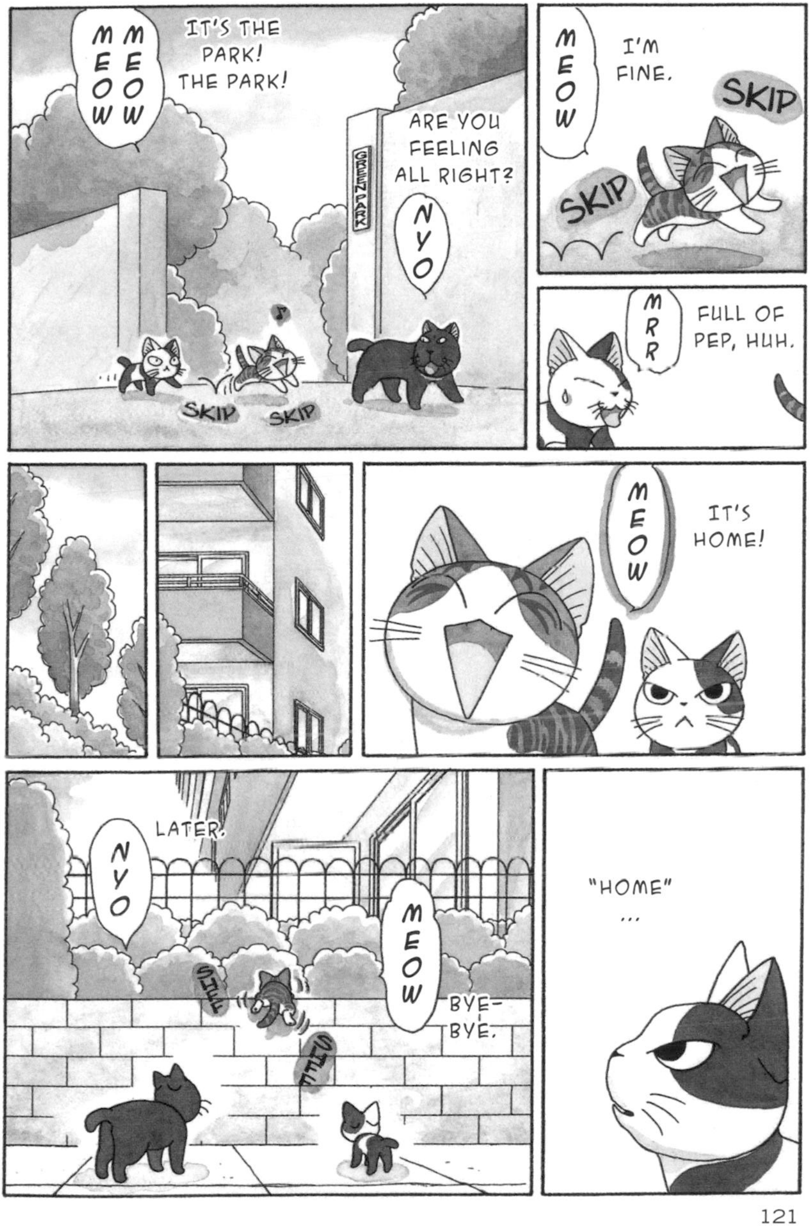
MEOW MEOW
IT'S THE PARK! THE PARK!
GREEN PARK
ARE YOU FEELING ALL RIGHT?
NYO
SKIP SKIP
MEOW
I'M FINE.
SKIP
SKIP
MRR
FULL OF PEP, HUH.
MEOW
IT'S HOME!
NYO
LATER.
MEOW
BYE-BYE.
"HOME" ...

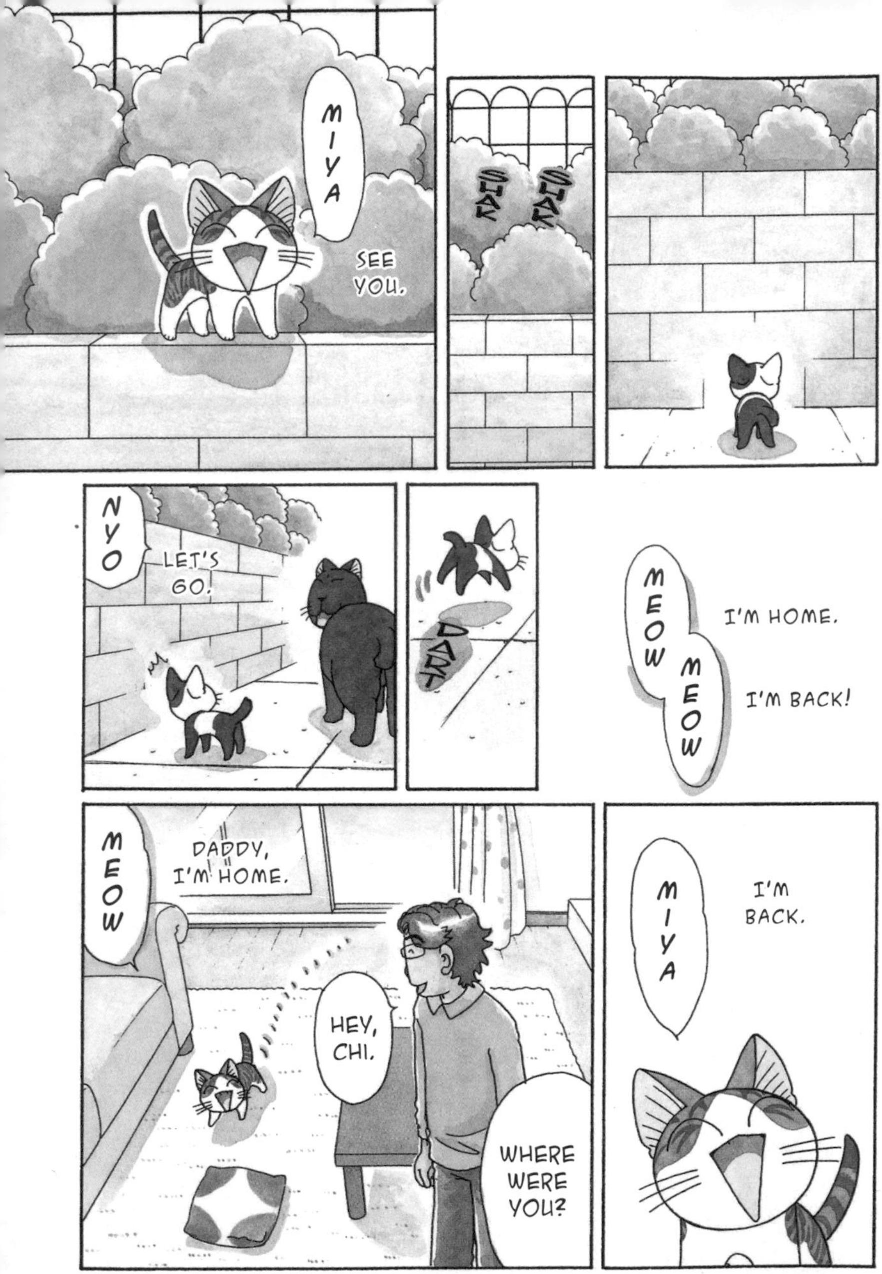
MIYA
SEE YOU.
SHAK SHAK
NYO
LET'S GO.
DART
MEOW
I'M HOME.
MEOW
I'M BACK!
MEOW
DADDY, I'M HOME.
HEY, CHI.
WHERE WERE YOU?
MIYA
I'M BACK.

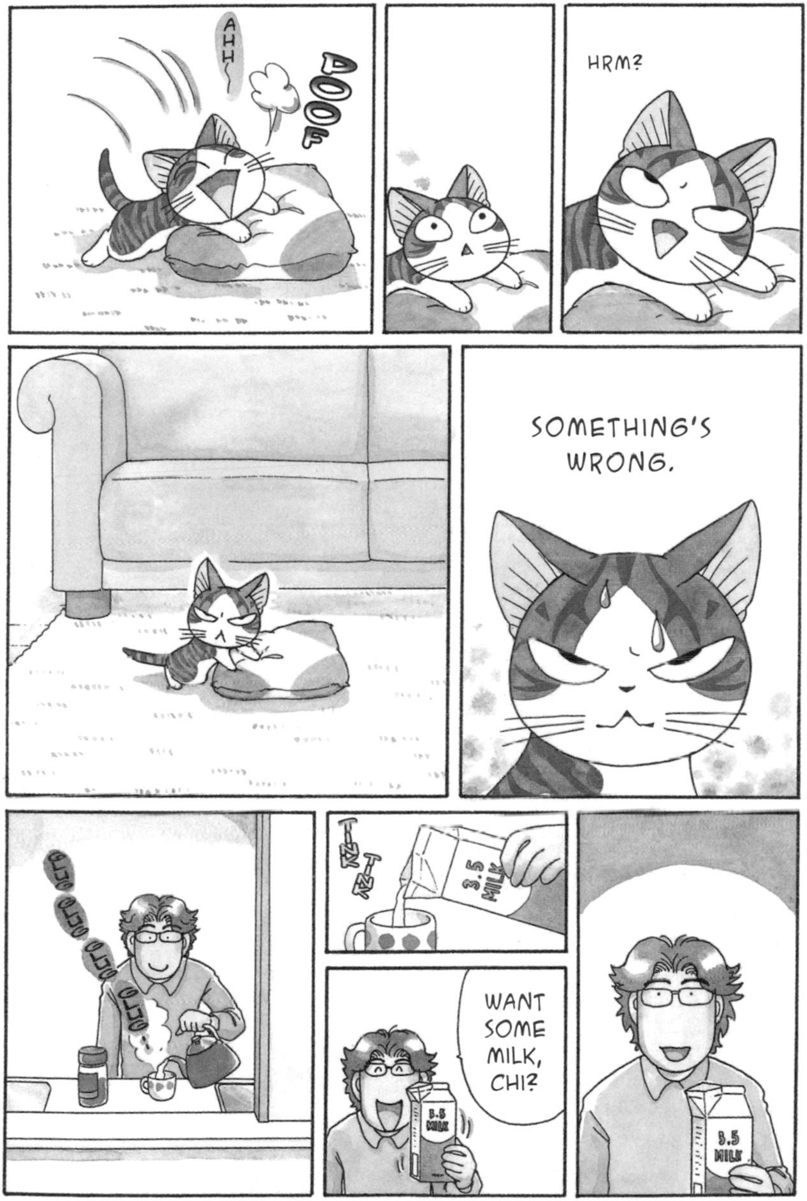
AHH~
POOF
HRM?
SOMETHING'S WRONG.
GLUG GLUG GLUG GLUG
TINK TINK
3.5 MILK
WANT SOME MILK, CHI?
3.5 MILK
3.5 MILK

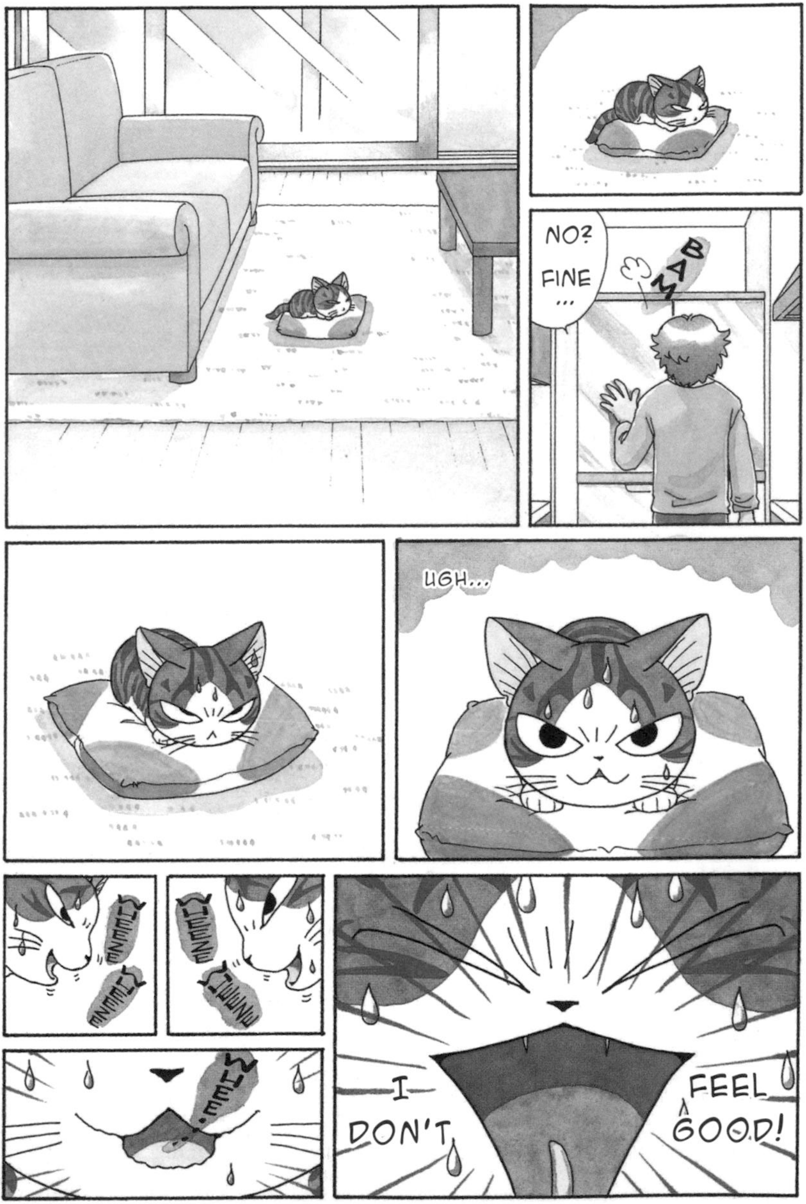
NO? FINE ...
BAM
UGH...
WHEENE
WHEENE
WHEE.
I DON'T FEEL GOOD!

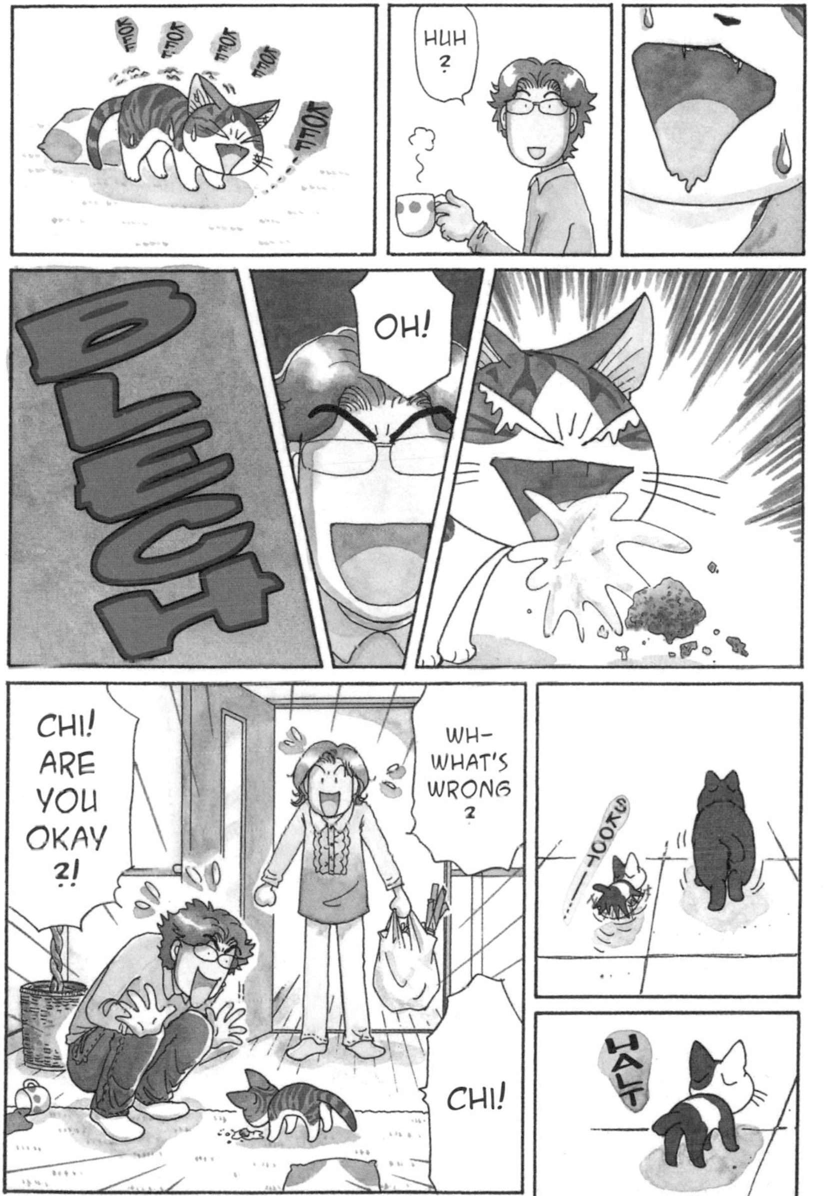
KOFF
KOFF
KOFF
KOFF
KOFF
HUH?
BLECH
OH!
CHI! ARE YOU OKAY?!
WH-WHAT'S WRONG?
CHI!
SCOOT
HALT

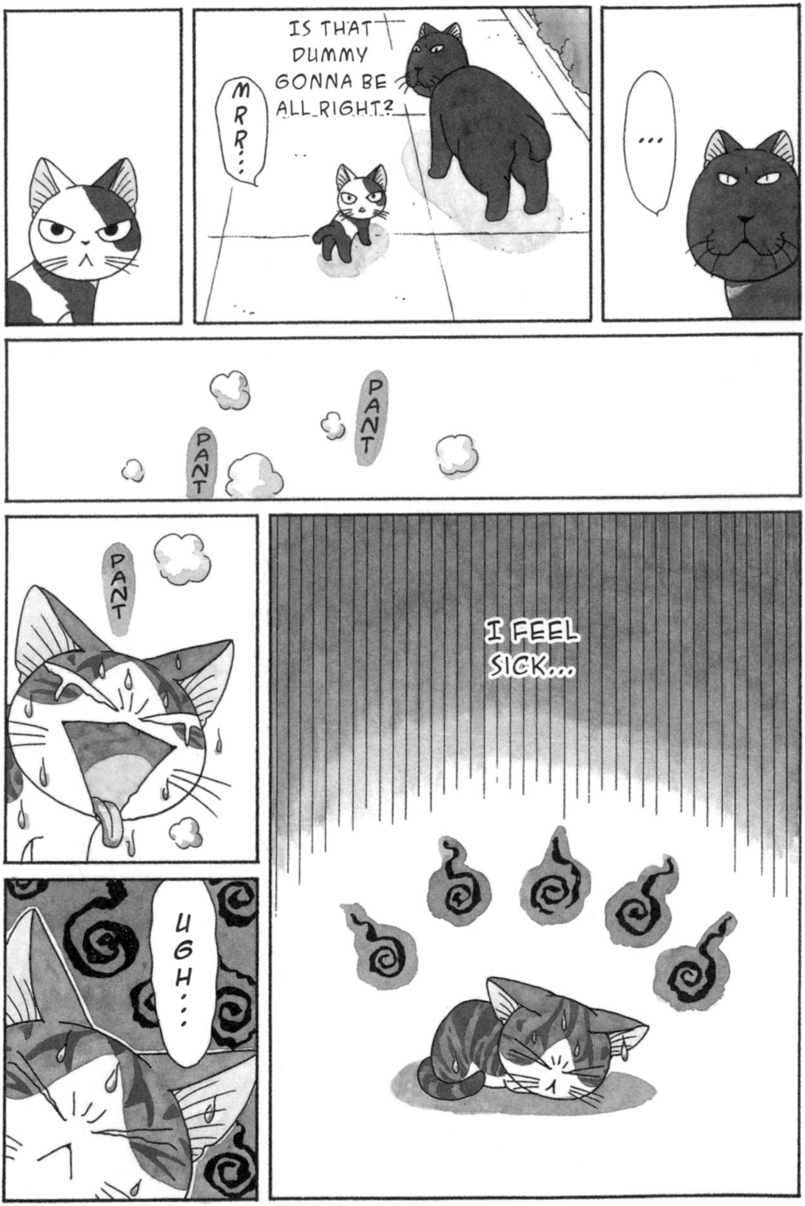
IS THAT DUMMY GONNA BE ALL RIGHT?
MRR...
...
PANT
PANT
PANT
UGH...
I FEEL SICK...

the end

homemade 127: a cat vomits

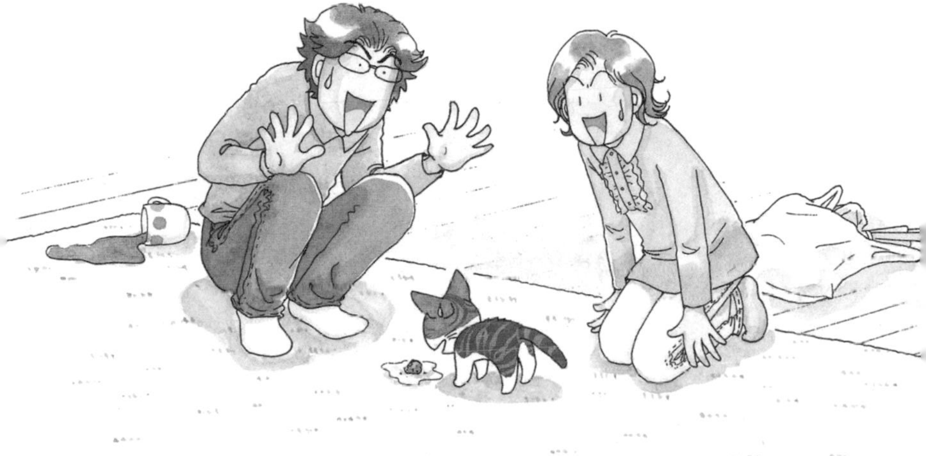

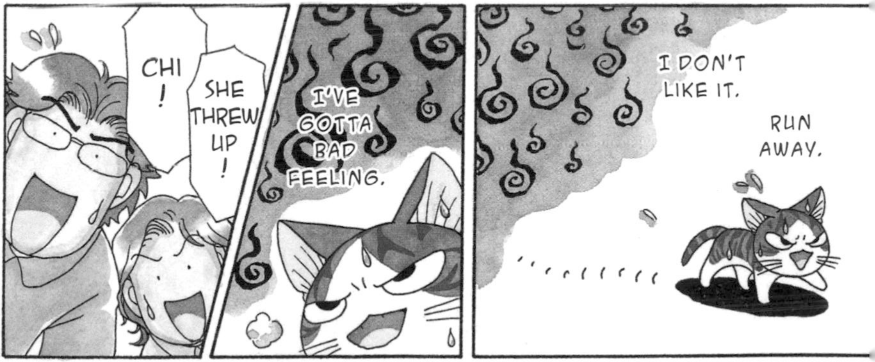
CHI!
SHE THREW UP!
I'VE GOTTA BAD FEELING.
I DON'T LIKE IT.
RUN AWAY.

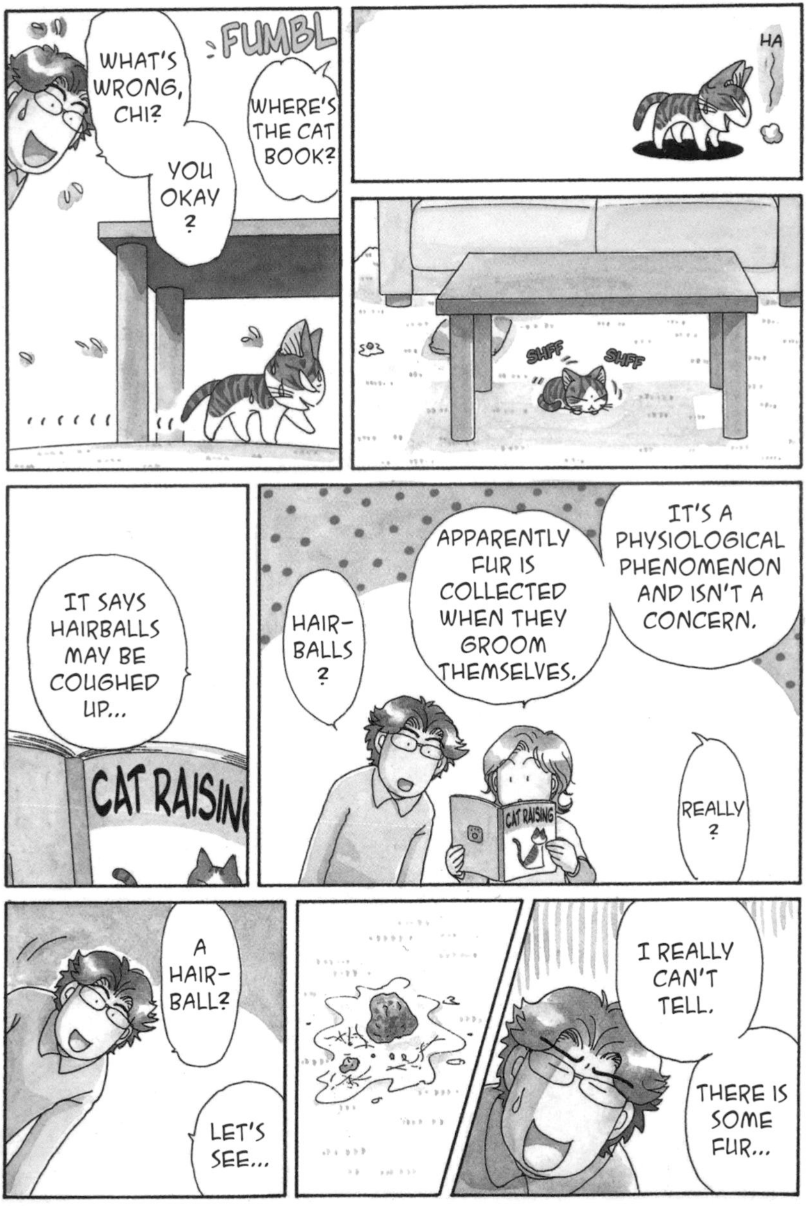
FUMBL
WHAT'S WRONG, CHI?
YOU OKAY?
WHERE'S THE CAT BOOK?
HA
SHFF
SHFF
IT SAYS HAIRBALLS MAY BE COUGHED UP...
CAT RAISING
HAIR-BALLS?
APPARENTLY FUR IS COLLECTED WHEN THEY GROOM THEMSELVES.
IT'S A PHYSIOLOGICAL PHENOMENON AND ISN'T A CONCERN.
CAT RAISING
REALLY?
A HAIR-BALL?
LET'S SEE...
I REALLY CAN'T TELL.
THERE IS SOME FUR...

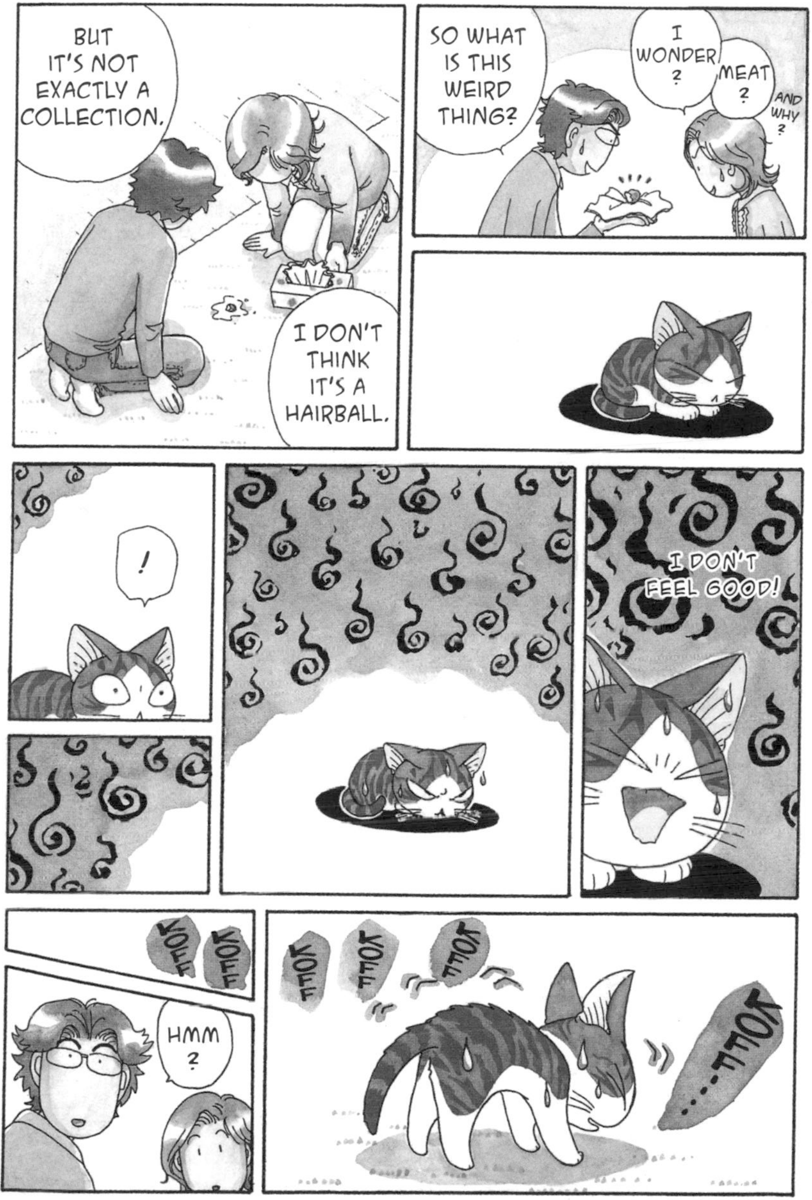

BUT IT'S NOT EXACTLY A COLLECTION.
I DON'T THINK IT'S A HAIRBALL.
SO WHAT IS THIS WEIRD THING?
I WONDER?
MEAT?
AND WHY?
!
I DON'T FEEL GOOD!
KOFF
KOFF
HMM?
KOFF
KOFF
KOFF
KOFF...

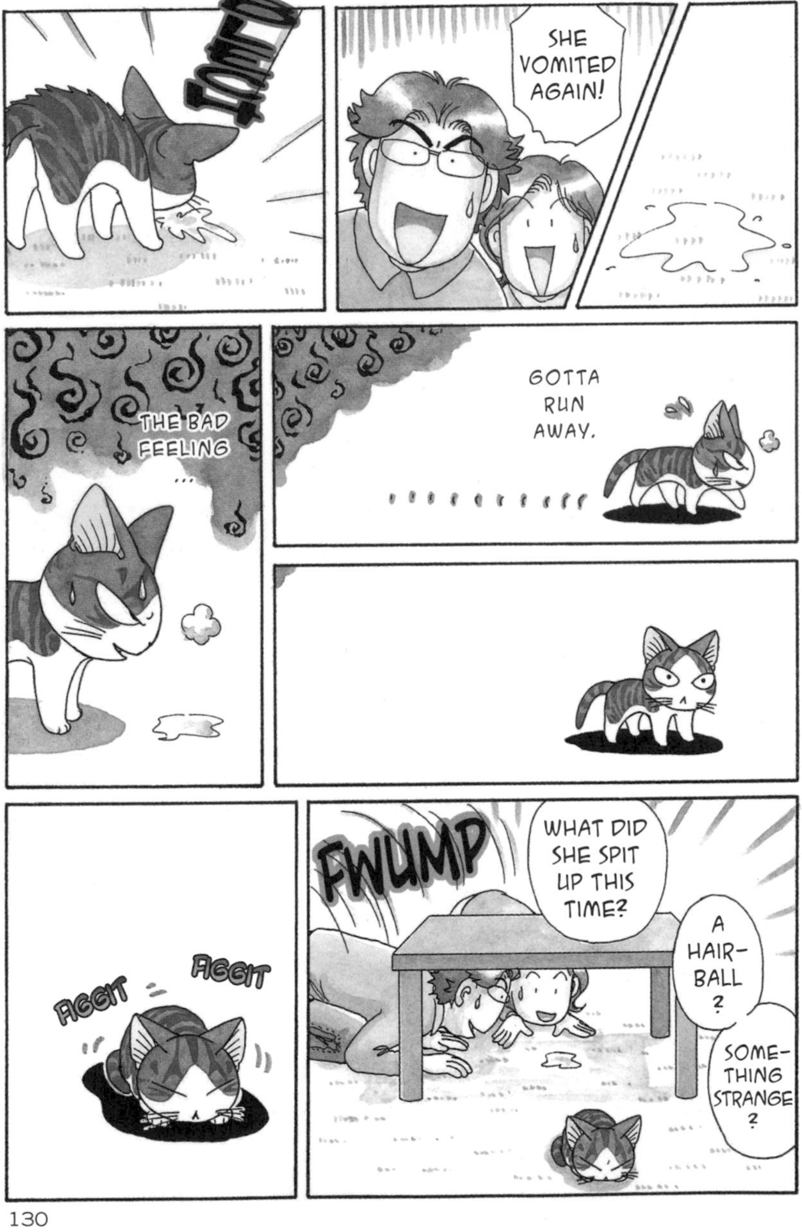
SHE VOMITED AGAIN!
THE BAD FEELING
...
GOTTA RUN AWAY.
FIGGIT
FIGGIT
FWUMP
WHAT DID SHE SPIT UP THIS TIME?
A HAIR-BALL?
SOME-THING STRANGE?

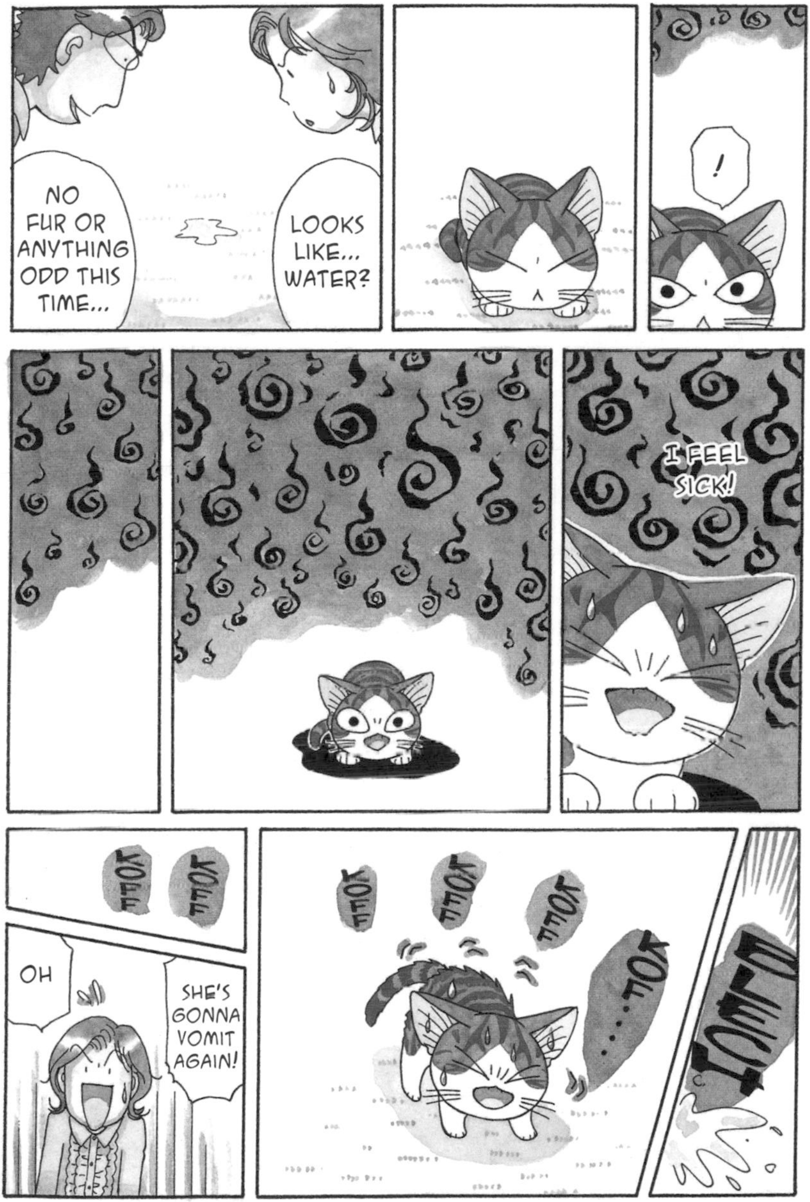
NO FUR OR ANYTHING ODD THIS TIME...
LOOKS LIKE... WATER?
!
I FEEL SICK!
HOFF
HOFF
OH
SHE'S GONNA VOMIT AGAIN!
HOFF
HOFF
HOFF
HOF....

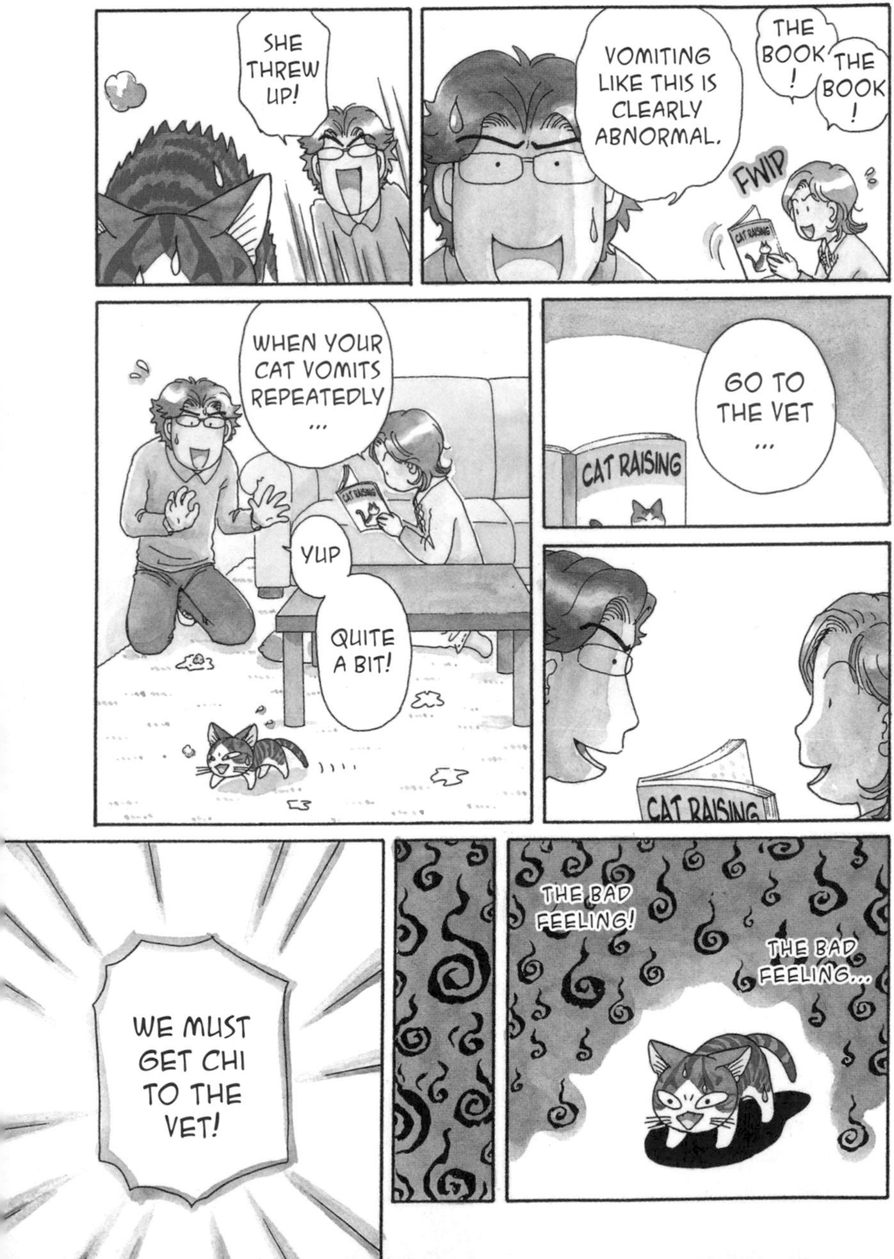
SHE THREW UP!
VOMITING LIKE THIS IS CLEARLY ABNORMAL.
THE BOOK!
THE BOOK!
FWIP
CAT RAISING
WHEN YOUR CAT VOMITS REPEATEDLY...
CAT RAISING
YUP
QUITE A BIT!
GO TO THE VET...
CAT RAISING
CAT RAISING
WE MUST GET CHI TO THE VET!
THE BAD FEELING!
THE BAD FEELING...

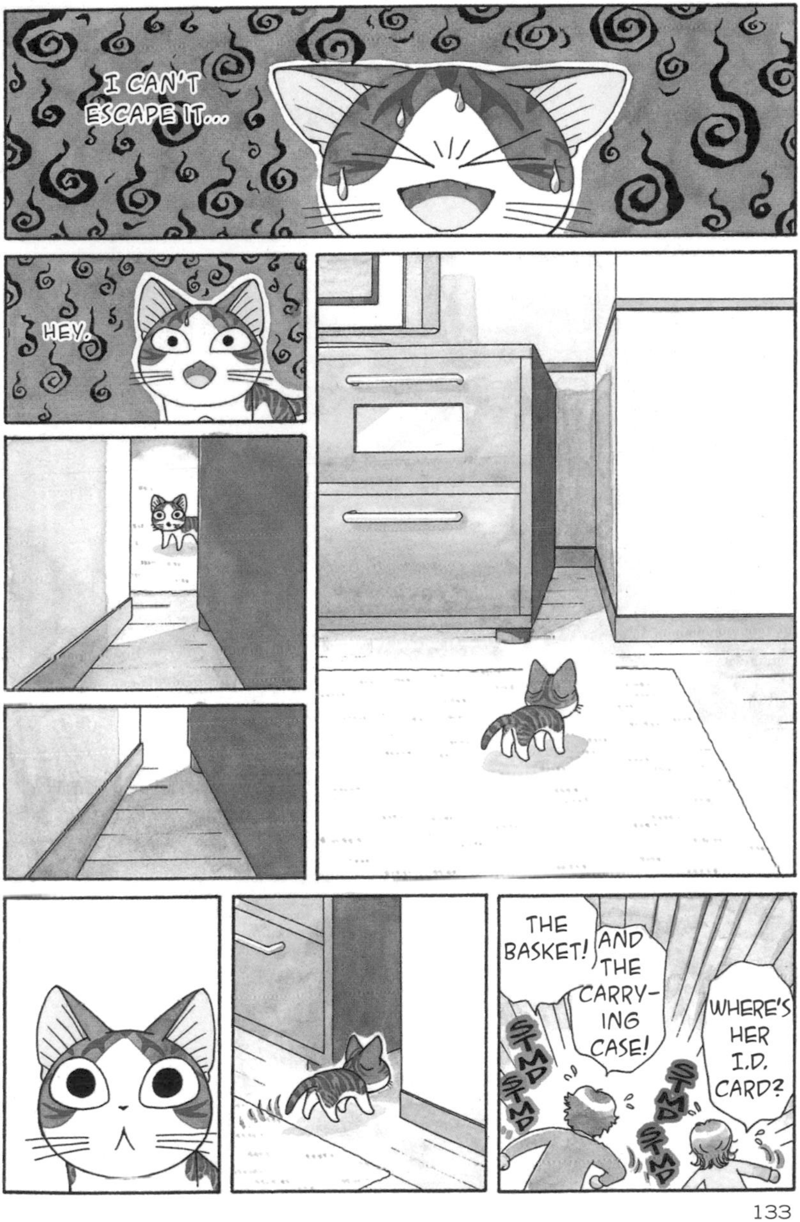
I CAN'T ESCAPE IT...
HEY.
THE BASKET!
AND THE CARRY-ING CASE!
STMP STMP
STMP STMP
WHERE'S HER I.D. CARD?

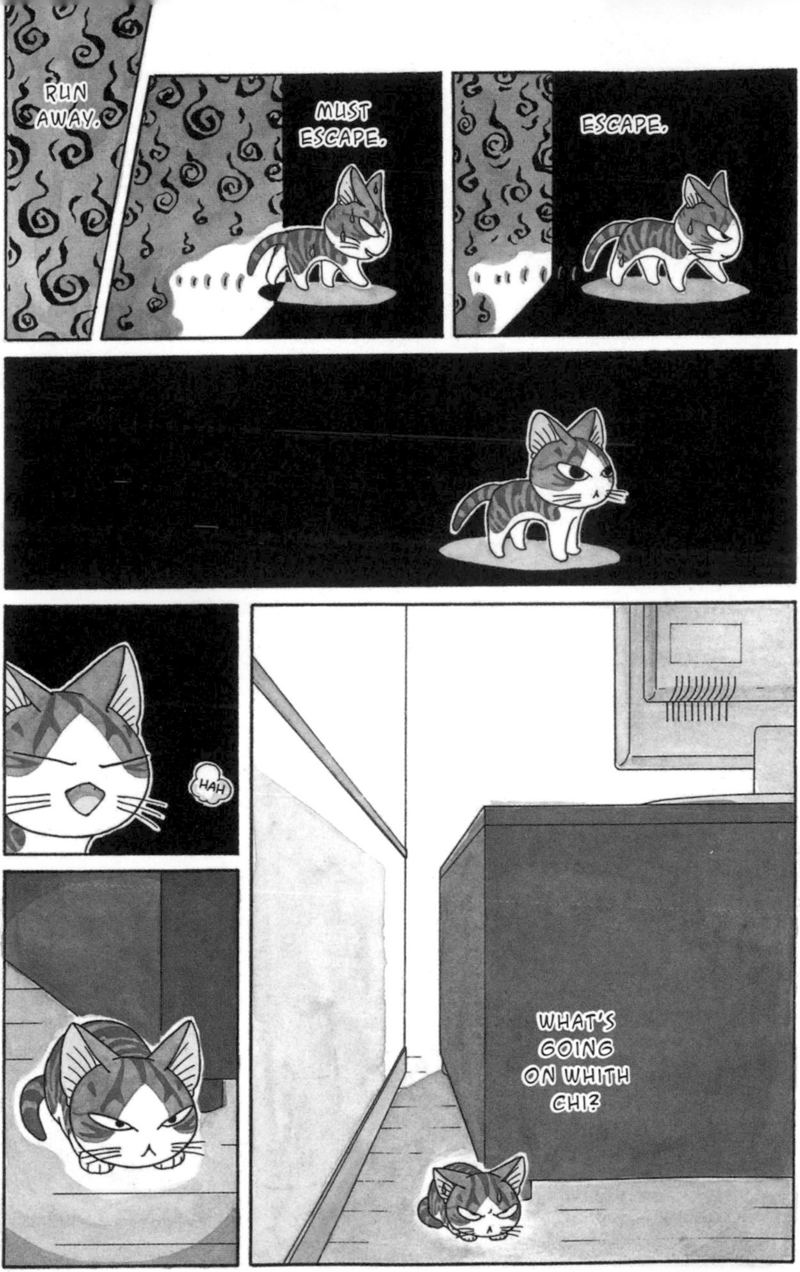
RUN AWAY.
MUST ESCAPE.
ESCAPE.
HAH
WHAT'S GOING ON WHITH CHI?

the end

homemade 128: a cat hangs in there

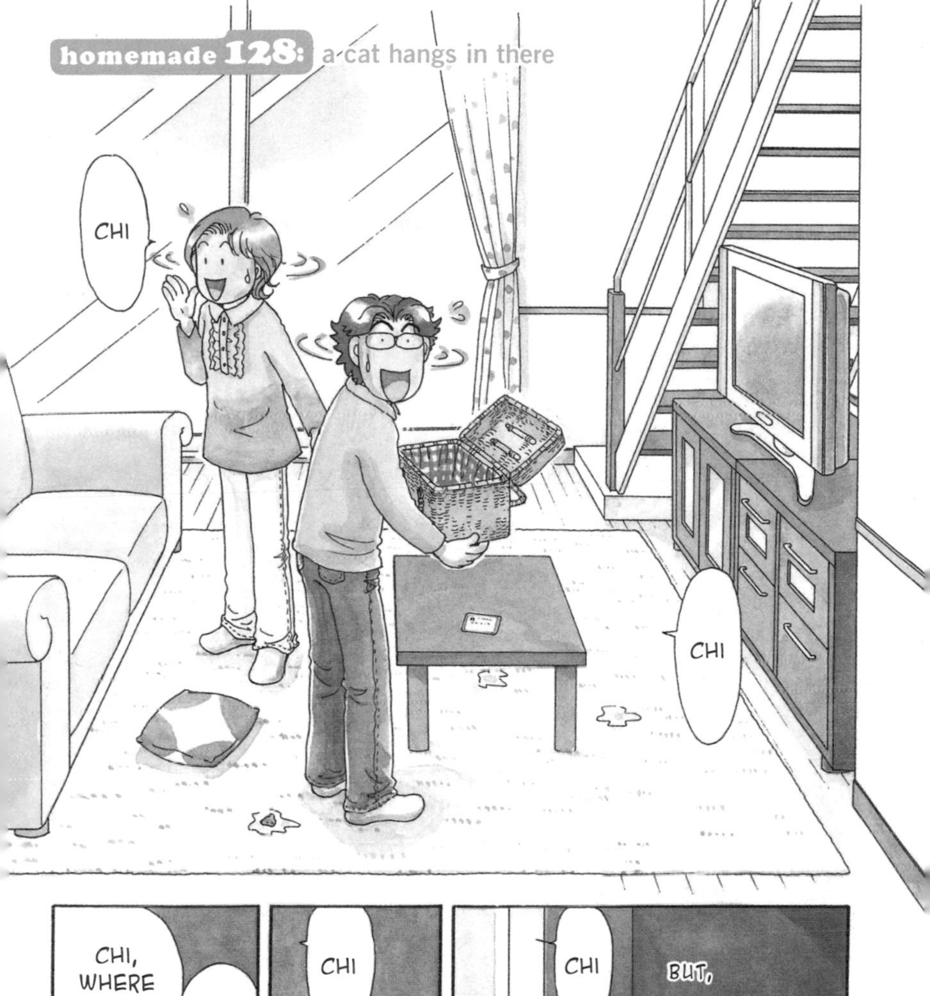
CHI
CHI
CHI, WHERE ARE YOU?
WHERE'S CHI?
CHI
THEY'RE CALLING.
CHI
BUT,
CHI WANTS TO STAY HERE.

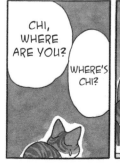

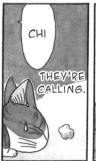

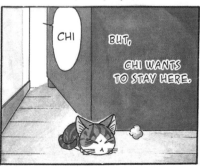

CHI, WE'VE GOT TO TAKE YOU TO THE VET.

WHERE COULD SHE BE IN THAT STATE?

Patient Registration Card
#1366 Miss Chi Yamada

CHI

IF I JUST STAY HERE...

!!

UGH

I FEEL BAD AGAIN...

KOFF KOFF

BLECH

OVER THERE

BY THE TV SET.

136

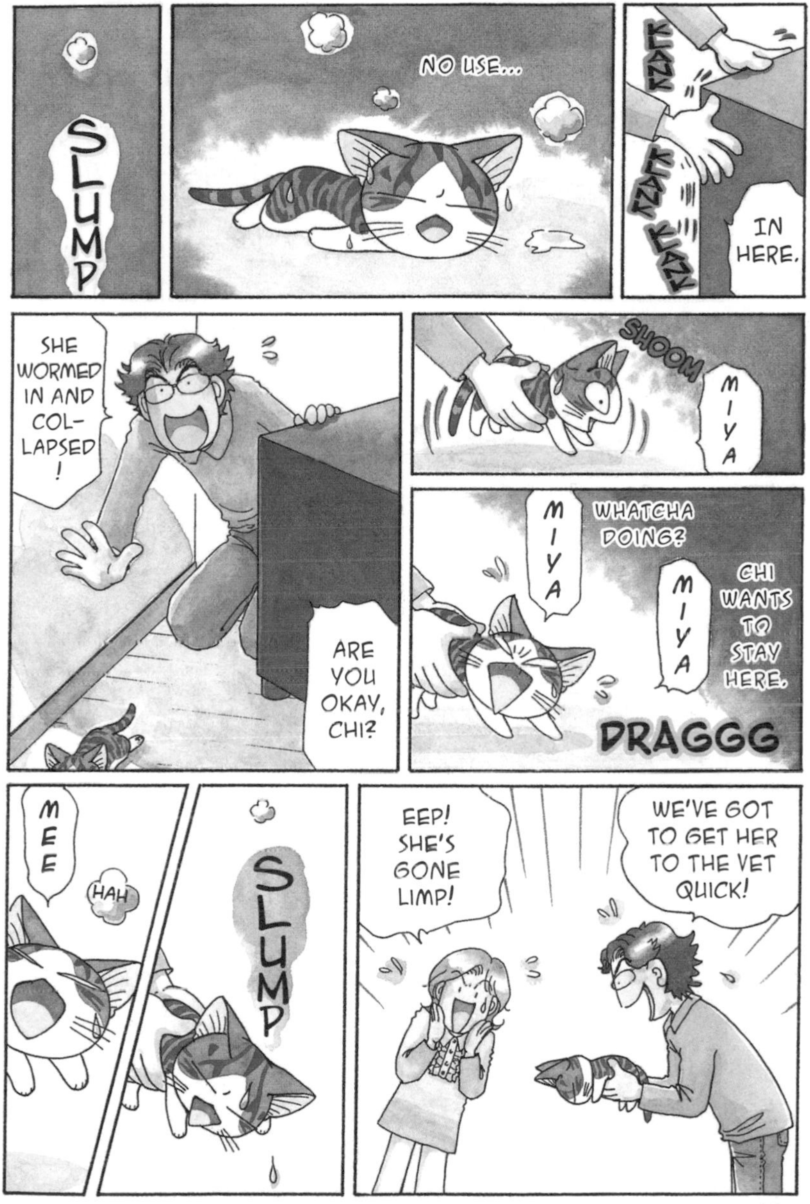
SLUMP
NO USE...
KLANK
KLANK
KLANK
IN HERE.
SHE WORMED IN AND COL-LAPSED!
ARE YOU OKAY, CHI?
SHOOM
MIYA
MIYA
WHATCHA DOING?
MIYA
CHI WANTS TO STAY HERE.
DRAGGG
MEE
HAH
SLUMP
EEP! SHE'S GONE LIMP!
WE'VE GOT TO GET HER TO THE VET QUICK!

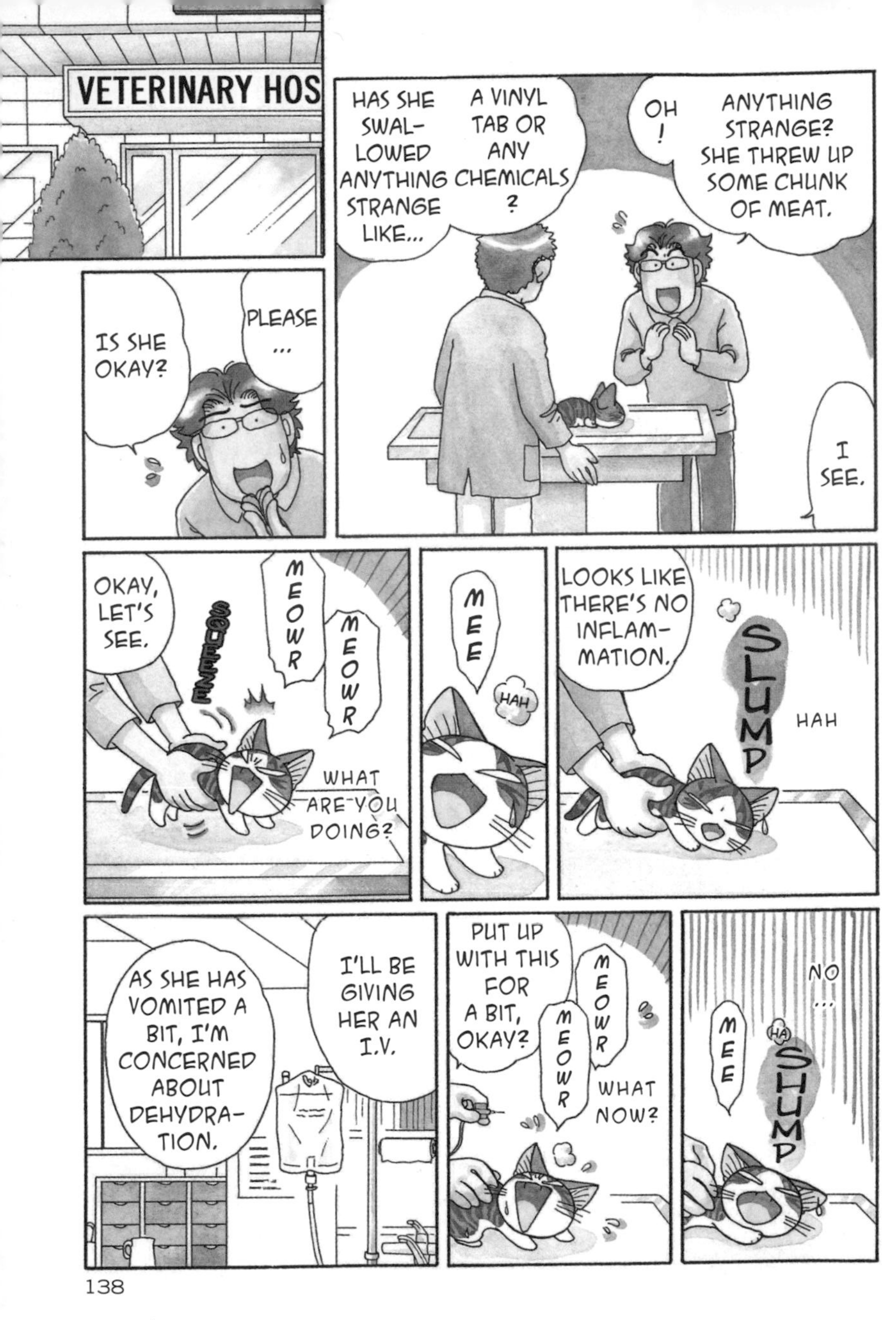
VETERINARY HOS
IS SHE OKAY?
PLEASE ...
HAS SHE SWAL-LOWED ANYTHING STRANGE LIKE...
A VINYL TAB OR ANY CHEMICALS ?
OH !
ANYTHING STRANGE? SHE THREW UP SOME CHUNK OF MEAT.
I SEE.
OKAY, LET'S SEE.
MEOWR
MEOWR
WHAT ARE YOU DOING?
MEE
HAH
LOOKS LIKE THERE'S NO INFLAM-MATION.
SLUMP
HAH
AS SHE HAS VOMITED A BIT, I'M CONCERNED ABOUT DEHYDRA-TION.
I'LL BE GIVING HER AN I.V.
PUT UP WITH THIS FOR A BIT, OKAY?
MEOWR
MEOWR
WHAT NOW?
NO ...
MEE
HA
SHUMP

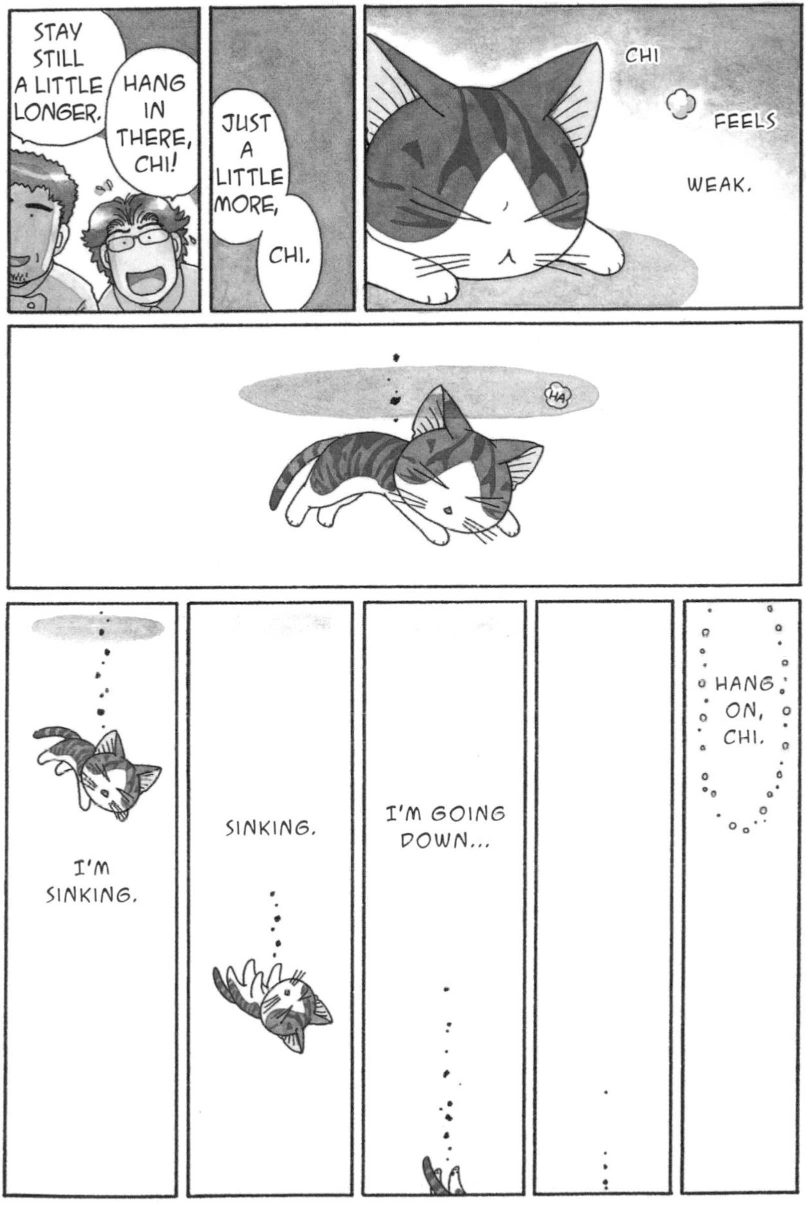
STAY STILL A LITTLE LONGER.
HANG IN THERE, CHI!
JUST A LITTLE MORE, CHI.
CHI FEELS WEAK.
HA
I'M SINKING.
SINKING.
I'M GOING DOWN...
HANG ON, CHI.

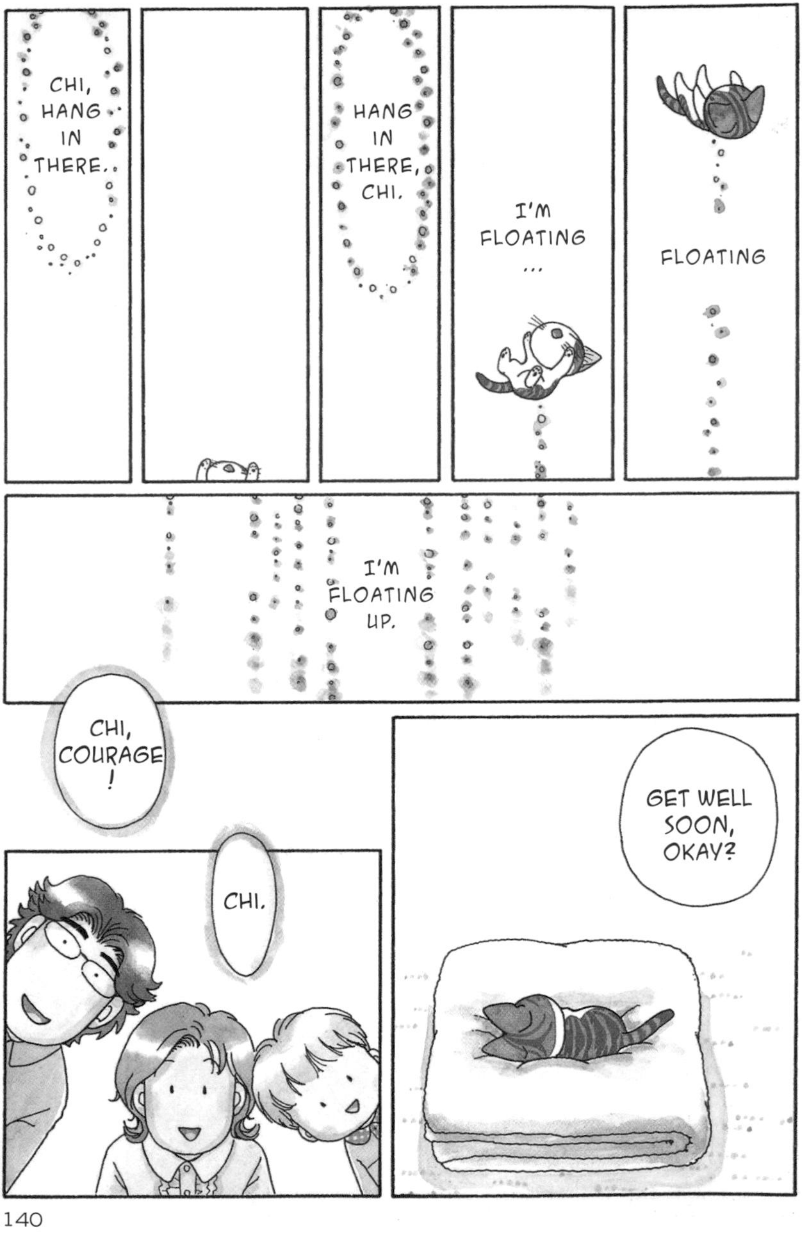
CHI, HANG IN THERE..
HANG IN THERE, CHI.
I'M FLOATING ...
FLOATING
I'M FLOATING UP.
CHI, COURAGE!
CHI.
GET WELL SOON, OKAY?

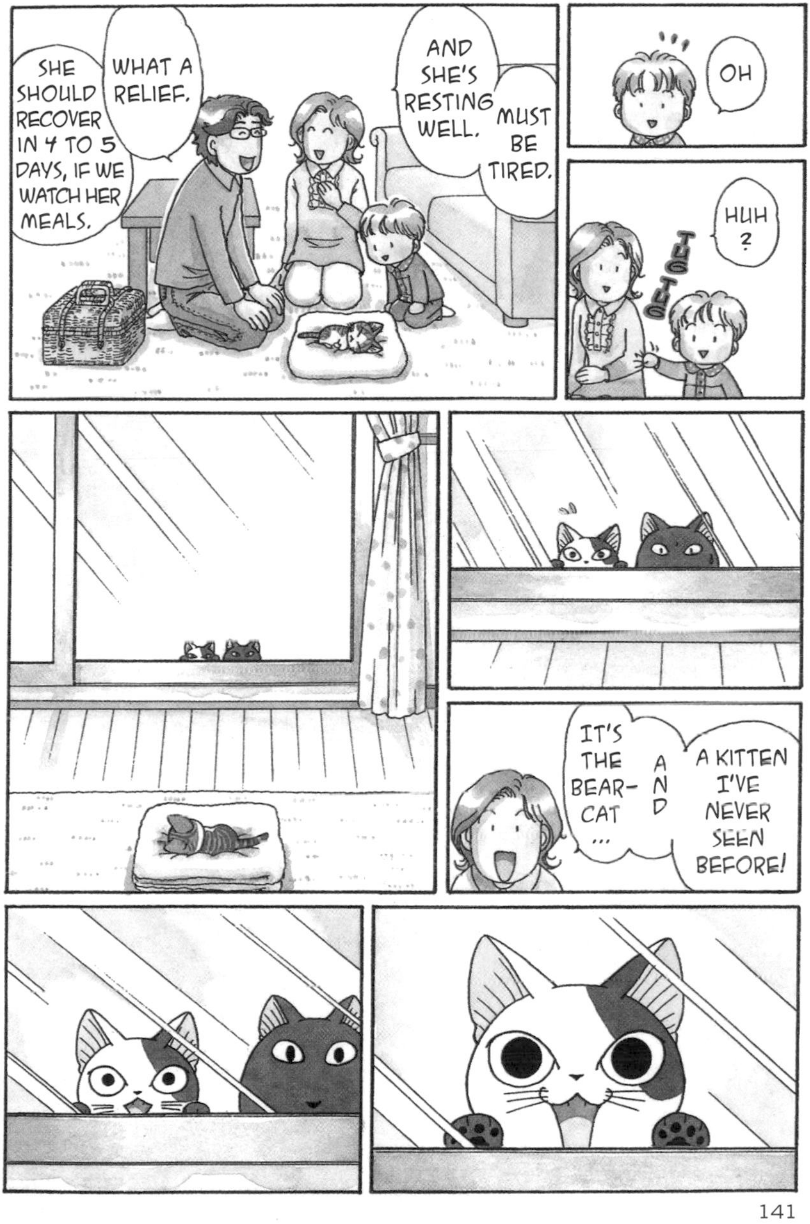
SHE SHOULD RECOVER IN 4 TO 5 DAYS, IF WE WATCH HER MEALS.
WHAT A RELIEF.
AND SHE'S RESTING WELL.
MUST BE TIRED.
OH
HUH ?
TUG TUG
IT'S THE BEAR-CAT ...
AND
A KITTEN I'VE NEVER SEEN BEFORE!

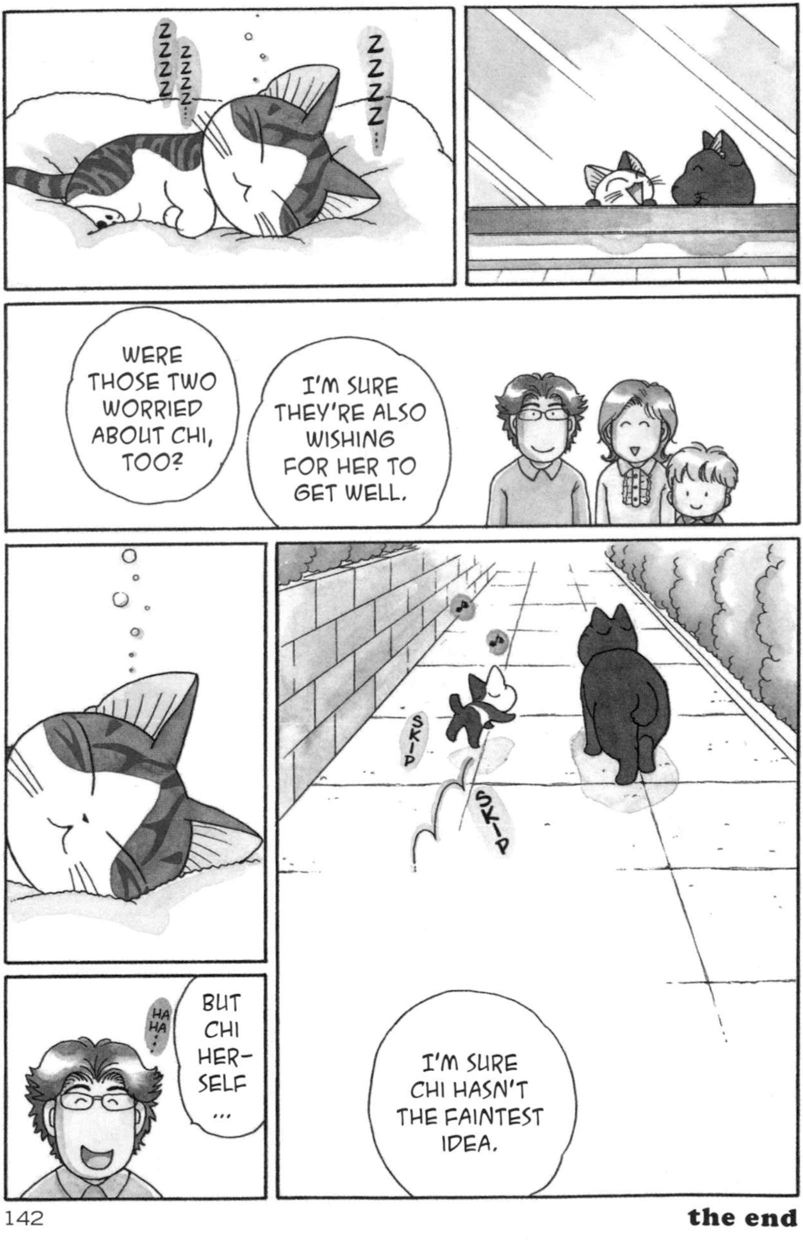
ZZZZ
ZZZZ...
ZZZZ...
WERE THOSE TWO WORRIED ABOUT CHI, TOO?
I'M SURE THEY'RE ALSO WISHING FOR HER TO GET WELL.
HA HA...
BUT CHI HERSELF...
SKIP
SKIP
I'M SURE CHI HASN'T THE FAINTEST IDEA.

the end

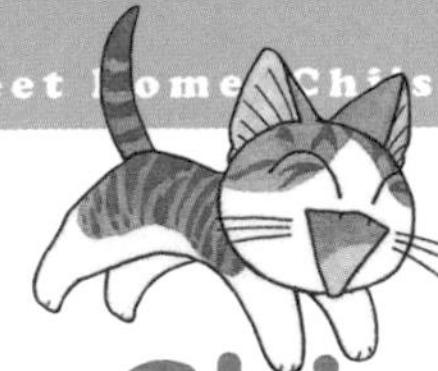

homemade special

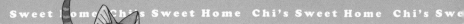

Chi goes global!

Chi's Sweet Home attracts not only the American and Japanese reader but is also widely read around the world. Editions released by each foreign publisher vary, though the comic's content always remains true to the original. So while one version may be in full color, others are in black and white; meanwhile, logos may differ and extras may change from those found in the original Japanese edition.

In this Homemade Special, reporters Blackie and Chi, having heard of such rumors regarding the various releases, visit a few of the many foreign publishers who have translated *Chi's Sweet Home* to interview them.

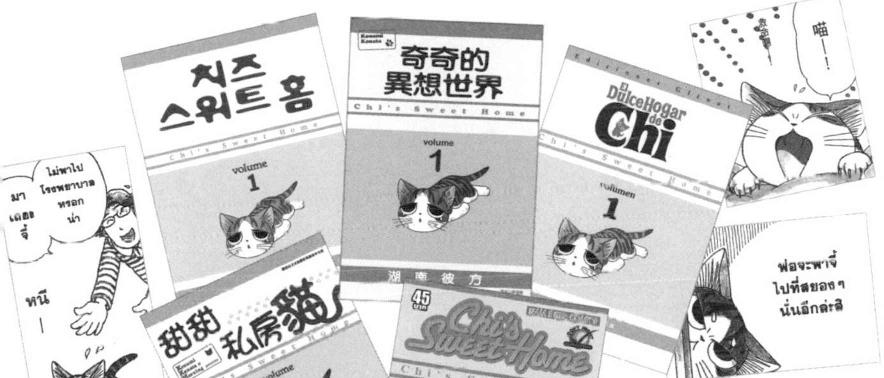
치즈 스위트 홈
Chi's Sweet Home
volume 1
奇奇的異想世界
Chi's Sweet Home
volume 1
湖南彼方
El Dulce Hogar de Chi
Chi's Sweet Home
volumen 1
喵——！
甜甜私房貓
Chi's Sweet Home
volume 1
Chi's Sweet Home
Chi's Sweet Home
Volume 1
Konami Kanata
FRAAAAAAAASH
替貓洗澡真是一件艱巨的工作！
喵呀！
喵呀！
喵呀！
洗澡和吹風筒明明是很舒服的……

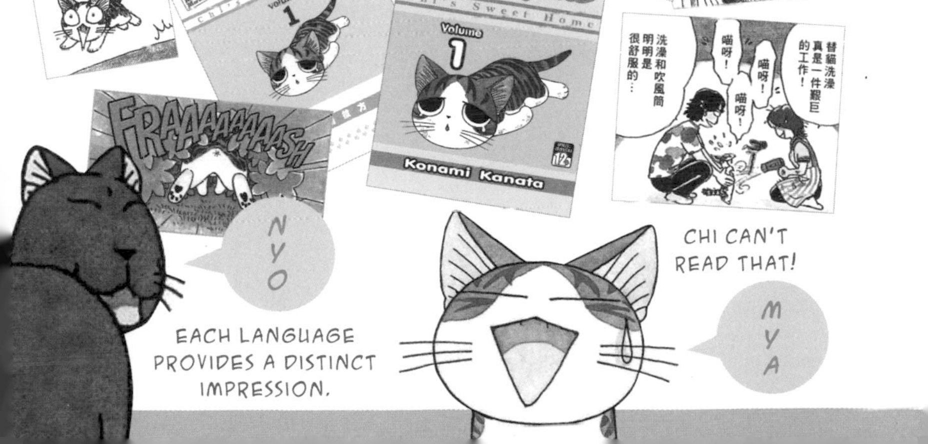
NYO
EACH LANGUAGE PROVIDES A DISTINCT IMPRESSION.
CHI CAN'T READ THAT!
MYA

It's Chi's Sweet World—a look at the

SPAIN
Ediciones Glénat

Glénat

The Spanish version launched in 2009, and as the entire staff loves cats we soon became big fans of Chi. When we came up with the idea of presenting our readers' cats as a book extra, we first started off with our own cats. By the second volume we began sharing images of our readers' kitties. Everyone in Spain is crazy about Chi's adventures, and cat-lovers just cannot get enough of her. We'd like to thank the author for creating such a fascinating cat world. We're looking forward to Chi's next adventure!

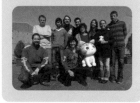

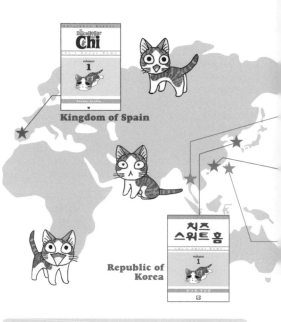

El DulceHogar de Chi
volumen
1
Kingdom of Spain
치즈
스위트 홈
volume
1
Republic of Korea

Other countries where *Chi's Sweet Home* has been published:

China Finland France

More countries across the globe are also looking to publish *Chi* as well!

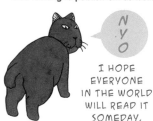

NYO
I HOPE EVERYONE IN THE WORLD WILL READ IT SOMEDAY.

The world of *Chi's Sweet Home* will steadily expand as long as cats exist!

South Korea
Haksan Publishing, Co.

(주)학산문화사

In South Korea more people tend to have dogs as pets rather than cats. But recently the number of cat-owners has been growing and an increasing number of cat-themed books have been published here. Among them *Chi's Sweet Home* we feel stands alone at the top. One reason for this is how it doesn't just emphasize cuteness but depicts a family story, where Chi and the Yamadas live together in harmony. While cat-lovers cannot resist grabbing a copy once they see Chi on the front cover, others find themselves attracted by the warm and fuzzy drama illustrated in this series' pages.

As the first volume debuted here in early 2010, we know there is a long road ahead for Chi, but we'll be watching over her until she finds her true sweet home someday in the next volumes. Fight on, Chi!

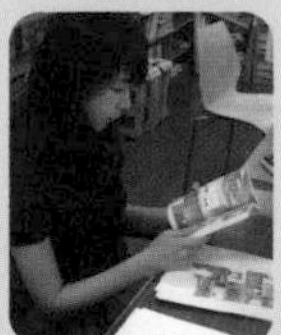

many publishers now releasing this comic.

Red-hot interviews with the many foreign publishing houses who are releasing international editions of *Chi's Sweet Home*! What about Chi intrigues fans from other countries? Let's go ask them!

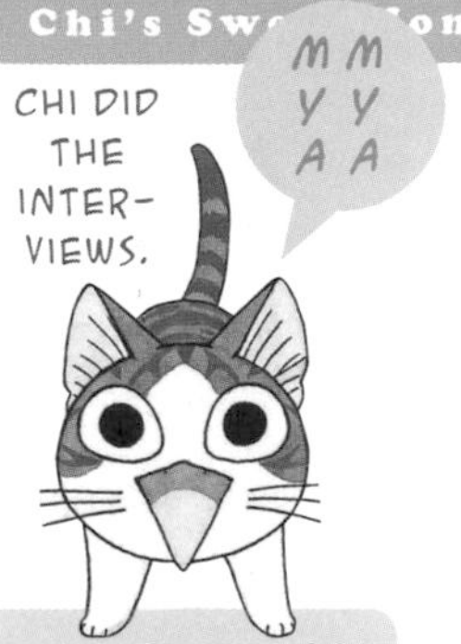
CHI DID THE INTER-VIEWS.
MMYYAA

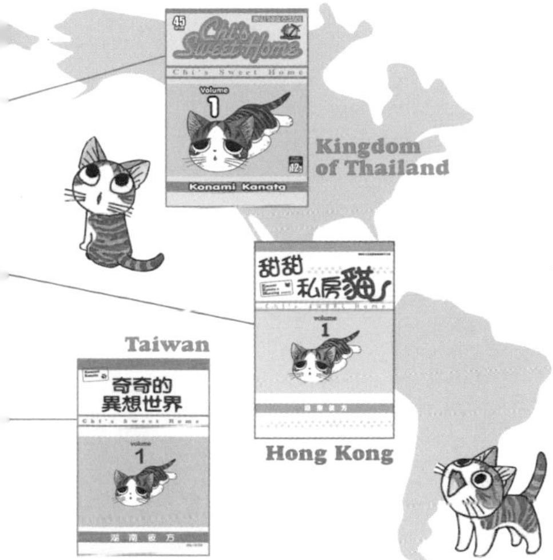
Chi's Sweet Home
Volume 1
Konami Kanata
Kingdom of Thailand
甜甜私房貓
Hong Kong
Taiwan
奇奇的異想世界

Thailand
Siam Inter Multimedia, PLC.

SIAM INTER Multimedia

I wasn't much of a cat fan before, but upon reading this comic I came to the realization that, yeah, cats have all sorts of cute sides to them! To tell the truth, I was a little concerned about selling *Chi's Sweet Home* in Thailand. I mean, our heroine Chi is always nude! And she is almost too sexy on the covers of volume 5 and 6. (Laughs) Still, I desperately want to read the next installment.

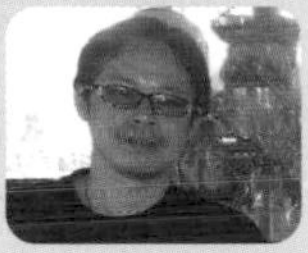

Taiwan
Sharp Point Press

尖端出版

Congratulations on the release of *Chi's Sweet Home* Volume 7! I am certain that anyone who experiences Chi's cuteness will shout out, "How cute!"
Taiwanese readers are also greatly looking forward to more of Chi's adventure. We hope Chi will gleefully continue to saunter on and give everyone who reads this comic joy!

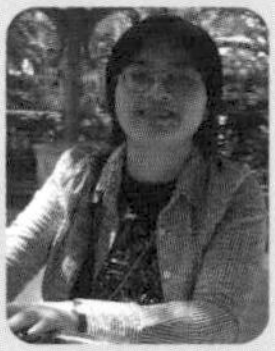

Hong Kong
Rightman Publishing, Inc.

正文社 www.rightman.net

I think I first ran into Chi in a toy store. At that time, I wasn't at all sure whose home Chi came from... And to think that I would eventually become a comic editor and would once again meet with Chi... I guess it was fate. (Laughs)
Chi's Sweet Home is very popular in Hong Kong. Men and women alike, everyone loves to read *Chi* because she is just so adorable! Cat-owners of course empathize with Chi's every movement. But we also feel readers who live cat-free lives also read the comic and find Chi's mildly hyper and occasionally sulky antics quite interesting.
I hope Chi will continue to be a bundle of cheer and that more people will come to love her. Good luck, Chi!

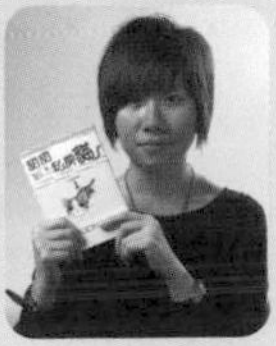

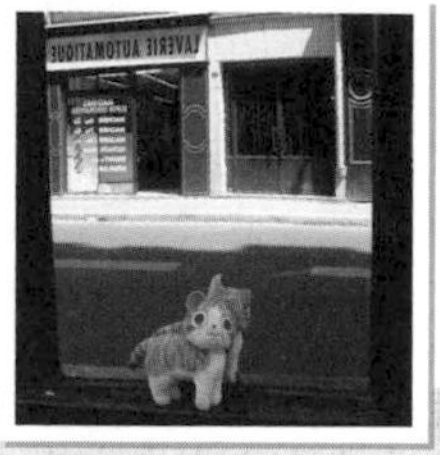

Our Humble Reporter Chi Reports from Paris!

A French version of *Chi's Sweet Home* debuted in late 2010, published by Glénat Editions. So, Chi went on a business trip to France and was tasked to guide a tour of Paris after her meeting!

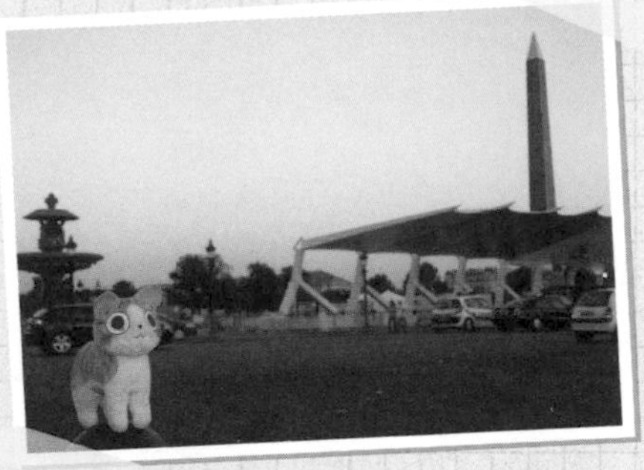

1 Place de la Concorde

Arrived in Paris!

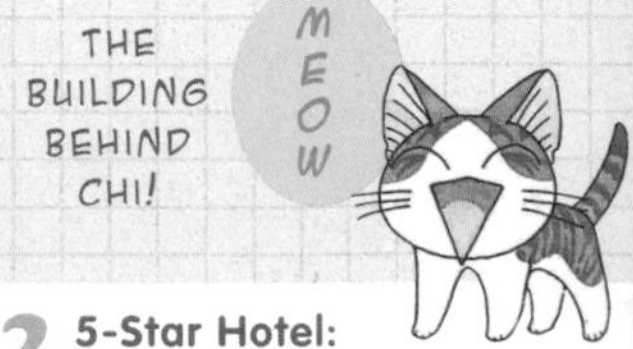
THE BUILDING BEHIND CHI!
MEOW

2 5-Star Hotel: Hôtel de Crillon

Chi wants to stay here, too...

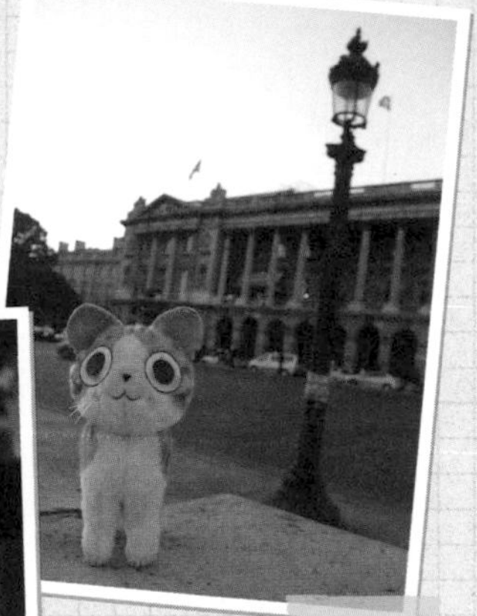

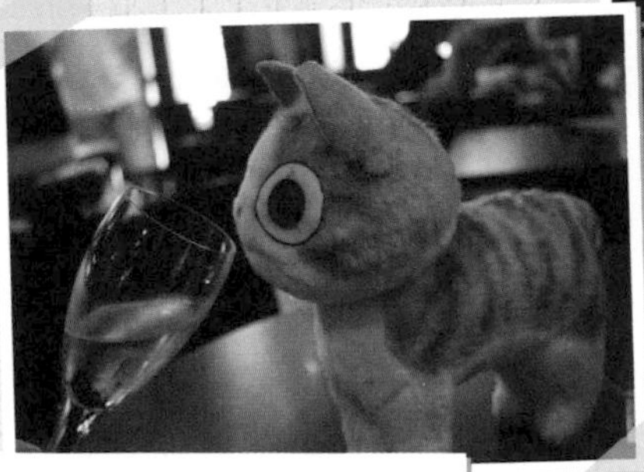

3 At a restaurant. Chi's first glass of champagne!

Smells good...? Hey, it's alcohol!

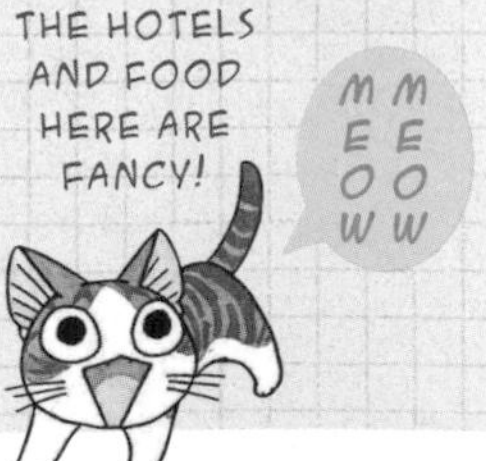
THE HOTELS AND FOOD HERE ARE FANCY!
MEOW MEOW

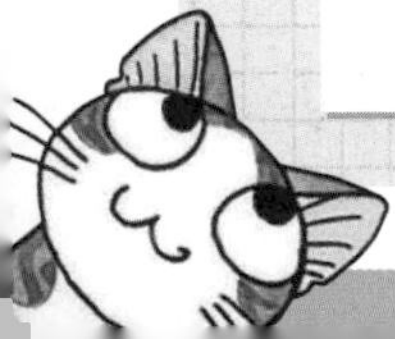

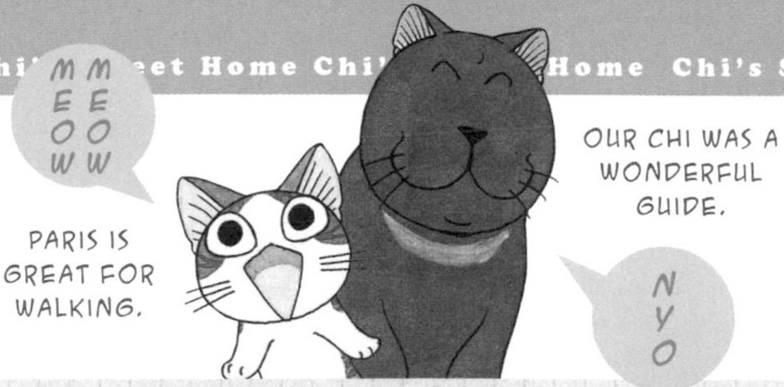
MEOW MEOW
PARIS IS GREAT FOR WALKING.
OUR CHI WAS A WONDERFUL GUIDE.
NYO

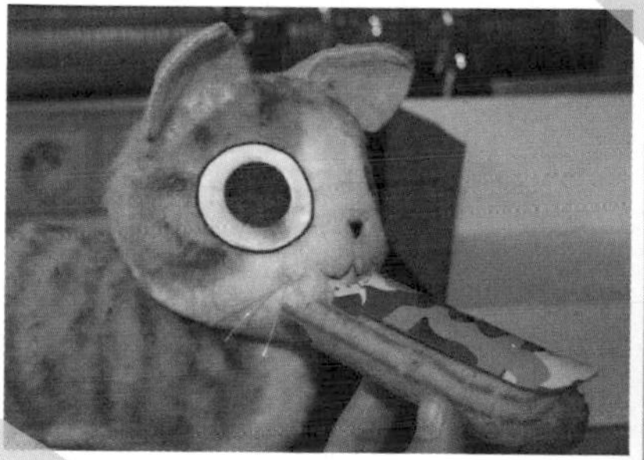

4 Eating a fauchon éclair

What's this?! Delish!

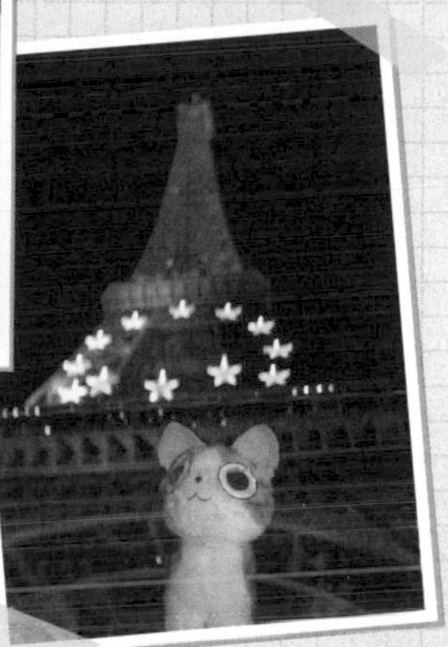

5 The Eiffel Tower

It's beautiful. Paris sure is nice!

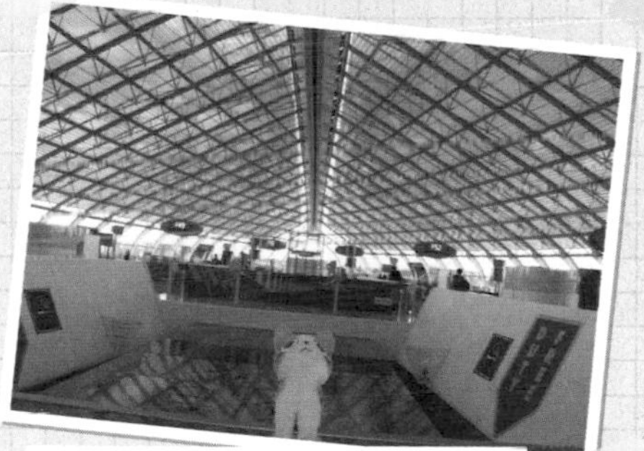

6 Charles de Gaulle International Airport

What a huge airport! Okay, my business trip is all done!

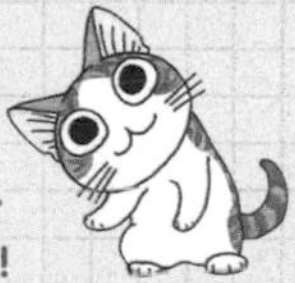

Follow more of Chi's global adventures on her Japanese website!
http://morningmanga.com/chisweetravel

And find more Chi fun at her English language site...
http://www.chisweethome.net

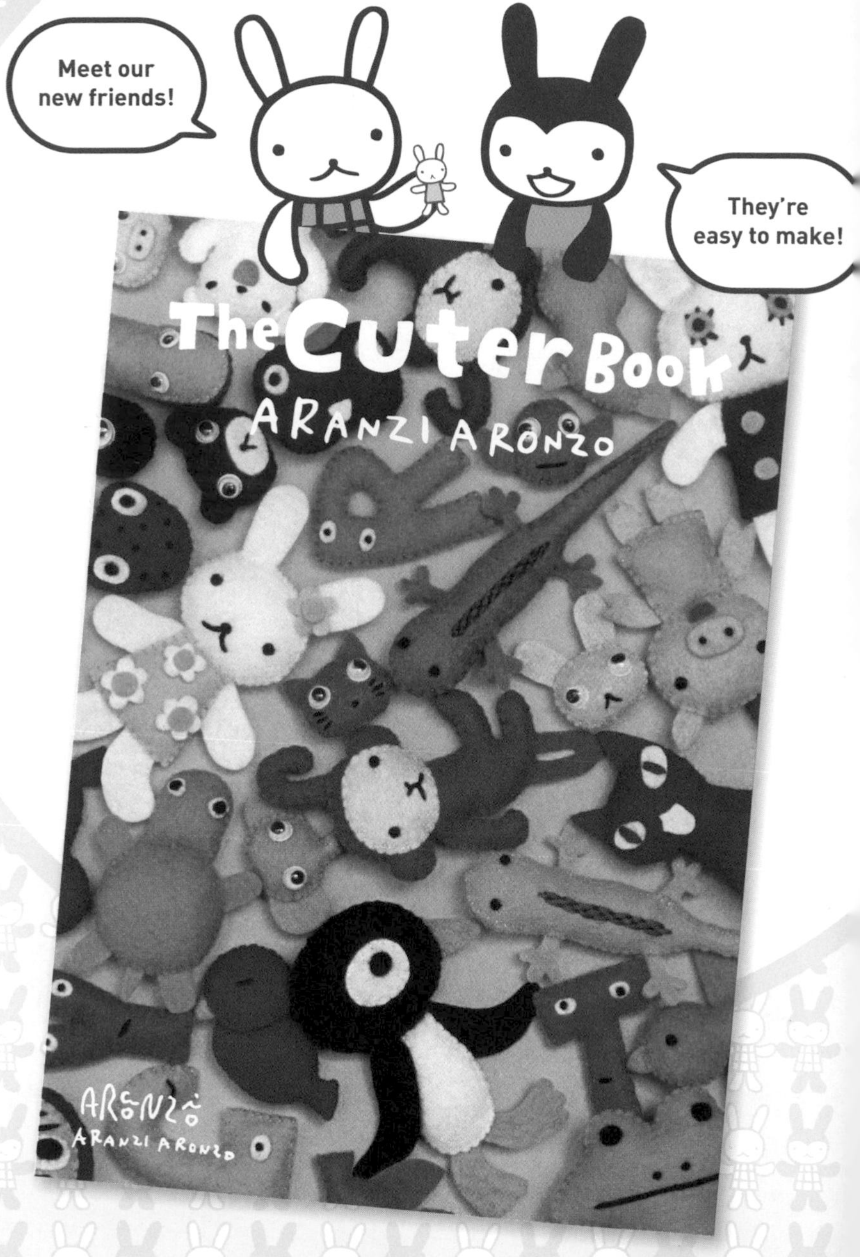

Meet our new friends!
They're easy to make!
The Cuter Book
ARANZI ARONZO
ARANZI ARONZO

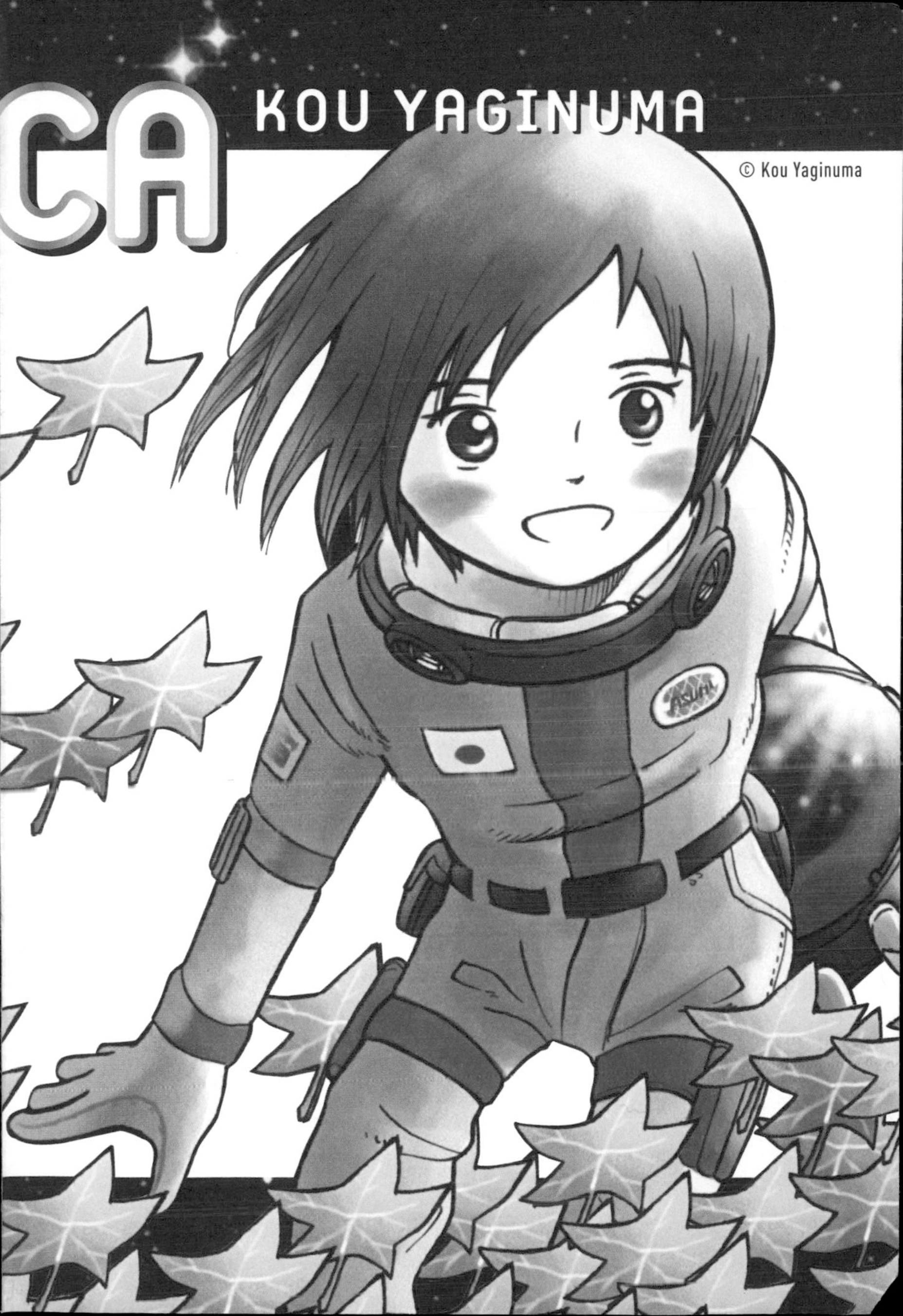
CA
KOU YAGINUMA
ASUMI

Chi's Sweet Home, volume 7

Translation - Ed Chavez
Production - Hiroko Mizuno
Tomoe Tsutsumi

First published in Japan in 2010 by Kodansha, Ltd., Tokyo
Publication for this English edition arranged through Kodansha, Ltd., Tokyo
English language version produced by Vertical, Inc.

Translation provided by Vertical, Inc., 2011
Published by Vertical, Inc., New York

Originally published in Japanese as *Chiizu Suiito Houmu* by Kodansha, Ltd., 2008-2009
Chiizu Suiito Houmu first serialized in *Morning*, Kodansha, Ltd., 2004-

This is a work of fiction.

ISBN: 978-1-935654-21-6

Manufactured in the United States of America

First Edition

Third Printing

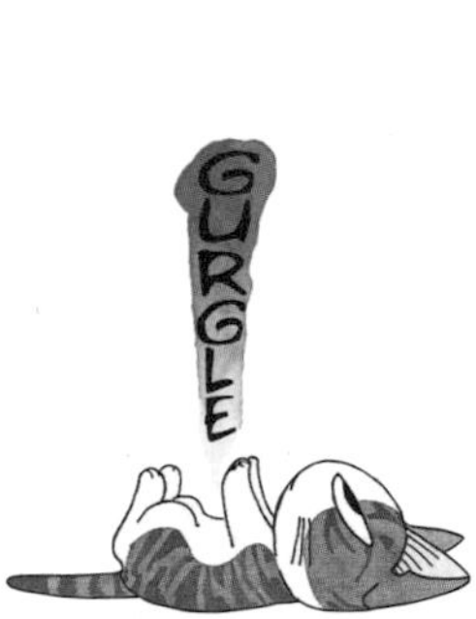
GURGLE

Vertical, Inc.
451 Park Avenue South, 7th Floor
New York, NY 10016
www.vertical-inc.com

Special thanks to: K. Kitamoto